UNANIMOUS VERDICT

JAMES A. KIDNEY

© 2009

ISBN: 1-4392-1454-9

ISBN-13:9781439214541

See what others have to say about Unanimous Verdict and read suggested Book Club questions at unanimousverdict.com

Visit www.amazon.com to order additional copies.

This book is dedicated in loving memory of

Arthur Zilversmit
and
Daniel M. Kidney II

Table of Contents

PART ONE: THE CRIME

PART TWO: THE DEFENDANTS

PART ONE: THE CRIME
Prologue: March 27, 1954

Corporal Walter Earle's principal goal was to travel his journey of life suffering neither physical nor emotional discomfort. Achieving this meant following only one rule: Avoid risk. Corporal Earle did not expect or desire riches or advancement. Any such passion implied ambition, and Corporal Earle had none beyond receipt of his monthly paycheck from the District of Columbia, which employed him as an officer for the Metropolitan Police Department. Joining the force upon graduation from Coolidge High School in 1949 was not in conflict with his life goal. Earle's father had been a policeman for 25 years. His firearm was holstered, except for practice drills, for a quarter century — until a comfortable retirement. It required only a few years of service before the older Earle acquired sufficient seniority to select a weekday shift. Thereafter, Corporal Earle's father never missed either dinner or a weekend at home. This was young Walter's model for success — to be just like his Dad.

When the younger Earle joined the force five years ago, his father offered advice which Walter eagerly absorbed. "If you should be so unfortunate as to encounter a crime in the making," his father said, in one of the longest conversations Walter could recall having with him, "do not intervene to stop it. Instead, make yourself scarce and wait until the crime is over and all the bad guys have left the scene. The force has detectives. They should be made to work. They need

1

crimes to solve. Your job is not to lose your life or the District will have to waste good money training a replacement. One day you'll get a desk job, and then you won't have to worry about such things."

Corporal Earle was practicing his father's lesson on a cold, damp Saturday morning near the end of March, 1954. He was crouched behind a line of parked cars while viewing the double-door entrance to a warehouse across Second Street in Southeast Washington, near the Anacostia River. Earle knew the neighborhood well because it had been his beat for over seven months. The warehouse was one of several on his rounds, along with a Capital Transit bus barn, a cement plant, a couple of liquor stores and a single block of three-story row houses, most of them containing enthusiastic patrons of the liquor stores. Earle liked his beat because it was unimportant. Serious crime was rare among the resident middle-aged drunks, most of them colored, and the warehousemen and bus drivers, all white, who quickly departed for Anacostia, Arlington, Northeast D.C., Maryland and other white neighborhoods immediately after their shifts. Earle calculated that within a year his seniority would allow him to work the same day beat Monday through Friday, thus achieving an important career goal. An inside desk job would come in time.

Avoiding risk requires an alert mind, though not an especially bright one. Corporal Earle's nightmare was to bumble into a dangerous, but avoidable, situation and suffer a painful injury – or worse – because he had missed warning signals. The young corporal made it a point to be very familiar with the physical details of his beat and the routine

Part One: The Crime, Prologue

of neighborhood inhabitants. He had been instructed at the police academy to look for the unusual because it might be a sign of crime. Since coming upon a crime was exactly what Earle was afraid of doing, he learned his academy lesson well. Consequently, he knew a Mr. Grossman operated the warehouse. He knew Grossman lived somewhere in or near Hyattsville, Maryland, a few miles away. Earle also knew that Grossman closed his warehouse with a large padlock on the double doors every Friday afternoon at 4 p.m. and did not reopen until 7 a.m. Monday. On this Saturday, the padlock was missing from the door. Earle never knew Grossman to leave his building unlocked. The missing padlock probably meant thieves had invaded the building to pilfer whatever they could find of value, which Earle knew would not be much. Grossman's warehouse contained tires, a couple of old automobiles and a great many boxes of dull documents stored at the request of downtown law firms and some government agencies. The thieves would be disappointed. This was even more reason for caution. The bandits could be armed and they might be angry at the lack of loot — perhaps angry enough to hurt or, God forbid, kill a police officer.

Mindful of his father's advice about the benefits of delay, Earle waited behind the automobiles a half hour, long enough, he calculated, for any burglars to take what they wanted and leave. Fortunately, the area had little weekend pedestrian traffic and there were no passersby inquiring why a young uniformed police officer was crouched alone behind a car in mid-morning for 30 minutes with his pistol at the ready pointing at a brick warehouse barren of activity.

3

Unanimous Verdict

Corporal Earle debated whether to use the police call box two blocks away to summon assistance. But doing so before adequately assessing the situation entailed another kind of risk — ridicule from other cops, including accusations of incompetence and cowardice. "There's Corporal Earle, scared to death by a broken padlock." He could hear the scorn even as he worried for his safety. The officer weighed the risks of physical injury versus harassment while watching the warehouse and decided it likely was safe to enter the building before calling for assistance.

After exactly 30 minutes, Earle moved across Second Street, SE quickly, in a crouch. He stood only when he reached the brick warehouse wall to the right of the double doors, holding his body tight against the wall. Hearing nothing from inside, Earle pushed the door closest to him inward slightly until he could see the first few feet of the north side of the interior. Transom windows just under the roofline shed light despite the overcast day. He heard nothing. He saw stacks of bankers' boxes, presumably containing documents, and a collection of large construction equipment, such as earth graders and a steamroller, parked neatly in a line. Nothing appeared to have been disturbed.

Earle was now convinced that the warehouse was unoccupied. He pushed the door farther inward until it met an obstacle of some sort when it was halfway opened. The obstacle caused a squishy resistance to Earle's pressure on the door, but did not block the door from opening. Earle entered the warehouse and circled behind the door. His nose hit on a brown leather shoe. It was attached to a foot that was attached to

4

Part One: The Crime, Prologue

a body hanging from a rope tied to a beam supporting a loft area above the door. Earle stepped back to get a full look at the body. The person was well dressed, in a dark suit, dress shirt and tie, as if going to a job interview. Blank bug eyes stared vacantly toward Earle. A tongue was visible, hanging an inch from the mouth, made slack by a hanging jaw. Although the face was slightly distorted and the neck pulled to the right by the rope, the object hanging from the rafter was clearly a young male. He was also a Negro.

Jesus Christ! Earle thought as he raced to the callbox. A lynching!

Chapter One: Mrs. Virginia Van Dyke, April 23, 1954

Neil Endicott was awakened from a sound sleep at 8 a.m. by a phone call from his answering service. The service told him a Mrs. Van Dyke called at 4 o'clock the previous afternoon and that she wanted to speak to him as soon as possible. The number she left was a LI, for LIncoln, exchange, which meant the caller worked or lived somewhere on the edges of downtown D.C. "Van Dyke", Neil thought. – very Dutch, perhaps very rich. Just another angry wife who needed pictures of her husband in "the act" with his girlfriend. She would only be Neil's third client since quitting the police department and setting up his one-man detective agency, but the work already bored him. Chasing errant husbands and wives was like repairing a flat tire on Connecticut Avenue at rush hour – dangerous only if you were stupid and careless, but never glamorous or challenging.

Neil's tiny Capitol Hill studio apartment was furnished with a bed, nightstand and bureau from his boyhood bedroom in Chevy Chase. He had added a floor lamp and a second-hand green stuffed chair, which was ugly but comfortable. The walls were bare except for a mirror over the bureau. A 25-cent Pocketbook Mike Hammer novel was on the bedside stand along with a photograph of his sort-of-but-not-really girlfriend Jennifer in a dime store frame. The entire apartment could be crossed in fewer than five steps to a small refrigerator and an electric stove. Neil did not have to open the refrigerator. He knew it contained only three bottles of Ballantine Ale, a half-eaten bag of potato chips, stored in the fridge to protect it from roaches, and about a half-pound of sliced bologna from the DGS market. The two-door cupboard mounted above the stove contained only Melmac place-settings for 2 1/2 people. (A dinner plate had melted when Neil tried to reheat some coffee cake to give Jennifer "breakfast in bed" on her birthday. He learned that although Melmac is nearly unbreakable, it is not oven-proof.) Neil was not unhappy with his Spartan accommodations. He was a bachelor and his quarters satisfied his needs, even if they appalled his mother and amused his girlfriend.

Neil showered, brushed his teeth, combed his hair and put on his skivvies and a T-shirt before returning Mrs. Van Dyke's call. If he was going to meet her today, he would wear his one sport jacket, one of three ties and one of two dress shirts. He had no choice in dress shirts, since he wore one the day before and it required more time to air out, in Neil's judgment, before it could be worn again.

He dialed the number. The phone rang three times. "Hello," a woman's voice answered.

"Is Mrs. Van Dyke there?" Neil asked.

"Speaking," the woman said. The voice was firm, a little bit guttural, but not loud. It was conversational, accustomed to doing business on the telephone. It was the voice of an older woman.

Neil introduced himself.

"Yes, thank you for returning my call," Mrs. Van Dyke said. "I would like to speak to you about retaining your services. You

Chapter One: Mrs. Virginia Van Dyke

are a private investigator, correct?" She enunciated each word with precision.

"Yes Ma'am."

"Can you come over to my house to discuss the assignment?"

"Yes, I believe I have some time today, though I have several appointments." Neil told himself this was not a lie since he was due at his parents' house for dinner that night.

"Are you free at 10 o'clock this morning?" Mrs. Van Dyke asked. Neil said that he was and Mrs. Van Dyke gave her address. Neil was surprised. It was in the 300 block of T Street, NW, about four blocks east of Griffith Stadium in the Howard University area. Given that geography, it was certain that Mrs. Van Dyke was a Negro.

"Excuse me Mrs. Van Dyke. I think there has been some mistake. I am a white man and I take it from your address that you are a Negro woman." Neil immediately regretted what could be interpreted as a hostile tone. He did not know how to handle the situation because he never had encountered the prospect of working for a colored person. Mrs. Van Dyke did not sound as if she noticed.

"Well, yes, Mr. Endicott, but are you saying that you have a policy of not accepting colored clients?"

He had no "policies" of any kind, other than to try to make a living from detective work. He was not complying with that policy very well at the moment, a thought which led him to a maneuver to back away from Mrs. Van Dyke which would be economic, not racial.

"No, my firm has no discrimination policy, but my fees are very substantial and I've found that few people can afford them. There are several reputable colored private detective agencies in town which are probably cheaper. I could recommend one or two if you give me some time to check around." Neil had seen a couple of small ads at bus stops for colored agencies but knew nothing about them. He hoped they were in the Yellow Pages.

"This job really requires the services of a white man, Mr. Endicott. I heard you were somewhat new to the business, and thought you might be reasonable."

Neil was surprised that she knew something about him. She had done some research. Her point that he was new to the business was a sharp one that hurt. He did not like his experience questioned, especially by a colored woman. Her requirement of a white detective also made Mrs. Van Dyke suspect. Neil wondered if she might be looking for a beard or front-man for some sort of swindle. A young white man could add legitimacy to a colored grifter's confidence game.

"Yes, but I've enjoyed considerable success and I charge accordingly, just like the other detectives in town." Neil wanted to end the conversation right now.

"How much do you charge, Mr. Endicott. I have some means."

Neil aimed at a figure he was sure she could not afford. "I charge $500 a week plus expenses."

"I can afford that," she responded without hesitation. She did not retreat; she advanced. "I expect that the work will take at

Chapter One: Mrs. Virginia Van Dyke

least two weeks. Of course, we can't know until you are finished. Mr. Endicott, it is very important work. I understand that you had a brief career in the police department and are well-regarded there. That is another important reason I need to hire you specifically." Neil was a little flattered as well as concerned that she knew so much about him. Having claimed to require a high salary, Neil now was tempted to take the job. He decided to test Mrs. Van Dyke's bona fides.

"Thank you for the compliment, but where did you learn about me? How do you know I was with the police? How do you know what my reputation was at the department?"

"I will tell you that when you come to my house this morning. You have the address. Can I count on you at 10? No obligations of course – for either of us." Mrs. Van Dyke knew she had won. Neil acknowledged her victory by consenting to the visit. He put on his navy sports coat, his white dress shirt, a pair of charcoal grey slacks and a blue and yellow regimental striped tie. Everything but the pants was a Christmas or birthday gift from his parents since Neil was discharged from the Marine Corps a year earlier.

The Eighth Street streetcar passed in front of Neil's apartment in a three-story row house that had been divided – with difficulty – into six tiny apartments. The streetcar traveled north to Gallaudet College for the deaf, then west on Florida Avenue. Two evidently deaf students exchanging hand signs got off at the Gallaudet stop. After that, Neil was the only white person on the streetcar. He disembarked at Rhode Island Avenue, Northwest. It was a short walk to the 300 block of T

Street. The warm weather of the previous day had moved on, replaced by an unusual late April chill. The temperature would not reach 50. Neil shivered and regretted not wearing a coat.

The row houses Neil passed on his way to Mrs. Van Dyke's home were the same Victorian architecture as those on Capitol Hill. Most appeared to be at least as well maintained. The dominant color was red, either red paint or unpainted red brick, but the blocks were also dotted with tasteful tans, browns and other earthy tones, trimmed in complementary black, white or cream. Some houses had small lawns with azaleas in bud, prepared to bloom in only a couple of weeks. A few had handsome turrets topping bay windows in the front parlor. Others boasted front porches, some with roofs and others with bare awning rails, awaiting warmer weather that would bring colorful canvas coverings.

This was LeDroit Park, home to D.C.'s "Talented Tenth" as W.E.B. DuBois, the colored writer, labeled the educated, well-to-do black middle class. DuBois hoped the fortunate would lead the other 90 percent of their race to equality in the United States. Neil had driven through LeDroit Park in the past, probably with his parents looking for street parking to attend a Senators game. As a native Washingtonian and regular reader of his father's newspaper, *The Evening Star*, he knew LeDroit Park was home to prominent blacks, including Mary Church Terrell, who was the first colored person on the D.C. school board and was now, at age 90, helping to lead a sometimes raucous, but mostly peaceful, drive to desegregate the city's restaurants

Chapter One: Mrs. Virginia Van Dyke

and theaters. Neil had encountered picket lines outside the National Theatre and downtown restaurants. He greeted the picketers pleasantly. He supposed he hoped they would win their campaign, but he was mostly indifferent. He couldn't afford anything but the movies, which permitted Negroes in the balconies. His only fancy restaurant meals were as a guest of his parents.

Neil read somewhere that LeDroit Park was no longer the neighborhood of choice for well-to-do colored folks. Like their white counterparts, residents were abandoning the areas close to downtown. Upper Sixteenth Street and Georgia Avenue, near Walter Reed Army Hospital and on the way to Silver Spring, Maryland, was supposed to be their new enclave. The area even developed its own nickname: The Gold Coast. But everything Neil saw on his trip to through LeDroit Park to Mrs. Van Dyke's was neat and well-cared for. Obituaries for the neighborhood were at best premature, he thought.

Mrs. Van Dyke's house was painted a light yellow with cream trim. It was one with bay windows and a turreted top. There were two other houses like it on the block, one of them adjoining the Van Dyke place. It was painted red with black trim. A teen-aged colored boy was in the neighbor's tiny front lawn planting two boxwoods in front of the window to the English basement. He looked up as Neil dropped the brass knocker on Mrs. Van Dyke's paneled front door. Within seconds, the door was opened by a woman who introduced herself as Mrs. Van Dyke. She welcomed Neil. Before she could close the door, the teen-age boy raised his voice to be heard.

13

Unanimous Verdict

"I'm sorry about your boy, Mrs. Van Dyke," the child said. "I liked Clayton a lot. He was always friendly to me. It's a damn shame. My Momma and I are prayin' for you and him, Mrs. Van Dyke."

"Bless you Leon," Mrs. Van Dyke answered. "Please tell your mother that I thank her for her prayers. And thank you, too."

"Yes'm," the boy said, returning to his yard work as Mrs. Van Dyke closed the door.

Before Neil could fully take in either his hostess or her home, he felt obliged to say something about the yard boy's remark. "Did something happen to your son, Mrs. Van Dyke?"

"Yes, he was murdered. That's what you are here to talk about."

"I'm so sorry, Ma'am. Have they caught the killer?"

"Before we get started on all of that, Mr. Endicott, will you have some tea? Some coffee? A sweet? Please have a seat."

"Yes, coffee, please. Black." He dropped into a loveseat in the bay. Behind it were green potted plants and grasshopper-green draperies. Thin white curtains, which permitted sunlight to flood the room, covered the windows. An oval coffee table stained a deep mahogany was in front of the loveseat. It was intricately carved around a raised edge. The loveseat had claw feet, also darkly stained, and was upholstered in a red and yellow floral pattern on a neutral background. A fireplace was to Neil's right. Above the mantel was a large painting of a man the color of charcoal holding a pipe in his lap with his left hand. His right thumb was hooked into the jacket of a three-piece suit.

14

Chapter One: Mrs. Virginia Van Dyke

The viewer's attention was drawn immediately to the subject's eyes. They were a lighter color than the skin, surrounded, of course, with white, but also appearing to reflect light from the pupils in a way that animated him with emotion. One could imagine the subject either angry or intensely studying the artist. The artist deserved praise for a painting that did more than freeze a man expressionless at a moment in time. Or perhaps the subject himself was so compelling that the artist only accurately captured a picture of an extraordinary man.

The remainder of the living room was filled by a baby grand piano bearing a number of framed pictures upon it and two stuffed chairs identically upholstered in a kind of oriental pattern whose principal color theme was red. A thick oriental rug covered the floor, and more photographs were hung on the wall on either side of the entrance to the foyer on Neil's left. The wall photos were all black and white, some now yellowing, of colored people, some of them obviously dating to the last century. Additional lighting was provided by floor lamps at either chair. A ceiling light was not turned on. An ottoman in matching upholstery was placed in front of one of the chairs. The room was tasteful but comfortable, intended for both entertaining and daily living. The room would not be out of place in Chevy Chase or even the wealthier Foxhall neighborhood, Neil thought. If he had suddenly been dropped into Mrs. Van Dyke's living room, he would not have guessed it was the home of a colored woman, but for the pictures and the portrait.

Unanimous Verdict

That he even briefly carried such a thought puzzled him.

Mrs. Van Dyke returned with the coffee from the kitchen at the rear of the house, passing through the dining room. She was of average height, but carried herself in a very erect manner, almost ceremonially, which made her seem taller. There was no hint of either slouch or jauntiness. Her walk was not slow; it was measured. Her dress was very formal for the morning, perhaps in anticipation of a professional visit, but more likely because it was her habit to always be well dressed. She wore a black wool suit, white blouse, hose and black dress shoes with two-inch heels. Her skirt reached a fashionably stylish but modest level about two inches below her knees. The suit was obviously tailored to present Mrs. Van Dyke's figure proudly, but with dignity. Mrs. Van Dyke deserved more credit for the effect than the tailor, however.

Mrs. Van Dyke had a long, graceful neck, unmarked by wrinkles or sagging, adorned with a simple string of pearls, which led to a head with slightly graying hair pulled tightly into a bun at the back. The hairstyle seemed to stretch her face taught. In fact, her skin was very smooth and her features sharply defined. Her skin was deep black silk, tempting to touch, stretched over high cheekbones. She had full lips painted a bright red and a slightly flat, wide nose. Neil usually perceived the prominent features of many Negroes as rough and unattractive, especially on a woman, but Mrs. Van Dyke's mouth was erotic, her face inviting. Her eyes were dark and, at the moment, welcoming. But Neil guessed they revealed nothing involuntarily.

Chapter One: Mrs. Virginia Van Dyke

"Well, Mr. Endicott, as you can see, I *am* colored. But perhaps you also can see that I can afford your fees." Mrs. Van Dyke took a seat in the upholstered chair across the fireplace from Neil after handing him his coffee and waving her arm around the room at the costly furnishings to illustrate her point. She set her own cup of tea on a side table. "Are you prepared to consider taking my case or would we be wasting our time talking about it?"

"As I told you, Ma'am, I have no race-based policy for my clients. I'm sorry if my remarks caused you any embarrassment."

"From the redness of your face, Mr. Endicott, I do not believe it is I who am embarrassed." Mrs. Van Dyke leaned slightly forward, as if preparing to share a confidence. "Let's get right to the point. As you learned walking in, a little prematurely perhaps, my son has been murdered. I want to hire you to find out who killed him."

Neil took a deep breath. Such an assignment was far beyond his skills and experience. He could not in good conscience accept the matter even if offered by a white woman.

"Haven't the police investigated the killing?" Neil asked. It would be rude to turn down the job without the courtesy of some basic questions and the details of a murder were almost always interesting.

"No, they have not. My son was beaten and then hanged nearly one month ago. The police began an investigation, but within a few hours of the murder they were told to treat the death as a suicide. Clay's death was definitely not a suicide. I saw the body. The police admit privately he was beaten but say he then hanged himself. This is nonsense, which even the police have a hard time with. I'm hiring you to investigate and to identify the killer."

Neil considered that despite her evident sophistication and intelligence, Mrs. Van Dyke was a mother and was unwilling to accept that her son killed himself. He could not imagine the pain to a parent of such a death. Perhaps he could help her come to terms with the death by drawing out some other facts before he rejected the assignment.

"Don't you think Clay might have been beaten by someone and then hanged himself? Maybe he was upset or not thinking right. He may have been in great pain and thought this would end it. Suicide is always a mystery. I mean, we never really know why they do it."

"I claimed the body from the coroner and had him autopsied at Freedmen's Hospital. The coroner's office wouldn't do it. They said Clay clearly was a suicide and there was no need for an autopsy. The doctors at Freedmen's said even a visual examination showed that Clay probably was dead before he was hanged. His head was fractured. Something about the morbidity and the location of the blood and stuff. Apparently this kind of thing happens all the time when a black man dies under mysterious circumstances. The Freedmen's doctors said they get these kinds of cases every three or four months where the coroner has ignored obvious causes of death of a Negro and refused to perform a public autopsy. I'm sure if you talk to your friends at the police department they will confirm it."

The words spilled out of Mrs. Van Dyke's mouth as she began to lose her composure. She pulled a handkerchief from a pocket of her jacket.

Chapter One: Mrs. Virginia Van Dyke

"I'm sorry, Mr. Endicott. It is very difficult. I try to be clinical about this so you will have the facts, but Clay was a good boy. I miss him terribly. He deserves the same justice as anyone else. I deserve the same justice.

"I took the autopsy results to the police earlier this week, but they refused to change their position. I don't understand it. I don't understand why they won't treat my boy's death the way they should, the way the evidence directs."

Neil was not particularly surprised that the death of a black man was treated so dismissively by the police and the D.C. government. The number of colored cops on the force was infinitesimal. A dead colored man wasn't going to receive the same police resources as a white one. The white-run city government and the newspapers collaborated with the cops in tolerating the differing treatment, the first for budget and political reasons and the other because colored crime victims just weren't good copy. Editors didn't want to spare a reporter to cover the crime or the family of the victim like they did for white folks. Neil didn't worry if the system was right or wrong. That was just how it was. In an ideal world, it would be better, but lots of other things would be, too.

"I assume you gave the police any information you had. Who would have killed him? Did he have any enemies? Was he into any kind of bad crowd? The police need leads to pursue a crime." Neil was tap dancing. He was looking for an opportunity to back out.

"I gave them the names of some of his friends and people he knew at work. I don't think the police ever contacted any of them."

"Well, Mrs. Van Dyke, I would love to help you, but the police have more resources than I do. I assume most of Clay's friends were colored, and a colored detective would surely be able to gain their confidence more easily than I could. That is important if they have any useful information, especially if it somehow implicates them in some kind of suspicious conduct." In case that was not enough to change her mind about hiring him, he added this:

"I'm also pretty green at this job, despite what I told you over the phone. I don't think I'm ready yet for a murder investigation. And while I do have a lot of police friends, I got bored with patrol duty after fighting in Korea. For now, anyway, I'm on my own. So I don't have much experience, not enough, at least, for something this serious. A missing child, as opposed to a murder investigation, maybe I can handle that. Crawl around for evidence of cheating, yes. Murder, no."

Mrs. Van Dyke tilted her head slightly, her mouth tightened and her dark eyes, again dry, seemed to darken further. She was looking skeptically at Neil. Then she addressed his objections.

"Mr. Endicott, I am well aware that you are inexperienced. You were not my first choice for this assignment. I have contacted nearly every white detective I could locate. One or two had a reputation for taking money and not doing the work. Most of them turned me down

Chapter One: Mrs. Virginia Van Dyke

as soon as they heard my address, as you tried to do. I interviewed one other private investigator here last week. He said he would take the job, took a check from me, but I have not heard from him since. Yesterday, the check came back to me in the mail with a note from the investigator saying he did not have the time to do a proper job investigating my son's death."

Neil was a little chagrined to be such a desperate choice, but Mrs. Van Dyke's narrative reminded him that he wanted to know the source of her information about him disclosed on the phone. "How did you hear about me, then? I'm not even in the Yellow Pages."

"We share a mutual acquaintance. She brought up your name when I mentioned how difficult it was to find someone. You do know an Alice Henshaw, don't you? She said you were a novice, but a well-intentioned young fellow with police experience. She thought you would take the job. She didn't think you would turn me down because of my race."

Alice. Although nearly 20 years his senior, Alice and her husband Max were good friends of both Neil and his parents. He knew Alice had liberal views, but was puzzled how she might know Mrs. Van Dyke. Mrs. Van Dyke's professional inquiry now turned into something close to a request from a personal friend, one Neil liked very much who was dear to him. Nor could Neil turn down Mrs. Van Dyke's request without repercussion. Mrs. Van Dyke undoubtedly would tell Alice, who would be disappointed in Neil, if not angry. Worse, if she thought he was acting for racial reasons. Alice would misinterpret his indifference as bigotry if he turned down the job. She knew he was not overwhelmed with clients.

"How do you know Alice?"

"She is a member of the NAACP. You know what that is, don't you Mr. Endicott? My neighbor, Mrs. Terrell, helped found the NAACP. Poor thing. Ninety years old. She's feeling very poorly. Anyway, we have an active chapter here in D.C. We have several white members, including Mrs. Henshaw. We meet twice a month, but have been meeting more frequently during this campaign to integrate the restaurants and theaters. I just hope Mrs. Terrill lives to see us prevail. We will prevail, Mr. Endicott." She stated the outcome as fact, not hope.

Neil recalled Alice mentioning she joined the NAACP and made Negro friends in the organization, but she said nothing about assisting the latest desegregation drive in the city. Neil suddenly had the sensation that his conduct was being monitored; that Alice was tracking his and asking Mrs. Van Dyke to report on him. He did not like it.

"I appreciate Alice's vote of confidence," Neil said, finally deciding he could provide objective reasons to turn down the assignment that might satisfy Alice. "But I am still white and inexperienced. You would be better off with a black investigator. Surely there are some in town who could satisfy your needs."

Mrs. Van Dyke's tightened mouth relaxed a bit. She had an answer for this objection. "I already have retained a colored detective to work with you. He is very good. His name is Lorenzo King. He has investigated murders. You might learn from him. He is waiting to see you this afternoon. We thought it might be more convenient for you to visit him, since he has an office." The knowing reference to an office stung Neil since he was very conscious of not having one. "Mr. King recommended that I retain a white man to deal with the police. He also thought that, given the seriousness of the issues, having a white man in tow when Clay's friends were questioned might give proper weight to his inquiries."

She had thought of everything. This guy King's plan was a reasonable one and Neil was Mrs. Van Dyke's last chance for a white investigator.

"In addition, Mr. King and I agree that Clay was murdered by a white man." Her face hardened as the subject moved to speculation about the perpetrator.

"You can't know that, Mrs. Van Dyke. What is your evidence?"

Mrs. Van Dyke allowed herself a sigh. She was tired of doing battle with the callow young white man before her. "The evidence is that my son is – was – an intelligent American Negro who knew full well the horrible history of lynching in this country. Every adult Negro in this city, and probably in the entire country, knows that history and knows that the white man, whole crowds of white men and women, sometimes, lynched colored men for amusement. They lynched colored men for crimes they did not commit. They lynched colored men to 'show them a lesson.' And they didn't just do it in the South,

Mr. Endicott. They did it in the Midwest and even in the West. My late husband and I followed this subject carefully on behalf of the NAACP. There have been over 2,000 lynchings that we know of in this century alone."

Mrs. Van Dyke raised her voice as she spoke. Her nostrils noticeably flared and her eyes burned with intensity. Neil could not know how often talk of race discrimination overwhelmed Mrs. Van Dyke's genuine gentility and grace, causing her to rage. This white Chevy Chase boy seemed ignorant of or, worse, indifferent to the Negro's constant awareness of color. Even in LeDroit Park, comfortably insulated from the worst of white bigotry, race issues traveled every day with Mrs. Van Dyke. In a perverse tribute to those who bought, transported and caged their ancestors, many black people hated members of their own race in direct proportion to their skin color. The blacker a man or woman, the purer their African genes, the more likely they would be discriminated against by lighter skinned Negroes, most of whom presumably descended from European masters in the more recent genetic past. Lighter skin was a sign of good fortune as well as of brains, beauty and talent. Dark skin, such as that possessed by Mrs. Van Dyke, suggested stupidity and even savagery, especially if joined by Negroid facial features. It was a form of collective racial self-hatred that was never far from Mrs. Van Dyke's consciousness. The very reason whites discriminated against blacks was the reason blacks discriminated against each other. Mrs. Van Dyke and her equally dark husband, as well as other dark skinned men and women, battled a dual

Chapter One: Mrs. Virginia Van Dyke

black-and-white discrimination which, especially in the higher strata of Negro society, was a constant presence. Color was a constant presence with Mrs. Van Dyke, even among her own people.

"My son knew the symbolism and horror of lynching. Even if he took his own life, he would not do so by hanging himself. He would not reduce himself to a racist cartoon of a helpless black man. But a white man, a man who hated my son or wanted to send some sort of message to other blacks, he would hang him from a warehouse rafter. A Negro man would not do so. A Negro man would not multiply his sin against my son with a sin against his own race. A white man would do so, and I can envision him cackling as he did it. That vision of evil haunts me."

Her message delivered, Mrs. Van Dyke relaxed her body into her chair and considered how she was demeaning herself by begging this spoiled son of privilege to overcome his casual racism and accept a handsome wage for taking on her son's case. Were it not for the love of her son and the need to avenge his death, this woman of great achievement would not have groveled in person and by telephone before half a dozen more mature and experienced white men soliciting help. She certainly would not have tolerated the insolent interrogation by this Endicott child which forced her into roads she wished not to travel once more, including the ugly history of lynching. She was nearly sixty years old and had tried to live a constructive, perhaps even inspiring, life against difficult odds. But even as a grieving widow, ninety years after the Emancipation Proclamation, she was treated as little better than a field hand by a white man who had achieved very little himself, but who assumed, by virtue of nothing but his birth, that he was the superior one in the room. She choked back her anger and despair. She needed this young man's help only because of *his* color.

"Mr. Endicott, I can see you are resisting this. I pray it is not because of my color or assumptions about people of color. My son was a good boy. He had a very successful father, who never pressured Clay to equal his success. But I think Clay felt he failed us somehow. Perhaps parents send signals to their children that they don't intend. I don't know. But you must understand a mother sheep is always most tender to the weakest of her lambs. Clay's sister always has been strong and made her way. Clay was weaker. More confused, perhaps. Please take this on, if only to help an old woman with her grief."

"You are hardly old, Mrs. Van Dyke."

"I am older than you think. I have good health; I always felt the Lord blessed me and my family. But a parent, no matter how successful in other ways, measures her success by the happiness of her children. My son did not live his allotted years, and I am afraid we had something to do with it. Something that made him lose his way. I need to know why he was murdered. That is almost as important as who killed him. Did he die doing something good or something evil? Was he protecting or attacking someone?" This was mostly true, except that her first priority was to capture the killer and see him dead,

Chapter One: Mrs. Virginia Van Dyke

by her own hand if necessary. Christian charity and forgiveness were no match for the murder of a son.

"You may not like the answer, Mrs. Van Dyke. It might show he hanged himself despite what you say about him. Perhaps you should leave it alone. An investigation will not bring him back, and could add to your sorrow."

"A child always is a gift, Mr. Endicott. Clay was a special gift because we got to pick him out. He was adopted, you see. I could not have more children after Christine was born. We chose him. We could have chosen some other baby, or not adopted at all. We have an obligation to both of our children, but only one of them could have had other parents – could have led a different life. We don't know what that life would have been, but I am called to know and remember my baby's life, which includes his death. He is my responsibility, including his memory. I need to know if we could have protected him from this fate." Mrs. Van Dyke again reached for her handkerchief. She made no sound, but tears slid down her face.

"Where is your husband, Mrs. Van Dyke," Neil knew he could not continue to resist the woman's entreaties. Perhaps together with this other fellow, King, they could persuade Mrs. Van Dyke not to waste her money after a few days of investigation.

"He died two years ago; sudden heart attack. Have you heard of Elmer Van Dyke?"

"No Ma'am, I'm sorry."

Unanimous Verdict

"He was a law professor at Howard University. He taught different courses over the years, but mostly he taught criminal procedure and landlord-tenant law. Other professors liked to focus on constitutional law in the classroom and appellate and Supreme Court race cases in their work outside the classroom. Elmer picked a different path. He called the other professors 'glamour pusses.' He meant it jokingly – he called them that to their faces. He appreciated the importance of their work. But Elmer felt that these big federal desegregation cases were like water wearing down a stone. They might cause the rock to move or to wear away over a long time, but immediate change was barely perceptible. Do you understand? He thought representing a handful of people to sit at the front of Greyhound buses or attend white law schools, things only a few colored folk ever came into contact with, incidental things, was kind of the 'Talented Tenth' serving the 'Talented Tenth.' You have heard of the Talented Tenth?"

"Yes ma'am," Neil lied. He could figure it out from the context of the message. He didn't need all the information he was getting about a dead dad. He wanted to move to something more constructive without showing disrespect.

"Anyway, Elmer wanted a more immediate impact for the less talented 90 percent of coloreds. So he worked the D.C. Municipal Courts representing poor folk charged with crimes or trying to prevent foreclosure of their homes or eviction from their slum apartments. Not just colored, but anybody who was too poor. He persuaded the courts to let these people be advised by Howard law students. The

28

Chapter One: Mrs. Virginia Van Dyke

white schools, Georgetown and George Washington, are letting their students do the same thing now, but Elmer started it. He also lobbied the White House and the bar association to appoint more Negro judges to the local courts.

"I know I go on about him. But I am so proud of him. All those years we were raising our kids and I was so happy. These last two years have been a struggle. First Elmer and now Clayton. Both died out of nowhere." Speaking proudly of her husband's work helped to dry her tears. The handkerchief was returned to her pocket.

"He sounds like a fine man. I wish I had met him." Neil hoped he did not sound patronizing.

"Alright, Ma'am, I'll take the assignment – for now." Neil was anxious to end the sparring with his new client and begin his investigation. "But I warn you not to expect too much. Can we agree that either of us can cancel at any time? It wouldn't be good for either of us to go on a wild goose chase." Neil figured he would be out of the case in a week.

"Yes, Mr. Endicott. And I will stick by my bargain – $500 plus expenses. Let me give you a week in advance."

The terms of the engagement were settled. It was time for an interrogation.

"Tell me what you know about your son's death."

"All I know is what the police told me and what I know about my son. I already told you why my Clayton would not have hanged himself and why his death must be murder."

"I understand that, Mrs. Van Dyke. But it will help the investigation if you tell me what the official story is. Who did you talk to at the police?"

"A Detective Jeffords at the Southeast District substation on Capitol Hill. Clay died in a warehouse along the river in Southeast a few blocks from the substation, so he was assigned the investigation."

"I know Jeffords. He's a straight-shooter. I'd be very surprised if he lied to you and even more surprised if he dropped the case for any improper reason." Neil was a rookie patrolman in Northeast before he was sent to Korea. Jeffords was his sergeant. He was a solid cop and a Marine veteran. Jeffords suggested Neil join the Marine Reserves to supplement his police pay so he could move out of his parents' house. Neil never blamed him for the consequences of that decision.

"He gave me a copy of the police report. He wouldn't give me any other materials, including photos of Clay's body. He said it would upset me too much. But I identified his body at the morgue and he was awfully beat up. The doctor at Freedman's said the body had been cleaned up by the coroner's office before I saw it, so you can imagine how bloody and bruised he must have been. Added salt to the wounds that the D.C. government gave Clayton a bath but not an autopsy. He didn't need no bath."

The police report contained no further specific information about the condition of the body, other than that it was hanging from the rafter supporting a loft about 10 feet above the concrete floor, a standard hemp half-inch rope around Clay's neck. A step ladder was

Chapter One: Mrs. Virginia Van Dyke

on its side nearby. The report assumed Clay used the ladder to loop the rope around the rafter and himself before kicking it away as the final act of his life. The cause of death was listed as "suicide." The report was signed by Officer Walter Earle.

Mrs. Van Dyke told Neil that, according to Jeffords, the warehouse was owned by a Mr. Grossman, who locked the warehouse Friday afternoons before going home. However, Grossman gave copies of the padlock key to several of his customers who occasionally required access to the warehouse on weekends. The clients liked having a key because it gave them control over their property 24 hours a day. The cops had a list of Grossman's customers who had a key. Most of them were law firms and government agencies. The White House had kept a spare presidential limousine at the warehouse until Grossman started handing out keys over the protests of the Secret Service, which then moved the car to another location for storage. The police told Mrs. Van Dyke that Grossman was not a suspect in her son's murder because he had a strong alibi and a few years earlier he had cleared a Secret Service security review. Mrs. Van Dyke protested to no avail that just because a man wouldn't murder a President of the United States didn't mean he wouldn't murder a colored man.

Jeffords also told her that Clayton Van Dyke appeared to have been beaten about the head and torso before he was mounted from the warehouse rafter. He said there was blood on the warehouse floor, an indication that Clay was beaten at the warehouse before he was hanged. No sample of the blood was taken at the scene because the death was

31

deemed a suicide. Grossman washed the floor when he returned to work the following Monday.

Neil was mildly surprised no sample was taken to compare Clay's blood type with the blood at the scene. Evidence Clay was beaten where he died could rule out suicide and point directly to murder. Neil doubted the sole reason for the indifference was that Clay was a black man. The MPD detectives he knew had no special brief for the colored, but most of them would rather investigate a murder than a suicide, regardless of the victim's race. For some reason, before Monday when Grossman came to work, the decision was made not to investigate. Therefore, there was no need to spend departmental money on a blood analysis. He kept his musings to himself, but addressed the possibility of police misconduct with Mrs. Van Dyke indirectly.

"Surely your husband had connections at the Courthouse and at Howard Law School. You are friends with Mary Terrell. Why don't you and your friends and the NAACP put some public heat on the police to investigate this? That might produce better results than Mr. King and I can."

"I thought of that. Everyone is sympathetic, but nobody is enthusiastic. The law faculty is anxious about the school desegregation case at the Supreme Court, which of course includes D.C. schools. They don't want to get on the wrong side of the police or be responsible for any racial disruptions before that decision comes out. Mrs. Terrell and the local NAACP don't want any distractions from the theatre

Chapter One: Mrs. Virginia Van Dyke

demonstrations. They all say they'll help, but later. I want to get some action now."

Neil asked for pictures of the entire Van Dyke family and any recent pictures of Clayton with his friends. Mrs. Van Dyke handed him some framed pictures from the top of the baby grand.

Neil examined closely Clay's 14-year-old black-and-white high school graduation picture and a family picture taken in color shortly before Elmer Van Dyke's sudden death. The face, especially the younger face, was familiar.

"Elijah Lincoln." Neil called out the name spontaneously, without any thought.

"I'm sorry, Mr. Endicott. Did you say something?"

"No ma'am. It's just that your son reminds me of someone I knew in Korea." Neil quickly recovered his composure and looked more carefully at the more recent family photograph. The Van Dykes were a handsome family, but Neil was immediately struck by how much lighter Clay was than either of his parents or his sister. He also was noticeably taller than the rest of his family, about four inches taller than his father, who was not short. Mrs. Van Dyke said Clay was six feet four inches tall, but that there were boys at Dunbar High School much taller. Clay stood out because of height, she said, but he was not especially unusual.

In answer to the inevitable question, she said Clay had not played varsity basketball, preferring to spend his time playing the trumpet with the school orchestra and his own jazz quartet. Clay's eye coloring could not be clearly discerned from either photograph, but Neil's suspicion that the young man did not have the deep brown or black eyes typical of a purely African Negro was confirmed by his mother. Clay's eyes were hazel, with a distinctive smattering of yellow flecks. Nearly everyone remarked on his eyes when he was a child, his mother recalled.

"He was hardened by his wartime service. He wanted to fight, but the Army made him a cook down in Louisiana. It was hard on him." Mrs. Van Dyke stood and retrieved another picture, this one of a young man in uniform. "When he got back home, he didn't want to continue with his education or use his music talent. He got a job driving a truck at the public library. But mostly he got excited about militant race ideas he picked up in the service. He wasn't active helping people like his dad was. He wanted to stir things up. He laughed at my NAACP work. He said desegregation not only is useless, but works against the black man."

"That was the only thing we really fought about." The elegant demeanor crumbled slightly as Mrs. Van Dyke reached into the recent past with thoughts of her son. Again, tears began to gather and fall down her cheek. The handkerchief came out.

Neil compared the first two pictures and noted to himself how much change nearly a dozen years caused. The high school graduate's features were soft, his smile bright and cheerful. Clay's hair was carefully clipped short for his graduation picture. The graduation picture was of a clean slate, anticipating the future with eyes that twinkled and an

Chapter One: Mrs. Virginia Van Dyke

optimistic grin. Fourteen years later, the same face was experienced in hardship, disappointment and anger. Features pliable in youth had hardened, the mouth tight, the eyes glaring. The other three people in the picture were smiling naturally, but Clay's grin was forced, more grimace than smile. Aging accounted for part of the change, but Clay also had become both tougher and sadder. He was different, and not in a good way.

Still, the resemblance to Elijah Lincoln in both pictures was haunting.

Chapter Two: Lorenzo King, April 23, 1954

Neil closed his notebook about 12:30 p.m. and thanked Mrs. Van Dyke for the information about her son and the check she handed him to pay for his first week of work. Although Mrs. Van Dyke had cried more than once during their meeting and had described intimate details of her dead son and of her family, the parting was distant and formal. A businesslike handshake was extended. As Neil walked through the door held open for him by his hostess, he sensed that she was relieved to be done with him.

Lorenzo King, the Negro private investigator, expected Neil at his office on H Street, NE at 3 p.m. Neil decided to take the streetcar to the Southeast Division police substation in the meantime. He called Detective Jeffords on Mrs. Van Dyke's telephone and arranged to meet him there at 1 p.m. He told Jeffords he wanted to talk about the Clay Van Dyke case.

The Southeast District division headquarters offices were across the Anacostia River. Under pressure from the local community and the small Capitol police force, the Department erected a sub-station on Capitol Hill to which Jeffords was assigned. Jeffords was a second father when Neil was a private walking a beat in Northeast D.C. and Jeffords, in uniform then, was his sergeant. Jeffords was a Marine in the war, but unlike Neil's real father, a World War I veteran, or his brother, Jeffords wore his Corps experience quietly – pride without braggadocio. He also was a friendly counselor who saved Neil's job and maybe a life or two before Neil's Korean tour of duty.

Neil nearly caused a riot in his rookie year on the force. A six-year-old white boy was reported missing in the Brentwood section of town the night before. His picture was printed in both *The Post* and *The Times-Herald* along with a short story suggesting he had been kidnapped off the streets. Brentwood was mostly white; Neil was patrolling in Ivy City, which was black, but only a couple of miles from the missing boy's house.

Ivy City was poor, but working class. It wasn't known as dangerous. The residents mostly kept their distance from the young white patrolman and he from them. He knew the names of very few people on his beat. He was a stranger. Neil assumed that was the way it was supposed to be.

It was winter. The day was bright but cold, with temperatures well below freezing. It was just the kind of day on which Neil enjoyed walking a beat in his heavy police-issue overcoat, which added girth to his still-adolescent frame. He wore his plastic-brimmed police hat low, tipped down to hide the top half of his face in shadow The sidewalks and curbs were broken, low on the city's list for repair. Neil kept his eyes to the ground, both to avoid tripping and to further disguise his youth from those he passed. He was only a year out of high school. He was young. On the beat he felt even younger. The uniform was a disguise. He was acutely aware of his own color and of his own pampered background. He was embarrassed to be a figure of authority. He did not know how to approach people on his beat. He told himself that regardless of all that, if anything happened on his beat, he would prevail. Neil was the cop. He was supposed to be in charge.

The young patrolman was watchful as an explorer in a strange land, but was specifically thinking of little more than the cold air he saw coming from his mouth, when he heard a child's frantic scream. He quickly traced the sound to the rear corner of a frame house with peeling white paint and a sagging front porch which had two window screens resting against the rails. A colored man was trying to hold on to a screaming youngster who, at least from a distance, looked like he could be white under his leggings, jacket, mittens and cap.

"I guess I wouldn't have done anything with just a man struggling with a screaming boy," Neil later recounted to Jeffords. "But it looked like a white boy. He looked well-dressed for the cold. And that kid was missing in Brentwood. I had to check it out."

For the first time in his young career, Neil pulled his police-issue revolver from its holster and advanced toward the back of the house. He moved slowly, partly from uncertainty and partly to give the man plenty of warning. He did not want to startle him, which might further endanger the child.

"Hands up. Hands up, you over there. Leave the kid alone." His voice cracked through the dry air, carrying the entire block. Black occupants of the neighboring houses quickly appeared on porches, sidewalks and at side doors to see what was causing the police to take up arms. Neil quickly calculated he was two blocks from the nearest call box. He couldn't get any help.

"Pulling your firearm was your first mistake. Shouting was your second," Jeffords later told Neil as they relived the situation. "You had no cause for either."

The man struggling with the child appeared not to hear the officer's cry, so Neil shouted again, repeatedly, each time with greater urgency. "Stop. Hands up. Leave that child alone. Stop. Hands Up." More residents came outside. Some grouped behind Neil to better see what was causing a ruckus. The colorful housecoats, hats and jackets were bright in the sun, contrasting sharply with the dead grass of winter on the lawns and the dull gray and black of the salt-stained sidewalk and street. Neil ignored the shouts of "What's goin' on?" and "Leave him alone" and "Go home, cop" that angrily trailed him up the side yard. Neil was friendless; he had no allies, only restless enemies.

"You should have listened to those people," Jeffords said. "Maybe asked some questions." Neil didn't.

Suddenly the Negro pulled the boy to his body. The man was on bended knees and the boy was up against his chest. The man pulled the boy's face into his armpit and held his hand over the back of the boy's head. The noise from the boy's screaming ceased. Neil did not know whether he had stopped screaming or his screams were muffled by the man's body. Nor could he tell if the man was comforting the boy or muzzling him. Only after the boy was tightly against him did the man look up at Neil. His eyes were opened wide. They were bullets launched into Neil's own eyes – threatening, angry and resentful. Neil was confronted by an angry black man and behind him was an angry black crowd. He was frightened. He was in danger. He needed help. He leveled his pistol. The crowd behind him screamed. Neil couldn't make out what they were saying. All of his attention was on the man and boy in front of him.

"Let the boy go. Let him go."

The man pulled the boy tighter. The boy tried to put his arms around the man, a child's hug. Neither said anything.

"Let him go," Neil repeated. He had no idea what to do next. The crowd was yelling. "Let him go. Let him go." A rock flew by Neil's temple. Another hit him square in the back, harmlessly thanks to the padding of his overcoat. Neil turned and pointed the gun at the crowd, which halted its advance and further increased its emotional pitch, acting as one. "Get out of here whitey." "Don't need no white cop." "Put down the gun." "That's his kid. Leave him alone."

"Awright, awright. Break it up. Break it up." The comfortable baritone was familiar, its timbre distinct from the higher pitched screams in the crowd. The two dozen or so Negroes gathered near Neil calmed quickly, the angry threats replaced with friendly "Hello officer" and "Howya doin' sarge?" and "Jeffords, this guy is a jerk." Sgt. Jeffords moved easily through the crowd, shaking hands and greeting many by their first name. He said nothing to Neil until he was at his side, then, quietly, unheard by others: "Put that damn thing away before you hurt someone. That's a father and son. Nothin' wrong here. Apologize and leave. The prowl car is on the street."

Then Jeffords turned to the Negro man and his child. When the father broke his grip on him, the child turned toward the two police officers. He was wiping tears from his black eyes that had fallen down a face the color of coffee-and-cream with a spoonful of pure terror. He definitely was not the missing Brentwood boy.

"Howdy, Jacob. I'm sorry about this. Private Endicott didn't know of your affliction." Jeffords shook the colored man's hand, and then turned to Neil. "Mr. Robinson here has a bad case of the stutters, Endicott. I'm sure when he saw you he just clammed up. I think you scared his little boy. What's his name Jacob? He wasn't born when I was on the beat. Congratulations."

"B-b-b-b-o-b-b-b-y, O-O-Officer Jeffords. His m-m-m-m-mama n-n-n-n-named him just to m-m-m-make me c-c-crazy." Jeffords waited patiently to be sure the man was done speaking.

"Well, she sure done that." Jefferson patted the older man gently on his shoulder as both of them laughed.

"You got something to say to Mr. Robinson, Private?"

Neil was silent in the prowl car most of the way back to the station house after extending his apologies to Mr. Robinson. Jeffords made him repeat the apology so the crowd could hear it. Neil didn't know what to expect. Perhaps his career was over. Or he would be a private forever.

In sight of the Northeast Division station, a practical question occurred to him.

"How did you show up?"

Chapter Two: Lorenzo King

"Why, Esther McCormick called. Don't you know Esther? She's practically the mayor of that block. Hasn't she offered you her cinnamon crumble cake?" Jeffords was jovial. He didn't seem angry. The warm reception on his old pre-war beat brought back happy memories of a simpler time in his life and in his country.

"I don't know any Esther McCormick."

"Yeah, I don't think you know anybody on that beat. I had that beat before the war. Wasn't any oldern' you." Jeffords didn't say he had made friends on the beat. He didn't have to.

"You made a lot of assumptions out there that were wrong, Endy. You did it because you don't know your beat. You don't know the people."

"I don't know how to talk to 'em. We got nothin' in common, Sarge."

"How do you know unless you talk to 'em? They got families. They go to school. They got jobs. How're you any different? Plus, while you're walkin' that beat you all share the same little spot of earth and got the same goals for that piece of earth and are tied to each other by that earth. Preserve and protect. That's what cops do. That's what they're supposed to do, anyway. You do that – protect that earth and make friends of those strangers you share it with eight hours a day instead of treatin' 'em as strangers – you'll get a good return."

Jeffords never mentioned the incident again, but every month he asked Neil about Esther McCormick's cinnamon crumble cake until Neil finally brought him a piece, courtesy of Mrs. McCormick, one of Neil's new friends on the beat.

Unanimous Verdict

That was in 1949. In 1954, fresh from Mrs. Van Dyke's house, Neil received a friendly greeting from Jeffords and two or three uniformed officers at the substation who knew him from his work on the force. Jeffords invited Neil to join him in a small inner office used for interrogations. It was furnished only by a steel table and four steel chairs and was meant to be uncomfortable.

"Welcome back, Endy. I mean, welcome back from Korea. I don't think I've seen you since you rejoined the force." Jeffords added: "I'm sorry you decided to quit. You'd be off patrol and a sergeant after a couple more years. You were a good cop." Jeffords said the last sentence like he meant it. He did.

"Thanks. Just impatient, I guess. Tired of taking orders. Good to see you again, Sergeant. I guess it's detective now. Congratulations."

"Thanks. I miss the uniform sometimes. Life's a little easier as a beat cop. I don't miss being a supervisor, though. Keeping track of guys like you was like herding cats."

"You still eatin' Mrs. McCormick's crumble cake?"

"Naw. New Division. But I also heard she passed."

"Too bad. She was a sweet lady — once I got to know her."

The men exchanged a knowing look.

Small talk done, Neil asked Jeffords to tell him all he knew about the warehouse death. He carefully did not call it a murder.

"Not much to tell. Officer Earle found him hanging in the warehouse. It was clear he was beaten up some place. Our surmise is

44

that he hanged himself." Jeffords, who was looking directly at Neil throughout the conversation, turned his head away at the last sentence. He was like Neil – a poor liar.

"You don't believe that, Bob. That's ridiculous." Jeffords looked across the table a few moments in silence, his icy blue eyes probing Neil's hazel ones, not quite sure what he was looking for.

"I consider you a friend, Endy, as well as a good cop."

"Bob, you taught me to be a good cop. Even a poor cop would know this smells bad. If there's something else about this case, I need to know it." Jeffords paused a few more seconds.

"Listen, Endy. The official position is that it was a suicide. You want anything else, you have to promise you never heard it from me. This has to be Marine-to-Marine, OK?" Jeffords frowned and didn't wait for an answer. Endy was young, but he could be trusted. He already owed Jeffords a lot.

"Guy was colored, but he didn't deserve to be murdered. Nobody does. And even a bigoted cop – which I'm not, as you surely know – doesn't like to be told by some civilian to kill an investigation."

"Why aren't they playing this one straight?"

"We heard it direct from the Commissioners' offices. It's all politics. I'm told there's never been an officially recorded lynching in D.C. and nobody wants to wreck the record, especially now."

"What's so special about now?"

"Maybe nothin'. Maybe that's a catch-all excuse. Hell, for all I know there've been lots of lynchings in D.C., but not officially.

Unanimous Verdict

"Look, Endy, you grew up here, right?" Jeffords leaned across the bare steel table as if to share a confidence.

Neil nodded.

"Then I shouldn't have to tell you this city is run like a plantation, from sanitation to high society. The House District Committee is made up of Dixiecrats. They want to keep the place under congressional control and no one else on the Hill has the balls or interest to fight them. The city's half black or better and nobody in the Great 48, especially in the South, wants the Negro to have political power in the capital of the country. The Commissioners have to march to the beat of the southerners, but since they are appointed by the Dixiecrats, they probably agree with them anyway. The point is, the colored man has no friends in high places here. The opposite."

Neil knew that no resident of the District of Columbia had cast a ballot in the last sixty years. The Constitution did not provide for representation of the District in Congress or even a chance to vote for the President. Congress eliminated the elected office of mayor after a scandal late in the last century, and the city had since been run by committees of the Congress and three commissioners appointed by the President with congressional approval. The southern Democrats controlled the city through the committees, vowing no racial liberties would be permitted. D.C. was mostly segregated by culture and custom, but less rigorously and with greater local disapproval than in the states south of the Potomac. But the House District Committee was a firm bulwark against any risk of either black political power or serious racial desegregation.

"Ok, Ok, I know all that. What's it got to do with Clayton Van Dyke's death?" Neil was impatient with Jeffords' political history lecture. Like Jeffords said, Neil knew.

"Simple. The Supreme Court's about ready to rule on school segregation, including in D.C., and there's that protest about theatre segregation. The powers-that-be are afraid Van Dyke's death will be called a lynching – which it probably is – and that might create enough sympathy and outrage to turn both issues to the advantage of the colored. Moreover, in case you hadn't heard, we're in a propaganda war with the Communists. The Reds like nothing better than to rub our noses in racial problems. A lynching in D.C. may not make headlines in Alabama, but it sure will in Moscow and the rest of Europe. One little dead guy, black or white, amounts to nothing compared to international politics."

Neil was immediately struck by a familiar theme. He scowled at the thought that D.C.'s colored leadership and the racists on the Hill were both so worried about the schools case and integrating theatres that neither group would investigate – or force an investigation – of poor Clay Van Dyke's murder. They didn't know it, but the blacks and the racists who hated them were united on this issue for the present, albeit hoping for different outcomes.

His mind flashed again to Elijah Lincoln, Clayton's look alike. Same theme. Abandonment.

"And you go along with this bullshit?" Neil asked, knowing the answer he would get. "We let a murderer go free in D.C. 'cause we're worried about some crappy newspapers in Europe? It's crazy."

"I hate it. But I've got a family and a career. Van Dyke will be forgotten soon. What if I went public with this? I probably would be ignored or be viewed as a crank. *The Post* might make something of it, but at the end they'll get stonewalled. And I would be out of a job for nothin'."

Neil winced that Jeffords didn't see his father's newspaper, *The Star*, as an ally, but he was probably right. Even the more reliably liberal *Post* probably wouldn't spend any political capital or financial resources on the story. Nobody in the city establishment cared what the third paper, a tabloid called *The Daily News*, wrote. It was thought to be aimed mostly at a colored audience anyway and operated on a shoestring. Despite these realities, Neil felt obliged to challenge his old boss.

"You might get some traction and be a hero. The kid comes from a pretty prominent family. His dad I guess was well known at the Courthouse. His mom's a big deal at the NAACP. It won't go down quietly."

"Yeah. I'm surprised we haven't heard a lot of noise yet. But Negro protesting is a long distance away from an official finding of a lynching. The best I can do is give you some information and hope you can find the killer. Maybe we can go public if we have iron-tight evidence against a suspect. Who're you working for, anyway?"

Chapter Two: Lorenzo King

"His mother. I know you talked to her, and she has one page of the file. She asked me to get the rest of the record and any pictures."

"Can't do that. But I will let you look at them here. Same ground rules: You didn't get anything from the Metropolitan Police Department." Neil agreed. Jeffords moved a thin folder that was at the end of the table which Neil had not even noticed and put it in front of his visitor.

Neil opened the folder. The first page, the closing sheet, was identical to Mrs. Van Dyke's copy, except that hers was a Photostat. There was only one other page in the report. It contained a one-paragraph description of the crime scene and the condition of the victim. A stepladder was found nearly under the body which Clayton would have stood on to toss the rope over the rafter and then kicked aside after looping the rope around his head – if he really committed suicide. There was a reference to some blood on the warehouse floor, which the report asserted came from the victim without any evidence the blood was typed or otherwise matched to Clayton. The report concluded that the victim suffered injuries around the head and neck consistent with repeated beating with feet or fists. No examination was made of the torso, a job left for the coroner.

The police report was followed by a one-page form from the coroner. It offered a more technical description of the injuries to the body, including extensive neck bruising caused by the rope. Although the report found torso bruising in addition to injuries to the head and neck, presumably from a beating, the coroner concluded no autopsy was necessary because death was by suicide/hanging.

Two glossy color photos — one taken of a naked Clayton Van Dyke's front and one of his back — were all that remained in the folder. Neil was repulsed, but tried to maintain a professional cop's emotional distance and a studied demeanor. The face in the picture was bloated and heavily bruised, especially noticeable because of Clay's light skin color, which emphasized the red swellings, some of them tinted with darker dried blood. He was barely identifiable as the same young man in the family picture Neil saw at Virginia Van Dyke's house. His torso bore bruises that were wide and crossed the front and back of his body. Neil surmised these could have been a result of beatings with a two-by-four or something of similar size. Only Clay's legs escaped injury.

Neil closed the folder, disappointed. He understood why the police were unwilling to share the photographs with Mrs. Van Dyke. To do otherwise would have been almost sadistic. But the second page of the police report and the coroner's report offered no clues or leads.

"Bob, is that really all there is?" Jeffords didn't immediately respond. Instead, he heaved a regretful sigh and looked at the ceiling, almost as if he was surprised to find himself in the interrogation room. His mouth turned down at the left corner and he again sighed, this time more like a scowl.

Chapter Two: Lorenzo King

"I knew you would ask that, Endy. I don't want to lie to you, and I don't want to mislead you." Jeffords paused, like a diver about to take the plunge.

"We have direct proof that this was a murder."

Neil considered the disclosure carefully, weighing it with everything else he had learned that day.

"Other than the evidence of beatings, it's not in the files."

"Of course not. I was told to destroy it."

"What is it?"

"I'll show it to you."

"I thought you destroyed it?"

"I'm not that dumb. Failing to follow-up an investigation is professional misconduct, which can get you fired. Destruction of evidence is a crime, which can land you in prison. I'm not the only one who knows about this evidence. Officer Earle knows, as well as a couple of other cops, the Chief, at least one city commissioner, and I'll bet he told a congressman about it. What goes around comes around. Like you said, the Van Dykes are a prominent family in town. Even if they are Negroes, they might get some action on this some day. I personally hope they do. Nobody will be able to nail me for destruction of evidence if that happens. Like I said, I got a wife and kids.

"Wait here." Jeffords left the room and returned only seconds later. Neil calculated he was gone just long enough to reach his desk and come back. He had a single half-sheet of typing paper in his hand. "You can look at it. Same ground rules."

51

The note was in block handwriting, in pencil, the kind of writing that anyone could duplicate and that can't be tested successfully against a writing sample. It said:

NIGGERS – KEEP TO YOUR PLACE – OR DIE!

Both men were quiet a moment so that Neil could digest the message and its implication. It left no doubt Clayton Van Dyke's death was a lynching, whether by one man or a mob. He was killed by a white man or white men. Not to a scientific certainty, or even to a level of proof necessary at a criminal trial, but it was unthinkable that another black man would write such a note.

Jeffords finally broke the silence. "It was pinned to his shirt."

"Did you do any follow-up, any checking with his friends, associates, to see if he had any enemies, any run-ins with whites?" Neil asked.

"That would be the next step, I guess. But we got cut off at the knees before that could get started. We haven't done a damn thing except collect evidence at the scene and send the body to the coroner. Oh, and cover up the whole damn thing. That too." The presence of the note in the room – the physical proof that could be held in the hand that a man was murdered, that he probably was killed because of his race, and that the government of the District of Columbia, run by the Congress of the United States, was doing nothing to catch the killer – rekindled Jeffords' anger. Anger was in his voice as he grabbed the paper back from Neil, his hands shaking in barely controlled rage.

"I hope to hell you find out who did this. This man deserves justice. His killer needs to be caught. Any goddamned southern Senate asshole or know-nothing D.C. commissioner who doesn't believe that needs to be strung up himself. And I promise you this: If we find some dead white guy was the victim of a violent crime, just give me the word that he killed this kid and I'll make sure he gets the same investigative treatment Van Dyke is getting – none!"

Neil chewed his lip. The veteran officer was licensing him to commit homicide. Neil had always thought Jeffords' friendships with the Negroes on his beat were just for the job. He was wrong. Jeffords didn't like the colored getting the short end. It was another surprise in a day full of them, and the day wasn't half over.

"Might not even be a white guy," he mused. "This note could be intended to throw you off. The note proves Van Dyke was murdered, although the beating pretty much told us that."

"Hard to believe somebody would be like that to their own race," Jeffords replied, shaking his head.

Jeffords wouldn't give Neil a Photostat of the note, but let him copy the contents on another sheet of paper.

The younger man thanked Jeffords and shook his hand. The crime and the cover-up were monstrous, but Neil took some comfort in Jeffords. He was proof there were decent men in the police department. Neil would die before betraying his trust.

Unanimous Verdict

The substation was not far from Pennsylvania Avenue, SE, where the Capital Bank of Washington was located. It was known as a Negro bank, and it was where Mrs. Van Dyke maintained her account. Neil arrived there just before the bank's closing and cashed Mrs. Van Dyke's $500 check. The teller asked for two forms of identification and conferred with his manager, who placed a phone call, presumably to Mrs. Van Dyke, before cashing the check. He clearly was anxious about giving so much cash to a walk-up white man from the account of a middle-aged black woman. Neil couldn't blame him. It was a first in his life, too.

Taking advantage of his newfound wealth, and noting that it was almost 3 p.m., Neil took a taxi across the Hill to the office of Lorenzo King. Along the way, he pondered the purpose of the nasty note. Maybe the note was a ruse to throw off the police. But more likely the killer wanted to communicate something. But what? To whom? He couldn't have known the investigation would be suppressed. Was the note specific to something Clay did? Or was it just a racist taunt intended for the newspapers, something to create panic and cause riots? Neil concluded that the note was not much of a clue to the identity of the killer, but it sharply increased his own interest in solving the crime. Whoever wrote the note was a monster.

Although he had lived in Washington all of his life, Neil had never set foot on H Street, NE, which was the principal "downtown"

Chapter Two: Lorenzo King

Negro shopping area. It was the colored woman's equivalent to the white woman's F Street, NW, which was home to all the major department stores – Woodward & Lothrop, Garfinkle's, Hecht's, Lansberg's and, a couple of blocks south, Kanns. None of them overtly discriminated, but, except for Kanns, the prices were high and little effort was made to attract a colored clientele.

The H street shops were smaller, just storefronts 18-feet wide, connected in block-long brick rows, interspersed occasionally by a larger store. Each store had display windows on either side of the entry door. Because of their small size, the stores tended to specialize in a particular line of products. There were shoe stores, handbag stores, women's clothing stores, men's haberdasheries, hardware stores and appliance stores. Professional offices for doctors, lawyers, realtors and the like occupied the two or three stories above the retail shops. Neil spent a few moments eyeing the windows in the shops around King's office. The merchandise seemed different – more colorful than that offered on F Street, even whimsical sometimes. The haberdasher's window displayed a blue pin-striped three-piece suit that any lawyer or congressman could wear proudly. But in the other window was a bright red suit on a mannequin which also wore white patent leather shoes. Neil thought of his father in such a suit and laughed to himself. He had never even wondered where black folk purchased their clothes. Now he knew. Shopping might be more fun on H Street, he thought – if he were a colored man.

Unanimous Verdict

A second story window above a shoe store garishly advertised "Lorenzo KING of Private Investigators" in bright Chinese red letters bordered in gold. Neil opened the street level door and climbed stairs to King's office. He opened the office door without knocking, expecting to find an outer office with a receptionist. Instead, he stepped directly into King's office. It was elegant.

The walls were paneled in a tightly grained wood that was stained a deep brown with hints of red and was maintained in a bright polished shine. Matching built-in bookcases lined half the room on both right and left walls. The book bindings were worn, suggesting that the volumes were referred to frequently. Neil had no opportunity to review the titles as he tread on the thick grey pile carpet in the direction of a battle-ship sized desk of darker stain than the walls which fully occupied the space in front of two of three sash windows overlooking H Street. Atop the desk was a large brass pen and pencil holder engraved "J. Edgar Hoover FBI Crime Fighter". It also bore the red, white, blue and gold FBI seal. Otherwise, the leather-covered desk surface was marred only by a short stack of typewritten papers. The owner of the desk was turned on his chair with his back to the office entrance, looking out the window. As Neil continued his stride forward he said, "Mr. King? My name is Neil Endicott."

The man turned in his chair. "You don't knock, Mr. Endicott?"

"I'm sorry sir. I expected a receptionist."

"No, we are a low overhead operation here. No receptionist.

Chapter Two: Lorenzo King

These fingers do a fine job of typing. Don't need to pay anyone to do it for me." He rose from his chair.

"Are you busy? We have an appointment I think."

"I'm as busy as Christ at a cripples convention, son. But you are correct. We have an appointment. Please sit down."

As Neil sat on a somewhat scratched Chippendale dining room chair, which served as King's guest chair, he tried to assess his host. His first thought was that Lorenzo King was a black Moses in a three-piece suit, if children's Bible illustrations were accurate, only a lot fatter. His face was the color of strong black coffee. It was encircled by a pure white beard and a thick frizzy mane of white hair behind a four inch bald spot running from his forehead to the middle of his scalp. Other than his color, his features were not pronounced. His nose was almost Roman, with just the slightest additional flare at the nostrils. His lips, to the extent they could be assessed between a thick white mustache that met the beard below his mouth, were not distinguished by size, but the flesh was quite reddish.

Neil's initial impression was that King was a jolly man, not only due to a Santa Claus sized body but because he laughed and his dark eyes twinkled when he squeezed by the desk to welcome his guest with his mildly sacrilegious simile about Jesus. King reached out his right hand to welcome Neil and grabbed Neil's arm with his left hand, forcing it up and down until Neil wondered if King was selling him something.

Unanimous Verdict

Neil took advantage of the few seconds King required to maneuver back to his desk chair to examine the walls in the front half of the office. Rather than bookcases, the walls were covered with framed certificates and award plaques. There was one for "Valor In Law Enforcement" from the Alabama State Police. Another was for "Heroism Including Risk of Life" from the Neshoba County, Mississippi sheriff's office. Clarendon County, South Carolina, had awarded King the "Distinguished Civilian Service Award" and Henrico County, Virginia something called the "Distinguished Crime-Fighter Award." Another plaque was engraved "Official Kentucky Colonel".

"An impressive collection of awards."

"Yes, I helped a lot of colored folk in those states and the authorities were very appreciative," King said, adopting a serious mien. "In Alabama I stopped some crackers from whipping on the skull of a colored man. In Mississippi I single-handedly stopped a lynch mob and in Kentucky, why I personally desegregated every restroom in the state." With the last "achievement", the serious mien fell away, replaced by another loud laugh and the clapping of hands.

"God, I love to give that speech! Especially to white folk. Takes a minute or two for them to get the joke. Colored folk don't need the speech. They get it as soon as they read the words on this gimcrackery.

"Of course, J. Edgar Hoover just loves the colored folk. You can hardly stop him from giving out these pen and pencil sets to any

Chapter Two: Lorenzo King

Negro caught walking in front of the Department of Justice." He laughed again at his own sarcasm while Neil squirmed with the red face that King anticipated and loved to cause. "I'm surprised a good detective like you didn't notice something about all these awards, young man."

Neil decided to take the bait. "None of them have a name of a recipient on them."

"You win an award, too. Take one off the wall!"

"No thanks. I think you deserve to have all of them," Neil said, trying to get into the same spirit of fun as his host. "Where did you get them?"

"Some are real that I found in flea markets and the like. A couple of them I just made up and passed copies out to friends and good clients. Not surprisingly, the most popular are from Mississippi and Alabama. The belly of the beast. I have to make fun of those places once in a while. They are the two best examples of the many places in this country where the inmates run the asylums!"

The jokes now exhausted, King turned serious again.

"Mrs. Van Dyke told me you were going to the police before coming here. Did you find anything out?"

"Hold on, Mr. King..."

"You can call me Lou. It's not really short for Lorenzo, but I like it. Common man sound."

"OK, Lou. Don't we first have to talk to each other a little bit? Kinda feel each other out and see if we can work together on this before we start exchanging confidential information?"

King stared scornfully for a moment before responding.

"What is it that you need to know? We were both hired by Mrs. Van Dyke to find out who killed her son. That's all that's necessary."

"Well, I disagree. I'd like to know a little about you – how long you've been in the business, what kinds of cases you've handled. Get to know each other."

"That would be a one-sided conversation, wouldn't it?" King's eyes narrowed under his furrowed snow-white brows. "I mean, I've been at this business over 30 years. I understand you've been at it about 30 days."

"Six months, but I was a cop before I went to Korea and for a year after I got back." Neil wondered if everyone he met already knew his background. At least it seemed every colored person he met that day did.

"How long before Korea?" King asked.

"Two years. Walked a beat in Northeast."

"I don't think that's long enough to have to polish your badge."

"There's no call for that." Neil was now flushed. He was embarrassed and angry at the same time. King was being disrespectful to him and to the badge. Neil thought he had been diplomatic and didn't deserve the abuse. "We're going to be partners on this thing, so we have to get along."

Chapter Two: Lorenzo King

"*Partners?* Are you serious? You are only on this case for one reason, which ain't none of your doing — you are white. Mrs. Van Dyke had to almost beg you to take the case and she isn't sure yet that you really are dedicated to finding out who killed her son. I've been a private investigator in this town since 1922 and a friend of the Van Dykes since they came to town. I may not have a fancy receptionist or an office on Connecticut Avenue, but I am successful by any standard you want, especially compared to those walrus faced racist PIs downtown who can't find their ass with either hand.

"I'm happy to *say* we are partners working together, for the sake of appearances. Hell, if we have to do so to please some redneck for the benefit of the case, you can even *say* I'm working for you. But the truth is, I know what I'm doing and you don't. Some politician said being vice president ain't worth a bucket of piss. Well, I'm the president of this operation, and you are the vice president. Now, do we understand each other?"

Neil had not been chewed out so aggressively since he was a Marine recruit. He was not going to stand for being remonstrated by some colored combination of Santa Claus, Moses and The Kingfish.

"The only shit around here is what you are swinging, Father Christmas. I've been on the D.C. force a total of three years. I walked a beat in Northeast and learned plenty. I was a Marine and lost a helluva lot of buddies and nearly my own life in two years in Korea. You say you've been here since '22. That means you missed the wars, both of them. Sitting around on your fat ass collecting phony awards and looking for missing dogs and cats, I'll bet. As for Mrs. Van Dyke, she's right that at first I didn't want the job. But now I do. There aren't many times you can work for good money *and* for the right thing, but this is one of them. I probably want to solve this as much as you do. So I'll forget what you just said. But we will be partners. That means equals. I'll listen to you and you listen to me. Do we understand each other *now?*" Neil expected to be ejected from the office. Part of him hoped to be ejected so he could work the case alone.

King rubbed his face and turned to the window. The back of his head was all white hair. He said nothing for at least a minute, instead humming to himself a tune which Neil did not recognize. Neil was calming himself after his emotional speech. He regretted bringing up his Korean War experience and comparing it to King's non-existent war record. It was a cheap shot. But he didn't regret it enough to apologize. King's shots were cheap, too.

Finally, King turned to face Neil. "Mrs. Van Dyke is expecting us to find out why her son died," he said gravely. "She is counting on us to show her that her son did not die for no purpose in this life. I think waiting for us to give her an answer is what will sustain her through the sudden loss of her husband and her son. Without that, I'm not sure she will be with us long. That's a long way of saying she needs us – both of us. We can't bring her any message if the investigation vehicle is driven on two flat tires – you and me – or if we are sparring like two rabbits in a bag. Maybe I spoke too harshly. I'm sure you did. My career is not to be ridiculed. But we have no choice but to work together, so

Chapter Two: Lorenzo King

I emphasize *together.* Let's just agree that the best idea, the best strategy, wins, regardless of who it comes from. Can we agree to that?"

Neil would not take the bait to apologize for himself, but nodded his agreement to terms of a cease-fire meant to save face.

"Just remember this: My loyalty is to Mrs. Van Dyke. That's not just because she is my client. She is my friend. I won't compromise that."

"Agreed," Neil said. "I wouldn't expect anything else."

"And one other thing. If I sense that you are patronizing me because of my color, or treating me as anything but an equal or better in this case, I'll let you know and give you a second chance. If you fuck up again, you are out. Virginia – Mrs. Van Dyke to you – told me you are just what we'd expect from a Chevy Chase boy. That means a walking around collection of bigoted prejudices based on the three M's. Not mean, exactly, just casually accepting that you're better than any black person 'cause you're white."

"That's not fair. I was very courteous to Mrs. Van Dyke."

"Exactly. Courtesy prompted by overturned low expectations. I heard you couldn't hide your surprise at how well Virginia lives. How fine she dresses. And how she speaks as well as you do or better. Sometimes she felt you were gawking at her. Don't you think she's developed a sixth sense about such things? She knows a patronizing attitude, especially from a young fella' who's ignorant about black folk."

Neil was too surprised and stunned to fight back. He had been ambushed by King and Mrs. Van Dyke. They were minimizing him;

making him small and ashamed so that they could control him, Neil thought. He was not going to let anyone do that to him, especially a couple of Negroes. The war would go on. For now, however, there was no point in continuing this battle. He would back off.

"I'm sorry that Mrs. Van Dyke felt that way. Please apologize to her for any hurt feelings. It was totally unintentional." He wasn't going to otherwise answer King's personal attacks or agree to any conditions he laid down. "Let's drop this for now and focus on our jobs."

"Just don't forget what I told you. I'm not happy to be working with a white man, especially a new-born. Now tell me what you found out at the police station."

Neil shared everything he learned with King except the existence of the handwritten note. He definitely did not trust King and revealing the note might cause King to inform Mrs. Van Dyke. The note was explosive. It would be enough to prompt the NAACP and the colored community to go to the newspapers and push for an investigation regardless of other considerations. Sharing it with King also risked breaching the commitment to confidentiality he gave Jeffords. The rest of the information from the police files did nothing except to confirm what Mrs. Van Dyke and King already knew.

"Not much to go on. Of course, you didn't know Clayton Van Dyke. I assume Mrs. Van Dyke told you her son was a little bit of a black nationalist?"

"She mentioned it briefly. Based on what you said, maybe she thought I'd gawk at her if she talked more about it – like looking at a zoo animal."

Chapter Two: Lorenzo King

King ignored the jibe. "He picked it up during the war. Guess it was the first time he really was exposed to some bad racists. Kinda' cloistered from that stuff up in LeDroit Park. Howard University, Dunbar High – Clayton was with the crème de la crème until the Army. I'm sure he knew about racism – he surely went to the movie theatre and had to sit in the balcony – but he never before experienced the brutal stuff that colored men face in the South and in poor communities all over all the time.

"A man like Clayton, a man who assumed he was as good as any white man and better than most – and rightly so – wasn't gonna' turn tail. He fought back for a while. Did some time in the brig for fighting white GIs. Hardened him. Made him tougher. Made him hate white folks.

"You ever heard of the Nation of Islam or Wallace Muhammed?"

"No. Never."

"Well, they are a race group. Mostly in Detroit. I guess their closest ancestor is Marcus Garvey. You probably heard of him. Garvey wanted to take the colored back to Africa or set up a section of the U.S. for black folk. Nation of Islam is similar, but they talk tougher. They want nothing to do with the white man, 'cept maybe to kill 'em, if you took 'em seriously. I don't take 'em seriously, but Clayton did."

"Do you think that had anything to do with his killing, his attitude about race, I mean?" Neil hoped King believed this was a possibility since it was the only lead they had right now.

65

"Maybe. Maybe not. White folks are always ready to believe that any time a colored man talks up it's a reason for some racist cracker or another to kill him. But you know we got some evil black folk around D.C., too. They might have done the deed. Clay didn't hang out with white folk much, except maybe at work."

Neil was tempted to share the note from the crime scene because it seemed to establish a racist motive for the slaying. Instead, he asked: "Did Clayton have any drug problems? Alcohol? Hang around with a bad crowd?"

"He liked to hang around in the bottle clubs after hours listening to jazz. He'd likely run into white folks there. Maybe he smoked a little of the Mary Jane. Common in a musician crowd, you know. He drank a little. I don't know his friends. I'm way past the age of stayin' up until the wee hours carryin' on, so I never saw Clayton socially except at his parents' house."

"No girlfriends?"

"Not that I know of. Didn't you ask Mrs. Van Dyke about that?"

"Same answer from her. She doesn't know much about his social life."

"Could be a problem at work. Can't really see the public library crowd killin' anybody, but stranger things have happened. Plenty of preachers killin' folks or gettin' killed," King said.

"I once had a case where a deacon of a local AME church close to downtown was murdered. Cops didn't pay much attention to it and the widow hired me, just like Mrs. Van Dyke did. Turned out the deacon and his preacher got in a fight over whether it was OK to substitute grape juice for wine at Communion. Preacher shot the deacon dead and took the body down the street and left it in front of a bar hoping people would figure that's where he was shot. Lots of witnesses, but they were scared to turn in a preacher. I had to do a lot of persuading. Preacher's in prison now. I heard he's got quite a following behind bars. Anyway, I would be surprised — but not shocked — if some angry librarian wiped out Clay. Most anybody can kill if they're mad enough."

Neil was impressed with the story, but wondered if it was true. "How many murders have you solved, anyway?"

"Solved? You mean so the police make an arrest and the guy is tried and convicted? Not many. Three I can think of offhand, including the preacher I just told you about. My job isn't to find the bad guy, just to get my client off. Sometimes he is the bad guy, but the evidence the cops have still might be wrong. Justice is the government's job, not mine. Mostly I develop good evidence and give it to my client. Sometimes it identifies a killer. The client takes it from there."

"You mean they extract their revenge based on what you tell them?"

"I don't ask. Look, the justice system in this city — hell, in this country — is run by whites for whites, which means it comes down hard on colored folk committing crimes against white folk, or even if they're just suspected of committing crimes. But black-on-black crime? Forget it. That's mostly do-it-yourself work to get any justice at all. If I ain't convinced the evidence shows another guy is guilty, I don't give it to the client. I just try to get the client off."

"So you're the jury?"

"You can look at it that way. So what. Clayton's murder proves my point quite well. No investigation. Just another nigger dead. If another colored man killed him, then they say 'who cares?' If a white man killed him, then it's 'he probably deserved it.' Either way, no investigation, no justice. You can't defend it, but you have to live with it best you can. If we figure out who killed him and the cops don't do nothin', then there's other solutions."

"So what's your suggestion?" Neil had no good ideas and decided to let King take the lead. He admitted to himself that King had a lot more experience, if any of his stories were even half true.

"It's Friday. Big night at the jazz joints and bottle clubs. I think Clay was partial to the Blue Mirror. Let's see what we can dig up there."

"I have an engagement for dinner," Neil replied. "How about we meet at the Blue Mirror around 11?" He had been to the Blue Mirror once or twice. It was a mixed race crowd. Good jazz, lousy food.

"Fine. No point in getting there any earlier. I suspect Clay's buddies won't even start their evening until 11. It'll give me time to take a nap, else I won't make it to the wee hours."

Chapter Two: Lorenzo King

Neil rose to leave, but felt obliged to do more to heal the breech erected earlier in their conversation. "It's too bad we got into a fight right away. I hope we can work well together."

King was in no mood for further apologies. "If we don't, I'll bounce you from this case like a harlot workin' a revival meeting." He grinned and shook the hand Neil offered while showing him to the door.

"By the way, when you were insulting me you mentioned something about a Chevy Chase boy learning about coloreds from the 'three Ms.' What are they?"

King's grin disappeared as he looked Neil squarely in the eye. "Mammies, maids and movies," he replied, closing the door.

Chapter Three: Problems with Parents, April 23, 1954

It was 5:30 when Neil left King's office. He was due at his parents' house in upper Northwest at six, but paying for a taxi to take him that far was extravagant, even with $500 in his pocket. It took one bus and two streetcars, including the long ride on the L-4 line practically to Chevy Chase Circle. Neil reached his destination about 6:30. His parents lived in a trim stucco house on McKinley Street, east of Connecticut Avenue. It had a broad front porch that Neil loved when he was a child because he could pretend to study while looking at passing cars and pedestrians.

Both his brother's and his sister's cars were parked on the street. Neil entered the house without knocking. He still considered it "his" house, as part of the Endicott family. The Endicotts were the original owners. They had two children when they bought the place, and did not anticipate a third, who was Neil. Neil had to room with his brother, Norcross, until the older boy went to war after graduating from Georgetown University in 1943. Sister Nancy left the house when she married a man named Brad Gifford in 1947. Neil returned to the house after his stint in Korea was over in 1952 and did not move to his own apartment for a year. Finally, after more than 32 years, the senior Endicotts had the house to themselves. It suddenly felt too large.

Neil's father, Samuel, and his brother were seated in two Queen Anne chairs located at either end of a well-worn sofa on which Brad Gifford was sitting. They were having a drink when Neil entered. No one rose, but all three waved a hand in greeting.

71

"You're a little late, Neil. Anyway, glad you could make it. Would you like a drink? I had planned gin and tonics, but it's a little chilly tonight. Not spring yet. How about a scotch and soda?"

"Sure, Dad. Thanks. Where are the ladies and the kids?"

"Grace, your mother and sister are in the kitchen. I think the children are in the den watching television," his father said. "Did I tell you we got a television? Very fancy one, too. An RCA. It's also got a radio and record player. I got the office to pay for it."

"How did you do that?" Neil was impressed that his parents finally had bought a television set.

"To watch the Army-McCarthy hearings. I argued I needed one to keep up when I wasn't at the office. I'm surprised I sold them on the idea, since I'm in the office all the time. Let me mix you that drink." He headed for the kitchen. Neil took a seat on the worn sofa next to his brother-in-law.

"So, old man, how's the detective business treating you?" his brother asked in a manner that suggested he didn't care about either the question or the answer.

"Not bad. I just got a big assignment." Neil hoped to whet his brother's curiosity. His family was critical of his latest career choice and Neil could not resist the chance to promote it.

"Big? What's big?"

"Five hundred a week plus expenses."

Chapter Three: Problems with Parents

"Jesus! That's what Dad makes. Maybe more. Pretty good wages for a guy like you." Neil knew that in his brother's view a "guy like you" meant a guy without any college. "What evil things do you have to do to make so much filthy lucre?"

"A man died earlier this month. The police have ruled it suicide. The victim's mother thinks it was murder and wants me to investigate."

"Murder? That's the big leagues. Aren't the police investigating? Why did she pick you? Do you have any experience at that stuff? What do you think?" His brother's curiosity was easier to spark than Neil had imagined.

"Slow down, brother. Do you want me to answer all those questions or just the last one?"

"All of them. But wait 'til Dad gets here." As if on cue, Samuel Endicott appeared bearing a tray with four drinks which he offered to his sons and son-in-law before taking his own and sitting.

"Dad, Neil's got a job for some old widow paying him $500 a week. He's supposed to track down a murderer."

"Hold on," Neil said. "I didn't say she was a widow, although she is. She is a mother. And I don't know about tracking down any murderer. We have to at least figure out if it was a murder first. The police say it was a suicide."

"We?" his father asked. As an editor, he was always alert to a change in pronoun.

"I'm working with another guy. He's a PI, too."

"What's his name?" Samuel Endicott prided himself on his knowledge of people in Washington. Many names passed through his hands as managing editor for news at *The Star*. Because of both his job and his distinguished New England family name, the Endicotts frequently attended White House state dinners and embassy functions at which Sam met many of the city's movers and shakers. He probably knew the guy working with his son, he thought. Probably a PI at Metro Detectives or Five Diamonds, the biggest private agencies in town. Their clients could afford to pay that kind of money.

"Lorenzo King."

Samuel Endicott was puzzled. "I never heard of him. Is he a D.C. private dick?"

"Yes, he is. Office on H Street in Northeast."

"H Street Northeast! Is he a colored guy?"

"Yes, Dad," Neil said, a touch wearily.

"That explains the big fee, anyway." A grin broke across Norcross' thin, sallow face. "Narcotics, numbers, maybe prostitution. Big money in all that." Neil tried to laugh with the other men at his brother's observation, but could manage only a wan grin. He quickly turned serious and surprised himself with a little anger when he thought of Virginia Van Dyke.

"My client has nothing to do with any of that."

"Who's your client, for goodness sakes?" his father asked.

74

Chapter Three: Problems with Parents

"That is confidential information." Neil wasn't about to alert his father to the possibility the police were covering up the death of the son of a prominent black family.

"Was the victim colored?" Samuel Endicott asked.

"I don't think I'm at liberty to talk more about it," Neil said.

"Fine, don't tell us. But at $500 a week, I'll bet it's a white victim who was found dead in a black neighborhood. Probably some guy who went to a bottle joint on the wrong side of town, got drunk and had some kind of fatal accident. Or maybe he was killed by a colored guy. That's why you need a Negro PI. Am I right? Because he can get information from the coloreds you can't?"

"You got it Dad," Neil said, knowing the subject would be dropped now that his father could claim to have figured out the mystery.

"You see, Norcross. Your brother isn't wrapped up with drugs and prostitution, after all." Neil's father clearly was relieved. "But I really wish you'd reconsider this detective business. Now you're associating with coloreds. Nothing wrong with that, I guess, but it's more than a little below you and it just proves how crude this whole private detective business is."

"You don't like colored folk much, do you, Dad?" Neil couldn't recall his father ever talking about Negroes, not counting the Endicott's housekeeper.

"Look, we brought them over here and now we have to live with them. I've got nothing against them. But they kind of rut in their own kind of culture. It's nothing a self-respecting white man wants to get into. We shouldn't mistreat the Negro, but we really have little in common." Samuel Endicott spoke as a man expressing a commonly accepted truth, such as that the sun would rise tomorrow or that spring rain was good for flowers. Norcross and his son-in-law nodded their agreement. Neil was silent. His mother entered the room, guaranteeing a change of subject.

"Why hello Neil. I'm so glad you could come. It's just like old times having all our children in this house again. And now their children, too." His mother thought her life pretty much ended when the kids left the house. She was genuinely rejuvenated when they visited, especially with grandchildren.

"Hi Mom. Glad to be here. I guess it's getting pretty crowded in the old place."

"Plenty of room for more, dear. We're keeping space for your kids when you visit with your wife."

"Please, Mom. Nothing in sight on that score right now."

"What about that nice young woman you brought around last time. What's her name?"

"Jennifer, Mom. She's just a friend."

"For now, maybe," Mrs. Endicott said. "You never know."

"No, Mom, you don't."

"Anyway, it's time for dinner." The men in the family trooped into the living room to take their seats. Nancy and Norcross's wife, Grace, were already seated. The four children, two for each of Neil's

Chapter Three: Problems with Parents

siblings, sat around a card table under the arch which separated the dining room and living room. They already were pushing and shoving and playing with their food. The eldest was six.

Neil knew what the menu would be: Dry, overcooked roast beef, lumpy mashed potatoes, green beans or broccoli, also overcooked, soft, mushy rolls that were nothing more than a flavorless excuse for eating butter, and a cake. The rolls and cake were always purchased from Schupp's Bakery on Connecticut Avenue. Only the cake would be delicious. Everyone knew, but no one said, that Mrs. Endicott was a terrible cook. Her daughter and daughter-in-law were no better. All the men claimed ignorance about all kitchen activities, including washing dishes. Making accommodations to bad food was the cost of admission to the Endicott family. Once they all were seated, conversation would be lively if the usual pattern was followed. The quality of the food was secondary, since there was not a gourmand in the group.

"So, Brad, you've been quiet. What's going on with your business?" Norcross asked as his sister delivered serving bowls of vegetables to the table and his father circulated a pitcher of iced tea. Brad had completed a B.S. in biology at an obscure Midwest college. He never clearly explained how he escaped military service and the Endicott men, each of whom was a Marine in different wars, did not press him for details out of respect for Nancy and fear an honest answer would cause bad blood. As a result, however, Brad was forever condemned to be an outsider among the veterans. The Endicott women welcomed Brad. He was more relaxed and accommodating than Samuel and Norcross,

77

who never entirely lost the erect bearing, stern manner and expectation of orderliness characteristic of Marine officers. They prided themselves on their manliness. Brad told Nancy privately that taking pride in just being a man, which was an accident of birth, was silly and that the Endicott men had plenty else to be proud of, except maybe Neil. The Endicotts all maintained a trim physique, with only Samuel starting to show a small pot belly, nearly forty years after his discharge. Brad's belly already hung well over his belt and he didn't care. Neil, who "only" was an enlisted man, was more like his mother. The Marines had toughened his body, but he somehow escaped the service much less influenced by his enlistment than his father and brother. Even so, he, too, thought Brad a lightweight who left little impression.

"Oh, not much," Brad responded to Norcross's question as he cut a one-inch slice of butter from the stick and applied it to his potatoes. "We acquired some property in Bethesda. One hundred acres. We expect to put some high quality shops there and about 150 homes. You know where Old Georgetown Road is? On the way to Rockville?" Brad was on the staff of a local real estate developer. He was salaried, but his purchase of a large, expensive, rambling house on Primrose Street in Chevy Chase Village, just a few blocks across the Maryland line, proved to the Endicotts that he was doing well. The house cost over $40,000.

"Christ that's far out. Have they even paved those streets?" Norcross said laughingly. Nancy jumped in to defend her husband.

Chapter Three: Problems with Parents

"I've seen the drawings of those houses. They are going to be very nice – little brick colonials. They are going to attract nice families with children. Maybe you should think about moving your practice to Bethesda, Norcross? You always talk about getting into the ground floor of some prosperous new neighborhood."

"I've been thinking about something like that," her brother said, suddenly serious. "There's too much competition around here. Might be wise to pioneer someplace like that."

"We would love to have you sign-on as a tenant," Brad said enthusiastically. "You can even help us design an office building you would like." This prompted several minutes of further discussion, ending with an agreement that Brad would take his brother-in-law on an inspection trip to Bethesda next week. Neil's mother and father then started reminiscing about auto trips through Bethesda when Wisconsin Avenue was unpaved and about the rural county seat town of Rockville, Maryland.

"I think Walter Johnson's farm was just off Old Georgetown Road," Samuel told the table. "Don't know if Hazel and the kids sold it off. I have a vague recollection they moved to Gaithersburg. They probably made killing on that Georgetown Road farm. Remind me on Monday, honey. Frank Stann should write an update about Johnson. Maybe pay his widow a visit." Stann was a popular sports columnist at *The Star*. Johnson, a Hall of Fame pitcher, was the best player the lowly Washington Senators ever had. He died in 1946. "Maybe you could have an office on Walter Johnson's farm!" the eldest Endicott said to his elder son with palpable enthusiasm.

Norcross carried the unusual name of his uncle, his grandfather and numerous grandfathers before him. His own young son was named Norcross to continue the line. The senior Endicott fought all attempts by friends and acquaintances to shorten his son's name to "Nort" or "Nordy" and the like. The son was now waging the same battle against the six-year-old friends of his son. To hear Norcross or Samuel tell it, the Norcross name crossed the Atlantic while Plymouth Rock was molten. Samuel Endicott shared this pride of ancestry, even though his older brother got the distinctive family name in his generation. His son was born before his nephew, so Samuel was able to steal the name back.

Norcross was a war hero. He joined the Marines in time for most of the major battles of the South Pacific and was prepared to lead a company into Japan if an invasion was necessary. He won two Silver Stars in quick succession on Guadalcanal and Tarawa. His father made sure stories of his heroism were printed on the front page of *The Star*. Even *The Post* printed a short item when Norcross got his second Star. After the war, Norcross returned to Georgetown and earned a degree in dentistry. He opened a practice near Chevy Chase Circle in 1950, just when the children of returning veterans were losing their baby teeth. He told his family that the practice was good, but that the suburban practices did better.

He and Nancy recently moved from a rented row house in Georgetown, near the university, to a large fixer-upper on McComb Street in Cleveland Park, closer to downtown than Chevy Chase.

Chapter Three: Problems with Parents

Only Neil, who was awarded a Purple Heart, but no medals for heroism in Korea, was not on the post-war track to affluence that was the God-given right of any kid who grew up in Chevy Chase and survived the war. He was not envious of his brother's success or his in-law, but he was a little jealous of the evident pride his father expressed over their achievements. He wanted to change the subject before the family again got around to pressing him about college.

"So, you guys got a TV, huh? What's the screen size?" Neil asked. "I think that's supposed to be important." He was glad his parents owned a television. His father rarely parted with a dollar for what he called "extras." His mother was not so cheap, but respected her husband's rules as the breadwinner. The family's radio, for example, was purchased long before the war.

"Twenty-four inches. Good reception even without rabbit ears."

"What did it set *The Star* back?" Neil asked.

"What does *The Star* have to do with it?" his mother interjected. The men at the table knew instantly that Samuel Endicott had not told his wife that the television console was bought by the newspaper. Neil shut up to let his Dad handle the situation.

"Damn, Neil. You've got a big mouth," his farther said angrily. Turning to his wife at the other end of the dinner table, he said, "I persuaded the paper to pay for it. TV covers more and more stuff, especially the hearings on the Hill. I persuaded them it was necessary for my job."

Unanimous Verdict

Mrs. Endicott turned red and excused herself from the table. She had spent the week excited about the $400 purchase, telling her friends and showing off the set to visitors. Not only was the console handsome with its cherry cabinet and three-speed record player, but it was a visible sign of her husband's success and, she thought, his love and respect for his wife, who had been requesting a set for months. At least, that is what Mrs. Endicott believed until Neil disclosed his father's secret.

There was a moment of silence after Mrs. Endicott left the room. Nancy initiated the bombardment.

"Terrific, Neil. Why didn't you just shut up?"

"Now Mom's in tears and the dinner is ruined, thanks to you," chimed in Norcross. Brad and Grace only looked knowingly at each other across the dining table, uncomfortable to be in the middle of another Endicott family fight.

"I didn't know you were keeping it secret, Dad," Neil said in his defense.

"Why should he have told Mom? He got to save some money and make her feel good. What's wrong with that?" Nancy kept up her attack.

"Now, now Nancy. Neil is right. I should have told him to keep it a secret. Your mother will get over it," he said. Norcross pursued another line of sibling torment.

Chapter Three: Problems with Parents

"Neil, you shouldn't be after Dad for the TV. What have you given our parents lately? Christmas cards? That was it last Christmas, wasn't it? Crummy cards. This detective business is a joke. Isn't it time you grew up? Isn't it a son's duty to make his folks proud?"

"Lay off, Nordy. I'll lead my own life, thanks." Neil used the hated nickname like a weapon.

"You're in a fine fix now," his sister said angrily. "No college, a crappy job and no prospects. I mean, nobody believes you can be some kind of *Boston Blackie*," referencing a radio and television program about a private eye. "Why don't you get your degree? You've got the Korean GI bill. You can still get a diploma before you're 30. Make something of your life." Neil's only thought – unspoken – was that the criticism came from a girl who spent two years at Mount Vernon College, a finishing school at best, and whose sole aim at the time was finding a husband.

Neil hunkered down in his chair and focused on Grace, who knew better than to step into feuds among blood relatives. She turned her eyes away from him. Neil always considered her lovely, but not especially bright. A good dentist's wife, he thought, while his siblings continued their attack. A good fit for his hero brother, who rarely expressed a thought more complex than how to fill a molar.

The raised adult voices quieted the children at the card table, but Nancy's last remarks were delivered with such force that one of her children started to cry. His mother was scaring him. Nancy cut off her rant to comfort her son in the living room. But Norcross wouldn't let go.

"Dad, can't you get him a job at *The Star*? The place is riddled with nepotism. Can't you get a share of it? Last I knew, your ink stained wretches didn't need a college degree. You don't have one."

"I'm not interested in the newspaper business."

Neil's father ignored him.

"That's true, I don't. But newspapers were different in 1919 and so was the country. Most jobs didn't require college. We pretty much expect at least some college for reporters now. Still, I probably could get you on as a copyboy or something if you were at least attending college. You aren't a Noyes or a Kauffman, of course, but I could hide you someplace." The Noyes and Kauffman families owned *The Star* and were notorious for favoring relatives for jobs. "If you'd rather sell ads, I could make inquiries in that department. A successful display adman makes good money."

"I'll repeat it, Dad. I'm not interested."

Mrs. Endicott returned to the dining room, recovered from her surprise, if not relieved of her disappointment.

"Are you all picking on poor Neil again? He's just testing his wings. He's still young. His father and I are very proud of him already. He's already been a policeman and a war hero. What more would you want of him? Just leave him alone." Mother's remarks were heartfelt and reasonable, Neil thought, but because she never criticized any of her children, her opinion about Neil carried little weight with his brother and sister.   And although everyone was too polite to mention it, the only medal he received was a Purple Heart for a shrapnel wound to his leg that took him off the front lines for less than a week.

"Thanks, Mom. I appreciate that."

"He's 22 and acts 16," Norcross said to his mother.

"I'm 24," Neil said.

"So it's even worse."

"All right. Enough," Samuel Endicott said firmly as Nancy reentered the room, her son quieted in her arms. "Neil, I'm not so concerned that you don't have a stable home life, a family or a good career at this point. You are young enough to get all those things still, and maybe a college degree is overrated. I've done ok without one." Neil suspected this merciful dispensation would come at a price. His father's voice turned grave.

"What troubles me more than all of that is you don't have much drive to achieve anything, or even a cause or an interest that might drive you to make something of yourself. I don't want you to be uncomfortable, but we are all family and this is as good a time as any to talk about it.

"Are you interested in politics? I probably could get you a job on the Hill. A trade? I'll bet Brad could get you a job managing construction projects. Doesn't anything attract your interest?"

"Good God. In case you've forgotten, I've picked a career already. I'd call it a kind of law enforcement." Neil was fighting not to lose his temper or deliver a sanctimonious speech about the majesty of the criminal law. The less said about his work the better since three-quarters of his clients just wanted pictures of spouses having sex with other people.

"And your Mother is correct. We were proud of you when you went on the force. Even prouder of your war record and that you returned to police work. But this private investigative work is disreputable at best and might get you in some illegal activities at worst. The PI's I've met are mostly slovenly, with the ethics of a coyote. Private detectives are about as much like real police as professional wresters are to the Olympics. You must know that. Surely your ambition is not to be like those guys, is it? And now you're even involved with some colored business. You really can't get much lower, can you?" His speech completed, Mr. Endicott sat back from the table waiting for his son to respond.

"Would you feel better if I was involved with white crooks, like the Mafia, Dad?"

"Of course not. I don't hold anything against the colored. You were practically raised by a colored lady."

"That's not true." Mrs. Endicott put down her fork and appeared ready to bolt from the room again.

"Of course I don't mean that literally, dear. You were a wonderful mother. But Louella isn't like most coloreds. As a rule, they just aren't

Chapter Three: Problems with Parents

as smart or as honest as most white folk and many of them can be violent. You know that, Neil. I'd prefer you stay away from them."

Neil said only, "I think I'd like to play with my nieces and nephews before I leave, if you don't mind. Are we through?" Without awaiting a response, Neil rose and approached the child-laden card table. Fifteen minutes later, he was gone.

The weather was unusually cold. Perhaps it was the full moon, which was so bright that the street lights were almost unnecessary. The brisk air was a relief from the smothering confines of the house he grew up in and the hot breath of family criticism. Neil decided to head for Connecticut Avenue and walk toward downtown, taking a streetcar somewhere along the way when he got cold or bored. He needed to clear his head. There was plenty of time to meet King at the Blue Mirror.

Neil worked the family's dinner table conversation around in his mind. The theme was a familiar one: "What's wrong with Neil?" Only this time, race was interjected. Only a day earlier, Neil wouldn't disagree with his father's observations about race. Samuel Endicott would admit that they were generalizations, with lots of exceptions. He was a fair man. Yesterday, Neil would not have given his father's remarks a second thought. But tonight they were an itch in his head needing some scratching. Was his father prejudiced? Maybe, but no worse than most folks he knew except maybe Jennifer and her friends, who called themselves "liberals". But maybe Lorenzo King *is* a crook. That seemed unlikely, but Neil surely could not depend on him.

Unanimous Verdict

King didn't seem too serious with his goofy plaques and he was disrespectful of white people. His father's remarks were an insult to someone like Virginia Van Dyke and her husband, but what did he really know about them, either? Defending poor tenants sounded like do-gooder work, but landlords had rights, too. Poor people have poor habits and are unreliable.

It didn't matter. He had the $500. This would surely be his last case for a colored client.

I'll work this one for Elijah Lincoln, Neil told himself. He dismissed the thought instantly as foolishly sentimental. Elijah was dead on the other side of the world. He didn't give a fuck.

As he reached the avenue, Neil turned his thoughts to himself. His father was wrong. Neil didn't lack drive or ambition. He wanted to succeed as a private detective, if that was what he was going to be. He wanted to solve Clayton Van Dyke's murder. Wasn't that drive and ambition? No, he decided, not really. It was just a desire to complete the task assigned him. Finishing an assignment successfully wasn't the same as dedicating yourself to dental school, creating a practice and committing for the long-haul to provide for a family. Norcross's life wasn't exciting. It didn't appeal to Neil. But his brother had visible ambitions even now and was planning and plotting to reach his goals. Tracking unfaithful husbands and wives to get pictures of them fucking was not fulfilling an ambition, at least not an ambition Neil wanted to claim.

Chapter Three: Problems with Parents

Neil paused in his contemplations to ascertain his geography. He had walked far, farther than he had intended. He was at the Calvert Street Bridge, an informal border between the principally residential area of Northwest and downtown. He looked at his watch. It was only 9:30. He decided to walk through the Adams Morgan neighborhood in the direction of 14th Street and the Blue Mirror. He had plenty of time and he was bundled warmly in an old overcoat he had left in his parents' closet long ago.

Elijah Lincoln. This guy Van Dyke was the same light brown color as Elijah and had the same slick black hair. But Elijah wasn't especially tall and had black pupils on big white bug-eyes, like Eddie Cantor in the movies. Some guys even called him "Eddie." The two Jews in the squad sometimes called him "Cantor" and asked him to sing. Elijah didn't object, but he didn't sing, either. Neil would never forget the eyes. Neil probably was the last person those eyes had seen, except maybe those of some Red happily jamming a bayonet into Elijah's gut. Elijah said very little. He was a quiet Negro from Louisiana who never asked for anything. Who laughed at everyone's jokes. Who volunteered nothing, but was friendly when spoken to. Even the many bigoted men in the company enjoyed his presence sometimes after they found he wouldn't react to their evil name calling and nasty stories. Elijah would just walk away.

He finally spoke up through those eyes in the middle of Hell. Elijah's buggy eyes begged, doing the job his mouth could not as his chest heaved, trying to recapture air lost through a wound caused by a Red rifle round. Don't leave me, the eyes beseeched. I'm a Marine. I'm alive. Take me with you, Neil. By all that is holy you gotta' help me."

"No! No!" Neil screamed to his squad. "Marines don't leave Marines on the battlefield alive! He's alive! We can save him! We *must* save him." Surely the men heard him even as the shells exploded around them and bullets screamed past their ears and thumped into the rocky, snow-covered earth of North Korea. These men knew the informal but strictly adhered to code of the Marine Corps – Marines don't leave Marines behind to die. It was drummed into them from the first day of basic training. Doing otherwise was a sacrilege to the Corps. But the Jarheads removed Neil's bloodied hands from Elijah's chest, where they were trying to cover the ragged hole, trying to force blood, flesh, muscle and air back into place. The men lifted Neil to his feet, jammed his rifle into his hand and pulled him away. Cpl. Rudin dragged him by his pack strap 100 yards to the rear, over boulders and across a pencil-thin stream, until finally even Neil realized he could not go back.

In two more days, the Marine retreat from Chosin Reservoir was completed. Neil fought the war for another year. Chosin was the worst, but it was all bad. He saw many men die and even more wounded, some horribly. But he never saw the Marines leave another wounded man on the field of battle. Only Elijah. Nobody said Elijah was left behind because he was colored. Other Negro Marines were rescued.

Chapter Three: Problems with Parents

"As far as I'm concerned, he was a Marine first and a nigra second," Gunnery Sgt. Henderson, the highest ranking enlisted man in the company at the time, told Neil when he asked if Elijah was left behind because he was black. "Things was hot and gettin' hotter, Endicott. If we hadn'a gotten outta' there when we did, we'd all a died. Sometimes doin' what's right ain't the same as doin' what's best." Henderson was a career Marine from Texas who was openly scornful of putting Negroes into combat units with white men. The question of why Elijah was left behind was never a closed subject in Neil's mind. Elijah's pleading big dark eyes never closed for him, either.

Chapter Four: The Other Side of Town, April 23-24, 1954

The Blue Mirror was one of the better jazz joints in town. Some of the best known names in jazz played the Mirror, including Dizzy Gillespie, Washington native Duke Ellington, Count Basie and Billy Eckstine, but most of the time the bill was made up of lesser lights, known to, maybe even loved by, aficionados, but strangers to the casual fan. This was such a night.

The Maxwell Williams Quartet, a Baltimore-based group, was in the middle of its second set when Neil arrived. Neil classed himself a casual fan, but he recognized the song, "Jump, Jive 'n Wail", a lively swing number recorded by Louis Prima. Several couples were jitterbugging on the small dance floor, but most patrons were seated at one of about 35 small round tables. The tables were covered in white linen and topped by a bud vase containing a rose, an ashtray and a candle like those purchased in Catholic churches for devotionals. Everybody had a drink; nearly everyone was smoking a cigarette; very few were eating. D.C. law required any establishment serving liquor to also offer meals. The Blue Mirror's food tasted like a grudgingly offered legal obligation, which it was. It was made worse by the heavy, sometimes choking, cigarette smoke.

Lou King was at a table near the dance floor. He was engaged in animated conversation with a young Negro man at his table. King waved to Neil, who was led to the table by the maitre de.

Unanimous Verdict

"Mr. Endicott, I'd like you to meet Albertus LeClerc. Mr. LeClerc, this is the man I was telling you about who is helping in my investigation," King said. King smiled broadly at the reference to Neil as his helper. Neil decided to let it go. "Mr. LeClerc is – or was – a friend of Clay's, isn't that right Mr. LeClerc?" King spoke loudly over the music.

"Yeah, I was his friend, at least when it came to partyin' at the clubs," LeClerc said. LeClerc stood to shake Neil's proffered hand. Neil struggled to conceal his shock. LeClerc was extraordinarily thin, as if he were starving himself. Although he was nearly six feet tall, he could not have weighed more than 110 pounds. His skin was deep black, but pallid, as if he had been dipped in dust. His face was narrow and boney, his cheeks hollow and his deep brown eyes protruded listlessly from shrunken sockets. He reminded Neil of the terminally wounded soldiers he saw in Japan. He immediately assumed LeClerc was a narcotics addict and simultaneously comforted himself that his father was home and could not see him now in the company of a colored drug abuser. Neil said nothing and took his proffered seat.

"It's very sad to hear that he passed," LeClerc said. He spoke softly, interrupting himself to take deep, long breaths. He was difficult to hear. "Clay was a decent man." Deep breath. "I can't believe he hung hisself." Deep breath. "I hope you and Mr. King here," deep breath, "find his killer." His bona fides established, LeClerc sat back, anticipating questions. A waiter took Neil's order for a Ballantine Ale.

94

Chapter Four: The Other Side of Town

"Did Clay have any enemies," King asked. "You know, people who didn't like him for one reason or another. Did he get in any fights? Maybe stole somebody's girlfriend? Things like that?"

"Naw, he didn't go in for things like that." Deep breath. "Clay was a peaceful guy. White people made him a little nuts," deep breath, "but, hey, ain't that true for all of us?" LeClerc looked directly at King, clearly excluding Neil from his frame of reference. He slumped further in his chair, exhausted by his speech.

"Well, what do you mean by 'nuts'?" King raised a snowy white eyebrow, asking the question in a way that emphasized to LeClerc that he wanted a thoughtful answer. He was able to speak more softly because the quartet had finished its set. King made the conversation conspiratorial to inspire LeClerc to provide information, as if doing so was his part of a cunning plot. LeClerc still was difficult to hear and gulped the air even while not speaking. Neil was grateful the tables were small so he could hear LeClerc but was annoyed by the deep breathing.

"He was kinda' focused on race. He said he drove out to the lilly white parts of town in his job," deep breath, "and it disgusted him to see how they had more books in the libraries there," deep breath, "and the buildings was much nicer." Deep breath. "He used to say the only colored folk in Chevy Chase was dem dat cleaned the mastuh's privies." Deep breath. Neil reddened slightly.

"Well, sure. That's a given," Lou replied. "That don't hardly make a man especially known for being nuts about race."

95

"He carried it further than that." Deep breath. "Clay wouldn't tolerate no racist remarks. These clubs, especially the after-hour bottle clubs," deep breath, "they get a mixed crowd and lotsa people get pretty drunk by four in the morning. Not Clay." Deep breath. "He hardly drank. But, man, he sure got pissed if some drunk white guy made some remark," deep breath, "or even looked at him like he was just thinkin' about some racist crack." Deep breath. "One time he overheard a white guy with a buncha other white guys at a table next to us talkin' 'bout coon huntin'." Deep breath. "Clay stood up and told the guy he was in his neighborhood now and," deep breath, "if he talked like that again he might never leave the neighborhood." Deep breath. "Looked like he meant it, too, though I ain't never seen Clay actually do anything like hurt somebody." Deep breath.

"Joke was on Clay, though. The white guy was talkin' 'bout real coon huntin'." Deep breath. "Had a brochure or somethin' for some huntin' lodge. He showed Clay. Clay said somethin' like," deep breath, "'Well, be careful how you talk aroun' here,' but that was just a face-savin'. He looked kinda' foolish." Deep breath.

"Sounds harmless enough," King said. "Doesn't strike me as a reason to say he was especially nuts 'bout race issues."

"Thas' jus' an example." Deep breath. "He was real sensitive. You know, he was pretty light skinned," deep breath, "and I know he was damned sensitive about that. Deep darkie like me, I'd love to been born lighter." Deep breath, laugh and cough. "'Scuse me. But Clay, he was mad about it. He

96

wanted to be black like his mom and dad." Deep breath. "He said bein' a black man is somethin' to be proud of and he felt kina' tainted by white blood. Sounded a little crazy to me — nuts." Deep breath, laugh, cough. "Scuse me."

"Well, that didn't cause him to actually do anything that might get somebody mad, did it?" King asked. Neil thought the line of questioning with LeClerc was pointless and he was getting restless. LeClerc was probably dying from his addictions. Looking at LeClerc, Neil figured Clay was involved with drugs, not the pointless dermatology of Negro skin colors.

"He tole me he was gonna find out who his real momma and papa were — what they call it, his 'biology parents'?" Deep breath. "I know for a fact he went to Chicago where he was adopted," deep breath, "and he sho 'nuf found out something. He jes tole me he had a clue." Deep breath. "He said he was goin' to Atlanta to find out more. I think he went, but I never saw him again." Deep breath. "He died jes after comin' back from Atlanta, I guess."

"What other friends has he got who he might have talked to about this?"

"He got a sometime girlfriend. Name's Audrey, Audrey Winkler. She works at the downtown library. But you might find her later tonight at the Slide Trombone." Deep breath. Cough. "Scuse me again. My breathin' ain't so good, as you kin tell."

"You mean the after-hours place up Sixth and Mass?" King knew of the place.

"Yeah, thas it. But watch out. Audrey gets kina' loaded on Friday nights." Deep breath. "Can't tell if she'll be a mean drunk or just a sleepy one. Try to catch her early." Deep breath.

Neil finally spoke up. "One other thing, Mr. LeClerc, was Neil involved in illegal drugs at all?"

LeClerc turned and stared into Neil's eyes a long moment. He turned up the right side of his lips into a sneer. He took a deeper breath than usual. "Y'all white folk always got the drug thang against the Negro, right? What about prostitution and numbers? Maybe Clay was the drug kingpin of Washington, D.C.?" LeClerc took several deep panting breaths. He was angry, excited and exhausted by his efforts. "LeDroit Park, Dunbar High, military service, good respected parents — don't matter to you people, does it?"

"Well, it looks like you have a drug problem. That's why I asked."

LeClerc's breathing moved from pants to a loud heaving noise which attracted nearby guests. "You cracker bastard!" LeClerc rose from his seat. Clearly, he was ending the conversation. "I used to weigh over 200 pounds and lifted weights. But I got the cancer a year ago." Despite his breathing difficulties, LeClerc was nearly shouting. "First in my lungs, and now it done spread all over. I only got months, maybe weeks to live. I got only one lung. Am I on drugs? Damned right. Prescription drugs, mostly for the pain now." Neil stood up. He was afraid LeClerc's loud heaving would cause the skeletal man to vomit.

Chapter Four: The Other Side of Town

"Well, I'm very sorry. I didn't know." Neil was now very red with embarrassment. But LeClerc wasn't through with him.

"You probably don't believe an ole nigger like me. I'll prove it to you." LeClerc lifted his white dress shirt practically to his neck, revealing a long scar of creamy brown, white and pink along his upper torso that stood out against his normal ebony skin and was pulsating in time to his heavy breathing. "So fuck you, whitey asshole. No, Clayton wasn't into drugs. He was a good man. Fuck you again." LeClerc wrestled his shirt back into his waist and resumed a frantic battle between breathing and coughing. He pulled himself upright despite his obvious pain, turned in an almost military fashion and marched with considerable difficulty — which translated from a distance to an exaggerated dignity — to the door, accompanied by the trumpet sound of his own forced breathing and a tympani of coughing. At least half the room heard and saw LeClerc's demonstration and was silent a few moments until the sick, angry black man left the building. When conversation resumed, it was almost whispered, with most patrons casting side looks at Neil and Lou.

"Well done. Very well done." King was more amused than sarcastic. "Didn't they teach you how to ask questions when you were a cop? You had no call to accuse the man of anything. He was trying to be helpful. Plus, I would have gotten there eventually about the drugs and all. Got to get his confidence first. Keep the conversation about Clay, not about LeClerc, at least, not so's he knows it's about him."

Unanimous Verdict

The quartet returned from its break. Lou and Neil listened to the music a few minutes to permit the crowd's attention to wander away from them. Soon, the incident was forgotten by all but Neil and King. King said he had no money, so Neil paid the check, including for Lou's Remy Martin and soda and LeClerc's Coca-Cola. Although it was still early – not yet midnight – they left the Blue Mirror, hailed a taxi and went to the Slide Trombone at Sixth Street, N.W. and Massachusetts Avenue.

You had to know where the Slide Trombone was before going there because it was a bottle joint, an illegal after-hours bar. D.C. law provided that all bars closed at 2 a.m. on Friday and Saturday, midnight on the other days of the week, far too early to accommodate the pressing need for fun of a generation raised on the Depression and two wars and now enjoying record prosperity, albeit under the threat of nuclear holocaust. War, bombs, and an uncertain world – these were good excuses for a drink at 3 a.m. for those so inclined to need one – either the drink or the excuse. Thus, the bottle joints met a pressing social need. They were called "bottle joints" because they originally were places for a patron to bring his own bottle. The joint provided the set-ups, music and sometimes food. Over the years, the more prosperous joints started supplying the liquor, too. The D.C. police were pragmatic about the bottle clubs, knowing some laws are unenforceable if they aren't supported by the public. They struck a silent bargain: If the bottle club patrons didn't cause trouble, the police would ignore them. Of course, some cops required a little extra cash

Chapter Four: The Other Side of Town

from the bottle joints to enforce the deal and sometimes a joint needed to be raided to satisfy the blue nose contingent in Washington, which was substantial. Otherwise, the rule was to live and let live.

Sixth and Mass was seedy. Not the worst place in town, but bad enough to scare off most white folk. Adding a little more excitement, the only entrance was from an alley, down some dimly lit steps to a basement door. The club was in the basement of a store that sold cheap furniture to poor colored families, on credit and at high prices. As they went down the basement steps from the alley, Lou told Neil to stand far to his right. He then knocked and stood in front of the peephole, a device leftover from the club's speakeasy days. The bouncer could see only Lou. Satisfied the patron was a black man, somewhat elderly, not likely to cause trouble, the door opened. The bouncer was surprised when Lou entered accompanied by a white man.

"He's with me. He's OK," Lou told the bouncer. "You know an Audrey Winkler?"

"Who wants to know?" The bouncer was appropriately large, tough, and ugly and spoke in a deep bass. He wore a suit that looked like it would tear when he inhaled and a bow tie that nearly strangled him.

"Lou King. You heard of me?" He didn't bother to introduce Neil.

"Why sure Mr. King. You the big time investigator, private eye type."

Unanimous Verdict

King accepted the compliment as a fact. "That's right. We are here to see Miss Winkler. It's business." He would show this white boy the difference between a career in private investigation and a hobby. King's name opened doors. He wondered what Endicott's would do. He answered his own question: nothing.

"She ain't here yet. It's only midnight. She usually comes in after the bars close. We ain't really open for business yet anyway."

"You don't mind if we stay, do you? Play the juke box, have a couple drinks. We won't be a bother."

"No, Mr. King. I'm sure that'll be OK. Impress the cops to have you here if there's any trouble." King smiled at the man's error. He was not a friend of cops. King made his money by working for defense lawyers.

The two men sat at the bar, which ran the length of the building. They were the only customers. It was nearly one o'clock. Lou ordered a Remy and soda; Neil a Ballantine. The juke box was playing something by Etta James. Apparently it was rigged to play without money for the benefit of the bartender, the bouncer and a couple of other employees until the place opened for business. Other than the music and staring at the bottles on the other side of the bar or into their own drinks, there was nothing to do. The two men were forced to talk to each other.

"What're we doin' here," Neil finally said, a little uncomfortable in a third rate bar in a bad side of town with a private detective he had never heard of until about 10 hours earlier. So far, he thought, all they had done was suck up about ten dollars of their expense account on

Chapter Four: The Other Side of Town

booze. "You can't think Clay was killed because he was angry about being light-skinned? That's crazy."

King stirred his drink lazily, trying to avoid looking at his aging self in the mirror behind the bottles behind the bar. It wasn't clear if he was considering an answer to Neil's question or ignoring him.

"You got any friends, Endicott? Any friends from high school or the army or the cops?"

Neil decided to play along. "Sure, I've got lots of friends. I grew up around here, remember?" As long as "around here" wasn't defined too narrowly, his assertion was a fact.

"Any of those friends real fat, or have a lot of zits on their face, or real ugly?"

"I suppose. One guy, Willie Max, was so fat he couldn't do a single chin-up in high school. Military wouldn't even take him. Musta weighed 300 pounds. Maybe five-six. Almost square. Shook like Jell-O when he walked. I'm not even sure if he's still alive."

"Do you think your friend, what was his name? Willie Max? Do think this Willie Max ever thought much about being fat?"

"I assume he thought about it all the time. How could he not? Where is this going, Lou?" Neil was getting tired of being interrogated for no evident purpose.

"You think Willie Max wanted to be fat, or be more like you and the other guys, meaning sorta normal," Lou said, sipping his drink and ignoring Neil's protest.

"Sure he wanted to be normal. Now that you mention it, I remember Willie crying a few times in gym class 'cause he couldn't do even the simplest thing. Sit-ups were impossible for him. I don't know, he was just good for nothing in sports. Last guy picked, that kind of thing. Got kidded a lot, too."

"So you'd agree that this fella's weight was on his mind always and caused him a lot of problems?"

"That's what I said ten minutes ago. Let's move on to something else. Clay Van Dyke for example."

Lou returned to his drink, stirring the mostly melted ice. "We are talking about Clay Van Dyke, Mr. Endicott. You told me a few minutes ago that it was crazy to think Clay was murdered because of his light skin. I'm telling you it's not so crazy.

"You white people walk around without a thought about your skin color. You are in the majority most places and in charge. You get to set the rules for 'normal.' But a black man, I don't care how dark or light he is, a black man *never* forgets about his color. Even if he's just among other colored folk, he's comparin' his color to the other folks. Now, you don't think that happened back in Africa, do you?"

"I don't know," Neil replied truthfully.

"Well of course it didn't. The black man was in charge then, 'til the white man came 'roun to buy some slaves. The black man decided what was 'normal.' This place here will fill up soon and there's a good chance you'll be the only white man here. You probably already wish you could jump outta your skin, and it'll get worse before the night's over.

Chapter Four: The Other Side of Town

"Your friend Willie Max was the white nigger in your school. He was the guy who didn't meet the standard. He never forgot it and you and your friends never let him forget it. Same thing with skin color. White folk never let coloreds forget they're colored. Jes bein' round white folks is enough. 'Course, white folk, they're aware of coloreds. But I bet that except when they are in the minority, white folk don't think of their own color, just the black man's color."

"I guess that's so," Neil responded, more in hopes of trimming the lecture rather than making it a discussion. "But I never heard some white person complain he wasn't white enough or was too white. You just are what you are."

"But some black folk are always wantin' what the white man's got. 'Causes other black folk to react the other way. Maybe Clayton was one of those. The big tragedy is that just like Willie Max, who wanted to be normal size, lotsa black folk look at themselves and wish they was lighter. White, for sure, but at least lighter. Like you say, most learn to live with the color they are – no choice. Some don't.

"I don't know why Clayton Van Dyke was murdered. Maybe it had nothin' to do with him being a Negro or his skin being light. But I do know this: Thinkin' his color had somethin' to do with why he died ain't 'crazy.' It's common sense."

Neil was silent. It had been a helluva day for a guy who never paid much attention to colored folk. LeDroit Park in the morning, a run down bottle club the next morning. Quite a range for one day. What would be a white parallel? Chevy Chase to Suitland, Maryland?

Unanimous Verdict

One thing was sure: At this point, Neil Endicott needed Lorenzo King more than King needed him. That might change, but as long as they were in the colored neighborhoods – and Neil couldn't see much chance they would not stay there for a while – King was the lead. Neil was the vice president – not worth a bucket of piss right now. He had to place his trust in this elderly snow white haired black guy and hope he could earn King's trust, too, eventually.

"I think Clayton was killed because of his color; not because he was light skinned, but because he was colored. We have direct evidence of that." Neil pulled his copy of the note found at the scene from his pocket and handed it to King. "You can't tell anybody we have it, but this was found on his body."

King studied the note. "Why didn't you show me this before?"

"I wasn't sure if I could trust you. A good friend of mine could lose his job, maybe even be prosecuted for giving me this."

"So what changed? You trust me now?"

"I'm not sure. But you have a lot more experience in these race matters than I do. I've got none. Except for freezing under the Korean stars with a few and walkin' a Northeast beat for a few months, I've had no real experience with colored people since I was a kid and…"

"Yeah, I know, you had a sweet colored gal takin' care of you while Mommy went to art galleries and ladies club meetings. Spare me the story."

Chapter Four: The Other Side of Town

Neil turned red for at least the third time that day. He didn't really deserve King's patronizing tone, he thought to himself. He was trying to be cooperative.

King returned his attention to the note. After committing it to memory, he gave it back to Neil. He said nothing. Neither did Neil.

In a few minutes, customers started coming through the door. It was nearly two a.m. Some of the men were dressed in colorful suits, one in a tuxedo. Most of the women wore gowns, lots of costume jewelry and high heeled shoes in which they could barely walk. Others were not so fancy, just jackets, no tie for the men and neat skirts and blouses for the women. Everybody was black and was having a good time. The average age couldn't be much above 30.

Half an hour later, the bouncer came over to Neil and Lou. He pointed to a short woman, with a figure that once was a knockout but was succumbing to rolls of fat visible under her thin black silk blouse. Her face was soft and very round. Her lips were full, covered with bright red lipstick. "There's Audrey Winkler," the bouncer explained. She was alone. Lou and Neil took their drinks and walked to her table.

"Miss Winkler? My name is Lorenzo King. This is my associate, Mr. Neil Endicott. We are investigating the death of Clayton Van Dyke. Mr. Albertus LeClerc told us you might have some useful information. May we join you?" King was formal with the woman. LeClerc warned she might be either a mean drunk or a cooperative lush. He needed to find out which Audrey Winkler he was dealing with.

Unanimous Verdict

"Oh God, Clayton! Yes of course. Please have a seat." Her words were slightly slurred. She already had too much to drink, but was still coherent. "Did you say you are police?"

"No ma'am, we are working for Mrs. Van Dyke. Private detectives." King pulled up a chair inches from the woman and offered her his business card. Neil sat across the table from the two of them. Chastised for the LeClerc debacle, he took a vow of silence. Audrey Winkler looked at him suspiciously, Neil thought, or maybe he was just jumping out of his white skin, as Lou predicted he would. He was the only white person in the place.

"Are you alone here tonight?" King asked.

"Yeah. Clayton used to come here with me. But I can't get anyone else to join me. LeClerc is too sick for late nights. Lots of my other friends gotta work on Saturday. Can you buy me a drink? Scotch rocks?"

"Certainly." King hailed the waiter and ordered the scotch and refills for himself and Neil. He wanted to get right to the point while Miss Winkler was sober enough to answer questions and because it was way past his own bedtime. "Mr. LeClerc told us that Clayton went to Chicago, where he was adopted, to find out something about his past. Is that right? Do you know anything about that?"

"Clayton was obsessed. He always wanted to find out if he had some white ancestor. He said he needed to know himself, know who he was, and couldn't do it without knowing why he was so light-skinned.

Chapter Four: The Other Side of Town

It was silly to me. I mean, he wasn't so light-skinned he could pass. He clearly was a colored man."

"Maybe he just wanted to find out who his real parents were. I think a lot of adopted kids want that." Neil broke his vow of silence and popped in with an obvious point.

"Sure, that's so. Maybe that was part of it. But Clayton was interested in Black Nationalism. Marcus Garvey, Muslim Nation, Liberia. Black separatism they call it. He was always raisin' money for one black cause or another, mostly to separate us from the whites. Pie-in-the-sky you ask me. Who wants to go back to Africa? I think he wanted to find a white relative and ask for money."

This was a new element. The possibility Clayton Van Dyke was extorting money from some previously unknown relative. Lou and Neil looked at each other with surprise.

"Did Clayton say that — that he wanted to get money from any white relatives?"

"Not exactly, but pretty close. He said he wanted to extract some vengeance against whatever white man raped his mother or grandmother, he wasn't sure which. He assumed some white guy took advantage of his power and authority and raped a black woman and got her pregnant. He wanted to find out who did it 'cause of the violence he assumed happened and because his own black blood got tainted, as he put it. I don't know. He went on and on about it. We broke up 'cause he got so boring with it. We were still friends, though." Audrey

Winkler adopted a distant stare into the rest of the room, which was nearly filled with customers. She was thinking about the past. Then a tear fell, followed by another.

"Clay was a wonderful man. He was gentle and kind and smart. But he'd go crazy over this stuff. Can you buy me another drink?"

"So he went to Chicago?" Lou was coaxing her to move on. He didn't want to be comforting a 30-year-old falling down drunk the rest of the night.

"Yeah, he went. I think it was in January. Took the train out there and went to the place where he was adopted. He had a friend out there. A guy he met in the Army. Earnest or Ezra or something like that."

"Last name or first name?" King was getting tired, but didn't want to have to go through the same drill again. He needed the information to be accurate the first time.

"First name. I don't know his last name. Can I get that drink?"

Neil made himself useful by signaling the waiter again, who came quickly. Neil didn't know if it was standard good service or to please the white guy. If the waiter expected a big tip, he'd be disappointed. A small stage was set up at the front of the club and some musicians were getting ready to play. There were a lot of them. Maybe it was a jam session.

"What else do you know about the Chicago trip," King asked, pressing again to get the story completed before sunrise and before the music started. He was too old for jam sessions at three a.m. and the cognac was giving him a headache.

"Well, he couldn't get anything out of the place where he was adopted, but this guy Earnest or whatever did. I don't know how. Clay told me he found out that he was actually born in Atlanta, but was sent to Chicago to be adopted. Sounds strange. He didn't know why. He wanted to go to Atlanta, and he did."

"When was that?"

"Soon after Chicago. I know he had to wait to get enough leave at work. He died early this month, I think. He went to Atlanta a couple of weeks before that. Train again. I remember he was mad about the treatment on the train. White passengers kept telling him to go to the back car, the 'colored car.' He wouldn't do it until a colored conductor told him his own life would be a lot easier if Clay went back."

King sighed. Standard practice on the railroads south of Washington. "Did you see him after he got back from Atlanta?"

"Yeah, I did. Couple times."

"What did he tell you?" King was getting tired of pulling this gal's teeth for answers. He thought she was stretching things out to get another drink.

"He didn't really say. He said he might have big news and he might not. He wanted to check with somebody. He wasn't as excited as after Chicago. He was more reserved. I think he maybe found out his dream wasn't going to happen. Wasn't no rich white man. That's the last time I saw him. Right here, right at this table." Audrey Winkler started to cry again. King pulled a handkerchief from his pocket and offered it to her. "Keep it," he said. Then, as a matter of form, he asked:

"Do you know of anyone who had a grudge against Clayton? Might want to kill him?"

"No, of course not. He was a good man, like I said. He went after me about my drinking and lately I've kinda gotten a little fat. You know, that's kinda' like married folk talk. I was expectin' to get back together and marry him one day." The tears came in a flood of loud sobs. For the second time that night the King-Endicott table was getting a lot of unwanted attention. King patted her on the back. Neil wondered if Miss Winkler was the kind of woman who fell in love with anybody who paid attention to her.

"Can I get another drink?" Miss Winkler asked.

"Of course," King said. "Thank you very much for your information." He left a twenty on the table to cover the tab plus a few more drinks for Miss Winkler. "I think that will take care of everything."

"That's very kind. Thanks," she said, her eyes already casting about for other company.

"I thought you said you didn't have any money," Neil said as they left the building.

Chapter Four: The Other Side of Town

"I didn't have any money to pay for your blow-hard performance with LeClerc, if that's what you mean." King looked at Neil angrily. "I'll pay for results."

"What are you mad about now?"

"Don't get me started."

"No, what?"

"White people – and black people. Everybody. I know this kid's parents," King said, referring to Clayton Van Dyke. "They struggled hard to get up the ladder and then they been pulling people to come up behind them. NAACP, Howard University Law School, Mr. Van Dyke's work in the court system. And most white people see their skin and treat them like any common nigger. And their son buys into that shit. He's all ripped about his skin color and who his granddaddy was and meanwhile his life is crap. That woman we just talked to, what was her name? Winkles?"

"Winkler."

"Yeah, Winkler. Clay could do much better than that drunk. He coulda' gone to college and made something of himself – more than a damn library truck driver. But the white man has got him all worried about his color 'cause the white man has made him think that's the most important thing of all."

"Well, maybe it is. I can't imagine many white men wantin' to be black." It was the wrong thing to say.

"Fuck you," King exploded as the pair reached the alley. "I'm going home. We can talk over the weekend. You got my card. I'll be in my office tomorrow."

King could walk surprisingly fast for a man his age and girth. He walked quickly away from Neil, clearly ending their conversation. He reached Massachusetts Avenue and stood at the curb on the north side of the street, which headed west, looking for a taxi. Neil soon joined him, even though he was not wanted, since he needed a taxi in the same general direction as King – east.

"Don't you live in northeast? That's the other direction," Neil said, trying to be helpful.

"You come and talk so polite to a man who just told you to fuck off? I'm tryin' to get rid of you for the night. I ain't no stupid peckerwood. It's three in the morning. Hard enough to get taxis for anybody, but it's impossible for a black man to get a taxi headed for northeast. Probably in any direction."

At that moment, a taxi heading west stopped at the curb. Neil politely made way for King to get in. When the driver saw which man was his fare, he sped away. "See," King said. "Fucker," he yelled powerlessly at the fleeing taxi. The two men continued to wait.

"Look, Lou, you can't blame me for the whole race situation in this country. I have always tried to be polite, not use hurtful words or be mean to black people. It's unfair." Neil was trying to calm the waters. "Let's do like you said this afternoon: try to cooperate for Mrs. Van Dyke's sake." King did not respond. Another taxi pulled up in front of Neil. This time, Neil opened the door, took a seat and motioned King to join him. As King did so, Neil got out of the car on the driver's side and instructed the driver to "take this man where he wants to go. No crap, please."

"I don't carry no coloreds this time of night," the driver said.

"Well, he ain't goin' anywhere 'til he gets home. He'll stay in your taxi all night if he has to. So this is an exception to your rule. I got your cab number and I'll find you if I hear you haven't taken him directly home. No more crap," Neil said, surprised at his vehemence and conscious that he was putting on an act for King. He was *Helping The Negro.*

As Neil started to close the taxi door, King said only, "I'll take care of it. Talk to you tomorrow." The driver took a closer look at King in his rear view mirror. King's three-piece suit and the fact his English was better than the cab driver's was enough for the driver to decide it was a safe fare. He drove off after the door closed. Neil saw the driver make a U-turn at the next intersection while he waited for his own taxi to take him home, which required another U-turn. King didn't know it, but at three a.m. cabdrivers didn't want to go anywhere but northwest D.C., whether the fare was black or white. Color isn't the only thing that counts, Neil thought to himself as he was driven home. Geography can be destiny, too.

Chapter Five: The Chief I, April 24, 1954

Weary of reading the same document several times without finding a shred of reason, the Chief Justice of the United States removed his horn-rimmed reading glasses, rubbed his eyes and sighed. The few pages of typescript in the middle of his otherwise cleared desktop caused him deep anxiety. He feared that his rookie term was going to conclude a failure.

The Supreme Court's 1953-54 term ended in a little more than six weeks. Its most important case, potentially one of the most important cases in the Court's history, had yet to be resolved. That case, *Brown v. Board of Education of Topeka, Kansas* and companion appeals from three states and the District of Columbia to be decided at the same time, was going to strike down as unconstitutional legal racial segregation of schools in 17 states and the District. That much was decided. Six justices out of nine were in favor of such a ruling.

The Chief, as the Chief Justice was called inside the Court, knew that *Brown* by itself would not really end separate schooling of Negroes and whites. But it surely would *start* the end of something. Whether that was to be school segregation, civil order or the power and majesty of the Supreme Court, no one knew.

The Chief lost no sleep over his own vote. He had allowed the State of California to assist the federal government in impounding American citizens of Japanese extraction in camps during World War II. God had granted his Norwegian soul the opportunity to make amends and — he acknowledged the vanity — surely to stand taller in history. Others on the Court were not so charitable or farsighted, especially Nathan Bedford Farwell, the author of the pages on his desk.

"This piece of racist crap isn't going to see the light of day on my watch," the Chief exclaimed angrily to his empty chambers. Since it was a Saturday, the Court building was nearly empty. Only a few clerks were around scribbling madly to complete what they hoped would be end-of-term opinions minimally rewritten by the justice to whom they were assigned. The justices had agreed not to involve the clerks in the drafting, compromising, rewriting and discussion in the *Brown* case to insure the decision was not leaked to the public before it was announced. The Chief could not vent his frustration to his own clerks, as he frequently did.

"It's a disgrace. Fuck Farwell." The Chief was surprised by his intensity and coarse language as soon as he spoke. He never used such words in public or private conversation. They welled from sources the man viewed by most Americans as a moderate preferred not to visit.

The Chief was a politician to the bone. He was not appointed Chief Justice because of judicial brilliance. He was a competent Alameda County prosecutor and later California attorney general, then governor. But his first job as a judge was to head the highest court in the land. The Chief Justice owed his prominence in national affairs to politics, not to the law. His strengths were leadership, persuasion and compromise. He would need these attributes and more, the Chief thought, if he was going to curb the egos of the eight other prima donnas on the bench. *Brown* was the first important test of his abilities.

As a political animal, the Chief knew that the *Brown* decision must be a unanimous one to have the legal *and moral* authority necessary for it to be obeyed and enforced. Dissents, no matter how well-intentioned, would be used to excuse Jim Crow laws – laws that separated blacks from whites with the goal of keeping the former socially and economically inferior to the latter. Jim Crow laws already struck down by the Court continued to be practiced unabated in some especially truculent areas of the South. Rail cars leaving Washington for the South still were segregated after they left Alexandria, Virginia, just across the Potomac River from the Court, although laws requiring such segregation had been declared unconstitutional several years ago. The Chief also knew that state colleges and universities in the South admitted those Negroes they specifically were ordered to admit by the Court, but used multiple tactics and outright contempt of the Court's orders to avoid enrolling other colored students. More seriously, Negroes continued to be disenfranchised throughout the South as one state after another cleverly subverted court decisions intended to remove obstacles to exercising the right to vote. Racist southerners, like most people, read and remembered what they agreed with. They used dissents to justify continued Jim Crow practices and ignored or belittled the true rulings of the courts that condemned their practices.

The South's resistance to earlier judgments had an unexpected result: It reinforced the will of at least six justices, including the Chief, to eliminate all remaining legal segregation and, therefore, any ambiguity that segregation was unconstitutional. Piecemeal approaches aimed at weaning the South from its racist laws had instead strengthened the political will of the southern whites to more vigorously promote their race discrimination, going so far as to run their own candidate for president in 1948 on a purely segregationist platform. The Chief knew from discussions with other justices that it was clear to the majority that since a battle must eventually be joined, peaceful or not, the stakes must justify the tumult. Only the death of Jim Crow in all his visages was worth the struggle.

But the Supreme Court only issued opinions about the law. It had no power to enforce those judgments. It relied on the other branches of government in the state and federal systems. Only a unanimous verdict, one tolerating no dissent, would have the moral and political weight to be enforced. Even then, it was not certain that the politicians, the police and the public would join the Court's call, instead exposing the justices as nine powerless old men.

Two justices – Robert Jackson and Tom Clark – reluctantly were leaning toward a dissent. Justice Farwell was neither reluctant nor leaning. His feet were firmly planted in favor of continued segregation, not just in schools but in all areas of life. No reasoning would change his vote. It was his draft dissent from the anticipated six justice majority opinion that occupied the Chief this Saturday morning.

If nothing else, he hoped to persuade the justice from South Carolina to tone down his rhetoric. Even Farwell should not want to incite riot or disobedience to a decision by a majority of his own court. Or would he? It was not beyond the Chief's imagination that a nutty old Confederate sympathizer like Farwell would put himself and his ancient causes above the general welfare. These thoughts caused a slight tremor to run through the Chief's body.

The pages on the Chief's desk contained the following draft of a dissent from Justice Farwell in *Brown v. Topeka Board of Education*:

The majority today completes the usurpation of the rights of the States of this Union to preserve and foster their own social and educational traditions which they have relied upon for decades. Today's subject is once again the public schools. Tomorrow it will be housing or employment or even marriage. The logic of this decision knows no bounds in the mischief it shall create in what heretofore have been natural, largely benign, relations between the Negro and the white man.

The minority of this Court bows to no one in its respect for the Negro. But history has proven time and again that the white man and the Negro both desire to conduct their business, social, family and personal affairs separately, preserving the dignity and separateness of each race. This Court does the Negro no favor by requiring him to compete directly with the white man in public schooling. God has decreed that the black man's strengths shall differ from those of the white man. The history of the world, not only of the United States, shows that, in general, the Negro's strengths are not those of the white man or, indeed, of the Oriental or the Arab or even of the

Mexican. Physical labor and manual trades have been the Negro's contribution, as was predicted by the great Negro leader Booker T. Washington. The Negro race has been freely allowed to realize the fruits of its labor in all regions of the nation, commensurate with its level of skill. It is true that a few black men and women, such as Washington, have contributed to the liberal arts or sciences. This illustrates that Negroes are free to realize their God-given exceptional talents even in a segregated society. That so few Negroes achieve such recognition is clear evidence that few are capable of doing so.

It does no good to decree in law an equality which does not exist in nature. When the Negro is forced by law to compete directly with the white man, it shall be the Negro who suffers. The statutes which the Court declares unconstitutional this day are a shield for the black man, not a burden. They shield the black man from the truth, established by the Bible and by scientific genetic examination. The truth is this: that the Negro is assuredly a creature of God, worthy of respect, but he is different from, and not the equal of, the white man. This Court and the black race shall rue the day that the shield is removed and the differences are mercilessly exposed to the detriment of this previously protected minority.

All pretense of abiding legal precedent or of respecting the important cultural differences among the regions of this great nation, are now stripped away in an exercise of judicial supremacy– nay, judicial arrogance and dictatorial self-righteousness – not heretofore seen in our history....

Chapter Five: The Chief I

A call to arms, the Chief said to himself as he put down his glasses and furrowed his forehead to favor a deep frown. "Another civil war. That's what that war-loving, Negro-hating bastard wants. Resurrecting the stars and bars. What an ass. He won't get it," the Chief muttered.

He would have preferred that fate put *Brown* and the race cases sure to follow on some other Court's doorstep at some other time. Accepting that it was his burden, the Chief assigned himself to write the majority's opinion. He had already jotted down a theme on a yellow pad that he hid in a desk drawer, waiting for the right time to expand upon it. "To separate [Negroes] from others of similar age and qualifications solely because of their race generates a feeling of inferiority as to their status in the community that may affect their hearts and minds in a way unlikely ever to be undone," he wrote. He had shared it only with Felix Frankfurter, who suggested substituting "hearts and minds" for the Chief's words.

The Chief knew his job was to obtain a unanimous vote among the nine justices. No newspaper or magazine commentator expected a unanimous result with Farwell on the bench. Neither did the Chief. But he had to try. Anything less was failure. Although striking down legal segregation was sure to light fires of both freedom and hatred, there was no choice but to expect – or hope – the nation would survive and be a better place. Perhaps, the Chief thought, his grandchildren would not be burdened by the prejudice even he could not wholly discard in his own heart.

Unanimous Verdict

As winter melted into early spring, the Chief devoted nearly all of his time off the bench to maintaining a plurality of six votes to strike down segregated schools and pondering how to persuade the holdouts to make the decision unanimous. He regularly visited his allies – Black, Douglas, Burton, Frankfurter and Minton – to reinforce their commitment with hearty good cheer developed from many years of greeting political supporters. But the uncommitted justices, Jackson and Clark, were indifferent to his camaraderie. Jackson was not even around the Court. On April 1, he was hospitalized with what he reported his doctors describing as a "mild" heart attack. Jackson was still working and writing those opinions assigned to him before he got sick, but the Chief had not raised *Brown* on his visits to the hospital. Doing so was not a task the Chief was looking forward to, but the matter was sufficiently important even to threaten a fragile recovery.

The Chief comforted himself with the observation that Farwell's dissent was so crude, rabid and indefensible that the holdouts would side with the civilized majority. He could not envision Robert H. Jackson voting to sustain segregated schools, especially not if he was identified with the raw racism of Farwell's dissent. Jackson was a believer in judicial restraint, but he also took leave from the Court nearly a decade earlier to prosecute Nazis at Nuremberg. He understood that something evil, such as imprisoning and killing Jews, was not made right merely by making it a law. There was nothing about Jackson that suggested he believed in subjugating Negroes. He was from upstate New York and presumably his sympathies were shaped by the abolitionist history of the region. If he really was very sick, he would not want sustaining racism to be among his last acts. The Chief immediately dismissed the last thought from his mind as both morbid and frightening. However he voted on *Brown*, Jackson was a good man whose death would be a loss to the nation.

Clark was more difficult to assess. He was a Texan with no record of opposing segregation. He, like the Chief, facilitated the impoundment of the Japanese-Americans early in the war. He was a senior organizer of the project while with the Department of Justice. The Chief had not talked to Clark about their mutual experiences, but he assumed that Clark must have some regrets about his role. Farwell would have mentioned if any other justice were thinking of joining his dissent. The Chief assumed Clark would vote with Jackson, not Farwell. Would they dissent? Or would they set aside legal formalism to vote for justice?

These thoughts were interrupted by two knocks on the door of chambers, a private signal that the Chief's secretary wished to see him. "Come in, Janet," the Chief said loudly enough to penetrate the thick, wooden door. His secretary entered with some papers which she put on the desk, at the same time announcing that "these were delivered from Justice Jackson's chambers this morning." The Chief thanked her and she left. He turned to the papers she deposited and read them eagerly, expecting to see a memo from the former Nazi prosecutor announcing he would join the majority – a bright and hopeful antidote to the malicious poison of the Farwell dissent. But the message from

Jackson could be read in the Chief's face, which reddened easily when he was angry or excited. As he read, his skin purpled.

> Chief: As matters now stand, I plan to deliver the following dissent in *Brown*. I believe that Justice Clark plans to join me. I cannot let that damn fool Farwell's racist meanderings be the sole basis for opposing the majority when there are more rational and important reasons for holding one's nose and continuing to tolerate such laws if truly "equal" facilities can be provided. I can't let Farwell speak for the traditional legal views. By the way, I appreciate you not bringing up Brown while I was in the hospital — but I could see you chomping at the bit to do so. I'm home now. Drop by to say hello.

It was signed, "Cordially, Bob". The second page was a separate memo to all of the Justices. It said only Re: Brown (Jackson Dissent), followed by this text:

> JUSTICE JACKSON Dissenting. I cannot concur with the majority and must disassociate myself entirely from Justice Farwell's dissent. The statutes overturned today are indeed odious, but they were approved by the elected representatives of these four states and, for the District of Columbia, by the Congress. Each statute provides, consistent with *Plessy v. Ferguson*, decided nearly sixty years ago by this Court, that equal school facilities be provided separately for white and Negro races.

Chapter Five: The Chief I

The evidence demonstrates that Topeka, Kansas, does provide equal or nearly equal facilities for both races, proving that the rule of *Plessy* can be satisfied. The evidence also clearly establishes that the District of Columbia, Delaware, Virginia and South Carolina have failed to provide the equal educational opportunities mandated by the laws of those jurisdictions struck down today.

There is evidence, however, that these jurisdictions and others, undoubtedly fearing the Court would rule as it has today, are feverishly devoting treasure and labor to bring Negro schools to a level equal to, or nearly equal to, white schools. They should have a chance to do so. The Constitution properly forbids me and my colleagues from imposing our personal views on the South or any other region of the country, else I would join the majority. Consistent with our limited powers, the states should be afforded an opportunity to comply with their own statutes and *Plessy* before we take the step required by the majority. I dissent. JUSTICE CLARK concurs.

The Chief read Jackson's memo and the dissent three times before laying it on his desk. He stood to walk around chambers in hopes of allaying his anger. "God damn it!" he shouted to the walls of his office, not caring if anyone heard his exclamation through the marble. Didn't Jackson understand? Farwell's opinion gave the white trash, racists and know-nothings the seemingly rational, unbigoted arguments they needed to oppose the Court's majority.

Unanimous Verdict

Jackson's opinion also would provide cover for the more sophisticated and polished racists, north and south, as well as for their peers in the top law schools and corporate law firms that defended the *status quo*. The latter group pretended that the law imposed an orderliness and predictability it never really had so that power was retained by the wealthy individual and corporate clients of those same lawyers. Jackson's dissent, including his childish belief that the states would somehow equalize educational opportunities for people they hated once legal threats disappeared, would give all but the most dedicated abolitionists reason to ignore segregation. "Leave it to the states" meant "leave the slaves to the overseer and don't bother me about it." The Chief paused to write a note to himself that if Jackson maintained his dissent, the majority opinion might include some reference to slaves, overseers and "states rights"

The Chief surprised himself by his populist reaction. As Chief Justice, he was at the summit of The Law. He was meant to assure the rowdy populace of America that The Law was just, reliable and worthy of respect. But the Chief was frustrated because at this moment he was less successful doing what was both just and respectable than he was when he governed the entire state of California.

He considered that perhaps Jackson was the more responsible justice, trying to keep a respectful if hypocritical lid on an emotional issue. Why not leave it to the legislative branch? But the solons across the street under the Capitol dome were never going to pass a law or offer a constitutional amendment to end Jim Crow. Southern

Chapter Five: The Chief I

Democrats dominated both Houses. They blocked consideration of any civil rights laws. Their focus now was on Communism, a miniscule threat to domestic peace but a diversion from more important issues.

The Reds used America's mistreatment of Negroes as a propaganda advantage. Especially in poor African nations, expected to soon become independent of their colonial rulers, the Communists promoted on their newswires, radio transmitters and in diplomatic missions pictures and descriptions of Negro slums only blocks from the Capitol. The Jim Crow laws would be as well known to the black Africans of the Belgian Congo as to Alabamans if the Russians had their way. A Supreme Court decision affirming legal segregation would be handing them a loudspeaker.

"Thus concludes the political sermon," the Chief said to his imaginary congregation, smiling at the futility of lecturing to himself.

The Chief buzzed Margaret on the telephone intercom and asked her to call Justice Hugo Black's chambers, then changed his mind and told her he would walk there. He knew Black was in his office because they had encountered each other in the underground garage. Black had kidded the Chief for about the one hundredth time that only he got a chauffeured limousine while the associate justices drove themselves to work. Congress appropriated funds for one only a few months ago, without any urging by the Chief, but Black pretended the luxury was provided at his request.

Unanimous Verdict

The Chief met no one on his walk through the marble corridors to Black's chambers. No natural light entered the corridor. The incandescent lights in the chandeliers were placed long distances apart and only some of them were lit on the weekends. The absence of staff, reduced lighting, the cold marble walls and floors and the finish of the office doors made the corridors of the Supreme Court dark and uninviting. The Chief was reminded of a tomb. He missed the colorful politicians, lobbyists and hangers-on who always were present outside the governor's office and created a lively atmosphere in Sacramento.

The Chief entered Black's outside reception office, which was furnished nearly identically to the Chief's. Black's secretary said, "Good morning Mr. Chief Justice. Go right in. Justice Black is expecting you." Margaret obviously called ahead to warn Black of his visit. The Chief thanked the secretary and opened the door to Black's chamber. He noted jealously that Black's windows had a southern exposure, admitting the late morning light. Black rose from behind his desk to greet the Chief and they shook hands.

"Well, what pressing matter causes you to hike to my humble abode?" Black asked cheerfully, the older justice again referencing, by inference, the higher rank held by the younger man.

"Have you seen the latest from Jackson?" the Chief asked, attempting a casual air, emphasized by taking a moment to examine some of the pictures on Black's wall from his career as a U.S. senator from Alabama.

Chapter Five: The Chief I

"Of course," Black said, resuming his seat behind his desk. The Chief sat in the guest chair without waiting to be invited. "He's defending the Order of Legal Formalism," Black continued, "but I can't blame him for wanting to disassociate himself from that bastard Farwell."

In the short time the Chief had been on the Court, Black had become his best friend, though they did not always agree. Black had mentored the Chief through the term, advising him of the unwritten but still highly formalized rituals of the Court and the wide differences in personality among the justices. Black also matched the Chief's intolerance of fools, procrastinators and obstructionists, which included most lawyers and some of the other justices. The courtly, almost frail, Southern senator and the younger rough-hewn Western prosecutor were only different on the outside. They could speak to each other in ways they could never speak to their other colleagues.

"Bob just has not thought this through," the Chief responded. "If he votes with Farwell, his reputation will be badly tarnished, if not ruined. Farwell's opinion smokes. Bob's dainty regard for limits on judicial power is going to get burned by the fire. He'll just be remembered as another justice to vote for segregation."

"Oh, I don't know. You haven't been here very long. You get used to significant decisions, both making them and dissenting from them. I grant you this is high up on the significance ladder, but Bob will survive. His legacy is likely to be his Nuremberg

131

work, anyway. In any event, you won't get anywhere threatening him about his reputation." Black turned to another strategy. "What if Farwell withdrew his draft opinion and just dissented without any opinion at all?"

"Do you think that would satisfy Bob, and maybe Tom, and they would go with the majority? Neither of them likes these laws. It's crazy for them to dissent."

Black, who had lost most of his white hair and had a much paler and thinner face than the slightly jowly, ruddy Chief, put his feet on his desk, considering his answer.

"Well, you either haven't talked to Bob or maybe you weren't listening. Nuremberg didn't just teach him how horrible a government can treat its people, but also that government power has to be limited — vigilantly so. That includes the courts. There were no divided powers after Hitler took over. Maybe Bob figures that segregation will die of its own weight some day and it's more important to preserve a federal system. It's helpful to have the states keeping the feds honest."

"Hugo, that may be his view, but what about the reverse? It's our job to review these state laws. Making millions suffer for errors of government — at whatever level — sounds more like the Nazis than overturning a few state laws that are reprehensible."

"Point taken," Black replied. "Let me talk to him. We're friends, and you're still the new boy on the block." Black changed the subject slightly.

Chapter Five: The Chief I

"Bob may decide to switch because of Farwell, but it won't be to protect his reputation. It will be because Farwell genuinely is the evil face of racism. I know. I grew up with his type.

"Farwell is an insult to the South. His appointment was a travesty. I think the Old Man regretted it from Day One. It was a bone to the Dixiecrats. Elevating a racist South Carolina Supreme Court justice to this Court just to please Jimmy Byrnes is a scar on FDR. He replaced one South Carolina racist with another." Farwell was appointed to replace fellow South Carolinian Byrnes in 1942. Byrnes was now the governor of South Carolina and a leader of Southern opposition to desegregation.

The Chief waited patiently while Black told his story again. He knew the justice could not contain himself when Farwell's name was mentioned. Black hated him — a strong word, but not an overstatement. If Farwell had any genuine friend on the Court, the Chief could not identify him.

"What do you know about Farwell that isn't in the official bio?" the Chief asked. He was fishing but needed a hook.

"Why? You mean is there a skeleton in his closet? Chief, we don't go about things that way at the Court. You have to keep your old political tricks out of here. I don't like Farwell, and I want this *Brown* decision off on a good foot, but you've got to respect this Court first and foremost. We got the majority. We don't need him."

Unanimous Verdict

"It was just an idle question," the Chief said, putting it aside but not forgetting it. "You know damned well how difficult this desegregation is going to be. Surely you haven't gotten so liberal in the law that you don't keep up with your racist friends from Alabama who are going to blow up when this decision comes out. We need a unanimous verdict. We can't let Farwell be the Karl Marx of a Southern revolution. His dissent will be the racist manifesto."

Black was amused by the Chief's association of the wealthy, elitist, racist of South Carolina with the founding father of Communism. Even Joe McCarthy couldn't find many Reds in the South. But what the Chief said about racists was true. You could not be a politician in Alabama without their support. At least, not an *elected* politician. As newspaper articles reminded him – often – Black briefly joined the Ku Klux Klan in his younger years. He told people he regretted it – which he did – and that he thought it was just something to join to help himself get elected, itself hardly a badge of honor. He wasn't sure if that was his only motive at the time, but his brief membership embarrassed him now. Black loved the South and Alabama, but he knew that after 15 years on the Court, voting with the majority on the race cases and in most other "liberal" causes, he was unelectable in his home state. He was glad the Court was a lifetime appointment.

"I guarantee you that you can't paint Farwell as a Communist if that's what you're aiming at with that Marx reference. I'm sure Farwell would prefer a comparison to Tom Paine." Black chuckled as the Chief waved his hand, dismissing his own analogy as inapt. "As for whether

Chapter Five: The Chief I

there's any dirt, Farwell is from a different state and never served in Congress. I never even encountered him until he got to the Court and I took an instant dislike to him. I'm a poor source for that kind of information, even if I was of a mind to give it to you, which I'm not. I know he comes from one of those families that got rich from cotton. Still has a big estate, I think. His father was once governor. That probably put him on the state supreme court. The family owned slaves, I'm sure, and I believe Farwell still has some sharecropping on his farm.

"That part of South Carolina may not be the poorest, but it's among the meanest," Black continued, enjoying both the attention of the Chief and the sound of his own voice. "I think if you look at the record you will find that there were lynchings in that part of the state before the war, maybe a lot of 'em. It's not surprising how he comes out on these votes. That's how he was raised. He may be rich, but he still was raised in a latrine. It's tough to blame him if he's still got a lot of shit on his shirt."

"Hell. The man is 70. He ought to have overcome his childhood prejudices by now," the Chief retorted. "This is 1954, not 1864. Look, can you ask some of your Southern buddies about Farwell? See if you can get something on him. I'm not going to blackmail him, but it may be necessary to discredit him in some way if he insists on this dissent."

Black turned very serious. The Chief wasn't getting the message through the friendly banter. The warning had to be made clear. "I won't do it, Chief. I think you're overreacting. And even if you're not, we probably all have a skeleton or two in our background. It offends me that you are even speaking this way. We all did things when we were younger that we regret. I'm sure you've got lots of stuff in your closet. We don't play that way here." Black stopped. He did not want to lose his temper. The Chief was his friend, but his office had to be respected, too.

The Chief knew he was being chastised by the most senior justice on the Court. He politely retreated from Black's office, taking the unusual and certainly unnecessary step of reminding his friend that their conversation was not to be shared with anyone else. "Of course, Chief," Black replied, "and I am also going to assume that you were just running that blackmail idea up the flag pole to see if anyone saluted. Nobody did, so burn it." The Chief didn't respond, but shook Black's hand and left.

That was the difference between a legislator like Black and a governor or president, the Chief thought as he returned down the dark corridors to his own office. Black was content to let everyone have their say, as they did in the Senate. He didn't understand, or perhaps chose not to care, that policies had to be executed if they were to be any good. That's why it was called the executive branch. Ike would eventually have to enforce the law. At least, the Chief hoped he would. Dissents by Farwell, and especially by Jackson and Clark, would make that task much more difficult. Perhaps it was just an old governor talking, but the Chief believed that as the man named by the President to head the Supreme Court, and as the man speaking for the majority on an important issue of law and social policy, he had to do what he could to help the President execute the law. That meant no dissents. A unanimous verdict.

Upon returning to his office, the Chief asked Margaret to call Louis, his messenger, to his chambers.

Chapter Six: Lessons In Black and White, April 24, 1954

Neil was awakened by his alarm clock at nine a.m. It was Saturday, April 24. He was used to getting by on less than six hours of sleep, but he regretted the four or five Ballantines he had at the Blue Mirror and the Slide Trombone. He felt fat and slow. But as he recounted in his head the events of yesterday, he was in awe of himself for how much he had accomplished. He obtained a lucrative assignment and already had a helpful lead from Audrey Winkler. Then he thought almost simultaneously of his family and Lorenzo King – all the bad news in one grouping. Neither had much respect for him, for entirely different reasons. His family because he has a colored client and no career; King because he is white and hasn't any experience. He was a reluctant choice for Mrs. Van Dyke. At least he liked her. Neil loved his family, but at this moment he wasn't sure he liked them much. He neither liked nor loved King, and the feeling clearly was mutual.

Neil decided to stop by the central branch of the public library on Mount Vernon Square. Although it was a Saturday, some of Clay's co-workers might be there. It would give him a chance to do some investigating without King along side. Then he'd swing by King's office. He'd probably spend an hour or two at Pennsy's Bar for dinner and see if Jennifer could spend the night. Before he did anything else, though, he wanted some breakfast. He also needed to talk to Alice Henshaw, whose recommendation to Mrs. Van Dyke had mixed him up in matters he wasn't certain he could handle, matters of race and homicide.

Monica's Bakery was actually a full-fledged restaurant, albeit one with Formica tables and a linoleum floor. It was basically a hash-and-eggs place where you also could purchase baked goods. It had a full menu and you could get a beer. The food was greasy but everything tasted like it looked and the portions were adequate. The place was best known for its no-nonsense waitresses, gum-snapping clichés of the pink and blue collar workers who were leaving D.C. for Prince George's County as more colored moved into their neighborhoods. Still, Monica's was in no danger of closing soon. There weren't any fashionable restaurants on the Hill. Monica's and Pennsy's Bar were about as good as it got.

Monica's was always crowded on a Saturday morning, which is why Alice Henshaw was working. As day manager, she was on duty Tuesday through Sunday, but weekends were the most crowded. Alice was nearly 20 years older than Neil, and her husband, Max, was 10 years older than Alice, but Neil had known them as a child before the war and they still treated him with the tentatively expressed concern reserved by adults for other people's teen-agers.

Neil could not resist the opportunity to spend time with Alice. He recently admitted to his father, who had hired Max as a photographer before the war, that Alice gave him what Neil called a "low grade burn," meaning his attraction for her was controlled, but pleasantly warm and exciting. Neil, who never spoke so candidly about women and sex

Chapter Six: Lessons In Black and White

with his father until returning from Korea, was surprised his father understood immediately. Although he didn't say so, Neil suspected his father carried the same burn.

"Low grade burn? Never heard that term used in quite that way. Interesting," his father said. "I think a healthy guy knows a lot of women who make him feel that way. Attracted, but not realistically available. Keeps life interesting."

Alice Henshaw interested Neil because she was an older woman but still a beauty. Nearing 45, her hair – very dark, black or close to it – showed no gray and framed a face with equally dark eyes and brows. Her sharp features, supposedly the product of a remote Creek Indian ancestor, had softened slightly over the years, adding to her beauty rather than detracting from it. Her figure was slight and her skin always looked at least lightly tanned, even in winter, another product of her Indian blood. Her legs were muscular and well-defined. Because of her coloring, Alice rarely wore stockings. When her legs were crossed and her light cotton dress or even the pink waitress uniform tightened over her thighs, it was impossible for Neil not to entertain a carnal fantasy. He never knowingly hinted at this attraction to Alice, but Alice knew she still appealed to men and sometimes her expression suggested she knew Neil was not different.

She exchanged a light kiss on the cheek with Neil, but gave him no preference for seating. Rank and friendship meant nothing at Monica's – everybody was treated the same way, which wasn't all that good. Sometimes service was prompt; sometimes not. Compliments and complaints were met with equal disregard. Neil asked Alice if he could talk to her for a few minutes. She told him she had a break scheduled in twenty minutes. It took nearly that long for Neil to get a table. He had just ordered ham and eggs when Alice joined him.

"So how's the private eye business," Alice said. When she was at work, Alice adopted the customer-be-damned attitude of the waitresses. It wasn't the real Alice, who could be much softer, but a disguise she could not resist wearing because it was fun and kept her focus on the job. Neil went right to his point, conscious that Alice's break was a short one.

"Alice, I've got a Negro problem."

Alice looked at him with amusement. "That usually means a "white guy" problem," she replied. Neil ignored the slander.

"I'm working on an assignment with this Negro man. He's older, maybe about 60. He's another PI. We aren't getting along very well, but we have to work together. He acts like he's always kinda' disgruntled or angry at me. I think he hates white people."

"Why do you think that?" Alice thought it difficult to believe anyone could dislike Neil Endicott. He was sweet, even innocent in a way, despite his combat experience.

"He said so. He says whites have made Negroes so conscious of their skin color they can't get away from the subject. He says whites control what's 'normal' and normal is white. At least, that's one reason he said he hates whites."

"But he's working with you, isn't he?"

Chapter Six: Lessons In Black and White

"Yeah. But that's because we have a colored client. I can't tell you more than that about the assignment, but it's a good one. We need to work together and I was hoping you could help me. You get along with Negroes."

Alice laughed out loud. "Neil, I get along with Negroes if they can get along with me. But this is a segregated southern city, claims of northern politicians notwithstanding. I socialize with black people sometimes – NAACP, sometimes a neighborhood function has a few coloreds. But I don't know that I'm a good candidate for race-mixer of the year or anything like that. Also, I'm assuming you are working on the Clay Van Dyke case. Didn't Virginia tell you I recommended you for the job?"

"Yes, she did. And thank you. But I can't tell you any more about the case. I do need help on this race issue. It's not Mrs. Van Dyke. It's this other investigator. I don't know anybody else to go to. It's kind of personal."

"All I can tell you is that what this man told you is true. You know that. It can't be a surprise to you that whites have been running and ruining the lives of black folk for 300 years. Of course color is important. Biologically, it's all that makes us different. The white man has used the difference to keep colored people down – no education, no civil rights, need I go on? You have heard of slavery? Didn't they teach you about slavery at that segregated high school you went to?"

"Ok, ok. I wasn't really challenging the idea. I need to know how to work with the guy."

"You have to live with him. You say he's around sixty? He's got his own business? He's not going to sweat much over what a young guy like you thinks. He probably sees this as a chance to vent some anger. I can't blame him.

"Speaking of race and anger," she continued, idly stirring her break coffee, "Kenny was the target of his first racial slur yesterday afternoon walking home from school."

"It doesn't sound like Kenny to use such language."

"It wasn't Kenny. I said he was the target of a slur. Some colored kid pushed Kenny off a swing at the playground and called him a 'white peckerwood cracker' or something like that."

"The playground? Negro kids don't go to white schools," Neil said.

"No, but it wasn't at the school. It was at Stanton Park. There are a few swings, a see-saw and a jungle gym. We've taken the kids there for years and now that he's nearly 10, Kenny can go by himself. He passes near it on the way home. It could have been at school. After school, anybody can use the playground. But it wasn't. Kenny ran home in tears. Max called me at work and I came home to talk to him. Max doesn't do well comforting the kids. He's from the school of the stiff upper lip. He knows he's lousy at it so he called me. I think Kenny was more shocked than anything – both at getting bounced from the swing and being called a name."

"I'm surprised this hasn't happened to him before."

Chapter Six: Lessons In Black and White

"If it has, he didn't mention it. You know, this neighborhood — these blocks, actually — are almost all white, but it changes quickly. If you go farther north a mile or so, you hit the colored shopping district on H Street. So Negroes pass through here all the time. Max and I kind of like that. There actually are a couple of colored families living in the next block, which is good. We'd like to have some Negro friends besides my friends at the NAACP. But D.C.'s still basically a southern town. Max works at home and Monica's is white, white, white and she wants to keep it that way. So we don't meet colored folk at work. At least the kids see colored folk and I guess they run into them at the parks. It's not like where you grew up and there aren't any colored kids."

Neil pondered the last remark as his platter of ham and eggs was delivered to the table. It was true that Chevy Chase had no colored families he was aware of, but he knew Negroes. His Dad was accurate, if insensitive, the night before when he suggested that the colored housekeeper, Louella, had practically raised the Endicott children while their mother tended to numerous charity and social events. There was hardly a drive during the war Mrs. Endicott was not involved in — rubber, bandages, war bonds. Other kids were in the same situation and Neil knew their housekeepers, too. But every night, Louella and the other housekeepers caught the streetcar at Connecticut Avenue for the long journey to wherever it was they came from. When Neil was small he asked Louella where she lived, but had no clue then or now where "Benning Road" was, except that it was in a corner of the District far from Chevy Chase.

"Well, I wouldn't worry about that. I had no colored friends and none of my friends had colored friends and we grew up just fine. I don't want to sound harsh, but I would think you don't want to make a political statement through your kids. You get the best for them you can afford — best neighborhood, best schools — and that usually means no coloreds. So what?"

Alice's dark eyes rarely changed expression, but Neil could see her body tense slightly and she stared over Neil's shoulder, avoiding eye contact. "If by that you mean we are integrationists and want our children to be integrationists then you are correct that our politics are reflected in how we treat our children. But how is that different from your family? *The Star* takes that typical wishy-washy attitude toward civil rights — always 'soon but not now'. That's how you were raised, except maybe more 'never' than 'soon'."

"My Dad is the managing editor for news at *The Star*, not an editorial writer, as you well know, so don't be so quick to confuse the two," Neil countered, regretting that he was at risk of upsetting Alice and himself on such a pleasant early spring morning. "You know Dad's no bigot."

"Do I?" Alice responded. "I don't think I've ever talked about the Negro problem with you or your Dad. But I do know *The Star's* newsroom is lily white. I think the same is true of the pressroom. It's probably true of *The Post* and *The News*, too. I'll bet your Dad is for the Negro in theory but doesn't see much need for one working for him."

Chapter Six: Lessons In Black and White

"Is that so different from everyone else?" Neil replied. He knew the defense was weak, but he thought Alice had identified his father's position accurately, given the senior Endicott's views about how the colored lived.

"Unfortunately not. But that doesn't make it right. Some day it'll have to change."

"Would you send your kids to an integrated school?" Neil asked.

"Of course. Wouldn't you?" Neil let the question stand unanswered. It was rhetorical, since he had neither wife nor kids. But as he spoke, he pictured Lou King explaining the "three Ms" by which whites learned about Negroes. He conceded King's point to himself.

"What did you tell Kenny," Neil asked, desperate to change the subject.

"We – Max and I – told him about bigotry. It seems that our child rearing, which you question, at least succeeded in making him accept that there are black and white people without ever actually thinking there was some other difference. It's probably just that he never thought much about it. Maybe we sheltered him too much, since obviously race issues are going to be with us for a while and he's got to learn about them some time. Anyway, we tried to be balanced. We told him bigots could be black or white or even Indian. They all shared the same characteristic: They all judged folks based on their skin color, even if they knew them and should know better. You know, all very northern liberal despite my Southwest heritage."

Unanimous Verdict

"How did Kenny respond?"

"He shocked us. He asked if 'nigger' meant colored people. We told him that was a horrible, bigoted term for the Negro and asked where he heard it. Turns out some of his classmates – can you imagine, just nine or 10 years old – were saying that if they had to go to school with niggers their parents would move to Maryland, where there weren't so many niggers."

"From the mouths of babes," Neil said, trying to suppress a grin at the picture of 10-year-olds tossing racial slurs like sailors.

"Neil! It's not funny. It's horrible. You sound like a racist yourself. Is that how you feel?" Heads in a public place turned to look at Neil for the third time in less than 24 hours as Alice made no effort to lower her volume. Neil swore he never would have another encounter about race in a bar or restaurant.

"Well, I don't think I am. I just haven't given these issues much thought. I don't have kids, I don't generally work around black folk and it's just not a big issue with me. I'm just trying to scrape up a living right now, which is why I'm trying to get along with this King guy but he doesn't want to cooperate."

"Look at it this way. Colored folk have had to hold their tongues for white folks for years and years. The tables are turned in your case. I guess you need this guy for your job. So now it's your turn to keep your mouth shut."

"But he sees everything in black-and-white, so to speak."

Chapter Six: Lessons In Black and White

"Listen to yourself. You aren't any less color conscious than he is. Maybe I'm too Pollyannaish, but I'd try to look at the man as a partner. You don't have to like him, but try to get to know him. Get past the color. Maybe it won't work; maybe it will.

"Speaking of work, I have to get back to it. And those ham and eggs aren't getting any warmer."

The D.C. central library was in a white stone beaux arts building that was over 50 years old in the middle of a small, deteriorating park. Inside, it was indistinguishable from any other library — shelves of books, a circulation desk and a couple of offices with half-height walls so that the occupant could see what was going on in the main room. The area was well lighted, with large chandeliers supplemented by desk lamps on each reading table. Neil went straight to the circulation desk and asked a thick, middle-aged white woman with grey and white hair if she knew Clayton Van Dyke. She only knew his name was Clayton and that he had committed suicide. Neil showed her his PI license and said he was working for Neil's mother to find out some information. The clerk told him that Neil could find a co-worker in the basement whose name was Louie who might know more about Clayton. She showed him the door to the basement.

The basement was even more utilitarian. There were workbenches supplied with glue, tape and other materials to repair books.

Unanimous Verdict

Next to them was a machine of some sort which Neil assumed also was connected with book repair. A binding machine, perhaps? He didn't know. Farther from the steps was a warehouse area which also could be entered through a garage door. That door was open to take advantage of the cool breezes and sunlight. The basement was slightly damp, with a mildew smell, and needed the fresh air. The mildew can't be good for the books, Neil thought. There were fluorescent shop lights over the workbenches, but otherwise the basement was illuminated by naked incandescent bulbs hanging from the ceiling under small tin shades. The place was gloomy and uninviting. A lousy place to work, Neil told himself. It was no wonder Clayton drove all around town in his library delivery truck, if only to stay away from this basement.

The truck, a step van with the words "D.C. Public Library" stenciled on the sides, was backed into the driveway at the garage door. A husky black man in dungarees and a tan work shirt was loading books, magazines and newspapers into corrugated boxes. Several such boxes already were loaded onto the truck. They were marked with the names of branch libraries – Adams Morgan, Cleveland Park, Brentwood, Anacostia, etc.

"Are you Louie?" Neil called out to the man.

"Yeah. You here about the job?" The man stopped his work, drew a bandana to wipe his hands and approached Neil, eventually extending his right hand. Neil took it and said:

150

Chapter Six: Lessons In Black and White

"No. I'm here about Clayton Van Dyke. My name is Neil Endicott. His mother has asked me to look into some things since he died."

"I thought you were here about the job. Clayton's job. It's vacant of course. I'll help you however I can if you're working for Mrs. Van Dyke. Name is Louie Charles." Louie's face was sober, unsmiling, but his voice was friendly. He was well-spoken. Likely well-educated. Like Clayton.

"How well did you know Clayton?"

"Very well. We went to Dunbar together. He helped get me this job. You know, I can't believe he killed himself. Clayton just wasn't like that. He had plans. I saw Mrs. Van Dyke at Clay's funeral. She was telling everybody that Clayton didn't kill himself. Are you here to find out if that's true?" Louie's eyes probed Neil's, as if they could confirm Neil's honesty or convict him of lying. They had done so in the past.

"Yes, that's pretty much it," Neil replied, wanting to disclose as little as possible. "Any ideas?"

Louie sat on one of the sealed boxes on the warehouse floor and waved his hand inviting Neil to do the same. "I think he was murdered."

"By whom?"

"I don't know. But he was awfully excited about something he found out in Chicago. Not so much so when he got back from Atlanta.

That was all just in the last couple months. Maybe something, maybe nothing."

"Do you know Audrey Winkler?" Louie scrunched up his face as if another bad odor had been introduced to the warehouse.

"Of course. She works here. She thought she was Clay's girlfriend for a while. I can't see that drunk killing him, if that's what you're after. Only thing she can lift is a glass of scotch. She couldn't kill Clay and then make it look like a hangin'. You be barkin' up the wrong tree."

"No, I'm not suggesting that," Neil replied. "But she indicated that Clay was very... ahh,.." Neil wanted to be careful. He wanted to be sensitive. "... concerned about race issues." That was better than saying Clay was obsessed about his skin color.

"Name me a colored man or woman over about five-years-old who isn't. But I get where you're goin'. When he got back from the war, for a while all he could talk about was how bad whites treat the Negro. But, you know, I had a lot of friends from high school fought over in Germany and Italy. Lost some of them. The ones that came back, they all were pretty angry. They got treated the same way as before they left. I don't think they expected that and it made them mad. Clay was no different. He settled down after a few years."

Louie Charles continued, his eyes now focusing past Neil as he thought about his dead friends, both Clayton and those who died in battle. "Lately, he was talkin' about going back to college. I think he knew he was too old, but he was thinkin' 'bout it."

Chapter Six: Lessons In Black and White

Then the young Negro's tone turned angry. "Anyway, I asked them what did they expect? Black man raises his cotton and fights his wars and neither way is the white man going to give him a break. Hope you don't mind my speaking so frankly, mister." His last sentence was a courtesy, delivered as a curt command. Neil had been verbally pushed around like that by colored folk a lot in the last 24 hours, which didn't make it easier to take. As before, he ignored the tone of voice as the price of information.

"Yes, I can see how they would be upset. Did Clay tell you about his Chicago trip?"

"He expected to find out about his birth parents. All he learned is that he was actually born in Atlanta. That's why he went to Atlanta. When he got back, he said he was pretty sure who his real parents were, but he was going to confirm it. He said he might need one more trip, but maybe not. He said another trip might not be worth it. He said there were good ways to be born and bad, and that his was bad. I asked him what he meant, but he shrugged me off. That was a month ago, a Friday. Next thing I know, people are telling me here on Monday that Clay is dead. A suicide. That's all I know."

"Did he say who he met or talked to in Chicago or Atlanta?"

"I don't know about Atlanta. But he said he was going to find an old Army buddy in Chicago to help him out, maybe put him up."

"Do you remember his name?"

"Heck, I've met the guy. He came through D.C. a couple years ago and Clay introduced me to him. He was Clay's hero. Name is Ezra Lowell. Big guy. Very much a Black Nationalist type of guy.

Runs some kinda' political operation in Chicago. Sort of like Wallace Muhammed, Nation of Islam stuff, but different. No religious stuff, Clay told me. I think I got some pamphlet Clay brought back with him from Chicago. Would you like to see it?" Neil nodded.

Louie crossed the warehouse floor to a set of lockers in the far corner of the basement. He opened one locker and rummaged through it before returning with a pamphlet. It was a single piece of typing paper, printed on front and back in three columns, divided into three parts along the long edge and folded so that it was a small six-page pamphlet. The first page was all large type. It said:

JOIN THE
BLACK NATIONAL STRENGTH PARTY
400 East 64th Street
Chicago, Illinois
JO 8-3304

Ladies and gentlemen of Color: CAST OFF YOUR CHAINS.
FIGHT BACK. THE COURTS WON'T DO IT.... THE
PRESIDENT WON'T DO IT.... THE NAACP CAN'T DO
IT ... THE POWER IS YOURS AND YOURS ALONE!!!

At the bottom, in much smaller type, was written: Ezra Lowell, Party President.

Chapter Six: Lessons In Black and White

Neil noted there was a union button on the last page, but otherwise did not read the document.

"May I keep this?" he asked Louie Charles.

"Sure. I got no use for it. It's a Chicago organization."

"Did Clay say anything else about this Ezra Lowell or the Black National Strength Party?"

"I know they got to be friends during the war. I know Clay said he agrees with Ezra that the black man got to fight for his own rights. White man can't be trusted. Can't say I disagree. Been proved time and again by my lights."

"Do you know if this guy Lowell or his organization are violent, or encourage other people to be violent?" Neil already concluded he would need to go to Chicago to find this man Lowell. He needed to know if Lowell was dangerous.

"Clay wasn't violent. I don't think he knew how to be. I don't know about Lowell. He's a big guy. Very muscular. I think Clay said Lowell once was in some gangs. He might be violent. I just don't know. You white folk like to assume all coloreds is violent though, don't you?"

Neil ignored the comment. "Do you recall anything else Clay said about what he found out in Chicago or Atlanta? Anything at all?"

"No, but he was pretty excited after Chicago. I have to think he found out his father was white and some kind of big deal. Clay always assumed he was the son of somebody important. I always thought he was the son of somebody important already, since Mr. Van Dyke was pretty well known and did lots of good stuff. But Clay was looking for an important white man for his dad. I really didn't get it. I know this: if he found out his father, or grandfather or whatever was just an ignorant cracker, he would have been damned disappointed. I figure that's why he was unhappy after Atlanta. Things didn't work like he wanted. But he didn't explain himself at all."

This time, Neil knocked on King's office door before entering.

"Come on in. What're you waitin' for?"

"You told me yesterday I should knock, so I knocked," Neil said as he crossed the office to King's desk.

"Well, you were a stranger then. You ain't a stranger no more." King was jovial and alert. If he was suffering from the late night and the cognac, he was good at disguising the pain. He didn't appear to be holding any grudges against Neil, either.

"Anything new?" Neil asked.

"Naw, I just got here. My wife made me cut the grass and trim some bushes this morning. Workin' up a little sweat got rid of that damn cognac. Young man, do you own a house?"

"No. I live in an apartment."

"Well, stay in an apartment. Houses ain't nothin' but problems. Damned grass alone grows faster than a white man chasin' a dollar."

Chapter Six: Lessons In Black and White

King sounded like Neil's father, who hated yard work and household chores, claiming not to know one end of a hammer from the other. It had not occurred to Neil that King had a domestic life outside of his office, with a wife and house. "I didn't know you were married," he said.

"You never asked. Wife, two grown kids, house in the Trinidad area. Man, I got the works and got to work to keep 'em, too."

"What do your kids do?" Neil was a little chagrined. He knew that if King were white, dressed in a three-piece suit in a downtown office, he would have assumed he had a family.

"Son goes to Harvard Law. Graduates in a year. Daughter is at Cornell. Just a sophomore. She says she wants to go to medical school, but her mother and I hope she gets an M.R.S. degree. Medical school would bust us, and I'd like to retire some day."

"You must be very proud of them," Neil said.

"Well, sure," King replied as he began shuffling some papers on his huge desk. "But it ain't 'cause they're goin' to fancy schools. I'd be proud of 'em if they was on D.C. Sanitation. They're sweet kids and ain't addicts or alcoholics. That's the most a daddy can expect. That's the meat and potatoes. Everything else is dessert." Neil's brain flashed quickly on his own father's disappointment that his younger son did not go to college or have much prospect for a prestigious career. He wondered if King's kids knew how well they had it. He suspected that they did.

"So with an apartment, you musta' had some time this morning. No grass to cut. Did you find out anything?"

Unanimous Verdict

"Yeah, I did." Neil narrated the essentials of his trip to the D.C. library and pulled out the Black National Strength Party brochure. King read the entire brochure before speaking.

"Never heard of no Black National Strength Party," King said after completing his reading. "No particular reason I would have, I guess. Probably just local to Chicago. Lots'a these kinds'a groups around the country. You recall our discussion last night – early this mornin', I guess – 'bout Nation of Islam?"

Neil nodded.

"I guess this is a Little League Nation of Islam type organization. They're big in Detroit, New York, maybe other places for all I know. Don't know 'nuthin 'bout 'em bein' in Chicago. Maybe this Lowell guy has picked up the slack there. I don't follow this stuff much. Hell, I got enough problems bein' a Baptist. And I'm too old to tote both a grudge *and* a gun."

"I haven't read the whole brochure, but they sound pretty angry," Neil said.

King laughed.

"You're a funny guy, Endicott. Fuck yes they're angry. Whadda' you expect? But they probably ain't crazy or bug-eyed like you're thinkin'. Lots of 'em are recruited from criminal gangs and such, but the funny thing is, they join up with one of these political organizations and they go pretty straight. Even do good works.

"I can tell you're worried maybe ol' Clay was into something real bad with this guy Lowell. Maybe, but I doubt it. After you get past all the angry militant stuff, you see in this brochure that the Black National Strength Party or whatever it's called feeds the poor and has a school for the little ones. They got some kinda' mission on the south side of Chicago. Rough rhetoric and good deeds. That's typical of a lot of these organizations." King stopped short, as if he intended to say more on the subject but was struck by a different thought.

"You really don't know shit about black folk, do you Endicott?"

"I don't know. I served with some Negro soldiers in Korea. I told you I walked a beat in Ivy City for a few months." Neil heard the slightly mocking tone of Alice Henshaw at Monica's in King's question. "I'm not a biggot, if that's what you think. I can get along with Negroes."

King laughed again. Then he raised his pitch into what was supposed to be a sing-songy, falsetto imitation of a youngster and shook his head from side-to-side: "I can get along with Negroes." He laughed uproariously at his successful effort to shame Neil. "By that you mean you don't call 'em nigger or shine to their face and you tut-tut about how bad slavery was and ain't it a shame those po' colored folk can't hold a job. Ain't that how you get along with Negroes?" King adopted a mildly accusatory tone, the sound of someone playful who knows his gaming has caused a wound.

"You got no right to say that." Neil responded, more combatively. "Sure, I haven't had much contact with Negroes. But I don't want to see them held back. Why are we gettin' into this fight, anyway?"

Unanimous Verdict

"Because the obvious next step in this investigation is for one of us to go to Chicago to see this guy Lowell. It should be me. But I'm a witness in a trial coming up next week. It's a kidnapping. Serious charge but bullshit facts. I investigated it for the defendant. Have to be in town all week 'cause we don't know how many days the prosecution's gonna' take to present their case. So looks like we send the white guy to talk to the militant black guy. We can't have you actin' scared or as if this guy is a boogey man or somehow less than a full human being or he won't help us out at all.

"Unless these brain cells been totally dissolved by alcohol and old age, I'm sure this guy's gonna' be able to smell a condescending young cracker from a mile away and hate him immediately. That cracker is you."

King stood with his knuckles curled on the desk. "Look. I'll call this guy – what's his name? Ezra Lowell? – and try to set things up for you. Maybe he'll tell me everything on the phone and you won't have to go to Chicago. But I expect there's something about Clay's trip that's secret, maybe illegal, and he won't want to talk to a stranger without meetin' him face-to-face. It'll be your job to make sure Lowell doesn't think you're some Klansman or, worse, some country club rich guy who figures 'cause he tips his locker room attendant he's got the Negro race stuff covered."

"This is so damn unfair." Neil listened quietly to King's small lecture with a swelling sense of injustice. "I respect people black and white. I don't treat 'em no different."

160

Chapter Six: Lessons In Black and White

The room was silent as a grave.   After a long minute, King again spoke.

"I think you think you're right, Endicott. You're basically a good guy. You probably ain't a cracker in the sense that you want to go out and hurt black folk. You or folks in your family might even give canned goods at Christmas and put extra money in the offering plate for the poor, which in D.C. means mostly colored. That's important in a small way, I guess. But helpin' poor people to keep alive ain't the same as fightin' to make their life better. And that's what this guy Lowell is gonna' be lookin' for – somebody who's on the colored man's side. I bet he sees God-fearin' white guys bring canned goods to his mission all the time and then they high-tail back to Winnetka or wherever, breakin' their arm pattin' themselves on the back. He ain't gonna' tell such people deep dark secrets like we need. He'll just say 'thanks' and 'good-bye.'"

"Listen, you probably are right. But if you are, how can I gain Lowell's trust? I can't turn into Booker T. Washington all of sudden."

"Wouldn't help if you could, I 'spect. But if you can just look the guy in the face, talk to him like you would any white guy, and give him credit for being at least as smart as you are, you might pull it off. But really look at him. While you're talkin' to him, look into his eyes. Look at his nose. Look at his lips and his cheeks. And listen to what he has to say, the actual words and their meaning. Don't stare, but maybe if you look at his features, listen to the content of his speech instead of thinking how wonderful it is the guy can even talk, you might, maybe, really think of him as a human being just like you."

"I look at people" Neil said, sounding discouraged.

"Get past the color. Maybe even imagine them as having their own families, their own jobs, their own worries. And I definitely don't mean to pity them. Mostly their worries are like yours. Shelter, food, safety, education and the like. You don't need any pity and neither do they. If this guy Lowell thinks you pity him, your conversation is over."

"If it was that easy, we'd solve the Negro problem." he said, immediately regretting his comment.

"Ain't no 'Negro problem', Endicott. It's a white problem. And this stuff is like tips for play actin', not for solvin' any race problems. We are in a pinch. We can't make you no Paul Robeson, but maybe we can make you act like someone Robeson might talk to for half an hour. You got better ideas?"

Neil had none.

"He for sure ain't gonna open up to you, but he might let on what you need to know about Clayton Van Dyke. I'll try to pave your way with a phone call. Mark one thing, though: He'll never trust you."

"Do you?"

"I think under pressure from the cops or other white folk you'd open up faster than a Bible at a ladies prayer meetin'. But I'm willin' to be proved wrong."

Chapter Six: Lessons In Black and White

When he returned to his apartment, Neil made two calls. The first was to Jennifer. Neil wanted company. There was no answer at her apartment. The second was to Virginia Van Dyke, who was home.

Mrs. Van Dyke was cordial, but as Neil began to explain the results of interviews with LeClerc, Winkler and Charles, she cut him off. "Mr. King already has called and informed me of all that," she said. "He telephoned me only a half hour ago." Neil took the news calmly. Mrs. Van Dyke probably preferred to be informed of the status of the investigation by King, whom she trusted more than she did Neil.

"Then you can understand the purpose of my call, which is to get some more information on Clay's adoption. Can you first tell me where you adopted him? Was it an agency?"

"Elmer was an associate at a small black law firm. One of the firm's clients was a small adoption agency. It only handled colored children, of course, but it had a reputation for selectivity. Its clients came recommended by prominent Negro families. The agency assured us that the records of the birth parents were checked and that at least the mother had been interviewed and examined by a physician – not just to evaluate her pregnancy, but also to be sure the mother didn't carry any diseases or have a family history of illness which might be passed on to the child."

"What was the name of the agency? Does it still exist?"

"It was the Childress Agency. Named after the founder. I at first thought it was a typographical error when I saw the name. I thought it was the 'Childless Agency.'" Mrs. Van Dyke laughed

163

lightly at her own joke. "I don't know if it is still in business. We had to pay nearly $2,000 to adopt Clay. He was the only baby we looked at. He was a beautiful child. About four months old. He was healthy."

"Did you learn anything about his birth parents?" Neil asked.

"No. That information was entirely confidential. Obviously, we suspected that a white man might have been the father, since Clay was light-skinned. Or maybe his grandfather was white. We don't know and we didn't care. We just wanted our boy."

"When did all this take place?"

"Clay was legally adopted on June 14, 1922. He was born on February 20 of that year. Elmer's firm prepared the paperwork for the adoption."

"Was he born in Chicago?"

"We assumed so."

"Have you since learned anything more about the circumstances of Clay's birth?"

"No, we have not. Of course, we knew Clay was interested in that subject. We were warned many times by others who have adopted that that would happen. But as you have heard from his friends, Clayton was more interested than most, what with trips to Chicago and Atlanta and God knows where else.

"Forgive me Mr. Endicott for saying this, but I wonder if you and Mr. King are not off base with this speculation about his birth being tied to Clay's death. It sounds far-fetched to me. I mean, not

Chapter Six: Lessons In Black and White

only was it 32 years ago, but why would anyone wish to kill their biological son? It makes no sense. No sense at all."

"I'm inclined to agree with you, Ma'am. But this is the only exceptional circumstance we have so far. By-the-way, did your son ever mention an Ezra Lowell from Chicago?"

"Mr. King asked me that same question. Yes, he talked about Ezra Lowell and even brought him home around a year ago. He stayed at our house. I remember thinking I was sorry my husband was not alive to speak to him. Mr. Lowell is very well-spoken and very interested in politics. Although he is not a lawyer, he was conversant in the law, especially the law of civil rights. Elmer would have enjoyed talking to him. Clay was interested in civil rights law, too, but always in a more headstrong way — let's get it done now sort of thing. Mr. Lowell was more knowledgeable, more sophisticated, than Clay on the subject."

"Where did they meet? I mean your son and Mr. Lowell?"

"In an Army jail. Both of them got in trouble at Fort Polk in Louisiana. Clay said he was assaulted by a white soldier and fought back. They called the white guy the victim! Clay got off with a couple of months in jail and returned to active duty. He got an honorable discharge after the war, but he was pretty bitter about his treatment in the Army. They made him a cook and told him he couldn't fight. He never even left the U.S., which was a blessing to me but an insult to Clayton.

"I know Ezra served a longer time in jail. I think he hit a white officer. But I don't know what happened to him in the Army. He runs

165

a school and some kind of political organization in Chicago, according to what he told me."

"Did Mr. Lowell seem violent or militaristic?"

"No. Not at all. He was very well mannered. I think he was doubtful that white people ever would be of any real help to the blacks in this country, but that's a common feeling. I hope it's wrong, but surely it is reasonable to think that."

"Is there anything else you can tell me about Chicago that might bear on this?"

"No. That's about it. We lived there until about 1932. Then Dean Houston hired my husband for the law school. I don't think I've been back since before the war. My friends are here now."

Chapter Seven: An Evening at Pennsy's, April 24 -25, 1954

Pennsy's was one of several cheap bars on Pennsylvania Avenue, SE, within four blocks of the Capitol. It was near Seward Square between a gas station and a small grocery store. Bars like Pennsy's made no effort to attract the political crowd, despite their proximity to Congress. Senators and Representatives were barely aware of the vibrant Capitol Hill neighborhood to the East. Their focus — social, political and domestic — was on Northwest, where the moneyed folk resided in neighborhoods such as Foxhall and Chevy Chase or in high-rise apartments along upper Connecticut Avenue.

Capitol Hill's Victorian and Federal row houses stretched from behind the Library of Congress and the Supreme Court into the bent elbow of the Anacostia River on the South and East, and to H Street Northeast on the North. The neighborhood was predominantly white, its complexion darkening as one traveled farther in any direction except toward downtown, west of the Capitol. A new freeway planned six blocks south of Pennsylvania Avenue to whisk white politicians and their aides to equally white neighborhoods in Maryland and Virginia already was having a deleterious effect on the southernmost reaches of Capitol Hill, where the housing stock was in decline. There were plans to level residences near the freeway to construct high-rise apartments as public housing — very different from those on Connecticut Avenue. It was assumed that no self-respecting person who could afford to buy a home would want to live next to a freeway. The poor – all of them Negroes – would have no choice.

In the spring of 1954, Capitol Hill was a mix of teachers, civil servants and some of Washington's blue-collar workforce – the men who worked with pipe, iron and wiring which even a city as absorbed in policy and politics as Washington required. It was a neighborhood of a few thousand families, spiced with several hundred poorly-paid but ambitious young assistants who kept the paper moving in Congress and occupied single rooms in the residences of widows supplementing their pensions or in the four and five story apartment buildings that dotted those blocks closer in to the Capitol. Others, young and old, lived on Capitol Hill because they could not afford the rents in Northwest and had no interest in the burgeoning suburbs in Prince Georges County, Maryland, a few miles farther east, across the Anacostia. Neil Endicott, who was both young and broke, was among this last group.

Pennsy's catered to all of these crowds by being safe, fairly clean and cheap. It had hearty diner food, the beer prices were reasonable and the crowd was largely cheerful and well-behaved. The building was only wide enough for a laminate dining counter in front of the shiny chromed steel grill area that ran most of the length of the building on the left and a line of wooden booths across the linoleum floor on the right. The booths were as uncomfortable as a bus station bench when they were installed years earlier, but the shifting movement of a million bottoms had smoothed and worn the surfaces unevenly so that they were comfortable – if your butt was neither too ample nor too bony.

Chapter Seven: An Evening at Pennsy's

In short, Pennsy's was a place for the average person. Its patrons knew it and liked it that way.

In the early evening, the booths were packed with families looking for an inexpensive diversion from an evening by the radio or, in a growing number of cases, the television set. After 8, the crowd changed. It was younger and single, save for the few older men who nursed a beer until late, isolated from the young crowd, but not as lonely as they would have been by themselves in their barely furnished boarding rooms.

It being a Saturday night, Neil was certain some of his friends would be at the bar meeting other friends, hoping to pick up a new girl or pondering in isolation over a beer why the last girl walked out. If Jenny wasn't there, Neil thought, he would call and ask her to join him. He would even spring for the cab.

He was disappointed to find only Mike Q among those at the bar, sitting at the counter chewing on a sandwich, which he washed down with a bottle of Schlitz. The "Q" stood for Quantanapora, which Mike claimed was Portuguese. True or not, no one thought enough of the name not to shorten it, including its owner. He had been called Mike Q since grammar school.

"Well, if it isn't Lew Archer," Mike said, chewing his sandwich, making the name of the fictional detective in the popular Ross McDonald books sound like "larcher."

"Sam Spade to you," Neil responded. "Found any bodies in the trunk of those jalopies, yet?" Mike Q sold Chevys, including used ones, at a dealership on Georgia Avenue. The two-tone colors of the new cars were popular and a lot of GIs, even nine years after the war, were just coming into their own financially. They could afford a new car – or maybe a second one – so Mike was making a good living. He let everyone know it, too, particularly the girls. But cars bored Neil, who couldn't envision either needing one or affording one in his current situation. Since Mike loved to talk about cars, he bored Neil.

"Looks like I'm gonna sell three cars this week, Neil. We can't keep 'em on the lot. One guy bought a beauty of a Bel-Air for cash – cash! He pulled a wad out of his pocket and peeled off over $1,500. I never saw anything like it, I tell ya.. I was fuckin' impressed. It's the Eisenhower economy, I tell ya." Mike relied on variations of "I tell ya" to punctuate sentences empty of either interesting information or original thought. Neil assumed that the habit had something to do with pushing cars.

"We are gettin' three more Corvettes on the lot next week, Neil. One is already sold but I can get you one of the others. Which would you like, white or red? Now's the time to get one. You'll be able to get all the pussy you want with one of these Corvettes, I tell ya."

"I read in the papers that Ford's coming out with its own sports car in the fall," Neil replied, knowing this would cause Mike to drop the sales pitch and start defending the Chevy, which he proceeded to do as Neil ordered an open-faced roast beef sandwich and a Ballantine Ale. Neil thereafter responded to Mike's dull analysis of automobiles only as bar protocol required, with a series of grunts between bites of food

170

Chapter Seven: An Evening at Pennsy's

and swallows of beer to pretend Mike was keeping him entertained and informed. Experience taught there was no reason to worry that Mike's soliloquy about the virtues of the Chevrolet would end before Neil finished his meal.

Just as Neil began debating with himself over whether to call Jennifer and stay at Pennsy's, or just go home, the lady in question walked through the door and greeted the pair at the counter. An exchange of glances informed Neil that Jennifer knew she was as welcome as headache powder for a hangover. All three waited patiently to grab a booth while one of the last families in the bar paid its tab and departed. Soon after they were seated, the trio was joined by Jennifer's friend, roommate and chauffeur, Lisa McCartin, who had parked her car. She marched to the booth, her pretty face pinched and stern.

"So, what's up with the baboons you call politicians, Lisa?" Mike Q laughed at a line he had used a dozen times without causing anyone else to break a smile.

"It's McCarthy, McCarthy, McCarthy all the time," Lisa said angrily, holding an unlit Camel in her left hand and sipping Jennifer's Schlitz with the other. "I am so sick of him, and so is everybody else for my money. I don't think he's uncovered a single Red in the government. Now he's going after the Army. These investigative hearings are so loathsome. Even the right wing Republicans are tired of him. I heard Ike would like to shut him up but doesn't have the guts to do so. We get more mail about McCarthy than about social security benefits or the bomb."

Unanimous Verdict

Lisa worked for a senator, mostly answering constituent mail, giving special visitors tours of the Capitol and otherwise doing whatever chores she was assigned. Those who didn't know Lisa assumed she was eye candy and maybe something more for the senator, a liberal Republican from the Northeast. She probably gave the adjective "flaming" to redheads due to her hair, which she maintained at shoulder length, ending with a looping curl. Her hazel eyes were large and luminous, her skin delicate, clear and very pale, broken by a constellation of freckles that were more beige than brown and barely noticeable. At about five-eight she was neither too short nor too tall, and she kept her body in athletic condition by playing tennis frequently, preferably indoors because she burned so easily. Her figure was seductive — not so much breast to clearly define all that was under her dress, but enough to make men want to find out how much more there really was.

"McCarthy may not be the best guy to go after the Commies in government, but he pretty much is the only guy doing it," Mike said. "You don't really believe that the Russkys haven't got spies in the State Department or the Pentagon, do you? There's even suspicion that Oppenheimer is a Commie, and he invented the A-bomb! They are there, I tell ya, but nobody wants to help him find them."

"What's the matter? J. Edgar Hoover isn't good enough for you?" Jennifer said, intervening early to avoid another tiresome political battle between Lisa, who studied the issues, and Mike, who acquired his facts and opinions from other Chevy salesmen. "I don't see him

Chapter Seven: An Evening at Pennsy's

coming to McCarthy's defense. The FBI's caught a few spies. If it were such a big problem they woulda' caught more, I suppose."

"Hoover's supposed to stay away from politics. He ain't said anything bad about McCarthy, either," Mike replied. "Russia got the A-bomb by spying. Maybe from Oppenheimer. That should be enough to show McCarthy's on the right track."

"You are both missing the point," said Lisa, who finished lighting her cigarette and offered the pack around the table with no takers. "It's McCarthy's methods that are the worst thing about him. He has this weasely little guy – what's his name? The Jew? Cohn, that's it. They put these little people who haven't done anything or maybe just went to some meetings, they put them under a spotlight and call them a Commie or treat them like John Dillinger. Their lives are ruined for nothing. Now he's getting worse, what with bringing up soldiers and charging them with being Reds. Those guys *served* their country and McCarthy's going after them."

Neil anticipated what was coming next. Jennifer always tried to bring him into political talk. "You were a Marine, Neil. Did you find Reds in the military?"

"You know what they say? There are no atheists in foxholes."

Jennifer registered her disapproval. "Oh, come on Neil. You were in the Marines for over two years. Did you run into any traitors? Any GIs who thought the Reds were right?"

"GIs are Army, Jennifer. I was Marines, a Leatherneck. Most civilians don't care about the difference, but Marines do."

Unanimous Verdict

"You are intentionally missing the point, Neil," Lisa said as she pushed her hair away from her face and broke her stern mien with a toothsome smile. "I like your hair, by the way. I hope you'll let it grow." The tension in her voice relaxed as she contemplated Neil across the booth. Was it Neil or was it just changing the subject? It wasn't hard to imagine Neil in a Marine uniform. At 24, his stomach was still flat in a boyish, six-foot figure which lacked visible hips or ass. He had a full head of sandy hair, not quite blond and with a hint of ochre, which caused some to accuse Neil of being Irish, despite his High Anglican surname. At Jennifer's urging, he abandoned the buzz cut sold for fifty cents by a barber across the street from the Marine barracks a few blocks away. The longer, thicker hair covered his scalp and seemed to widen his face. Now he looked like an adult, Jennifer said, instead of a baby warrior, and was more interesting to the young career women of Washington. Lisa's lingering look confirmed Jennifer's judgment.

"Hey, what about my hair? I'm growin' a DA," Mike Q interjected, jealous of Lisa's attention to Neil. Everyone else at the table was too kind to tell Mike his head really did look like a duck's ass thanks to all the Brylcreem that caused his thinning black hair to hold unusual and inhuman positions. Neil thought he probably could bend Mike's hair into different shapes, but he didn't have the courage to mix his hands in the grease and whatever insects were attracted to it.

"I'm sure you'll get the attention of all the girls, Mike," Jennifer said, her voice carefully modulated to a neutral tone so that

Chapter Seven: An Evening at Pennsy's

even Mike would know the remark was not exactly a compliment. All four friends laughed, joining the general gaiety reigning at Pennsy's.

Suddenly, the room was dead silent. All eyes turned to the front of the building, where three Negro men, probably in their early 20s, came through the door and walked to the cash register on the end of the bar. They didn't sit, but said something to the bartender. Silence continued for several seconds, then conversation resumed like a gentle breeze rustling tree leaves as those patrons in the front, who could hear what was said to the bartender, returned their gazes to their friends and awkwardly resumed conversation, studiedly feigning indifference to the Negroes. The bartender swiftly pulled a six-pack of National Bohemian Beer from a cooler. The Negroes paid for it and left. Casual conversation was soon again punctuated by laughter at Pennsy's, except at Neil's booth.

"God that is so disgusting. You might think they were Japs at Pearl Harbor or something." Lisa bit her lower lip, smearing red lipstick on her upper bicuspids. With the instinct women have for such things, she pulled a hankie from her purse to wipe her mouth.

"What?" Neil was genuinely puzzled at Lisa's anger. "Nobody did anything. They got their beer and left. Everybody's happy. Why are you upset?"

"Are you made of stone?" Lisa was so angry she nearly spit at Neil after replacing her handkerchief in her purse. "Didn't you see the hatred when those boys walked in here?"

"Oh, Lisa, I don't think you have a right to say there was hatred. Curiosity, maybe." Jennifer tried to calm her friend, but Lisa only got angrier.

"Maybe not hatred. Maybe contempt is a better word. They were just scared to death those boys would try to sit down at this crummy bar and have a drink. Why, maybe they'd even have the nerve to talk to a white man, as if it might infect everybody with a disease."

"Jeez, you're overdoing it a little, don't you think," Mike Q said. "They got what they wanted and the folks here got what they wanted — a little beer and a little peace."

Lisa slumped into the booth, her shoulders nearly meeting her ears. Now, her body said defeat. Quietly, only to herself, her eyes examining her folded hands on the table, Lisa asked: "Doesn't America mean anything anymore?"

Neil leaned over the table. "What? I didn't hear you."

"I mean, didn't we fight for a lot of principles against the Germans and the Japs? We were just kids then, but didn't it seem like everyone was pulling together? It was hard, but it wasn't mean. We had a few Negroes in Holyoke, but also lots of Italians and Poles. We had coloreds in my high school even. We got along."

"Yeah, what's your point?" Neil was more abrupt than he had intended, but Lisa was meandering. Maybe she was inebriated on a half a beer. Suddenly, he wanted to go home.

"My point is that it's all moving backwards. Now we're scared there's a Commie around every corner. Free speech isn't free anymore.

176

Chapter Seven: An Evening at Pennsy's

Black lists, A-bombs are bad enough, but we can't even find it in our hearts to help the Negro. We treated those boys like traitors – full of suspicion and, what was the word I found? Contempt."

"Oh, c'mon, Lisa. Coloreds are mostly happy. They don't wanna hang around with whites anymore than whites wanna hang around with them. I met a few Negroes in the Marines. Now I agree they ought to have equal rights and be able to vote and stuff. Nobody should have to face being beaten up just to vote or hop on a bus. But those boys found a place to drink their beer I'm sure. It just wasn't here. Not so bad." Neil thought he struck a tone of compromise and comfort. Lisa thought otherwise.

"God damn your Marine ass, Neil. Don't you have any feelings? Don't you have any emotions? Don't you have any opinions except that 'all is well'? I've known you for nearly seven months and have yet to hear you get angry or even mildly upset about anything except maybe a sports team or something. Isn't there anything important you want to stand up for? It's not like you have a family and a real job or anything you have to protect or to worry about. And it's not that you're not smart. You know what's happening, you read the papers. But you're a cipher, a nullity. Were you always like this – some damned spoiled Chevy Chase brat who had everything and never cared where it came from? Or did the Marines just tear out your heart and throw it in the trash with some Communist soldiers?" Lisa's voice carried across the narrow restaurant to the bar as she reached the end of her diatribe. She was emotional, but dry-eyed, maintaining a steady glare at Neil.

Unanimous Verdict

Although Neil thought she was ranting, it was clear that when Lisa stopped talking, she expected some answer to her questions. She kept staring at him in silence.

As he tried to shape a response, Neil didn't know whether to be embarrassed, angry or flattered – or all three. Clearly, Lisa had pondered Neil over their brief acquaintance and was genuinely interested in how and why he had come to be as he was. Neil was flattered to have captured the curiosity of a woman like Lisa. But he was angry and embarrassed at being ambushed during a casual social function and, irrationally, at failing to meet Lisa's vague expectations of who he should be. He was clearly muddled and surprised. Jennifer rescued him.

"That is totally unfair, Lisa. Neil volunteered to defend this country and paid a price. If he went off and raised pigs in Iowa and did nothing else he would forever have done more for the country than most of your pipe smoking, paper-pushing politicos will do in a lifetime. Neil's also right. Not just about the colored, though. Didn't you see the last Gallup Poll? Folks are happy in this country. They're optimistic. They're keeping Mike rich by buying his damned Chevys."

Lisa responded to Jennifer in silence, continuing to stare at Neil, who tried to maintain eye contact with her but used the excuse of signaling the waiter for a check to end the optical combat. Jennifer, who worked for a small public relations agency, tried to end the night on a positive note.

"Anyway, Lisa, I think it's great that you are so concerned about all these issues. We certainly need people like you, and I didn't really mean to be so hard on the paper pushers. But if we all shared your intensity, the world wouldn't be a better place unless we all agreed with each other. It'd be war." Jennifer laughed. Mike, supporting her goal, forced himself to laugh. He wanted to move back to the bar for another beer. His friends suddenly were like difficult customers.

They paid the bill and walked toward the door. Lisa grabbed Neil by the elbow and pulled him close to her. She wore a gentle fragrance, lost in the smoke, beer and Juicy Fruit of Pennsy's, except when, like now, she was close and intimate. "I didn't mean to be so hard on you, Neil. But I was thinking of you. If I didn't think you were cut out to be a hero about something, I wouldn't care so much. I believe a good person has to be committed to something – the Bill of Rights, desegregation, maybe even hogs would do. You're a good person, Neil." Before he could reply, Lisa pecked him on his cheek and walked ahead. Jennifer rejected his invitation to spend the night, citing the late hour and a promise to visit her mother in Baltimore Sunday. Mike stayed behind in the bar.

Suddenly, Lisa's "hero" was alone, walking home in the cool April night. Her words and her scent played inside him like a wistful tune.

With nothing better to do the next day, a Sunday, Neil decided to take a long walk. It was a bright day, with unseasonably warm temperatures – a perfect spring day in D.C.. He wanted a destination.

Unanimous Verdict

Though he knew it would be closed, he decided to visit the warehouse where Clayton's body was found. It was only about a half hour away on foot.

The first half of his journey to the warehouse was reasonably pleasant. He went west four blocks to Fourth Street then headed south for M Street. Fourth Street was lined with well-maintained townhouses typical of the Hill. The short blocks were shaded by oak and chestnut trees. But before Fourth intersected with I Street, SE, the neighborhood declined dramatically. The architecture was the same, but the structures were not well maintained. Paint was peeling, the yards were unkempt. There was more street noise, with people shouting at each other from their front stoops. This was also where the complexion of the residents turned quickly from white to black.

Neil tried to assess the people he saw without regard for their color, as instructed by Lou King. He could not do it. He could not look at the deeply dark-skinned mothers carrying 300 pounds under loose fitting thin cotton dresses that exposed thick folds of fat around their arms, waists, thighs, calves and even their ankles, and separate them from their race. Some of the women had hair that stood on end like straw in a field; others had hair that fell down their heads without any sign of having been combed. Many covered their hair with bandannas. Neil could not help but think of those women as Aunt Jemima on the pancake mix box or as the fat Negro woman on the cans of chicory some people added to their coffee.

Chapter Seven: An Evening at Pennsy's

The men were mostly asleep on chairs on the sidewalk or talking excitedly in groups. One or two of the younger men wore loud, flashy suits and colorful shirts, set off by ties of a complementary hue. The outfits were not to Neil's tastes, but he admitted they demonstrated a flair for a certain kind of fashion. Most of the men, especially the older ones, wore only dungarees or dirty looking slacks and a sleeveless undershirt.

Neil attracted only quick glances from the sidewalk and front stoop dwellers, who averted their eyes at the sight of a white man or gave a perfunctory nod, which he returned. Conversation stopped as Neil walked by, resuming immediately when it was clear the alien white man was not looking for one of them, which would only mean bad news.

Neil could not identify with any of them. He could not suppress in his mind that they were Negroes, that they were poor, and that they were very, very different from himself. He thought of King's suggestion that these people had the same worries white people did — shelter, education, safety, health and the like. Surely that was so. But the comparison was too generic, too broad to be helpful. Their concern for shelter was how to pay the rent and how to get the landlord to repair a roof that had leaked for weeks, not whether to buy a bigger house in Chevy Chase or retire to a small farm in Gaithersburg. Their concern for education was keeping their children in class past elementary school, or scraping up the money that even public schools were always demanding for activities of one kind or another. They were not worried about getting an B instead of a A in chemistry or deciding which college to attend. He imagined that the health problems of the people he was passing were different, too. They were not so worried about getting their teeth cleaned as they were about keeping the teeth they had left. Not going to the doctor for the kid's tummy ache was a given. Trying to get some free medicine to stop the screaming genital pain of gonorrhea or syphilis was important health care. Or trying to get any care to prevent death from malnutrition, neglect or disease. Neil imagined those were the concerns of the colored poor.

It was much easier to think of King as having problems Neil could associate with a white family. Or Mrs. Van Dyke. Both had the kind of concerns that came with a decent education and income. King's advice was unrealistic, at least when it came to the black poor. He wondered if King or Mrs. Van Dyke themselves really could stand in the shoes of the poor. He assumed they once could – they may have been poor themselves. But a successful life probably dimmed those memories or even suppressed them. Neil immediately dismissed such thoughts. King and Mrs. Van Dyke were heroes to their race.

The modest warehouse district began on the south side of M Street, SE. Clayton's body had been found in a warehouse at Second and N. Neil had no particular expectations about the murder scene and he was not disappointed. It was a brick warehouse with a flat roof, two stories high. The door was padlocked. There was no sign of occupancy this Sunday or any indication that a month earlier it was the scene of a killing. There was no traffic. Only a few cars were parked along the curb.

Neil stood for a few minutes looking at the building. At first, his head was empty of any thoughts except that the surroundings were dully industrial. It was an unremarkable place to live; a terrible place for a young man to die. Then Neil pictured Clay's high school photograph that he saw at Mrs. Van Dyke's. He recalled that Clay played a musical instrument – was it the trumpet? – and had his own jazz group. He pictured a high school boy with a light brown skin and a big smile enjoying a life not yet marred by Army racism that put him in jail or employment discrimination that kept him in a dank library basement. He imagined that Clay dreamed of becoming a star musician, or maybe an author or maybe even just a clerk with a wonderful wife and a handful of children whom he loved. He thought of Clay in Chicago as an even younger boy. He imagined him on the playground, maybe on a swing or a see-saw with other children, both black and white. Did Chicago playgrounds have tire swings like they had in D.C. when he was growing up? Neil could imagine Clayton's mother scolding him for leaving the neighborhood to innocently explore the nearby urban world or for spending his nickel on a candy bar as Neil used to do. Neil doubted that any scolding from Mrs. Van Dyke was harsh and imagined that Clayton loved his mother and father and that they never really scared him because he knew they loved him. He was their boy. They wanted no other boy. At least until they stepped out of the Negro world, life was happy, optimistic and full of promise for a young boy like Clayton Van Dyke.

A tear made its way down Neil's cheek. He was ashamed that he could not raise more sympathy in his heart for the poor people he had just walked by. He just had no room for them. His emotions were occupied by friends made in the war he saw suddenly lose their lives before they even knew what took them or, surely worse, die a slower death, watching their own guts squirt onto alien soil. His reserve unit was filled with boys from Anacostia, Suitland and Southern Maryland – sons of blue collar families, clerks and tobacco farmers. These soldiers were blown to bits or shot dead by anonymous killers. Then there was Elijah Lincoln. Neil knew almost nothing about Elijah except that he came from Louisiana and was a decent guy. Was he like the folks on the Fourth Street stoops? Would he have been like that if he lived. Would Neil judge him differently if he had? Who was Neil to judge, anyway, he thought. The men he knew in battle – black and white – were his friends and his heroes. Not one deserved to die. Didn't they have the same rights as anyone to enjoy the mystery of the story of their lives – to see how the story would end without being executed in the middle of it? Didn't their parents have a right to know that their sweet babies were born for a reason other than to die in a useless far away war?

Clayton Van Dyke's killing was more intimate, a murder by people he knew or for reasons peculiar to him. No matter. At that moment, Neil believed his heart was at one with Mrs. Van Dyke's. He would find Clayton's killer and make him pay. Mrs. Van Dyke deserved it. Clayton deserved it. For now, it was the closest thing he had to avenging the killings of Neil's young friends in Korea. Maybe his conscience would finally let him close his memory of Elijah's pleading eyes.

His walk back home began somberly as he turned over these thoughts. But his mood brightened as he passed a Negro church just as the congregation was departing. The women were beautifully dressed in gay suits and in dresses made of large, striking patterns or bold colors. They wore hose, high heels and amazing hats of every shape and size, from conservative veiled black hats to red, purple and green straw hats celebrating spring. Many of the hats were adorned with plants or even animal skins. The men could not match the colorful finery of their wives and girlfriends, but tried. Most of them were decked out in tailored pinstripe or dark blue suits, with pastel, wide-striped or white shirts with stick pin collars and ties that ranged from conservative regimental stripes to hand-painted pictures of patterns or zoo animals. The men, too, wore hats. Mostly fedoras in black, grey, white, tan or even red. The children were mostly dressed like miniatures of their parents, even to the stick pins and hosiery. Everyone was excited and talkative as they spilled out the double-door of the church, followed by the last bars of a lively spiritual about water, Jesus and heaven. If the Episcopal Church had such lively services, Neil thought, he might be a more religious man.

It was easier to apply King's suggestion to this crowd. They probably were as poor as the folks on lower Fourth Street Neil passed earlier, but spent a substantial part of their income on Sunday church clothes. Their appearance of being middle class and even affluent caused Neil to be more comfortable with the idea that not much separated him from these colored people. They could almost be his friends, if not his equals. Maybe economics divided people more than race. That made sense to Neil, except that even the Van Dykes had to live segregated lives.

Neil had thought more about race in the last three days than he had in his entire life, and thought about it more seriously. It was much more complex than he had imagined. Every time he drew a conclusion, something happened to confuse him again. LeClerc conformed to Neil's idea of a Negro drug addict, but instead he was a cancer victim – perhaps yet another innocent soon to be murdered by chance. A pleasant surprise that King had a family and house much like his parents really was evidence of Neil's low expectations of the colored race. Talk of Black Nationalism and hatred of the white man was accompanied by acts of kindness and charity such as feeding and schooling the needy. In the same one hour walk, Neil was repulsed and attracted by groups of black people he did not know. Perhaps he was a bigot. He no longer was certain that he was not. He puzzled over the matter until he got to his Eighth Street room.

Neil called Jennifer Sunday night. Her words were formal, her voice was cold, and she was indifferent to the fact he was traveling to Chicago for a few days. When he explained the reason, careful not to identify anyone by name, she surprised him by asking if he wasn't desperate in taking on a colored client. They didn't make any plans to

Chapter Seven: An Evening at Pennsy's

meet later in the week. After he hung up the phone, Neil strongly sensed that his relationship with Jennifer was over. He wasn't sure why. She was cordial at Pennsy's, even protecting him from Lisa's verbal attack. He also wasn't sure why he didn't feel bad about it. Though they had sex, the emotional connection never really got beyond friendship. He would deal with the situation when he returned from Chicago.

Chapter Eight: Chicago, April 26-27, 1954

Lorenzo King called Neil at his apartment Monday morning to convey the substance of his conversation with Ezra Lowell. Lowell was angry to learn that Clay Van Dyke was dead and that the police were treating it as a suicide. But, as expected, Lowell was non-committal about cooperating based only on a phone call from a stranger. He was willing to meet with Neil, King said. King said he told Lowell the purpose of the trip and that Neil was white. "I told him you was OK for a white guy. A little young and inexperienced, but that you wanted to help Mrs. Van Dyke and the memory of her son," King told Neil. "He just sort of grunted in response, but I took that as positive. He didn't say 'no.'"

"Then he didn't say 'yes', either?" Neil asked. He was stung by King's constant reference to his youth and inexperience. He was 24 and a veteran of a war and three years on the police force, for Christ's sake. Yet again, he let the insult pass without comment.

"No, he didn't say 'yes,' but he knows you're coming and I'm sure he would have said 'no' if he meant to say 'no'. I told him you would call him when you got to Chicago Tuesday morning to arrange an appointment. You have his number, right?" Neil still had the brochure. King wished him luck and hung up.

Neil boarded the Baltimore & Ohio's Capitol Limited Monday afternoon. The coach cars were about half filled. He found an empty row and took a seat near the window. He enjoyed train travel – the gentle rocking relaxed him and he could stretch his legs whenever he pleased. The line had cancelled a lot of underperforming trains recently, but there were few signs of economic troubles on the premier routes like the Capitol Limited.

He opened a new bestseller he had purchased, *The High and the Mighty*, as the train pulled out of Union Station. A few souls boarded at Silver Spring, Maryland, and the train began to fill up in Baltimore. That's where Neil lost his seating monopoly. A man in a brown suit with a bowler hat sat next to him. He was quiet for a few miles, but then asked Neil about his book. Neil tried to avoid engagement by replying curtly "OK," but the stranger would not take the hint. He wanted to talk.

"Name's Such. Emil Such." He paused a split second. "Don't think I caught your name, son." Neil closed his book and introduced himself. Such was the pastiest man he had ever seen. His skin was the color of Cream of Wheat, sprinkled with small blotches of pink. Tiny flakes of skin peeled from his face onto his brown suit jacket like powder off a two-day-old donut. Dandruff snowed onto his shoulders, creating an area of dry skin flakes from his shoulders to his lap. His eyes were tiny black orbs smashed into his mushy face like raisins into unbaked cookie dough. As they spoke, Neil learned why Such did not show his teeth when he smiled. They were crooked, uneven, crunched together until they overlapped and were stained brown with nicotine. After introductions, Such lit up. He did not ask for permission from Neil nor offer him a cigarette. His brand was Chesterfield.

Chapter Eight: Chicago

"Where're you headed to?" Such asked, brushing dry skin from his jacket. He did that often during the conversation without apology, although some of the flakes inevitably landed on Neil's pant leg.

"Chicago."

"You goin' to the convention? What was it? Neil Endicott? Do you mind if I call you Neil, Mr. Endicott?"

"No and no."

"What do you mean 'no and no'?" Such was puzzled and offended by Neil's abrupt reply.

"I mean no, I'm not going to a convention and no, I don't mind if you call me Neil." The smile returned to Such's face, slightly tightening his cascading jowls. He was overweight, mostly with a large pot-belly and in his face.

"Well I ask 'cause I'm going to a convention," Such said, as if Neil had either asked or cared. He leaned slightly to Neil's shoulder, as if about to disclose a confidence. "Aluminum siding. Greatest building material in the world. I manufacture it and install it. Largest retailer in Baltimore and D.C. Convention in Chicago." Such was in the habit of exhaling as he spoke. His breath was a combination of cigarettes and Life Savers. Neil suddenly imagined he was eating the ashes of burned s'mores seasoned with wet saliva. He looked around the car and saw no empty seats. He would tell a white lie in self-defense.

"I'm afraid I'm allergic to tobacco, Mr. Such. I'll have to ask you to quit smoking. I'm very sorry." Such was stricken with embarrassment, which caused the pink portions of his face to redden like Christmas tree

191

lights. He quickly stubbed out the cigarette in the ashtray provided in the arm of his seat. The price of losing the cigarette was more intense attention from Such.

"I am terribly sorry, Neil. Atrocious habit, I agree. Stuck with it since I was 12 and hard to break. Believe me, I've tried. I hope you are all right, really. You know, I take the motto of my business – 'The Only Paying Customers are Happy Customers' – and apply it to all of my life. I want people to be happy around me. I'm very, very sorry."

Such no longer spoke in a conspiratorial tone. He was loud and drew attention from the rows around them. A woman one row in front and across the aisle who was reading to a child turned and stared Such into brief silence. She was a Negro, smartly dressed as far as Neil could see, wearing a veiled hat. The child's head was in her lap. She read to the child in a gentle, quiet tone. Neil could not quite make out the words.

Such did not like being singled out and stared at.

"That nigra' woman starin' at me as if she was God's gift," Such said. "Don't get me wrong, I ain't no Baltimorean who hates the nigra. No sir. It ain't right that they gotta sit in different train cars and such. I ain't no bigot, no sir. Equal rights for everybody is fine with me. But we gotta' be careful the nigra don't get special treatment. No sir. Equal is equal, but everybody gotta earn equal. Lotsa' nigras don't understand that." He quieted a moment, looking expectantly at Neil for confirmation of his profound philosophy of equality.

Chapter Eight: Chicago

Neil paused for a moment before answering. A few days ago, he would have replied with a neutral "yeah, yeah, that's so Mr. Such" and resumed reading his book, hoping Such would shut up. Now, he felt compelled to explore Such's sentiments, which he sensed were neither genuine nor remarkable. They were similar to those of his family and friends, albeit in a voice of the lower class of whites and not that of the more refined residents of Chevy Chase. Neil decided to be indirect.

"Do you employ any Negroes in your business, Mr. Such?"

"Sure do. Why, you can't hardly avoid it in Baltimore. D.C. neither. Some of my best crews are the black ones. People think puttin' up sidin' is easy. But it's a complex job. You would be surprised how many brick or wood shingled walls look straight but are bowed, bent and crooked. To get a good look on the siding, you got to make it look straight. We do that with furring strips. That takes some talent. Got to get it straight and level. The nigras on the crews, they got a talent for that. I never get a complaint about my nigra crews." Such concluded as if the subject was closed. Neil wanted more. He set the bait.

"Yeah, but the white crews got to be better, Mr. Such, ain't that right?"

"Well, maybe. But they cost me a helluva lot more. Some customers in Baltimore and D.C don't want some nigra crew working around their house when they are at work or away, especially if they got kids. I'd say the white crews are no better than the nigra crews and they demand more money on top of that."

193

"And you pay it?"

"Of course. Whites can get jobs anywhere. The nigra's gotta' work for me if he wants to do aluminum sidin'. It's just the marketplace." Such wasn't stupid, just ugly. He could see there was a problem with his logic.

"Well, I guess what bothers me Mr. Such is that you're payin' the black man less than the white man but the black man does a better job. I thought you told me that the nigra ought to know his place. But isn't his place at pay at least equal to the white man if he does an equal or better job?" Neil was surprised by his own aggressiveness. He was challenging Such's racial views. He had never done that before with anyone, even the most prejudiced Southerner he had met in the Marines. But he was having fun boxing Such into a corner.

"Like I said, son, it's the market. I'd be happy to pay a black man the same, but I don't have to."

"But I thought you said you were in favor of equal rights – no special treatment – if I recall. If the Negro employee does as good a job or better than the white one, shouldn't they get paid the same, or even better? I guess I'm missing something."

Such sensed he was sandbagged. Neil's questioning was too lawyerlike. Too challenging. Neil wasn't a genuine working man like Such, who grew up in the stern but poor neighborhoods of German immigrants in Baltimore. Such felt threatened by a tougher intellect.

"Let me ask you this, Neil. Are you some kind of nigger-lover? I mean, why shouldn't I pay what the market demands, and only that.

Chapter Eight: Chicago

Believe me, if I had a problem, I mean a problem with a customer or a supplier, I would not ask some nigra to help me. They are good for manual labor, maybe even some precision work where the tape measure is the dictator. They know how to measure and cut. But I would wager that my dumbest white man is at least equal to my smartest nigra.

"Now, if you will excuse me, it is time for a drink." Such rose and departed for the club car and pointedly did not invite Neil to join him. He took his hat, a sign he was not coming back. Neil was happy to regain his monopoly on seating, if only for a while, and to lose such an ugly, smelly man as a seatmate. But for an instant, Neil was ashamed of his race. He gave up the feeling as pointless and looked out the window at the western Maryland countryside, wondering why any black person – any person – should be required to prove his worth to a man like Emil Such.

By Pittsburgh, Neil was asleep. He stirred when a stop was announced, but did not wake up until a conductor shook his shoulder and announced they had arrived in Chicago. It was 6:45 a.m. Neil retrieved his small overnight bag from the rack above his seat and departed into Union Station, which was mostly a bigger and more majestic version of Washington's Union Station. It was too early to call Ezra Lowell, too early to check into his hotel or to visit the Childress Agency. It wasn't too early for either breakfast or a consult with the telephone book, however.

The Childress Agency was listed in the phone book on a street Neil never heard of, but most of Chicago's streets fell into that category.

Neil had been to Chicago only once before, as a side trip during his short leave before heading for Korea. He recalled very little of the visit, other than that the bars featured Old Milwaukee, a beer which was weak and tasteless, but equal to any for getting drunk.

He ate a large breakfast at the station coffee shop and then hailed a taxi to the Conrad Hilton on Michigan Avenue. Neil knew his father stayed at the Conrad Hilton when he went to political conventions and on other missions for *The Star*, so he reserved a room for himself there. The rate was high at $15 a night, but Neil didn't know where else to stay. The desk clerk told him told no rooms would be available until noon. He checked his bag with the doorman and used a lobby pay phone to call Lowell. It was still only 8:30 in the morning, but the phone was answered on the first ring.

"Black National Strength Party Headquarters. All power to the people. Who is calling?"

"Neil Endicott. With whom am I speaking?"

"Ezra Lowell, Mr. Endicott. I heard you were coming. It is a little early. We are in the middle of our breakfast feeding."

"I'm sorry to bother you so early, but I thought we could make an appointment to meet later today."

"Where are you?"

"I'm staying at the Conrad Hilton. They won't let me check in until noon, though."

"The Hilton? Fine. I'll meet you there at 4 o'clock. Leave word at the front desk you are expecting me. I haven't been to the Hilton in

Chapter Eight: Chicago

a long time – maybe never – but a lot of these fancy hotels won't send a black man to a room unless they know he's expected. OK?"

"Fine. See you then."

Ezra Lowell hung up.

Neil consulted with the concierge about the location of the Childress Agency and obtained a city map. It was chilly so early in the morning, so Neil took another taxi to the agency.

Neil expected that the agency would be a stand-alone building or perhaps a church with a playground and dormitories and young orphans playing in the yard. He was surprised when the taxi discharged him in front of a modest eight-story office building just a few blocks southwest of the Loop. The building was neither old nor new. It probably had been built between the wars. No effort had been made by the architects to remind a visitor that Chicago was the home of inspired works of by Louis Sullivan and Daniel Burnham, among others. It was a plain concrete oblong with holes cut for windows and doors. It was in the middle of the block. A similar, but slightly taller, building was on the east side and a three-level parking garage was on the west side. Neil entered a small lobby through the double glass doors and found a building directory. The Childress Agency was on the third floor.

He took the elevator and faced a door marked with the agency's name as soon as he exited into the hallway. He opened the door without knocking and entered a well-appointed reception area containing a desk on the right and a claw footed sofa and two stuffed wing chairs on the left. A petite, pretty young Negro woman was behind the desk typing. She looked up when Neil entered.

"May I help you?"

"Yes, thank you. My name is Neil Endicott. I'm here about an adoption."

"I'm sorry, sir. But all of our children are colored. We don't let them go out to white folk."

"It's not about me, ma'am. I'm inquiring about an adoption long ago."

"Are you a relative?"

"No. But I have been retained by the adoptive mother, a Mrs. Van Dyke, of Washington, D.C. Here is my card." Neil handed her a business card. He had spent $8 for 500 embossed cards. He had about 475 left at home, less the four in his wallet.

"What is it you want to know?" She looked at the card and then looked up at Neil. His smile was not returned.

"I need to know the name of the natural parents of a boy adopted through this agency 32 years ago." Neil could not stop himself from taking a formal and mechanical tone as if giving his rank and serial number because he knew what the answer would be to his query.

"I'm afraid that's impossible. We are not allowed to give out that information."

"Are you in charge here? I really need to speak to someone in authority." The receptionist frowned and moved her head back. He was too aggressive. He softened and smiled at her. "I mean, I know the mother is very anxious about this. At least I should tell her I did my best by talking to the head person."

"I'm just the receptionist and secretary." At that moment, the entry door swung open and another small woman entered. She was plump, over 60, gray-haired and white. She limped and used a wooden cane with a handle that was supposed to look like ivory but probably was plastic.

The secretary greeted the new arrival warmly. "Good morning, Mrs. Childress. How are you?"

"I'm fine as long as I'm not walking. Thank you, Mildred." She did not break stride walking toward the far door, presumably to an inner office.

"This man – what's your name, I'm sorry?"

"Endicott, Neil Endicott."

"Mr. Endicott is here inquiring about an adoption from before I was born. I told him we don't give out information, but he insists on speaking to someone in charge."

"That would be me, Mr. Endicott, Clara Childress." She paused in her walk, switched her cane to her left hand and extended her right. Neil took it. Her firm handshake and strong voice belied her elderly appearance. "Why don't you come into my office so I can sit down?"

The inner office was furnished almost like the reception area except it had no sofa and the desk was far more substantial. The room contained a wooden crib with white eyelet bed clothes. Colorful stuffed animals were piled at one end. A Donald Duck mobile hung from the ceiling over the middle of the crib. Mrs. Childress snapped on a wall switch by the door as she entered which, in turn, caused a table lamp on the desk and two floor lamps to light. The Venetian blinds behind the desk were drawn. Mrs. Childress opened them to reveal another window across the alley which also had its blinds drawn. Both windows were at least six feet wide, double-hung and had aluminum frames. Very modern. Very utilitarian. Very dull, in keeping with the rest of the architecture. The short space between the buildings allowed very little natural light to enter the office.

The office also contained four five-drawer file cabinets lined against one wall which appeared to be custom built of fine hardwood, stained to look like cherry. Each cabinet had a key lock in the top right corner. The lock on one cabinet set was broken, replaced by an ugly exterior iron bar blocking access to the drawers and a padlock holding the bar in place through a steel device meant for that purpose. Matted, framed letters adorned the walls. Tributes from adoptive parents or social organizations? Neil could not read them, but assumed that, unlike those in Lorenzo King's office, these tributes likely were real.

When Mrs. Childress took off her coat and sat behind her desk, she was transformed from an overweight, somewhat dowdy senior citizen into an alert, take-charge executive. Her brown eyes widened and the desk hid most of her weight and her bum leg. Her demeanor said "this is my domain." She examined Neil and frowned.

"Why don't you start over again, Mr. Endicott. Tell me your business here."

Chapter Eight: Chicago

Neil repeated what he told the receptionist.

"What is your client's name?"

"Mrs. Virginia Van Dyke." Mrs. Childress, who was staring directly into Neil's eyes, almost challenging him to provoke her, broke the stare briefly, casting a protective glance at her file cabinets.

"Van Dyke. Van Dyke. Can't say I recall the name. Are you sure this is the right place? There are many adoption agencies in town. Is Mrs. Van Dyke colored? We only adopt to colored." Neil knew she was covering up. Her quick glance at the broken file cabinet gave it away.

"Yes, she is colored. She and her late husband, Elmer Van Dyke, adopted a boy a little over 32 years ago. You may have heard of Mr. Van Dyke, the father. He was a prominent colored lawyer here in Chicago and became a well known law professor at Howard University."

"I'm afraid I don't follow the affairs of colored folk very much, Mr. Endicott. We help poor colored girls who made a mistake to get on with their lives by providing their babies to wonderful parents who want them. We are a social service agency, but I don't personally have much to do with coloreds once I'm out of the office."

Neil was surprised that a woman in Clara Childress' position would be so dismissive of black folk.

"Social service agency implies not-for-profit, Mrs. Childress. Is that true of your agency?"

She resumed her frown. "We do make a little money for my husband and myself, but you could call it a salary. We are not a non-profit, but there is a lot of overhead."

"Where are the orphans, by the way?"

"They are housed south of here, near Hyde Park, where the rent is much cheaper. This office is more convenient for me and for many of our adoptive parents. We bring the children here for inspection by potential parents. That's why there is a crib in this office, in case you hadn't noticed, detective." Mrs. Childress could be pointed, too. "What do our internal operations have to do with your inquiry? What *is* your inquiry, anyway?"

"The boy who was adopted through this agency about 32 years ago is dead. His mother believes he was murdered. We know that this boy — a man, now, of course — came to Chicago to find out about his birth parents. Whatever he learned sent him to Atlanta. He apparently was going to visit somewhere else on this hunt before he was murdered. As you can see, the trail starts here."

"Why, that's horrible. A murder. And so young." Mrs. Childress said the right words but remained stone-faced. "But isn't it clear that if he came here and then had to go elsewhere he must not have found what he wanted in Chicago?"

"No. He told friends the trip turned something up. We are sure he must have come here, because no place else would make sense."

"What was his name?"

"Clayton Van Dyke."

"We have had no such visitor. Certainly, I would remember someone asking about his birth mother. Such requests are rare, and always are rejected. The birth parents usually never want to be reminded of the child they gave away. We respect that desire. Parent names are never given out. We don't disclose the names of the adoptive parents to the birth parents, either. Such requests are even more rare, but it happens. No adoptive parent wants their child to be surprised by meeting the natural mother or father. Once a child is out the door in the hands of loving parents, we don't speak of him or her again."

"But you do keep records?"

"Of course. The law requires us to. I would rather not, but it's the law."

"Are they in those file cabinets?"

"Adoption is our only business Mr. Endicott, so yes. But you are not allowed access to those files. No one except myself and Ms. Dickerson, whom you have met, is allowed access. I wouldn't even let my husband look at them, not that he cares."

"Those are handsome cabinets. Must be custom made. I see that one appears to have broken. Was that recently?"

Mrs. Childress again broke her stare to look at the file cabinet. She leaned forward slightly over her desk.

"Mr. Endicott, none of this is any of your business. The lock simply broke and we are waiting for the man who made those cabinets to come and fix it. No one broke in. Now, it appears we cannot help you, so I suggest you leave." The suggestion was spoken as a command.

"I never suggested anyone broke in, Mrs. Childress. You did that." Neil raised an eyebrow. He could not resist letting Mrs. Childress know that he knew. She was unruffled.

"Whatever. There is nothing mysterious about our broken lock, Mr. Endicott. I think this meeting is over."

"Ok. Thank you for your time," Neil said as he turned the doorknob to leave. He closed the door behind him as he entered the reception area.

"Oh, Mildred – isn't that your name?" he said to the receptionist on his way out.

"Yes, Mr. Endicott."

"Mildred is a very pretty name. My mother's name was Mildred," Neil lied. "By the way, do you remember Mr. Van Dyke, who visited here about a month ago from Washington, D.C.? He's the man I was talking about with Mrs. Childress."

Mildred licked her upper lip. She was uncertain about what she could disclose and what she could not.

"Yes, I remember him."

"Did he leave an address or telephone number?"

"I don't know. You should ask Mrs. Childress that question."

"Oh, I will. No need to bother her again today. Maybe I'll call for that information. Thank you. I'm sorry to bother you. Have a good day."

"You too," Mildred called as Neil left the office.

"Lying bitch," Neil said aloud as he entered the elevator where no one could overhear him. He wasn't referring to Mildred.

Chapter Eight: Chicago

Neil was dozing over the newspaper after checking into his hotel room when he was awakened by a knock on the door. He glanced at the alarm clock on the bedside table. It was only 3:30. Ezra was early.

"Telegram," the visitor called, knocking a second time. King was the only person besides Ezra Lowell who knew where Neil was staying. Neil opened the door and saw a medium-sized black man in a black shirt and black trousers, hardly the uniform of Western Union.

"Are you Neil Endicott?" the man asked.

"I am."

"The message is to get out of town. Leave well enough alone." The instant the words were out of his mouth the man brought his right hand around from behind his back. A sawed-off police billy club was in that hand. Before Neil could react, the billy club hit Neil squarely at his left temple and he fell to the floor.

Chapter Nine: The Chief II, April 28, 1954

"God damn it, Felix. We're issuing a decision about freedom and you want to make it as dry as a patent case! I can't soften it further and have it still make any sense. There's hardly any opinion in it, much less any robust defense of our decision. It lacks spirit or emotion when it should be rousing and boisterous."

The Chief tried to control his temper in front of the oldest justice. Frankfurter was the leading proponent of the view that the Fourteenth Amendment, one of the Civil War amendments to the Bill of Rights, required abolition of legal segregation. But his persuasive powers had failed to pull Jackson or Clark into the majority. So, Frankfurter was urging the Chief to further water down the majority opinion in hopes of attracting their two colleagues.

The Chief refused to do so.

"We enjoy solemn resolution around here, and you'll work yourself right into a minority of one if you try to rub folks' face in your righteousness. But I think we could make Farwell stand alone if we limit the decision clearly to these five cases. They can be sort of a laboratory for a couple of years. Then we can strike down the same laws in other states one-by-one if they aren't repealed. I've talked to Jackson. He's willing to consider joining such a decision."

"You talked to him in the hospital?" Jackson had been hospitalized on April 1 for what the Court told the press was a "mild heart attack". He was responding well at Doctors Hospital, but neither the Chief nor Frankfurter discounted the seriousness of a heart attack in a man 62 years old.

"Yes, I went by and we conducted a frank conversation. He's up to it. He's home now. You should visit him, too."

"I've visited him a couple times a week, but didn't want to raise business. Was he saying he *might* go along if we limited the decision that way? Or did he say he *will* go along. It could be a trap. We change it now, and there will just be pressure to change it again and make it even weaker. There isn't any guarantee that if we weaken the decision as you suggest we would gain any votes. In fact, we might lose the other four. Douglas, Black, Minton and Burton might write a separate opinion calling us cowards for limiting the decision. It would be just like Douglas to grab his own publicity. He'd want to write an opinion that grabs his liberal friends. Three or four opinions – that's a recipe for chaos."

Frankfurter nodded. He was impressed with the political skills of the new Chief and his ability to make reasonable forecasts about the impact of the Court's decisions. It didn't quite make up for his pedestrian understanding of the law, but it filled a needed niche on the Court. Other than himself, Frankfurter didn't know a good politician who also was a good lawyer. He was supremely confident of his own skills in both arenas. Frankfurter never heard of a skill he didn't think he could master, except perhaps American baseball.

Black and Douglas didn't like him. The feeling was mutual. Frankfurter thought both of them fit the law to their policy goals.

Chapter Nine: The Chief II

They thought Frankfurter was a rigid pedagogue from Harvard with a boundless ego. Based on his experience thus far, the Chief thought all three were right about each other most of the time.

In the case of *Brown*, Frankfurter applied himself vigorously, looking for and finding the best legal reasons possible for overturning segregation. Black and Douglas didn't need legal research to decide Brown. Neither did the Chief, though he was grateful for it. Frankfurter assigned the best clerk on the Court to spend a summer in the Library of Congress across the street examining the history of the Civil War Amendments. He did not find much of relevance to school segregation because there were not many public schools in the South in 1868 when the amendments were adopted. But now that public education was commonplace and a high school education required for many jobs, Frankfurter argued that school segregation defeated the purpose of the Fourteenth Amendment providing for equal protection of the laws. The majority's position relied a lot on the psychological and sociological "facts" set forth by the NAACP in their briefs, not all of which were widely accepted by academics. But Frankfurter believed his arguments provided solid legal reasoning in support of the majority decision.

"What I don't understand, is why Jackson and Clark are still dissenting when even you have come on board," the Chief told Frankfurter. "You and Jackson both talk about the importance of judicial restraint, but I'd wager you a morning doughnut that if we took a vote among the nine of us you would be considered more conservative than Jackson, 9-0."

Unanimous Verdict

"It's Farwell," Frankfurter said. "If we are going to sweep the laws of a score of states and the District of Columbia off the decks, Jackson wants somebody to stand up for judicial restraint who isn't also an obscene bigot and legal crackpot. He understands your argument about how a unanimous decision will have greater moral and political force, but you aren't going to get a unanimous decision. Farwell will never vote to eliminate legal segregation. And Jackson thinks you are using scare tactics against him and Clark. I think he resents your constant claim that a Court divided 6-3 will jeopardize our authority more than an 8-1 vote.

"Jackson and Clark wouldn't dissent alone. They both understand that the states are wrong on this issue. Jackson thinks it's morally wrong. I'm less sure how Clark thinks about the morality of it, but he won't stand by himself. He doesn't have the guts. And he won't stand with Farwell, either.

"So you've got three choices," Frankfurter concluded. "You can live with a Court split 6-2-1. You can water down the majority decision to limit it clearly and explicitly to the five cases in front of us, leaving an opening for the other states to change their practices before we tell them to. That's probably your best shot. That likely will be an 8-1 decision. Or you can get Farwell to change his vote, and that'll give you your unanimous Court. Of course, you are more likely to pull down the columns of the court building like Samson than get an old 'lost cause' Confederate bull like Farwell to vote to end segregation. It will never happen."

Chapter Nine: The Chief II

"My stubborn old Norwegian blood calls 'never' a challenge," the Chief responded. "Thank you for your insight, Felix. I feel like a rookie getting advice from Joe DiMaggio."

"Well, Mickey Mantle is doing pretty well in DiMaggio's place. Maybe you'll hit some homers yourself. But not this time."

The Chief was surprised at Frankfurter's extension of his baseball metaphor. He didn't know the ancient Austrian Jew was a baseball fan. He still had a lot to learn about his court colleagues.

Justice Farwell's office was next to Justice Black's. Farwell was second in seniority, behind Black, and his office was the same size as the Alabaman's, but otherwise completely different. Farwell chose to decorate his chambers with oil paintings of Civil War scenes in wide, heavy, gilded wood frames that even the National Gallery was rejecting. The pictures all included bearded Confederate generals in grey uniforms, usually on a black or white stallion standing on two legs over piles of dead Union soldiers. The generals wielded swords or pistols against some unseen hostile force off the picture to the right or left. Or maybe they were just celebrating the fact they had killed so many Yankees. These pictures were complemented by tarnished swords in brass scabbards bearing some insignia of the Confederate States of America, which also hung on the walls. The American flag with all 48 stars stood proudly behind Farwell's desk, but it was joined by a Confederate stars and bars battle flag of the same size, as well as the blue-and-white flag of South Carolina, with its distinctive crescent and palmetto tree design. Douglas, who was the smart aleck on the Court, called Farwell's office "a Coney Island of the Confederacy," even to Farwell's face. Farwell did not find any humor in the metaphor.

Farwell usually reinforced the bizarre sense of journeying into a history most justices thought best forgotten when he opened his mouth to speak in a heavy accent, one more closely associated with the deeper South than with South Carolina, Farwell's home state. Black, who retained a gentler, less pronounced, Alabama accent, joked that if Farwell tried to be any more Southern, he would be in the Gulf of Mexico.

The Chief was announced by Farwell's receptionist, a blue-eyed young blonde named Susie who was engaged to a clerk for Justice Minton. The inner office was indeed a sentimental museum of what segregationists, perversely, proudly called the "lost cause," – the Civil War.

Nathan Farwell was born only three years after Frankfurter, but looked at least a decade younger. Frankfurter's appearance and demeanor were that of an aging but respected professor and scholar, slow on his feet but still quick in his mind. Farwell's was of an active outdoorsman accustomed to livelier pursuits such as horseback riding and hunting, which Farwell did whenever he could escape the Court. But only those who shared Farwell's enthusiasm for the Confederacy and the last century identified his mind as an asset. Farwell's stomach was flat and muscular under his dress shirt, which was open at the collar. There was no trace of a jowl or second chin. His eyes blazed a

Chapter Nine: The Chief II

striking deep blue under a full head of hair that was only now, at age 68, more gray than brown. Although it was just late April, Farwell appeared to have been in the sun, his face slightly red in a fashion that spoke of outdoor exposure and good health, not high blood pressure or excitement like the Chief's frequently red face. The Chief was impressed by Farwell's good looks and physique, but not threatened. He stood a good four inches taller than Farwell, forcing the much older and more senior, but technically still lower ranking, justice to look up when speaking to him.

Farwell rose from his desk to shake hands in welcome. A visit from the new Chief Justice had been a rarity since formal introductions the previous October when the term began. Farwell resumed his seat behind his desk, inviting the Chief to sit in an armchair upholstered in rolled bright red leather and brass tacks, which was used as the guest chair. Farwell offered his guest an old lead ball of shot, another Civil War product, as he did to all of his visitors. The Chief accepted the souvenir, although it seemed more appropriate for a fawning South Carolina tourist than a Court colleague.

"Business or pleasure, Chief?" The Chief hid his surprise. The idea that Farwell expected the Chief to visit him for any reason but business showed how far removed Farwell was from a realistic idea of his own appeal.

"I want to talk to you about *Brown*. We haven't really discussed the case together. I thought it was a good time to do so. Have you a moment?"

"I always have time for you, Chief." Farwell's accent was heavy, intended to sustain his attempt at Southern hospitality.

The Chief found it difficult to listen seriously to anything said in a Southern drawl. The accent reminded him of bad movies made from worse novels. He knew it was his own flaw, a regional prejudice, but he couldn't help it. He had never heard a true southern accent until he went to college and it still sounded strange, including Black's. He tried hard to smother this distraction.

"Of course, you have reviewed my dissent. I'm afraid it is firm." Farwell clearly intended the Chief's visit to be short if it was to be about *Brown*.

"I'm not going to try to talk you into joining the majority," the Chief replied. "But I think you would be doing your country and this Court a service by merely dissenting."

"You mean not write an opinion? Just vote 'no'?"

"That's right. Or perhaps you could simply refer to your dissent in one of the other civil rights cases. *Henderson, Sweatt* and *McLaurin*, for example. *Hernandez* will be issued just a few days before Brown. You could cite that dissent, too." The Chief was referring to three civil rights cases decided by the Court in 1950. *Henderson* struck down segregated seating in railroad dining cars. *Sweatt* and *McLaurin* struck down Texas and Oklahoma provisions for separate but equal graduate and professional schools. Farwell was the lone dissenter in all three cases. In *Hernandez*, the Court was to rule 8-1 in a week or two that

214

Chapter Nine: The Chief II

Texas violated the Constitution by intentionally excluding Mexicans from the rolls of potential jurors. Another Farwell dissent.

"I beg your pardon?" Farwell leaned forward over his desk trying to contain his anger. He was known for his short fuse. "Those cases did not strike at the heart of Southern practices. Not many nigras use dining cars in the South because travel is too expensive. They usually bring along their sandwiches and such for long rides 'cause it's cheaper, if they can ride at all. Even fewer – almost none – get Ph.Ds or law degrees in the South. And *Hernandez* deals with Mexicans, not nigras.

"But almost every white boy and girl goes to school through at least the eighth grade. You and Douglas and Black and the others want them to go to school with nigras. Let me ask you this: Were there any nigras where your kids went to school? Any where Black's kids went? Douglas? I doubt it very much and if there were, they probably were high yellas."

"What's a high yella?" the Chief asked, fearful of the answer. He wanted to insist that Farwell cease the lazy, bigoted reference to "nigras" in his presence. He was convinced that Farwell, on whom a good Harvard education had been wasted, used the word intentionally, presumably to irritate his more liberal adversaries and to sound more genuinely "Southern." The Chief cautioned himself that now was the wrong time to take on one Farwell's several reprehensible personal characteristics.

"A light skinned colored at a minimum. More often, a light skinned colored trying to pass as a white person. Probably most of your colored friends are high yellas, if you have any colored friends.

"Let me tell you, Chief. *I* have many colored acquaintances — real darkies, some of whom have worked for my family for generations. I know the nigra. They can be sweet people, very kindly. That's why the women can be entrusted with our children. But the nigras of the South are culturally backward Africans, regardless of the shade of their skin. Mostly they are also plain stupid. We can argue 'til the cows come home whether they are made stupid or born stupid, but the result is the same. You put them into white schools and all the children will suffer, the bright ones and the dumb ones and especially all the ones in between, white and colored. We live with the colored. They are in and around us in the South. California, New York, Massachusetts, you got coloreds. Lots of 'em. But they are segregated every way *except* legally. So they don't go to the same schools because they don't live in the same neighborhoods you do. You don't see 'em except when they make your bed.

"Look at Douglas, for another example. The Great Liberal of the Court. He lives in Washington State and hightails it out there as often as I head for South Carolina. He hikes and boats and lets the press know about it all the time. How many times have you seen a picture of him with a nigra in Washington State? Never. There ain't no nigras in Washington State, and if there were, you can be damned sure Douglas, who is a mean SOB anyway, wouldn't be hanging around with them."

Chapter Nine: The Chief II

The Chief was a bit taken aback. Farwell accusing Douglas of a mean heart showed stunningly poor judgment. The Chief was familiar with all of Farwell's other arguments. They were the commonplace sentiments of bigots everywhere, sometimes dressed up by politicians, academics and newspaper editorial writers in a vain attempt to hide their roots in ignorance, fear and hate. The observations about northern liberals stung, because they were true. But the racial prejudices of the North were a much larger problem than was before the Court. Even a unanimous decision in *Brown* would not change men's hearts. If practices were forced to change, hearts might, too. *Brown* was only a first step.

"We aren't remaking society, Nathan. We are just trying to decide a public schools case."

"Bullshit. You are trying to remake society in the South. That's my point. Only the South will suffer drastic change. Believe me, it'll be violent. There will be resistance. Byrnes in South Carolina, Talmadge in Georgia and a lot of other Southern governors are already threatening to close down all the schools rather than integrate them. That'll end education for nearly all coloreds and a lot of poor white kids when the only choice is to pay a bundle for some private school.

"You are overreaching here even more than in *Sweatt* and those other cases. I'm just sounding the alarm. The majority is the aggressor. It's an abuse of power at the expense of southern children. Overturning segregation is immoral. White southerners are not immoral and they won't let you get away with it."

Unanimous Verdict

"But you don't really want to see violence, do you? Don't you want to help the medicine go down here? You don't want to be a symbol of race hatred and division, do you?" The Chief paused to look around at the symbols of the Confederacy on the walls. "Or, maybe you do. Is that it, Nathan? You want to lead the Lost Cause? Be some kind of martyr? You're a little old to get back into politics, aren't you?"

Farwell leaned back in his chair and put his feet on his desk. He was shod in riding boots. He adopted a contemplative air. He lowered his volume. "Violence is something that people bring on themselves. Actions spark violence. People act irresponsibly or antagonize other people by being disrespectful of their deeply held beliefs and customs. Serious consequences result, legal and illegal.

"You know I run a plantation of considerable size – River's Edge. Been in the family since right after the Revolution. We managed 400 nigras at one time on our plantation. My Mommy and Daddy and my grandparents before them treated them kindly. Even so, there were times when one or two would step out of line. Couldn't fire them, and after the Civil War we couldn't sell them. They had no place to go. They'd just hang around River's Edge if they were fired, making a nuisance of themselves. So we punished 'em. Corporal punishment. Mostly it was mild; sometimes the thrashings would get a little out of control. All of it was technically illegal, of course. Assault. Felonies. Nobody enforced it. No Negro went to the county sheriff. They understood the need for order and for the protection of my family. Everything stayed on River's Edge. Mostly that was a happy result. Everybody had work and nobody got out of line very often."

Chapter Nine: The Chief II

The Chief listened to Farwell's speech in shock. A Justice of the United States Supreme Court was admitting his family routinely assaulted Negroes years after emancipation.

"You look surprised, Chief. Don't be a baby. Everybody did it. All the plantations in Aiken County, hell, in the South, did it. Couldn't keep order otherwise. You cannot tolerate disorder and disobedience on a cotton or tobacco farm at harvest time. Not possible and still make enough for everybody."

"What does this have to do with *Brown?*" The Chief was morbidly fascinated by watching the physically elegant Nathan Farwell devolve into an evil torturer as he nostalgically recalled the "pleasures" of his childhood. But the Chief pressed on with his mission, which now looked more hopeless than when he entered Farwell's chambers.

"It means this. It means that the people who control things in the South are accustomed to handling them their own way, without interference. Sometimes that way is not the way city folk and northerners and folks who like to ride boats down the Salmon River or whatever think it should be done. Southerners are used to being mistreated and looked down on by the North. We are used to overcoming hardship. We are used to beating our adversaries by trickery and guile if we cannot do it with guns and ammo. This *Brown* case will start a war. Believe me, it is one that you can't win.

"You asked if I wanted to lead this war, or be its martyr. The answer is 'no,' but sometimes events single out men for leadership even against their will. This may be such a time. In any event, your visit has caused me to rethink my dissent. I might make it longer and angrier. I might not. I'll look at it again. But I plan to dissent in a loud voice."

The Chief saw the meeting was concluded. But he had one question left: "You talked about your parents beating and whipping Negroes. Did you ever do anything like that? Did you ever *kill* a Negro?" The Chief expected a violently negative answer to the suggestion that Farwell might be a killer. He was surprised when Farwell stared into the space over his visitor's head for a moment, thoughtfully contemplating his response.

"I said violence is caused when people depart from custom. I won't answer your question, because to do so gives it more dignity than it deserves. There were occasions in my time when people, even my loved ones, departed from custom. The consequences were not happy. You can assume that when I say leadership may be thrust upon me that I have the courage and experience necessary to lead successfully, to preserve the customs of the South."

The hairs on the back of the Chief's neck stood up. Farwell turned his eyes to the wall, seeing himself in one of his paintings of the Civil War. A general on horseback, riding over the dead to victory or, in some ways better, a glorious defeat for a grand cause.

As he did so, the Chief wondered if Farwell was mad.

Chapter Ten: Ezra and Neil, April 28-30, 1954

Neil felt the pain before he opened his eyes. It was at the back of his neck and on the right side of his head. There was more pain on the right side of his torso, near his kidneys, and his thigh ached worse than a charlie horse. He willed his eyes open. He saw only white. But if this was heaven, he would not hurt so much. This was not his room in Washington, either. He thought for a minute and remembered he was supposed to be in Chicago, but this was not in his room at the Hilton. He turned, causing greater neck pain, to survey his surroundings. He was in a hospital room. He heard snoring coming from the other side of the white cloth, which was used to divide his bed from another's. Except for the source of the snoring, no one else was in the room. Neil tried to rise despite the pain in many places. Before he could get out of bed, he felt a tug at his wrist. He was attached to an intravenous fluid tube. The bottle feeding the tube was nearly empty. Neil sat on the edge of the bed and pulled the cord which entered the wall at a point labeled "nurse call button." True to its promise, a nurse entered the room a few minutes later.

Neil was of the male school that believed all nurses should be petite, pert and sexy in a healthy, gymnast kind of way that kept their breasts high and firm, their stomachs flat and their legs gorgeous. He'd actually encountered some of those near-mythical nurses while on leave in Japan. Chicago was disappointing. His nurse was short, middle-aged and fat. She possessed a cheerful disposition for which Neil was not in the mood.

"Hello, hello, Mr. Endicott. How are we this afternoon?"

"Is it still afternoon?" Neil replied. Her voice made his head hurt worse.

"Wednesday afternoon, Mr. Endicott. It's nearly 24 hours since you became our guest."

It was then that he remembered being sapped by a colored guy at his hotel door.

"How did I get here," he asked.

"I believe the hotel called an ambulance. You were unconscious. You've been unconscious all night and all day. Do you feel up to a police interview? We don't like our tourists beaten up. Bad for business."

"Not the hospital's business," Neil responded. A feeble attempt at a joke that brought an over-zealous response from the nurse and intense pain in his head.

"That's very funny, Mr. Endicott," the nurse said as she screeched a high, loud, squeaky laugh. Neil couldn't imagine anyone living with that laugh and instinctively looked at the nurse's left hand for a wedding ring. She wore one. Neil wondered if her husband was deaf when she married him or became deaf by sticking pencils in his eardrums.

"I think you must be on the mend. I'm Nurse Plasko, by the way, but you can call me Prudence. Prudence Plasko. Part Polish, part Greek. Endicott? What's that? Italian?"

Neil rolled his eyes. "When can I get out of here?"

222

Chapter Ten: Ezra and Neil

"The doctor will be by in a half hour or so. If he says you can go, you go. The police wanna' talk to you. I'll call them."

A uniformed police officer arrived an hour later. Still no sign of a doctor. The officer was young, probably only a year or two on the force. Neil quickly let him know that he was a policeman, but didn't tell him he was now a private investigator. The rookie didn't even ask him what he did for living now, but loosened up a little in the presence of a fellow member of the Order.

Neil gave the officer a description of the man who hit him. When the officer heard the assailant was colored, he asked if it was Ezra Lowell.

"I don't know. I don't think so. I had an appointment with Mr. Lowell."

"I know. The desk clerk told us. About what?"

Neil had read the entire Black National Strength Party brochure and its contents were fresh in his aching head. "About their work with poor children. I'm a freelance journalist writing about poor children in urban areas."

"I thought you said you were a cop?"

"No, no. Not any more. Walking a beat was just too dull after Korea. On my own now. Freelance."

"I hope you're getting' well-paid for this article or whatever you're writin'. You know, this guy Lowell's trouble. He's got a political organization that wants to start a race war. I'd be careful with him."

"Has he gotten into trouble? Guns? Drugs?"

"So far it's all talk. He's got these programs for poor kids. Probably just a front. I'd be careful. If you wanna' write about him, you should look at the bad stuff, too."

"Does he look like the description I gave you?"

"I've never seen him. I'll pass it along and if he does, we'll bring you to a lineup or just show you his photo for an ID. How long will you be in town?"

"Depends on when I get out of here and get rid of this headache. A day or two, I guess."

"I'll get on it. And call the precinct if you find anything's missing when you get to your hotel. By the way, did the guy say anything to you? Kind of crazy to just knock on a hotel door and beat a guy."

"No. He didn't say anything." Neil could not describe the shouted warning without causing a lot more questions he didn't want to answer.

"Any reason someone would do this to you? Any enemies in Chicago?"

"I haven't been to Chicago since I was in the Marines and all I did then was get drunk and leave town."

"OK. Well, that's enough for now. You might get a visit from a detective, might not. Their call. But call the precinct if something is missing."

"Yeah, I got it. Thanks."

Chapter Ten: Ezra and Neil

The cop left. Neil hadn't given him much. Many times a cop interviewed a victim just so that if anyone complained, the department could say the matter was investigated. He thought this was just such a *pro forma* procedure. He didn't expect to hear from the cops again.

The doctor finally arrived with several X-rays. He pointed to various parts of the X-ray photographs, but Neil couldn't see anything the doctor pointed out to him. He suffered two broken ribs that would heal by themselves and a mild concussion. The doctor said he could be released, but that Neil should rest through tomorrow and not undertake any heavy physical activity for at least a week.

The chirpy nurse took the needle out of Neil's wrist. He dressed and went to check out of the hospital. Neil couldn't pay the bill because his billfold was either in his room or stolen. He gave his Washington address so he could be billed and took a short taxi ride back to the Conrad Hilton. The desk clerk inquired after Neil's health. Neil asked the clerk if Ezra Lowell stopped by. He had and left a message: "I was told you were beat up and in the hospital. They wouldn't tell me which one. Call me when you get back. Ezra Lowell." There was another message from Lou King. It was one word: "Call" and his phone number. Neil asked the desk clerk if he could describe Mr. Lowell. The clerk said he wasn't on duty at the time Lowell stopped by.

Nothing was taken from his hotel room. His billfold was not disturbed. Even the change on his dressing table was as he left it.

The beating he took was an exclamation point to the thug's spoken message, not a theft.

It was after 5 o'clock in Washington, so Neil called King, before he went home to the picket-fenced house.

King picked up the phone on the first ring. "I hate to say it, but your first impression of this guy Lowell might not be far off – he looks like a bad *hombre*," King told Neil without waiting for a salutation.

"I got beat up yesterday. Put in the hospital. Maybe Lowell did it, or put someone up to it."

"You hurt bad?"

"I spent last night and this morning in the hospital. I got a concussion and broken ribs, but other than the pain, I'm OK. I'm out now."

"So Lowell got tough. Endy, he's a killer. I checked him out with my friends at the FBI. Yeah, I got friends at the FBI. Sometimes ol' J. Edgar needs a colored guy to help out." Even on a serious matter, King could not contain his sarcasm about white law enforcement. He also must have talked to officers at the DC Police Department, since the only place Neil was called Endy was at the MPD. Still, an acknowledgment that his concern about Lowell was well-founded and a friendly touch, all in one conversation with King. Neil wondered half seriously if the white haired old gent had suffered a stroke that made him less hostile.

"He was charged with killin' a white guy back in '34 in Alabama. Wasn't caught until some routine fingerprint checking while he was in a military prison in Georgia. He was printed for some petty theft when he was a kid, but Alabama didn't send the prints to the FBI until the early 40s. War Department was draftin' lots of young guys who it turned out had criminal records, but the states didn't forward the prints to the FBI. Tightened up the process and Lowell got caught."

Neil could feel the unnecessary bureaucratic details of fingerprint recordkeeping foul-ups feeding his concussion and brought King's narrative to the present to lessen the headache pain.

"Well how is he out now and in Chicago? I thought they hanged black guys for killin' white guys in Alabama. Sometimes gave 'em a trial, but always hanged 'em."

"I got some friends of mine on the MPD to call down there to Mobile and find out. They found some guy who remembered the case. Lowell was sent to Mobile from Georgia after a dishonorable discharge. Mobile DA must have been a civilized guy and more'n likely overworked with all the new War Department facilities built down there during the war. That probably brought a lot of those uppity Negroes from the North down that caused trouble."

"My head is pounding, Lou. Get to the point."

"I am, I am. You need background on this guy and I'm givin' it to you. Plus I spent a couple hours on this on Mrs. Van Dyke's nickel and I'm gonna' give it to you, like it or not." Lou was impatient with Neil's impatience.

"Anyway, the victim was some kinda' rural cracker of no account. The only witness, the guy's mother, was either dead or moved outta' state. Nobody knew where she was. Only thing they could prove was flight from prosecution, which was obviously true. Lowell pled to that and got two years on a road gang. Guess he hightailed back to Chicago when he got out, probably around '44 or '45. Ain't much doubt he's a killer, though."

"Any motive?"

"You could say so. Lowell's daddy was murdered the day before Lowell killed this white guy. Doesn't take a genius to figure out a motive."

"That puts the killing in a different light, doesn't it? This guy Lowell may not be such a bad apple. I mean, back in '34, Alabama, wouldn't a colored guy expect that the cops wouldn't pay much attention to the murder of his father? That was around the time of the Scottsboro incident, wasn't it?" Neil asked, referring to the arrest of nine young Negroes for the rape of two white women in a boxcar in Alabama in 1932. They were tried in Scottsboro. Eight were sentenced to death. The trials were completed two weeks after the alleged rapes. The convictions were reversed by the U.S. Supreme Court because the defendants were denied counsel. Retrials and appeals took the rest of the decade. None of the men was executed for the alleged crime, but all spent a long time in jail.

"My, my, Endy. Some sympathy for the colored man? I thought you was a law 'n order cop?"

"Can the condescension, King. I've been beat up on this job for real while you probably just been beat up on a witness stand. The point is, Lowell might not be such a bad guy despite his record. I'm calling

Chapter Ten: Ezra and Neil

him after I hang up on you to see him. This time I think I'll see him where he dwells. Might be informative."

"Ok. Don't get mad. You know I like to bait the white guy. Best I can get for 300 years of slavery and repression.

"I'd reconsider visiting him where he lives, which can't be a very safe place for anybody. I haven't been to Chicago in years, but I'm not inclined to think it's become a better place for the black man or, especially, for the white guy in a black neighborhood. No picket fences, green lawns and picnics on Calumet Avenue. Just 'cause it starts with a "C" don't make it Chevy Chase."

"Jesus, King, will you cut it out! I've been around. I've seen slums. I can handle myself."

"Yeah, your accommodations of last night certainly is evidence of that!"

"You got anything else except gratuitous advice and insults?"

"You can ignore the insults, but consider the advice seriously. I don't want Mrs. Van Dyke to have to pay to haul your body back to D.C. for a funeral."

"Nice thought. Talk to you later." Neil hung up and dialed the number for the Black National Strength Party. This time he got a female voice on the other end who said Lowell was not in the office but that she would have him call back.

For the first time that afternoon, Neil examined himself in the mirror. His face was badly bruised on the right side, as was his torso. He couldn't see the back of his neck very well, but it, too, was bruised.

Unanimous Verdict

There wasn't as much evidence of a beating on his thigh, which took the least abuse. Overall, Neil felt he was lucky his jaw wasn't broken or his skull cracked.

His contemplation of himself was ended by the ringing telephone. It was Ezra Lowell. Lowell said he heard about the beating from the Hilton desk clerk when he arrived for his appointment. He inquired how Neil was feeling. They arranged to meet the next morning at Lowell's office, which was part of the Black National Strength Party headquarters and mission on East 64th Street between the Oakwood Cemetery and the Englewood rail yard. "Just tell the cabbie you want 64th and South Park," Lowell said.

It was a long ride down South Michigan Avenue and lesser-known streets to reach the Black National Strength Party headquarters. The trip was a living newsreel of economic decline from north to south as the fancy stores and office buildings got less fancy, dissolving into shabby, shabbier and finally slummy storefronts and houses. Liquor stores replaced shoe stores. Beauty parlors and barbershops replaced banks. Black pedestrians replaced whites. Cars from the 1930s replaced those of the late 1940s and the 1950s. Odors of rendering plants at the Union Stock Yards replaced the sweet breezes from Lake Michigan. The flatness of Chicago somehow emphasized the sad narrative. There were no hills or scenery to distract from the street-straight line of wealth to poverty. Neil was barely out of the taxi before the driver sped away, anxious to leave the neighborhood for the more friendly confines of the Loop.

Chapter Ten: Ezra and Neil

The building in front of Neil was long, low and made of brick. Wide steel casement windows that cranked open served as architectural grins onto the street, but most of them were closed or open only an inch or two because it was still cool in Chicago in late April. Although it was southeast of the stock yards, the area and the building were industrial, the railroad tracks visible across the street to the west. A faded sign painted on the brick above the front door said "Walczak Polish Sausage – The Best in the West." A more recent sign hung on a hook screwed into the painted front door. It said "Come In." Neil entered without knocking, as instructed.

Inside was a huge open room, probably 80 feet wide and twice as long. At least 100 colored boys and girls of various ages were in several different circles sitting on bare, wide planked flooring around older Negroes, most of them female, who appeared to be delivering lessons. A quick glance suggested that the latter group, the teachers, all looked younger than Neil. As Neil opened the door he heard the cacophony of dialog and laughter between teachers and students, each class seeming to compete with another to be heard. Within seconds, the huge space was quieted by the sight of a white man in a sea of blackness. Anxiety, or maybe it was just wariness, was palpable. What did the white man want? Was he trouble? Only when a large, older black man approached Neil and waved his arm in the air in a sort of signal did the chatter of learning resume. The man introduced himself as Ezra Lowell. Neil extended his hand. Lowell did not take it.

Unanimous Verdict

"I'm not trying to be rude to you, Mr. Endicott. But I make it a rule not to shake the hand of a white man unless and until I know I can trust him." Lowell's voice was deep and even, neither welcoming nor threatening, neither loud nor soft, but a very deep bass, a thick blanket of sound. Consistent with the spoken words, it conveyed suspicion. "This is the headquarters of the Black National Strength Party and of its community mission center. Would you like a tour?" He did not wait for an answer and Neil offered none, still surprised by the rejection of his extended hand.

"Most of the space is devoted to our mission work. As you can see, classes are going on now. We teach a full grammar school curriculum, grades kindergarten through eighth, which is certified by the Illinois Department of Education. Actually, our schooling is better than the public schools, white or colored. Our classes are smaller, our books, at least for now, are usually newer, and we make a point of teaching in every class something about the history of the black man. Sometimes it is in the context of something else – the Civil War, the Revolution, the World Wars, for example. Or science – lots of Negro contributions to science. Other times, it is separate. It is amazing, but the State of Illinois requires no instruction about sub-Saharan Africa – ever. Even in high school. But it requires a whole year of mostly European "world" history in the eighth grade and again in the twelfth. We teach about Africa in every grade. Some on the Caribbean and a fair amount on the native tribes of North and South America."

Chapter Ten: Ezra and Neil

Neil pretended to be impressed, but he was only bored. He was not interested in pedagogy of any color. You didn't need to know the history of the Belgian Congo to drive a truck, he thought to himself.

"Please forgive my enthusiasm. I should answer your questions. As you can see, I am very proud of our teachers, students and curriculum." Lowell's Alabama accent was evident in nearly every word he spoke. But his words bore no trace of what Neil thought of as the "lazy" speech of lower class Negroes. Lowell didn't slur his words, drop the end of words or use much slang. His sibilants were properly expressed. By voice alone, he could pass for a plantation owner, as far as Neil could judge, which was very little since he did not know any plantation owners. His voice was well-suited for radio. By voice alone, Lowell could have been a Dixiecrat senator. Neil knew one or two of those through his Dad, and they were on the radio and movie newsreels all the time.

Neil pretended to pay close attention to Lowell's description of the curriculum, but mostly he examined his host's appearance. Lowell was the color of milk chocolate, neither extremely light, like Clay Van Dyke, nor deeply dark, like Lou King or Mrs. Van Dyke. His face was clean-shaven, his hair short and neatly trimmed. His nostrils were slightly flared and large meaty lips turned from deep brown to pink, like a sunrise, unveiling well-tended teeth. They fit well with his face, which was round but not chubby. Neil guessed that Ezra Lowell appealed to women. Nearing 40-years-old, Lowell was conservatively dressed in an open-necked short-sleeved blue sports shirt, charcoal grey slacks and plain black Oxford shoes. Casual, but highly presentable.

Unanimous Verdict

Lowell's most distinctive features were his height and weight. He was at least six and a half feet tall and probably weighed over 250 pounds. The weight was well-distributed over the huge frame. He carried it effortlessly, with no fat visible. The short sleeves wrapped around muscular forearms. His neck was a hogshead of muscle, probably 20 inches around, cause enough to avoid closing top shirt buttons or wearing ties. On appearance alone, Neil would bet on Lowell against any prizefighter.

Lowell continued the tour. A dozen bunk beds were at either end of the large room, allocated by gender. "We are sanctioned by the city for group foster care," Lowell said. "Some of these kids got no one to take care of them." His guide looked at Neil to see if this news had any effect.

"Gee, that's too bad." Neil realized there was a script he had to follow as the visiting white guy. But he thought: Why can't these colored families stay around to take care of their kids?

Another area was devoted to an industrial-strength kitchen and dining tables and chairs. There was a small library of several hundred books and a play area. There were no desks, either in the school area or in the sleeping sections. Neil asked why, figuring it was only polite for a visitor to show some interest in the tour.

"If each child had a desk, there would be less space. Less space would mean we could serve fewer children. They are young and flexible. They can work on their laps or on the floor. They can also use the dining tables for homework after mealtime. But the truth is, we wouldn't turn down donated desks. We can't afford to buy any.

Chapter Ten: Ezra and Neil

"Actually, our most pressing need at the moment is to expand the bathroom facilities. As you probably saw from the old sign on the wall, this used to be a sausage plant. It closed during the Depression. That's why we have the big blowers in the ceiling and have any showers at all. Since the sausage plant didn't employ women, we had to build a second bathroom. But it has no showers. Can you help out with that, Mr. Endicott?" Neil sensed, accurately, that no white person came within Lowell's purview without being cultivated for a contribution. Neil was a barren field, however, since he barely supported himself.

After the mission tour was completed, Lowell led Neil to his office, which was really just a corner of the room separated by two "walls" of five-drawer filing cabinets. Presumably labels such as "School Bills" and "Enrollment Records" were for the mission and "Party Platforms" and "Registered Voters" were for the political side. The office walls were lined with political posters for the Black National Strength Party. The walls outside the office were adorned exclusively with drawings by the school children. Ezra Lowell opened the conversation after both men were seated, Neil in a straight-back wooden guest chair, Lowell in a cushioned office chair behind a standard issue five-foot gunmetal grey desk which was clear except for a blotter, a daily calendar and a telephone.

"I was very sad to hear about Clayton from Mr. King. How is Mrs. Van Dyke taking it? She is a sweet lady. After I met her on my visit to D.C. a year or two ago, I kidded Clay that I wished she was my mother. I loved my Mama, but in some ways, it's true."

"She is taking it as well as can be expected. I think she's focused on finding out if her son was killed and, if so, who killed him."

"Yes. Contemplating vengeance can delay the onset of grief. No question about that." Lowell looked directly at Neil as he spoke. Neil tried not to convey that he knew about the murder of Lowell's father's killer. "From what King told me, there's no doubt he was murdered. But what do I have to do with any of this?"

Neil did not answer immediately. Lowell surely knew how he was related to the investigation. Neil considered accusing him directly of faking his ignorance. But trust clearly was important to Lowell. Accusations did not engender trust. He also remembered King's advice after the disastrous interview with the cancer victim, LeClerc: take an indirect approach and avoid accusations if he wanted information.

"Mrs. Van Dyke told us about your visit and what good friends you were with Clay. Army buddies, I guess?"

"More like jailbird buddies. We met in the stockade at Fort Polk."

"Yes, that's what she said. But you became good friends. Did you meet any of Neil's friends on your trip to Washington?"

"A few."

"Do the names LeClerc or Winkler or Louie Charles mean anything to you?"

"I met Louie Charles. Was Winkler a female? There was some woman I met who worked with Clay and had a crush on him. I think she was named Winkler. Never heard of LeClerc."

Chapter Ten: Ezra and Neil

"That's consistent with what we heard from them. All three told us Clay came to Chicago to see you shortly before he died. Is that accurate?"

Lowell, who folded his hands on the desktop, leaning forward, during earlier questioning, threw himself back in his chair and swiveled it from side-to-side. "Why do you care? What does a trip to see me in Chicago in February have to do with a killing in D.C. in March?"

"We know from his friends and his mother that Clay was anxious to find out information about his birth parents. He wanted to find out why he was so light-skinned. I mean, not why, but who his white relatives are.

"I'm not sure you'd want Mrs. Van Dyke as your mom, by the way. She blames you for making Clay so conscious of his color. Actually, according to his friends, Clayton kind of resented his color because he thought it proved his African blood was diluted by white blood. Mrs. Van Dyke says you introduced Clay to Black Nationalism that caused him to focus on this issue. She isn't pleased about it. Frankly, I'm surprised to see that you are as light-skinned as you are. I expected to meet a very black African man."

Lowell started to stand. Thinking better of it, he remained seated. He could not remember so candid a conversation about skin color with a white person since he was thrown off a streetcar in Mobile nearly 27 years ago for standing in the white section. He resented the accusatory tone of this white man, but admired his drive on behalf of

Mrs. Van Dyke and Clay. He didn't fit the description Lorenzo King provided on the telephone a few days earlier, warning Lowell to overlook Endicott's casual racism and inexperience to help find Clay's killer. Neil seemed genuinely interested in finding out who killed Clay; not just in taking Mrs. Van Dyke's money. It was a risk for a white boy to speak so candidly about issues black folk kept to themselves, like color, especially to a big black man in the middle of the Chicago slums. Lorenzo King's suspicions were not supported by the evidence so far. But King was right about one thing: The guy didn't know much about Negroes.

"First off, Mr. Endicott, you are being a little rude here, but I'll assume it's all in the name of finding out who killed Clay and I'll let it pass. Second, Clayton Van Dyke was an adult the whole time I knew him and was a pretty smart adult at that. He made his own decisions about what to think. Third, it is true that my philosophy and that of the party I founded is Black Nationalism. But we don't put color on a scale and say 'not dark enough' or 'too much white blood' or anything like that. Lots of colored folk do that. We say that is bad, both morally and politically. It is divisive and it works in favor of the white man keeping his power. All you need to be is a Negro. We don't care if you are a high yella or your skin turns day into dark.

"Where am I? What number?"

"I think you are at four."

Chapter Ten: Ezra and Neil

"OK. Fourth. I don't have a problem with my skin color because I know I'm a Negro. I have been reminded of it every day of my life. I come from the rural south, where you know you are a Negro from the moment you are born, and if you forget that for even a minute the consequences can be pretty damned scary. Clay's life wasn't like that. Of course he knew he was a colored man. But he didn't much have to *live* like a colored man. He felt guilty about it, and he was confused. I think that's why he resented his light skin.

"It's just another way in which the white man has got the Negro down. He's forced us to live in such poverty and ignorance and powerlessness that when God puts a black man in a good place, with a good education and brains and money, the black man thinks he ain't a Negro because he ain't also a nigger. He's actually got some of what we are fighting for – a little power over his own life – and he feels bad about it. Thinks he needs to pick cotton to be genuine, as if we all carried around one of those tags on the mattresses. 'Genuine Negro. Do not remove.' The Germans put that kind of sign on the Jews to kill 'em. The Jews didn't need any sign to tell them they were Jewish. But the white man's got some Negroes so confused they need a symbol or sign to tell them they are really Negroes. Often that sign is poverty, ignorance and a very black skin." Lowell rose to his feet and pounded his right fist into his left palm while pacing around his small cubicle. He was orating now.

"And, by the way, there's a range of skin color in black Africa, too. Not like here, maybe, but not everybody's dark as in a white man's worst nightmare. They got albinos over there like here. Some places an albino is worshipped. Other places he's killed or treated bad. Color's an excuse for bad behavior the world over.

"Yes, Clay came here for help finding out about his birth parents, like he told his friends. I tried to talk him out of it. I told him it didn't matter. That his color wouldn't change and his parents wouldn't change. His parents are the Van Dykes. I told Clay to remember his Army days, which was the closest he came to being treated like a cotton picker in Alabama. I told him he'd paid his dues, as if being a Negro was a dues-paying organization. I told him to go back to school and resume playing his trumpet. He could be a jazz musician and a mathematician. Pride of race, Talented Tenth, all that stuff. Black folk need that kind of model and help, whether you believe in Black Nationalism or all that NAACP integration stuff."

Neil gulped. The conversation over Clay's visit to Chicago had suddenly turned into another lecture on race. Ezra Lowell's speech was more fluent and angrier than even Lou King's. In both cases, Neil had no basis on which to respond, or helpful comment, so he moved on, relying on the question used by every speechless detective.

"What happened next?"

"He would not take 'no' for an answer. He wanted to continue his little investigation."

"Did you offer him any help?" Lowell did not respond. He waited for Neil's next question. Here was where Neil needed to develop some trust. He resorted to the same tactic he used with King.

Chapter Ten: Ezra and Neil

He showed Lowell his copy of the note found on Clay's body. He let the big black man read it before speaking again.

"There isn't any doubt Clay was murdered and there's damn little doubt he was murdered because of his 'little investigation' as you called it. He found something in Chicago that led him to Atlanta that led to him getting killed. This note came from a man I know on the D.C. police. He will lose his job if his superiors find out he disclosed it. He was supposed to destroy it. I'm trusting you to help me keep my word that it won't get back to hurt him. But I also need you to trust me."

"If the police have this, why are they calling his death a suicide?"

"Because the Commissioners of the D.C. government, and maybe even the President who appoints them, don't want news there was a lynching in the nation's capital. They don't want it for a bunch of reason. They don't want to incite the D.C. Negroes. They don't want to sway the Supreme Court in the school cases. And I think they don't want the Reds to trumpet that a Negro can be lynched a few blocks from the U.S. Capitol. The Commies have been making a big deal out of the alley housing and the slums near the Capitol. They love to print pictures with a long view of the Capitol dome and slums a few blocks away. A lynching in D.C. would give them more ammo. So the whole thing is suppressed. If we find out who did it, Mrs. Van Dyke and her NAACP friends can stir up a pot of trouble if the cops don't pursue the case and convict the person or persons.

"But we need your help. You have to trust me."

Lowell was silent for a moment. "And I thought Chicago politicians were two-faced bastards. Got nothing on Washington."

"We aren't even talking about Congress yet," Neil laughed, grateful for a break from the gravity of the conversation.

Ezra smiled slightly, but was very serious. "If I were to cooperate with you, I'd be giving you evidence of a crime. I've been in jail twice already, once in the Army and once in Alabama. With my record, I'd get sent away for a long time in Chicago. It's high risk for me."

"I already have a pretty good idea of what you did. You helped Clay break into the Childress agency, break the lock on the confidential file cabinet and find his adoption records."

It was Lowell's turn to be surprised. The note had not surprised him; King told him about it as evidence that Clay's death had to be investigated as a murder. Lowell recognized that the white man's sharing it was intended to engender some trust. But King was totally wrong about Neil's talents as an investigator, which King had said were few. The guy already knew what Lowell didn't want to confess. If he wanted to turn him into the cops, he would have done so already.

"My real question for you," Neil continued, "is did you return the records to the files or keep them? We didn't find any at the Van Dyke's, and Clay was still living at home."

"We grabbed them at around eleven at night, took them to a place I know that can Photostat documents around the clock, and then we returned the originals. Clay took the Photostats. I don't know where they are."

"The files were obviously broken into. What point was there in making copies? Why not just keep the originals?"

"Because Clay visited the Childress agency earlier in the day and they were uncooperative. If we didn't replace the file, they would be certain Clay, or someone working with him, broke in and took them. As it is, I'm sure Clay was their prime suspect, but then they had to ask why his records were still in the file. It made good sense and we thought it worked."

Neil resisted pointing out that the plan didn't work since Clay was murdered.

"Did you read the records? Or did Clay tell you what they said?"

"We didn't have time. We didn't get the records back in the file cabinet until nearly 6 a.m., almost dawn. Then Clay caught the morning train back to D.C. I suspect he didn't read the file until he was on the train."

"Did you talk to him later, after he got back to D.C.?"

"The last I saw or heard from him was when I dropped him off at Union Station. Next thing I know, this guy King is calling to tell me he was murdered."

A female voice out in the large room interrupted the conversation by calling for Lowell. He left, giving Neil time to think. When he returned, Neil offered a proposition.

"You will have to duplicate the break-in and theft with me. Only this time we won't bother with a Photostat. We'll just take the originals."

Lowell's dark pupils stood out from the whites of his widened eyes as he looked at Neil in astonishment. "Hold on, man. I just told you I'd be sent away for a long time if I'm caught breaking and entering. It was unwise to do it once. I'd be a damned fool to do the same thing again. You are one crazy white guy to think I'd even consider it."

"Well it's a risk to me, too, and I didn't even know Clayton Van Dyke, much less call him my friend."

"Then why are you doing it? A private investigator isn't supposed to break the law. And for a colored guy?"

"I'm not sure. It probably makes as little sense for me as for you. But I like Mrs. Van Dyke. The DC cover up of Clay's murder pisses me off a lot. And now I've got my own little stake in getting back at whoever put me in the hospital. Maybe the least of it is that someone killed Clayton Van Dyke and I'd like to see him punished for it. It's enough. But I don't know the first thing about breaking and entering. I suspect you have some experience."

Twelve hours later, Neil and Ezra were in Ezra's 1939 second- or third-hand Hudson. They pulled up to the front door of the building housing the Childress Agency. Ezra said there was no point in parking the car anywhere else. They might need to make a quick getaway.

Chapter Ten: Ezra and Neil

He instructed Neil to stand over Ezra while he crouched to jimmy open the front door. A white man at the door at midnight would be much less suspicious than a black man at the door, although Neil's slighter frame could not completely hide the larger man from passersby.

Whatever Ezra did, he opened the front door in less than one minute without breaking the glass. Not a car or pedestrian passed by. It was a side street with no bars or other late night attractions. They entered and took the elevator to the Childress Agency. The office door was easily broken. The same was true for the door to Mrs. Childress's office.

As they shoved it open, they were met by the same man who beat up Neil two days earlier. This time, he was holding a .38 instead of a sap. He was not surprised to see the two men. They made lots of noise breaking down two doors. And he was expecting one of them.

"Well, well. Ezra Lowell. Didn't expect to see you tonight. This how you fund that mission of yours, B&E? How come you workin' with the whitey here? I thought you hated 'em."

The .38 didn't lessen Ezra's self-assurance. He towered over the gunman and moved toward him. "You seem to know everything, Lester. Tell us what you know about the death of Clay Van Dyke."

"Step back, Ezra. I don't want to kill you. You either, white boy. I don't know what you're talking about. I got a contract to beat up the white boy. I went easy 'cause I wasn't 'sposed to kill him. Guess he's got an important daddy or somethin'. Even in the dark it looks like I did a good job. Anything else, I don't know and don't want to know, especially if somebody's dead and I didn't get paid for doin' it. Of course, nobody said nothin' 'bout you, Ezra. Guess I can kill the nigger and nobody'd care."

Neil said nothing. He was more frightened than when he was in combat. This was a more personal threat — one aimed right at him. But even with the gun pointed at them, Ezra engaged Neil in casual conversation.

"White boy, Lester here — what's your latest handle, Lester?"

"Same as always Ezra, Lester Bark."

"That's right. White boy, some folks obviously gonna' call him Less Bark or Lesser Bark. Ain't no Big Bark as far as I know. Lester here is like a cheap paint brush. Got a dirty job, use Lester. Nobody cares if he's tossed out when the job's over. Still hangin' with the hookers, Lester? I heard one of 'em's your momma. Does you gotta' pay her when you fuck her?"

If Ezra's purpose was to anger the gunman, he was doing a good job. Neil wondered if Ezra was crazy. Lester had already expressed an interest in killing Ezra. Why provoke him? Neil prayed Lester remembered his assignment and wouldn't kill "the white boy".

"I should kill you just for that, Ezra. But I'm a professional." He reached for a folder on Mrs. Childress's desk, which was between him and the other two in the room. "I'm supposed to show the white guy that I have this folder. He can keep the page I'm going to hand him, then I'm going to destroy the rest of the folder right in front of you. That way there'll be no reason to come back. I don't know what it all means, but those are my orders."

He handed Neil a single sheet of paper. It was a legal form memorializing the adoption of a male Negro infant residing at the Childress Agency by Virginia and Elmer Van Dyke. Neil started to hand it back to Lester.

"You can keep that. That's what I was told."

"Who told you?" Neil asked. His words came with his first breath since entering the room.

"That's my business. Now, I'm gonna' burn up the folder and what's in it. Back off." Ezra and Neil stepped away from the desk as Lester pulled a Zippo from his coat pocket and snapped it open. He moved the folder so that it hung over the edge of the desk and started to light it, keeping the barrel of the pistol aimed in the general direction of Ezra and Neil.

Neil's evidence and his chance to catch Clayton Van Dyke's killer were about to go up in flames. His mind flashed on Virginia Van Dyke. So proud, yet so beaten. Before he could formulate any rational basis for his conduct, Neil vaulted across the desk head-first into Lester Bark's hand lighting the folder. Bark dropped the lighter and tried to pull his arm up and push the pistol between himself and Neil for a shot to Neil's chest. Neil had his hands around Bark's neck, pushing two thumbs into Bark's Adam 's apple. Ezra Lowell recovered from momentary surprise at Neil's sudden action in time to grab Bark's arm, pull it from between the two wrestlers and force the gun into the air.

It discharged, putting a hole in the ceiling and bringing plaster dust down on the trio. Ezra wrestled the gun from Bark's hand, pointed it at the other two and yelled to Neil.

"I've got his gun, Endicott, back off."

Bark let Neil climb off of him, grab the folder off the floor and move back across the desk to a standing position next to Lowell. Bark put up his hands.

"Now things are a little different, Lester.

"Does that look like what we came for?" Ezra asked Neil, never taking his eyes off of Lester.

Neil looked over the folder quickly. In addition to the formal adoption papers, there was correspondence between some outfit in Atlanta and the Childress Agency with dates early in 1922 and some notes on scrap paper. It looked authentic.

"Let me check the file cabinet and see if there's more," Neil said. The cabinet was unlocked – Mrs. Childress obviously admitted Lester and retrieved the file for him. She probably just forgot to relock the cabinet. There were no more folders marked "Van Dyke." If there was a folder marked with Clay's natural mother's name, there was no way to identify it since no one in the room knew who the mother was. There was no time to review Clay's folder carefully or to search through hundreds of adoption records in five large file cabinets looking for clues. Anyway, Neil considered, Mrs. Childress obviously believed that whatever damning evidence existed was in the file Bark was instructed to destroy.

Chapter Ten: Ezra and Neil

"I think that's it, Ezra." Neil used Lowell's Christian name for the first time. Neil was grateful that Ezra never used his name. He was never happier to be called just "white boy." "Should we take more files? Might put them off track,"

"I can't imagine that's necessary," Ezra said. "The Childress agency obviously placed an armed criminal in this office waiting for us. We may be guilty of breaking and entering, but he's guilty of armed assault. I doubt the people who run this place will be reporting anything to the police." Ezra motioned with the gun for Lester to precede him through the office door. Neil followed the two of them, propping up the inner and outer office doors in a semblance of a closed position. They took the elevator to the front door and entered the street. The Hudson was undisturbed. Ezra emptied the .38 of its cartridges and handed the weapon to Lester.

"As far as you're concerned, Lester, only the white guy showed up. You can tell the guy who hired you that you destroyed the folder or you can tell him the truth. The only thing you can't do is mention my name or even that two guys showed up for the folder. If I ever have reason to believe you did otherwise, I'm going to kill you. You know I will, too."

Lester, already short, appeared to diminish further as Ezra threatened him. He nodded his head, turned and ran down the sidewalk. When he was out of sight, Ezra started laughing and headed for the Hudson.

"Dumb jerk. Would you really kill him?"

"Won't ever come up. I assume you know I killed a white man in Alabama. I had good reasons to do it and I served some time for it. Folks on the south side of Chicago know only that I killed a white man. That's uncommon for a colored man to do. Makes a lot of colored scared, especially if they got no guts to begin with, like Lester. If you got the balls to kill a white man, they figure, why, it won't be more than swatting a fly to kill a Negro. The reputation helps. I wouldn't say it was worth the time served, but hell, if I got it, I'll use it." The Hudson started up. "Where to now?" It was only midnight. The last train to D.C. had departed an hour earlier. The next one would leave at 7 a.m.

"Back to the hotel. Next train isn't until tomorrow morning."

"What time?"

"Seven."

"I'll meet you at ten to."

"Why?"

"I'm coming with you."

"The hell you are," Neil exclaimed. He didn't need another Negro sidekick who enjoyed making fun of him. "Why?"

"Remember when we were interrupted this morning – I guess it's yesterday morning now – in my office by a woman calling to me?"

"Yeah."

"She told me that we'd just got a letter from the alderman's office saying the city funding we needed had come through. Big weight off my mind. I think I'm entitled to a little vacation. Washington, D.C. and Atlanta sounds like a good trip. Give you some company."

Chapter Ten: Ezra and Neil

"I can't stop you. But there's a good chance I'm going to resign this case if both you and King are going to team up. Mrs. Van Dyke doesn't need to pay for three of us."

"That won't happen. I'll pay my own way. I want to see how this comes out. We're obviously gonna' find some white man who was Clay's father, or maybe if he's dead, some other kin who killed Clay. We'll still need you involved, if only to give us some white skin in the game.

"Also sounds like you and this guy King have a sort of difficult relationship," Ezra concluded as the Hudson pulled up to the Conrad Hilton. "Maybe you need me to smooth things out."

Ezra pulled away as Neil replied, "Unlikely."

True to his word, Ezra met Neil at Union Station, ticket in hand. He also carried a two suiter piece of luggage made of cloth-covered cardboard that looked like it was both brand new and very cheap, which it was. This was to be Ezra's first trip out of Chicago since he arrived in the city after he was released from an Alabama road gang in 1944. He was dressed as he had been the day before, except for a change of shirt. When Neil greeted Ezra, he withheld his hand, not wishing to be scorned again. But Ezra surprised him by extending his own hand, which Neil grasped appreciatively. Neither man commented on the gesture.

Ezra grabbed the window seat. He explained to Neil that he wanted a good view because he had not traveled in nearly 10 years.

He then lowered his voice and added he also did not want to risk a white man hitting his arm or leg while trying to manage walking down the aisle of a swaying train. Once, on a troop train, a white man treated such an incidental touch as an intentional attempt by Ezra to trip him. He insulted Ezra and a fight appeared imminent until other soldiers intervened to end the matter. Ezra wanted nothing to interfere with the trip to Washington to find Clay's killer.

Neil was surprised that a white man would make such a scene and that Ezra would recall it so many years later. He was certain the white soldier forgot about it within days, if not minutes. Did Negroes remember every such attack forever, building a file in their head of slights by the white man?

Once the train was under way, and after a few minutes of idle chat about the condition of the train, the weather and how many days of travel Ezra packed for, both men reached into their bags. Neil had the folder from the Childress Agency. Ezra had *The Sea in a Bottle* by Albert Léon Guérard. Neil asked if it was a sea story.

"No," Ezra laughed gently. "The author is a literary critic and sort of a light-weight philosopher who teaches at Stanford. I read a favorable review in *The Times*. The reviewer said Guérard is a humanist who doesn't believe in the established religions. But he didn't sound like some kind of nihilist, like a Sartre. I'll let you borrow it if you're interested." His expectant look reminded Neil of King's expression when King told him about his wife and family, a look that anticipated a white man's astonishment and the Negro's amusement. Neil tried to cover-up by addressing something almost irrelevant.

"You mean the *Sun-Times*, don't you?" referring to the second morning paper in Chicago after *The Tribune*.

"No, *The Sunday New York Times*. We get it out here on Mondays. I have to take a trip to a Loop newsstand to get it, but they save it for me. The papers out here are terrible." Ezra opened his book and began to read it. Neil opened his folder and pretended to read it while considering the just completed conversation. He thought about his walk to the warehouse where Clay was murdered. It was less than a week ago, but felt longer. He could not imagine those poor Negroes reading philosophers, literary critics or *The Sunday New York Times*. It struck him that he couldn't imagine his brother, the dentist, or his brother-in-law, the commercial realtor, doing so, either. And certainly not himself. Neil began to read the yellowed contents of the folder, encumbered by a gnawing sense of intellectual inferiority to the man in the seat next to him.

The documents were bound at the top by a steel clip that went through holes punched in the top of the folder and in the documents themselves and was then bent and secured by another piece of metal. The whole contraption could be undone and the documents separated if necessary, but the documents were easily examined without doing so. The records were in reverse chronological order. On the top was an undated handwritten note in what appeared to be a feminine hand:

Any inquiries, call Aiken County, S.C., MAgnolia 843 immediately.

Peculiar, Neil thought. If the records were secret, why would someone need to be called about an inquiry? Mrs. Childress was adamant about not disclosing any information. And who would care about an adoption over 30 years ago except the infant looking for his birth family? Aiken County, S.C. must be rural. Five-digit telephone numbers were replaced by six and even seven digits in most big cities. Neil had heard of Aiken, but knew nothing about it. It was a long way from Chicago. Why would a baby put up for adoption in Chicago be of interest to anyone in South Carolina?

Next in the folder were several legal documents memorializing the adoption. Every page was stamped in red ink "FILED UNDER SEAL". They contained no information Neil did not already know. Another sheet listed four typewritten names, each of them introduced by "Mr. and Mrs." It was titled "Prospects." The Van Dykes were among those listed, but only their name was followed by the handwritten addendum "approved." These were obviously the names of couples introduced to the baby for possible adoption. Another document, also a single page, read:

Chapter Ten: Ezra and Neil

ACKNOWLDGMENT OF DELIVERY AND TERMS OF DELIVERY AND ACCEPTANCE

The Childress Agency (hereinafter, "The Agency") hereby acknowledges delivery of an INFANT NEGRO MALE (hereinafter, "said INFANT") by St. Mark's Christian Home, Atlanta, Georgia (hereinafter, "St. Mark's"). Said INFANT was born on February 20, 1922, has been examined by The Agency and appears to be in healthy condition.

IT IS AGREED between The Agency and St. Mark's that said INFANT is delivered for the purpose of putting said INFANT up for legal adoption.

IT IS FURTHER AGREED that St. Mark's warrants that all legal requirements of the State of Georgia for surrendering any and all rights of the birth mother to said INFANT have been complied with. St. Mark's further indemnifies The Agency for any costs or liabilities should it be determined that this warranty is invalid or breached.

IT IS FURTHER AGREED that The Agency shall not, under any circumstances, except breach of the warranty described herein, return said INFANT to St. Mark's.

IT IS FURTHER AGREED that The Agency shall not, under any circumstances, permit adoption of said INFANT to any person then residing in any of the several states of the United States which formerly were known as the Confederate States of America.

The document ended with three signature lines. Neil could read two of the three signatures. Over St. Mark's typed name was the signature of "Muriel Drucker." Mrs. Childress signed for her business. The signature for St. Mark's was dated February 24, 1922. Mrs. Childress' signature was dated March 1, 1922. Under those signatures was the following language:

> On behalf of St. Mark's, I certify the said INFANT was delivered in sound condition.

The signature below this sentence was illegible. It also was dated March 1, 1922.

There was nothing else in the folder.

Neil handed the folder to Ezra, who put down his book and began to read it. Neil stared past Ezra out the window at the steel mills of Northern Indiana without seeing them. He pondered many questions for which he had no answers. Were babies often transferred from one region to another for adoption? The baby who became Clay was shipped like a Railway Express package, signed for and delivered. Was that normal? He was sure that the last paragraph of the contract was not normal in an adoption. Who cared whether a baby was adopted in or out of a state that was in the Confederacy? Did a white father want the baby placed far away, afraid that an unsuspecting wife might notice the close resemblance of a local Negro child to her husband? Or did a Negro mother, proud of her infant son but forced to give him up, believe that he would have a better life outside the South? The Civil

Chapter Ten: Ezra and Neil

War had ended nearly sixty years before Clay was born. Neil knew that southerners, including most southern politicians in Washington, publicly worshiped the Confederate trinity – bigotry, state's rights and valor in a lost cause. But was anyone so beholden to these beliefs to insist on banishment of an innocent black baby from the South? Who could hate a baby so much to warrant such treatment?

There is a stronger emotion than even hate, Neil thought. It is shame. A white father ashamed of his rape. Or a mother ashamed of having been raped. The possibilities were endless if you were sufficiently imaginative. But all of them required emotional intensity – hate, shame and even pride came to mind.

Ezra interrupted Neil's contemplation. "There's something I don't understand about this whole thing. I don't mean that crazy business about the Confederacy, which is obviously weird. I mean how come a colored woman in the South went to some church home to have her baby?"

"Why not?"

"Money, for one thing. Not many colored could afford to pay for such a place. Maybe it was charity. But more than that. I'll grant you that Atlanta might be a more cosmopolitan place than Mobile or rural Alabama, where I grew up, but back in the '20s colored folk birthed their own babies. I never heard of anybody even going to the hospital to give birth back in those days." Ezra spoke softly so that others on the train would not hear.

"Maybe the white father paid for the care. Maybe she was ashamed and wanted the baby to be born away from home."

"Ashamed of what? Being raped by a white guy? She might be angry. She might want to get rid of the baby. And, yes, she might even feel ashamed of not being strong enough to fight him off. But where I come from, she'd stay with her own people. Not head for some charity place. I don't say it didn't happen. Lots of different kinds of people, and the world's always changin'. I just say I never heard of it and it wouldn't make sense where I come from."

"None of this makes much sense. What about this note with the Aiken phone number? What's that about? The paper isn't as old and yellow as the rest of the documents in the folder. Is it recent? Did they have five-digit numbers when you grew up in Alabama?"

"I can't remember. Didn't have a phone except when I lived in Mobile with a white family for a short time. I didn't use it 'cause I didn't know anybody else with a phone."

Both men were silent for a time, rolling possibilities over in their heads.

"We'll talk to Lorenzo King about what to do next," Neil said. He was uncertain whether to go to Atlanta or simply find out whose number was on the notepaper. Although the adoption papers raised interesting questions, it was not his job to determine Clay's biological parents; it was to find out who killed him. But Clay's trips to Chicago and Atlanta investigating the former were their only leads on the latter.

Chapter Ten: Ezra and Neil

Ezra and Neil resumed reading their books, but Ezra was anxious for conversation. "Were you always a cop before you were a PI?"

"I was in the war."

"You're a little young to have been in the war."

Neil sighed. "Not that one. Korea."

"Oh, sure. Sorry." Ezra softened a bit. "Were you in combat?"

"Yeah. Marine rifleman."

Ezra waited for more. There wasn't any more.

"Let me ask you a question, Ezra. That guy who held a gun on us, he said you hated white people. Is that true?"

"It was once. Now I just don't think about white people very much. When I lived in the South, there were white people all around and in my life. They owned the land. We paid 'em the rent. They pretty much ran our lives, if not day-to-day, then in general. And they were always around. For the usual reasons, I hated them."

"What are the 'usual reasons'?"

"Aw, man. You know. They treated the Negro like shit. Every time some colored guy tries to get ahead, he's pushed back down. Same is true in the North, except you can avoid the white man in Chicago. There's nothing I do that requires me to deal with a white person in my normal daily life in Chicago, except maybe a white bank teller or some store clerk."

"So they don't control your life in Chicago?"

"Sure they do. They keep us from moving outta' the slums. They keep us outta' the colleges. They provide us with crappy schools and then say we aren't educated enough for good jobs. But it's a lot more distant. More the system than any white guy you run into personally. In the South, it used to be that the white man needed us to clear his fields. That was a specific white man and his family and friends. It was the white farmer versus the colored field hand. They needed us and hated us at the same time. We usually hated 'em back. It was very personal. In the North, I don't think as many white folk hate us as just sort of try not to think about us until they need some job done they don't want to do."

"So you don't hate the white man like you once did?"

"I just decided I was wastin' too much mental energy hating the white man, worrying about the white man. Now I focus on black folk. If the white folk don't care about me, I ain't gonna' care about them. No profit in it."

"I'll ask it again: Do you still hate the white man?"

"I don't hate you, if that's what you're asking me. At least, you haven't given me any reason to. If you're asking me overall, then I say I don't give it much thought. But if you require a yes or no answer, then yes, I still hate the white man."

"Isn't that being just as bigoted as the white man?"

"No, of course not. The whites have all the power. I hate the white man for not sharing the power. If we got some of that power, we wouldn't have all these problems. Or, if we did, we could fight back. I don't think it's meaningful to talk about bigotry among people who haven't got any power." Ezra was having a hard time keeping his voice low as he warmed

Chapter Ten: Ezra and Neil

to his subject. A glance back from a young white woman in the next row caused him to return to a lower voice. He did not want any trouble.

"Is that what your Black National Strength part is all about — getting power?"

"Well, I suppose. But it's really more about getting money for my mission. The Democrats control everything in Chicago. There hasn't been a Republican mayor since I've been in Chicago and I don't expect one any time soon. They tend to the South Side. South Side's got a colored alderman. We get a share of the spoils. No way my little party is going to be a political force. But it helps call attention to the mission. The white politicians don't know how small my party is, but they throw us some money to keep us quiet. Doesn't cost 'em enough to care. Hell, anybody asks me, I'm happy to say I support the mayor, if that's what it takes. Some coloreds are afraid of anything about empowerment, but more and more think it's the only way. And I view the education of colored kids — the sound education of colored kids — as necessary to get power, if we ever do."

"Sounds like a political speech to me," Neil said. Ezra, who leaned toward Neil as he spoke to convey the force of his convictions, sat back in his seat and grinned sheepishly.

"Maybe some day it will be. For somebody. But no black man charged with murder is gonna' get elected. So I'm out."

"You must be excited about these cases at the Supreme Court about desegregating public schools."

Unanimous Verdict

Ezra laughed loudly, causing several other passengers to look at him. "You are one goofy know-nothing white man, Neil. What's the Supreme Court? Nine old guys without guns? If they rule the schools have to be desegregated, it'll be by issuing some pieces of paper. That's all. If pieces of paper made the black man genuinely free and equal, why, we'd already be as strong as Superman. Emancipation proclamations, constitutional amendments, Reconstruction laws, thick books by white sociologists lamenting the condition of the poor colored man – stack 'em up and they're probably as high as the Washington Monument. A few more pages won't make any difference."

"I wouldn't be so sure. There's a lot of goofy know-nothing white men who will take a Supreme Court ruling seriously."

"Oh, it'll be serious alright. Any black parents who send their kid to an all-white school in the South thinking the Supreme Court said it was OK, they're going to know it's serious. That kid will come home with a few broken bones, if he comes home at all. Who are those parents going to complain to? The Supreme Court? Is the Supreme Court going to send out a posse to go after whoever beat up the kid?"

"Well, you have to admit it will be a start."

"We've been in the 'start' position for nearly a hundred years. If Eisenhower sends in the troops to back up the Supreme Court, then I might agree with you. That ain't gonna' happen."

Chapter Ten: Ezra and Neil

During the rest of the trip, Neil finished *The High and the Mighty.* Ezra seemed lost in contemplation, looking out the train window. Neil borrowed Ezra's philosophy book and quickly fell asleep reading it.

Ezra was lucky, he reminded himself. He was riding in a clean train to Washington, D.C., a few dollars in his pocket, with a worthwhile, if perhaps futile, goal of finding a black man's killer. He was even sitting next to a white man and, for the moment at least, they were acting as equals. He was melancholy, nevertheless. Neil seemed to be a decent enough fellow. He showed guts going after Bark in the Childress office. But he was so clueless about the difficult lives of black folk that he actually believed that what the Supreme Court might do would make a difference to them.

Ezra had four years of formal schooling, all of it while his older sister was a housekeeper and cook for a family in Mobile that agreed to take 10-year-old Ezra as a boarder in return for yard work and serving as a messenger for the family business, a cotton brokerage. The white family thought of themselves as enlightened and did not object to Ezra attending the local colored school as long as his domestic chores could be completed. Ezra's sister was a bigger problem. She had no education and told Ezra that since he would be returning to the cotton fields north of Mobile, he had no need for one, either. She already resented his ability to read.

Unanimous Verdict

Ezra had taught himself to read with the help of a part-time preacher on the cotton plantation and the only book available to them — a well-worn copy of the Bible. He loved reading and wanted to read and learn more than Scripture.

The North Mobile Primary School for Colored was a four-room frame structure built for the colored in about 1900. In 1925, Ezra's first year, plumbing was installed at the back of the building — one bathroom for both boys and girls. Each classroom had a wood-fired heating stove, some old student desks handed down from the white schools, a teacher's desk and a bookcase, also all handed down from the white schools. The school was supposed to teach students through the eighth grade, so classes were combined among the four rooms. This was not a big problem. So few students continued to attend school after the fifth grade that grades 6-8 could be in one room. The children dropped out to return to the fields or to take jobs in town or to take care of their younger siblings. Sometimes, they and their families simply disappeared, moving away with no notice.

As the B&O coach moved through Youngstown on the way to Pittsburgh, Ezra thought once again of Mrs. Washington, his teacher during his last two years of school. Mrs. Washington was young, very pretty, and stern with her students. She told them she expected great things of them. She wanted them to attend Fiske University in Nashville, as she had done. She told them to be men and women of courage and responsibility. That required attention in class, she

264

told them. She brooked no horseplay. Ezra, who was serious about education, loved Mrs. Washington.

After a couple of years ignoring the approved school textbook misrepresentations of black history, Mrs. Washington taught them as lies. She concluded that it was not enough to teach her students the truth; they must be taught to recognize what was false. The Civil War was her passion. It was her revival meeting. Ezra Lowell had recited her lessons both to himself and to others many times over the years. It was why he personally taught the Civil War and Reconstruction eras to all of the students at his own school in Chicago. Doing so not only provided the colored children with a good education. It was a tribute to Mrs. Washington. He easily called up her lessons in his mind as his companion slept and the B&O traveled the tracks east with its calming bumpty-bump.

"Your book says that most slave-owners were kindly and that the slaves were satisfied with their situation until agitated by Yankee reformers. We know better than that, don't we class?" she asked. Her students responded enthusiastically with information about slave rebellions, the harsh living conditions of slaves and how they were forbidden to learn to read and write. Mrs. Washington did not sanitize her presentation for an impressionable age. If the monographs she had laboriously obtained from the libraries at black colleges to correct the school textbooks said there was rape, she described for the children what rape was. If the monographs described bloody, fatal beatings and whippings, her class knew about them.

Unanimous Verdict

"The Civil War was about abolishing slavery." Mrs. Washington called the textbook claims the war was about the rights of the states nonsense. "It was about the rights of the states to allow slavery, plain and simple. If the Civil War was about states rights, and the South lost, why is the South Jim Crow? Why is the Supreme Court declaring so many federal laws a violation of states rights? Looks like states rights is alive and well to me. It was states rights only to bring back slavery as Jim Crow. That's all the South cared about and they won in the end."

She brooked no defense of slavery, though many defenses were in the white written textbooks. "Eighteen hundred years after Christ. Thousands more years after the Jews found freedom from the Egyptians. In the United States, there was still slavery. No other great nation practiced slavery. No other great nation debated whether there should be slavery. Only our Founding Fathers, class, great as they might have been in other ways, did not see fit to abolish slavery. Instead, they counted each slave as three-fifths of a person. It is right at the front of the Constitution. It is in Article 1, Section 2. George Washington, Thomas Jefferson, Ben Franklin and the rest, they couldn't wait to call the Negro only half a man. They put it on page one of the Constitution.

"Now you look at yourselves, class. Are you missing your legs? Are you missing your arms? Is your head on the other side of the room? Are you unable to speak? Are you unable to think? Are you only three-fifths of a human being? No! You have everything the white man has. Everything the white woman has. You have everything except equality with the white man. You don't have equality only for one reason: The white man holds the power." Right on, Mrs. Washington. Ezra smiled into the train window. His life and that of every person of color he knew had taught him the truth of her words.

"Thousands of years after the last white slave in this world died, the South in 1861 was defending black slavery and most white southerners are still defending it. They went to war over it and they are still mad they lost. But they kept the power. They lost it briefly, but they took it back. And it is up to you boys and girls to take it from them again some day." Her class, fourth and fifth graders, was in rapt attention throughout Mrs. Washington's oration, but jumped from their seats, applauded and yelled when she concluded. At least for a day, these children were inspired to be courageous for their race.

Ezra and the other children needed Mrs. Washington's presentations. All of them heard adults complain about segregation and call the white man names. But few parents explained how segregation came to be, other than that colored folk used to be slaves. The assumption was that Jim Crow inevitably followed slavery, and there was nothing to be done about it. Not many parents knew the real history themselves. Mrs. Washington told the children their condition was not an accident, or an act of God or nature, but of politics and the domination of whites.

"What is created by man can be changed by man," she said. Ezra had a firm memory of Mrs. Washington sitting on the edge of her desk, facing the class, chalk in hand. "And that includes change by the colored man." She transitioned easily from the Civil War to the subject of Booker T. Washington, the only Negro held in high regard by the board-mandated history textbook. She gave Washington his due, reading portions of *Up From Slavery* and emphasizing that he was a reformer for his time. But she supplemented her instruction with lessons about W.E.B. DuBois, the Niagara Movement and the founding of the NAACP. These subjects, viewed by the school board as too radical, definitely were not in the textbook. Her coverage of all of these issues was so extensive that she could devote only a couple of days to World War I before classes were suspended for the summer.

Ezra remembered asking Mrs. Washington the question he asked himself when he was a youngster: Why do the whites hate the Negro so much? She looked at him with a gentle smile, her well-cared for teeth gleaming from her deep black face framed by carefully marcelled black hair.

"Why, Ezra, the reason is fear." Ezra in his re-imagining must have looked troubled, because his teacher went on to explain, addressing the whole class as a teaching opportunity. "Whites are not relieved by God of a conscience. They know they have enslaved and oppressed the black man for hundreds of years. If you did something like that, wouldn't you be afraid that one day your victim would want to pay you back? Especially if your victim could look around him every day and see that he was imprisoned by you? Look at the date in the first two or three pages of your textbook, where it says 'copyright'. What dates do you see?" she asked the class. Children called out a variety of dates: 1903, 1910, 1912. The latest was 1914, 13 years and one world war ago. "The white children do not have books that old. They wore these out and gave them to us. Every time you read these old text books you should be reminded of your mistreatment." Ezra's question had lit a fuse. Mrs. Washington warmed to her subject.

"How many of your parents voted in the Mobile election last winter? How many voted for president in 1924?" No hands went up. "Well of course not. The white man is so afraid of the colored folk that he won't even let us vote." Her voice was reverberating through the small frame school. She was shouting. She paused to regain her composure and lower her volume. "When we got the vote sixty years ago, we threw out all those segregation laws and tried to educate everyone and make sure everyone had enough to eat and that black men could vote. Now we got Jim Crow, lousy books and not a single black man in the Alabama legislature, even though we account for nearly half the population.

"Ezra, wouldn't you be wantin' to keep people down after treating them like that? Wouldn't you be afraid of what they might do if they had the power? Does that answer your question?"

Ezra, taken aback like the rest of the class by the flood of emotion he had unleashed in his teacher, meekly responded: "Yes Ma'am." But, Ezra considered, the question had remained with him for many years as he sought an answer for the modern-day: Why do they hate us so? Finally, he had given up his quest, concluding there was no answer any more rational than the one he got from Mrs. Washington in the sixth grade: They are afraid.

Unanimous Verdict

Neil's nap and Ezra's reverie were broken by arrival at Washington's Union Station shortly after 11 p.m. Neil was surprised to find Lorenzo King waiting at the gate to greet them.

"You don't look nearly as bad as I thought you would," King laughed, examining the red bruises still visible at the side of Neil's head. "You must be Mr. Lowell. I'm Lorenzo King. We spoke on the phone." King extended his hand. Neil noted to himself that Ezra took it without hesitation. For a moment, he was jealous of the bond between them. After further exchange of pleasantries, the three men went to the all-night coffee shop in the station to fill King in on the adoption papers. As Neil expected, King was not at a loss for an opinion about how to proceed.

"First, we don't tell Mrs. Van Dyke about any of this unless and until we have to. This may not lead us anywhere and I don't think we need to open additional wounds for a grieving mother by dwelling on the circumstances of the adoption or that Clayton committed a crime." Lou said this as an agreed conclusion, with no evident blame placed on Ezra, who had assisted in the crime.

Neil stirred his coffee and nodded. He was surprised that King did not question Ezra's arrival in Washington or his participation in the investigation. It was as if he expected it.

"Second, let's find out whose phone number is on that sheet of paper down in Aiken. We can do that easily. I'll just call the number and ask. Can't hurt."

"It might hurt," Neil replied. "It will alert someone to our interest in the case."

Chapter Ten: Ezra and Neil

"I'll just say it's the wrong number when I identify myself. Maybe you should place the call. Some folks think blacks and whites have different sounding voices."

"OK." Neil would spend the rest of the weekend considering if he had other objections. "I think I should also go to Atlanta."

"I'm going, too," Ezra said. "It's part of my vacation." Neil liked Ezra. He didn't mind his company. But he was unhappy when King said he was coming along, too.

"But I don't want to take the train to Atlanta," King announced. "You got a car, kid? Let's take your car."

"I don't have a car," Neil said. He was tempted to add that it was a sign of King's own prejudices that he assumed all white men owned cars. "Let's just take the train."

"I do not take trains to the South. I refuse to be shoved into a colored car."

"But those are illegal now."

"Not in practice. You start getting the pressure to change cars in Alexandria and it just gets worse as you move south. Most coloreds are embarrassed into moving. They won't force me to the back, but it's uncomfortable being pressured all the time. I'd rather skip it. Plus, I don't want to give Mrs. Van Dyke's money to the Southern Line."

"I agree," Ezra said.

"I thought you hadn't been on a train since the war. How do you know what the practices are on the Southern Line?"

271

"I trust Mr. King here. And I don't need any reminders about why I ought to hate the white man."

"Ok. Ok. I think I know where I can get a car for a few days. I'll work on it over the weekend. Let's meet in your office tomorrow to make that call."

"No. Tomorrow is Saturday. If it's a business, they might be closed. It can wait until Monday," King said with a finality that foreclosed further debate. "Mr. Lowell is staying at my house. I plan to show him the sights over the weekend. We'll see you Monday, Neil. Is 10 o'clock all right?" The two colored men rose to leave as Neil nodded his head.

"Don't you think you should consult with Mr. Lowell before making him stay with you?"

"I did. We spoke by telephone several times this week. He told me you did a fine job in Chicago." King and Lowell then left Neil with his mouth hanging open in surprise. They were working together behind his back. Not only were they not a team, but there was an implicit pact sealed by skin color that Neil was not a part of. Neil was angry. He needed a drink. He checked his watch and headed for Pennsy's.

As usual, the Inn was very crowded at nearly midnight on Friday. Neil squeezed through the door and looked for anyone he knew. There were many familiar faces of Pennsy's regulars, but he didn't know their names. He saw Mike Q. at a booth in the back. Mike was facing the front door, sitting with two people who were facing the back wall.

Chapter Ten: Ezra and Neil

Based on the head of hair, one looked as if she could be Jennifer. Neil pushed his way to the back of the bar.

"Hi, Mike." He looked at the pair of heads opposite Mike. "Jennifer, great to see you." He bent down to give her a kiss. She smelled heavily of alcohol. This was the end of her evening, not the beginning.

"Hello, Neil. I'd like you to meet Ryan Hobbs. He works with Lisa on the Hill." Drunk or not, Jennifer's introduction was coldly formal. Hobbs looked as though he'd just stepped out of a men's fashion magazine. The hairs on the back of Neil's neck stood up as his expectations stood down. He was out with Jennifer and Ryan Hobbs was in.

"How do you do, Neil. I've heard a lot about you." Hobbs' grin was like a spotlight. How could anyone in their twenties have teeth that looked like they never touched food? Hobbs' grip was firm – too firm. Was he making some sort of punctuation mark? A physical way of saying "I win – loser!"

"Not all bad, I hope." Neil needed a minute to catch his breath from this blow to his solar plexus. He turned to Mike Q.

"Mike, can you get me a loaner car on Monday?"

"Are you thinking of buying a car? I can't just loan one out unless you are planning to buy."

"Sure. I'm thinking maybe one of those two-tones you're always talking about." Neil didn't like lying to a friend. Worse, Neil probably would be guilty of car theft if Mike ever found out he drove the car to Georgia.

"A Bel Air? That's not for you. You need a 'Vette, I tell ya'. A Corvette. A Bel Air is a car for folks with kids and stuff, I tell ya'."

"That's all my budget can afford. I'd like to come out and pick one up to use for a day or two."

"That's Neil Endicott – big spender!" Jennifer said, sounding woozy. "Neil, at least your imagination is the same size as your budget." Jennifer was trying to be funny, but she was merely insulting. Neil ignored her. Mike, sensing a sale coming, did too.

"I think we have one that we repossessed. You can have it for a week. No more. And we will need a $100 deposit. I can bring it by your house. No problem."

"Great. Monday morning? Before 10?"

"No problem. But have the hundred ready."

Neil had only about $120 left from Mrs. Van Dyke's expense payment. He would drop by to see her over the weekend. With business matters settled, he turned to Jennifer and Ryan.

"Where you from, Ryan?"

"Cleveland. My father's into steel."

"He owns a big steel company," Jennifer squealed, the effects of alcohol and happiness.

"No. It's a publicly traded company. He's the chief executive."

"So why are you in Washington?" Neil ordered a Ballantine Ale. He hoped it came fast so he could drink it fast and run from Pennsy's before his small talk ran out and he risked saying something he might regret. Suddenly, his ribs and head began to hurt again.

Chapter Ten: Ezra and Neil

"Neil! What happened to your face." Jennifer finally saw he was wounded. Mike didn't notice.

"Ran into a door. The door won."

"How do you run into a door with the side of your head?" Mike asked.

"Confidential," Neil said, forcing himself to laugh.

"I got to *go* to the head," Ryan said, causing Jennifer to laugh again at the connection between Neil's facial injury and the slang for the bathroom.

"Me, too," added Mike. Both left. Jennifer wasted no time.

"Neil, I think I'm in love with Ryan."

"What's not to love? He looks like a fashion model."

"Yes, but you're cute in a different way, at least when your face isn't beat up."

"Thanks. That's the nicest thing you've said to me in weeks."

"No, seriously. It's not all physical. You know me better than that. But Ryan's really got his head on straight. He knows what he wants to do and he's got a plan to do it. I guess he's got what they call 'direction' in his life."

"Ah, yes. Direction. I didn't think you took directions from men very well."

"You know what I mean. Ryan respects me. He doesn't belittle me."

"Neither do I."

"I know. You belittle yourself instead. It's charming at first, but you can't live your life being so down on yourself. And you need to figure out what you're going to do with your life. I worry about you. I worry about how sad you are when you wake up in the middle of the night.

"I love you, too, Neil, but not in the same way that I love Ryan. I can see a life together with Ryan. I couldn't ever see that with you."

Neil's ale wasn't touched. His stomach was grinding. His head was aching. His ribs were killing him. Although she didn't intend it, Jennifer was torturing him.

"What are your plans?" Neil asked, looking again for a way out.

"We talked about getting married in the fall. I've met his parents."

"How long has this been going on?"

"I met him a month ago and things have been moving along. I didn't want to tell you until I was sure."

"So you were with him all weekend?"

"I was, but we were at Mom's house. I wanted to introduce her to Ryan. I couldn't very well tell you. I wanted to talk to you face-to-face." This was the worst. Neil knew he didn't love Jennifer. But he thought she could be trusted. He confided in her. She was his friend, at least. Did everybody he knew work behind his back? He was desperate to get outside where he could breathe and was away from people.

"Well, I hope we can be friends still," Neil said lamely. "Good luck to you and Ryan. Send me a wedding invitation."

Chapter Ten: Ezra and Neil

"We will. And don't be a stranger in the meantime." Jennifer rose as Neil did and gave him a wet emotional kiss as he started to leave the table. Neil did not return the passion. "Tell Mike he can have my ale. I didn't touch it," he said when Jennifer pulled away.

He kicked an empty can on the sidewalk. What was it she said? "Direction." He lacked "direction." What the fuck did that mean? But Neil knew what it meant. And he knew Jennifer was right. His life was a mess. Mrs. Van Dyke hired him as a desperate last choice. His girlfriend dumped him because he has no future. King and Lowell plotted together to take over the investigation and leave him behind. His own dad and his brother treated him like a house pet – cute, lovable and irresponsible. "His own little detective agency. So cute. When will Neil learn to roll over? Fetch the newspaper?" His anger, resentment and humiliation pushed up his adrenalin. Neil forgot his physical aches and pains, at least for the few blocks it took him to get home.

Chapter Eleven: Road Trip, April 30 - May 7, 1954

Mrs. Van Dyke said she expected Neil when he arrived on Saturday morning. She said Lorenzo King already had already reported to her. He needed money for a trip to Atlanta. Neil said he required the same thing. She wrote him a check for another $500 as she asked how the investigation was proceeding. Neil asked what King had told her. She said he was very mysterious, but that they were following some good leads.

"Did you know that Clay went to Atlanta shortly before he died," Neil asked.

"Why, yes. He said it had to do with his adoption. He was excited when he left, but when he returned he told me the news wasn't what he expected. He was very down and unhappy." This was consistent with what Louis Charles had told Neil at the library.

"Did he say why he was disappointed? What he had found?"

"No, and I didn't ask. I hoped this meant he would give up the folly of finding his birth parents, whether they are white or black. The less said of it, the better.

"I don't know why you think this has anything to do with his murder. Frankly, I'm disappointed in you and Mr. King for spending so much time and money following this angle."

Neil gave a moment's thought to showing her the note found on her son's body, but decided against doing so until the murderer was identified. The note was too brutal and he doubted Mrs. Van Dyke would be concerned about a white cop losing his job for a cover-up of her son's murder. She would release it to the press immediately.

"So far we haven't got any other leads. Your boy wasn't involved in crimes and didn't have any serious enemies that we know of. If you can think of something else for us to pursue, we'll be happy to, I'm sure."

Alice Henshaw answered the door when Neil knocked. She looked radiant in a yellow sundress, bare legs and open-toed sandals. She smelled of some fragrance that was clean, not overpowering, and not too sweet. Perhaps it was only her bath soap. Neil liked it. Her long hair was bundled at the back of her head, showing off the high cheekbones and permanently tanned skin of her Indian ancestry. Her green eyes were luminescent and happy to see Neil. He wanted her to hold him, to comfort him. He didn't know if he wanted her to mother him or make love to him, but he could accept either.

The odds that either of these fantasies would come true, not high to begin with, were lowered to zero when Max greeted Neil in the living room sitting in his favorite chair.

"Where have you been?" Alice queried before Neil could take a seat. "Your parents have been worried sick. You have not answered your telephone in days." No one but King knew he was going to Chicago.

"I've been around," Neil lied. "I don't stand by the phone waiting for my parents to call."

Chapter Eleven: Road Trip

"Well you should call them today to tell them you're OK. They've been calling us, as if we kept track of you. Max and Kenny rang your apartment doorbell last night, but no answer.

"Are you sleeping somewhere else?" Alice's last question rang with both curiosity and hope. "Jennifer's, perhaps?"

"Jennifer and I are kaput. No, I was home. Just keeping some odd hours lately. Lots of work."

"How are you getting along with that Negro detective, anyway?" Neil was startled. He had forgotten all about his conversation with Alice at Monica's a week earlier. He wanted to tell Alice that King and Lowell were ganging up on him, but he knew Max would not be sympathetic and probably would mention the situation to his father, who would find some reason for ridicule or offer useless counsel. As an answered prayer, Max used his cane to pull himself to a standing position and announced his departure. He had a wedding to cover at Foundry Methodist. Kenny was going to help him take pictures. It was a fifty-dollar engagement and Max could not afford to be late. Alice summoned Kenny, who was excited about helping his Dad. He hefted a bag of camera equipment, which was large and heavy for a boy his size. Max picked up an even bigger bag and they wobbled off to catch a streetcar.

Alice was standing as her husband and son left. So was Neil. Neil made little secret of his admiration as he again scanned her body. Alice gave Neil a look he had not seen from her before. Was she interested in him? In a different way than in the past?

Neil's emotions had been taut for days. He was excited about the investigation, but forced to temper his enthusiasm with his new Negro partners, who saw him as an outsider. Trying to deal with them was another source of tension. His girlfriend had dumped him. Neil was desperate for something to release the pressure – something exciting and care-free.

Alice resumed her seat on the sofa while Neil returned to the armchair. Alice crossed her legs, causing the sundress to rise and tighten around her thighs. The "low grade burn" Alice always gave Neil was suddenly many degrees higher.

"So, I was asking you about your Negro partner," Alice said matter-of-factly. Whatever unusual interest that had registered in her eyes while standing had disappeared.

"We've got another Negro on the case now. I think they are ganging up on me. They seem to be sharing information without including me."

"Example?"

"Well, I can't give you information about the case. But they are making arrangements, such as where this new guy should sleep. That's just what I know they talked about. It's not much, but I think there's more. I don't know if they don't trust me or just don't like me because I'm white."

"Could be either, or something entirely different. But I saw Mrs. Van Dyke this week at an NAACP meeting. She thanked me for putting her in touch with you. She said you are a sweet young man."

Chapter Eleven: Road Trip

Neil felt his face burn. He was a little old to treat "sweet young man" as a compliment. It was belittling. Everything that had happened to him since taking on the Van Dyke case made him feel small and useless except overpowering Bark, and he couldn't tell anyone about that.

"What do you intend to do about it?" Alice continued.

"I don't know."

"I have no suggestions except to stick it out. I doubt they're getting together is really directed at you. Probably just a couple of colored guys enjoying each other's company. Is this other guy older than you are?"

"By about 15 years, I'd say. Still, he's 10 or 20 years younger than the guy I told you about last week."

"Don't feel bad. I attend these meetings of the NAACP committee Mrs. Van Dyke is on. There are about six of us, including two men. I'm the only white person on the committee. The others socialize with each other all the time, as far as I can tell. I've never been invited to any of their houses except for committee meetings."

"Have you invited them here?" Neil asked. Alice scrunched her eyebrows together in a concerned expression, as if she had just been reminded of a problem.

"No, I haven't. That's a very good point. I think Max and I should invite one or two couples over for dinner. Good idea, Neil. I'm embarrassed for not coming up with that idea myself. I think we just get accustomed to our social rules and don't even think about them. Would you like to come?"

"I'm pretty busy."

"Oh, that's too bad. Why? Now that you've broken up with Jennifer I thought you might have more time. What's with the breakup?"

"She's found another guy. But she also said I lack 'direction' and don't have any plans for my life."

"Is she right?"

"I guess so."

"My, my. No direction. No plans. And all of 24 years old." Alice mocked Jennifer's concerns. Then she turned serious. "What do you believe in, Neil? It could be a cause, or a religion, or a calling. Like Max is called to photography. I'm trying to make my contribution, small as it is, to civil rights. Of course, I also have a family and have to work. Your Dad believes in journalism and I guess your Mom believes in caring for her family. What is your lodestar?"

"What's a lodestar?" Neil thought he knew the answer, but he was trying to buy more time for himself to come up with an answer to the question.

"It's a star used for guidance, but I'm using it to mean a guiding ideal."

"A long time ago, when I graduated from high school, I wanted to be a policeman. I guess I also wanted a family, a nice house, raise some kids. None of that is important to me now. I mean, it's important, but not for me."

"What caused you to change your mind?"

Chapter Eleven: Road Trip

Neil opted for the simplest explanation. "I was bored by the beat after Korea, and sick of taking orders about the smallest things. I wanted to be on my own."

"OK, but what about the rest? The family and stuff?"

Neil sat pensively. The Korea pictures came flooding into his brain as they always did when conversation turned metaphysical. Bodies blown up. Bullets through the heads of men you were just speaking to. The rattling of his Browning Automatic Rifle and the distant vision of men he had never met but still hated falling to the ground, anonymous victims of his personal killing machine. And, of course, the pleading eyes of Elijah Lincoln.

"I guess the war. Korea. All that death. For what? Now Korea is back where it was before the invasion. But even if it wasn't, why did all those people die? Wouldn't my kids just get sent to war? It doesn't make sense."

"That's crap Neil. I'm surprised at you. You came back from the war without physical damage. You are lucky, not someone to feel sorry for. You can do whatever you want. Those other guys died. It was terrible. What did you expect? It was a war."

Neil was taken aback by Alice's fierce reply.

"Remember, I lost a brother in Europe. My husband lost a leg. I guess that war was a 'better war' because we actually won, but that doesn't make things any better for my brother or my family. Mark is as dead in France as he would be in Korea or if he got hit by a truck on Massachusetts Avenue.

"What's your logic? Because we are all gonna' die some day there's no point in living? That's the point of living – live to the fullest."

"But I'm haunted by this. By these deaths. I can't get past it."

"Then see a shrink or grow up. But don't just wallow in useless memories of tragedies in the past. My Mom died of cancer when she was my age. Every extra day I live is a day in memory of her. If these guys in Korea were such buddies, maybe you ought to think about honoring them by doing something with your own life."

Alice stopped suddenly. Her words were harsher, her tone angrier, than she had intended. "I'm sorry, Neil. I didn't mean to get so upset. I guess it's because I worry about you. Would you like something to drink? I mean, I could get you a Scotch or a Coke."

"A Coke would be fine." Both of them rose and Neil followed Alice into the kitchen. Alice turned her back to Neil to reach for a glass in a cupboard. On impulse, for fun, Neil put his hands on her waist, spun her around with a glass in her hand and kissed her. He was gentle at first, but when she responded with her tongue, he pulled her closer and reached into her mouth with his own tongue. He pushed Alice's back against the sink and lowered himself, also pulling her forward so he could continue kissing her while exciting both of them. He was erect against Alice's crotch, hidden by at least two layers of clothing. He released Alice's back with one hand and moved the hand to her breast.

Chapter Eleven: Road Trip

At that point, Alice pushed him away.

"Is this what you want to do?" Alice said breathlessly, eyeing the bulge in Neil's trousers. Her voice was questioning, not angry, and left him the decision how to proceed.

"Don't you?"

"I don't know." She bit her lip. She looked frightened. Neil had known her for as long as he could remember. He had known her husband and was at her son's baptism. But she was gorgeous and sexy and utterly desirable.

Neil felt himself go limp. He realized he could not go through with it. He backed away.

"I... I'm sorry. I guess I should go now," Neil said sheepishly.

"Absolutely not. It was as much my fault as yours. You kissed and I responded. I am not going to let you leave feeling guilty about something that really never happened. Here. Drink this Coke." Alice poured one for herself and the pair went back to the living room and sat as before.

"Now that we've done that, let's agree not to do it again," Alice said.

"Would you have continued?"

"I don't know. Probably. It was exciting. But it would have been a foolish thing to do. I'm glad you stopped us."

"You did, with your question."

"But I asked that more for you to encourage me. You didn't. I'm grateful. Not many men could stop like that. Why did you?"

"Friendship, loyalty to you, Max and the boys. Making love to you would have been wonderful, but it would ruin our friendship. It would make us both traitors."

"Maybe. Maybe not. I've never cheated on Max, but lots of people cheat all the time and say they still love their spouse and stay friends with their lover. I wonder if I could be like that." She paused and considered Neil, her mouth turning to a half-frown. Her voice softened. Her tone was friendly but concerned.

"You have a decent morality, Neil. You worry about how you behave and how it affects other people. Lots of folks don't do that. You have a good heart. You have to find a place to apply it. You know what I think?"

"I have a feeling you'll tell me."

"I think you worry too much about pleasing your family, especially your Dad. He complains to Max and me all the time about how you should be on some big money-making project or joining one of the professions, a lawyer, a doctor or, of course, a dentist. The hell with that. I can't see you doing any of that stuff."

"I haven't done a very good job pleasing him so far. That's sure."

"But you still worry about it. It may come out as resentment sometimes, but it's in your head and it's a better reason for failure than your dead friends in the war. It's very Freudian to want to please your parents. But forget about it. Do what you want." Alice paused, considering what to say next. She reached a decision.

Chapter Eleven: Road Trip

"Your father wouldn't have done what you did just now."

"What do you mean? In the kitchen?"

"Yes. Years ago, when you were just a toddler, your father grabbed me in almost the same way. I was single, not even 20. Only he didn't stop. I begged him to stop, but he ripped my blouse off and started tearing at my skirt. He didn't stop until I grabbed his dick and squeezed it and twisted it as hard as I could. He yowled in pain." Alice smiled at the recollection. "I smile now, but it was horrifying. With you I was tempted to go ahead. I wasn't married then. I could do as I pleased. But I thought of your mom and the kids and how guilty I probably would feel later. Max isn't much in bed nowadays, and a younger man is very tempting. Maybe I was naïve then or I'm craven now. I don't know. But I didn't want to sleep with your Dad. He didn't care. If I hadn't struggled so much, it would have been rape."

"Jesus Christ!" It was all Neil could think of in response. Then: "Did you report him to the police?"

"Of course not. And we haven't spoken of it – ever. You are the only other person who knows about it. Please don't tell your father. It was a long time ago."

"Why are you telling me now?"

"I'd say there was a little incident in the kitchen just now that made it relevant. But also, I don't want you to think you are somehow less than your father or your brother and sister. Your Dad didn't do what's right with me and he has plenty of other flaws. You are flawed, too, like all of us. But you're at least as good as your Dad and likely better. Don't let him push you around."

"Ok. But that's quite a revelation. I always thought of Dad as the stalwart guy who kept his emotions under control."

"You only see him at home. Plus you're his youngest son. Max says he's known for a vicious hair-trigger temper at *The Star*."

Alice crossed her legs again and Neil was worried he would get excited again – physical intimacy seemed even more possible after a frank discussion and shared confidences. It was time to leave. He wasn't at all sure how resolved he was to keep his hands off of Alice. He thanked her and they shared a quick, platonic kiss on the cheek. He couldn't get the picture of Alice and even more intensely, the feel of Alice and the smell of her, out of his mind the rest of the day. He thought about her body as he drifted into sleep that night.

Neil was at King's office at exactly 10 a.m. Monday, May 3. He drove over in the nearly-new Chevrolet Bel Air which Mike Q. had delivered as promised earlier in the morning. Mike called it a "two tone green," but Neil thought it was more like green and turquoise. At least it had an automatic transmission. No radio, though.

King and Lowell were laughing when Neil entered. He thought they already were laughing about him, but Lowell explained that King was explaining the joke plaques on the wall. Neil asked the men about their weekend.

Chapter Eleven: Road Trip

"We saw enough granite to fill the Grand Canyon," King said.

"Lincoln Memorial, Jefferson Memorial, Washington Monument and the Smithsonian," Ezra added. "He ran me ragged. But we had fun. Met Mrs. King. She's a great cook. First home cooked meal in a long time. Ham, greens, yams — old fashioned cooking."

King quickly grew serious. "Let's make that call." He asked for the long distance operator and gave her the number. The only sound in the room while he waited for the connection was of his own pencil tapping his desktop. He handed the phone to Neil.

"Hello. Have I reached Magnolia 843 in Aiken County, South Carolina?"

"Oh, good. With whom am I speaking?"

"Mrs. Roach? This is Leopold Radditz, of Radditz Rugs in … in Aiken. I believe we have a rug to deliver." Neil paused.

"I was given this number. Where are you located?"

"River's Edge? I mean what street address."

"No street address?"

"I apologize for not knowing it. But the address I have says South Carolina Route 9."

"That's not around you. Then I have the wrong number. I'm sorry to have bothered you."

Neil hung up the phone.

"Leopold Radditz? Where the hell did you get that name?" Ezra asked, grinning.

"Name of a guy I knew in the Army," Neil replied. "I had a harder time naming any town in the area. I guessed that there's a town in Aiken County called Aiken. Guess it worked."

"What did she say? We couldn't hear what she said. What was the name again?"

"Roach. Mrs. Roach. Said the phone is at River's Edge. She was surprised that I hadn't heard of it. I guess it's a big deal in the county."

"Maybe it's some hotel or resort. Sounds like a resort," Ezra said.

"Anyway, we know the number is current and leads to a real place called River's Edge in South Carolina which is occupied by some woman named Roach. I guess the next stop is Atlanta, unless we want to just go straight to this Roach woman," Neil said, trying to gain control of the decision-making.

"Atlanta it is," King agreed. "If there is more information at this Christian home we should get it before we go down and confront this Roach woman. We need all the ammo we can get. But this sounds more and more like a dead end."

Neil crossed the Fourteenth Street Bridge into Virginia and picked up Route One south. It would take at least two days of driving all night to reach Atlanta, and then only if they didn't encounter traffic jams in any of the many cities and towns they had to pass through. Or get stuck behind a lot of slow-moving trucks on what was mostly a two-lane road. Neil's first surprise of the trip occurred when he suggested the three men divide the driving evenly.

Chapter Eleven: Road Trip

"I can't drive," said King.

"I ain't drivin' in the South," said Ezra. "Too risky. Some minor violation and I'll be here forever."

"Dammit. Why didn't you tell me before we got started?" The drive down to Atlanta on one of the most crowded highways in the country would be wearing. Neil should have been warned. "It'll take three days there and three back, then. I'm going to have to sleep."

"It'll take what it takes. You go ahead and sleep where you want. We'll sleep in the car."

"Mrs. Van Dyke can afford to put us all up. Nobody needs to sleep in the car."

"Ain't a question of money," said King slowly, his eyes reflecting the bright day, idly staring at the passing Fairfax County countryside. "We're in the great Commonwealth of Virginia now, boy. Then the Carolinas and Georgia. Not likely there's anywhere between here and the Florida Keys that will put all three of us up. Lots of places for a white guy, though. We'll sleep in the car." King was not angry or accusatory, just stating facts. The problem had not even occurred to Neil. Other than the trip back from Chicago with Ezra and military transport during the Korean War, Neil had not traveled with colored people before.

When they reached Richmond, it was time for lunch. Neil found a roadside diner just south of the city limits. He parked the car and got out. Ezra and King remained inside.

"Aren't you coming?" Neil asked.

"No. You can bring us something to eat in the car."

"Why?"

"Man, are you illiterate?"

Neil turned and noticed a sign in the diner window. "No coloreds." Neil returned to the driver's seat.

"What are you doing?" Ezra asked.

"We'll find someplace else to eat. Someplace they admit coloreds."

"You're gonna' be drivin' a long, long time," King replied. "Might find some place they seat whites in front and blacks in the kitchen, but you ain't gonna' find somewhere we can eat together."

"What about a place that serves coloreds? Won't they serve me?" Neil looked at Ezra for an answer.

"Don't look at me. I haven't traveled outside Chicago since the war."

"Yeah, they won't send you away. But it'll make the folks uncomfortable. Plus, I bet it'll take you forever to find such a place. Ain't likely they are sittin' right out here on the main highway. Even if some landlord was willin' to let 'em sign a lease, no colored place could afford the rent." Neil reminded himself that King had traveled the south before. "We're even more likely to starve together before we can all eat together south of the Potomac than in D.C."

Neil sighed and put the parking brake back on. He took his companions' food orders and went inside. He came out 15 minutes

Chapter Eleven: Road Trip

later with three carry-out meals in aluminum foil containers with paper tops and three bottles of Coca-Cola. They sat quietly while quickly devouring the indifferent diner food. When Neil was finished, he returned the car to the highway while his companions kept eating.

Less than two miles down the road, the flashing lights of a Virginia State Trooper's patrol car forced Neil to pull onto the shoulder. A uniformed officer wearing dark glasses came to the driver's side window and peered into the car. He asked Neil for his license and registration. The registration was in the glove box. The trooper had only a touch of southern accent.

"I'm sure I wasn't speeding, Officer." The trooper did not respond. Ezra and Neil were silent.

"I see this car is registered to Capital Chevrolet. You ain't Capital Chevrolet now, are you Mr. Endicott." It was a statement, not a question, but Neil answered "no." The officer reached in and took the keys from the ignition. "I'm afraid I'll have to ask all of you gentlemen to exit the vehicle."

"Why? What have we done wrong?" Neil asked. King and Ezra both immediately and firmly told Neil to shut up and do as he was told. After they were out of the car, the officer went to his patrol car and pulled his radio microphone through the car window. He made a call while standing on the shoulder. He remained there for nearly 20 minutes while Neil, Ezra and King variously stood on the shoulder or sat on a vehicle barrier. The officer finally approached them again.

Unanimous Verdict

"Capital Chevrolet says you borrowed the car for five days. This is day one," the officer said, returning the keys to Neil. "You planning to stay in the Commonwealth long?"

"No suh, Mistah Highway Patrolman. No suh. We headin' back to D.C. later today, suh. Mistah Endicott here, he just showin' us how easy and fun it is to drive this here Chevrolet automobile." King stretched the last word as "auto-moo-beel".

"Thas' right Mistah Highway Patrolman," Ezra chimed in. "Mistah Endicott say he get us a deal."

"I don't recall that I addressed you gentlemen. I'll talk to the white man here. You fellas can just shut up.

"Is what these niggers say correct, Mr. Endicott?"

Neil didn't know whether to punch the officer for his language or punch his colleagues for their outrageous performance. He satisfied himself by answering, "Yes, sir, it is."

"All right. You be outta' the state by the end of the day."

"Can I ask why you stopped us?" Both black men froze.

"Couple of boys down at the diner thought it was suspicious a young white boy traveling with a couple niggers and buyin' 'em food. Can't blame 'em. We don't much like nigger lovers around here. Just get out before it happens again."

The highway patrolman entered his car and took a U-turn to head north. The Chevy Bel Air resumed its journey south. Neil recalled Emil Such, his seatmate at the start of his train trip a week ago. Nobody had ever thought to call him a "nigger lover" in 24 years.

Chapter Eleven: Road Trip

Now he had been called that twice. Before taking on the Van Dyke case, he surely would have been angry. Now, although the words were mean and intended as an insult and a slur, Neil couldn't work up any anger. He was a little bit proud of the attacks. He didn't know what to make of such a reaction. Maybe it was because he was playing for the "nigger team" now, just temporarily. He wanted to win.

"What the hell were you doing asking that officer a question after he'd let us go?" King demanded. "Don't ever challenge the law in a southern state, especially if the cop's already said you can leave. When the cop says 'go,' you go, fast as you can."

"Well what was the deal with that Stepin' Fetchit imitation you guys put on back there?" Neil responded.

"Same set of rules. If a colored man wants to avoid trouble with the cops, start shufflin' and scrapin'."

"It's totally humiliating."

"Better than spending three days in jail."

Ezra nodded his agreement.

They were more cautious the rest of the trip. Ezra and Lou crouched to the car floor or lay down on the seat when they stopped to buy food. Neil parked the car far from the office for the two nights he spent in motels so that the clerk was unlikely to see the Negroes sleeping on the front and back bench seats.

Neil also called Mike Q. and told him he was enjoying the Bel Air so much he wanted it a few more days. Neil said he would reimburse the dealership for the extra time and miles. Mike checked with his boss and told Neil to return the car the next Monday, but be prepared to lose the hundred dollar deposit.

With no radio in the car, Neil required conversation to stay awake. But after the state police harassment, both Negroes were content to remain quiet, examining the countryside along Route 1. By the time they reached an area west of Norfolk, Neil needed to relieve both the silence and the tension he felt looking for ways to pass slow trucks when the highway narrowed to two lanes, as it did frequently in rural areas. They had been on the road over ten hours. Darkness had fallen an hour ago.

"Ezra, Lou tells me you served some time in prison. What was that like?" Neil did his best to make his question sound innocent. He told himself he had no motive but curiosity.

"That why you been so quiet so long? You been thinkin' 'bout that all this time?" Ezra did not raise his voice, but his response to Neil was an accusation rather than a question. "You worried about bein' in a car at night in a strange part of the country with a black ex-con? A killer of a white man at that? 'Fraid ol' black Lou and me might just up and kill you, right?"

"Hey, that's not fair. The only thing I'm afraid of is getting' hit head-on when I try to pass one of these trucks. Otherwise, I'm bored as hell and just tryin' to make some conversation to stay awake." Neil glanced to the back seat looking for support from Lou, who was sound asleep. "If you don't want to talk about that, let's talk about sumthin' else. I don't care."

Chapter Eleven: Road Trip

"How'd Lou find out about it?"

"He has some friends on the D.C. force. And they talked to someone in Mobile."

"Jes' good detective work, that's all." The mention of Lou's name stirred him awake. He was now sitting up, rubbing his tired eyes. "Didn't take a genius to look at that brochure of your organization and figure out you musta' had a run-in with cops somewhere. Didn't expect it would involve murder, though. Now that I've met you, it ain't a big surprise." Lou laughed at his own joke.

"What the hell do you mean by that?" Ezra growled. Neil was relieved Lou had diverted Ezra's attention to a man of his own color.

"Well, you're big, you're strong, you're black and you seem pretty well-spoken. That's gonna' piss off white folk, especially in a place like Alabama. If you killed a man, I bet he was goin' after you."

"Whadda you know about the south, King? Where the hell did you grow up? The Vatican? You seem pretty well off yourself. I bet right now you are farther south than you ever have been in your life."

"Almost. I had to go to Columbia once to investigate a case. After that trip, I swore I'd never again take a train to the south. And I haven't. Been down by car a few times to Richmond and Raleigh. Not as far as Atlanta, though.

"But to answer your question, I grew up on a tobacco farm near Upper Marlboro, Maryland. It was 'bout as southern as anywhere else, I guess. Not much schoolin' for coloreds there. Mostly just cut off tobacco leaves, store the leaves for curin'. Got paid by the pound sharecroppin'. My daddy grew a couple acres of other stuff, 'taters, vegetables and the like. He worked part-time as a janitor at the white school in town. I got the hell outta' there at 14 with my daddy's blessin' and moved in with a cousin in D.C. He and his wife both had jobs with the government. We did OK. Didn't meet no Popes or Presidents, but I went to school and graduated from Armstrong High.

"So that's my biography, such as it is. Now tell us 'bout your murder."

"Sound like the white guy's not the only one afraid some big Negro is gonna' kill y'all." Ezra glanced at Neil, who kept his eyes planted onto the highway. "I don't keep it no secret, though. I've told the story many times, including to Clayton Van Dyke whilin' away time in the stockade at Ft. Polk. It's a test of a sort. If folks who hear it are shocked, black or white, then I know they ain't got but at most a passin' understandin' of colored life in the Deep South. You'd be surprised how many folk, always black folk, ain't shocked at all, but come back at me with the same kinda' story about themselves or somebody they know."

Chapter Twelve: Ezra Lowell, 1931–34

As with all growing things, Ezra's hatred of white people began small. At first it was directed mostly at Mr. Bonhomme, the white man who, in Ezra's view at the time, ruined Ezra's life at age 14 in 1931 because he took the word of a white boy against Ezra's for a minor offense. Ezra knew he did not steal cash from Mrs. Bonhomme's purse. But Bonhomme refused to believe the neighbor's boy had done so, and sent Ezra back to his father and sharecropping, telling Ezra on the way out the door that he was lucky he wasn't going to jail. With that, Ezra's formal schooling was over, along with the much softer life of living in Mobile in the attic room of a large house in the plush Garden District tending to the landscape and delivering messages for Mr. Bonhomme's office. Now he was back on the red earth of central Alabama, living with his drunken father, picking cotton bolls to pay the rent and tending a few acres of land to feed himself and his Dad. His life was over before it began, Ezra told himself, a daily mantra that shaped his hatred and ripped away at his soul like a sharp chisel.

Ezra spent hours hoeing his father's rented land, and many more hours in the hot sun dragging a cotton picker's bag behind him, feeling it dig into his neck and shoulders as it neared 100 pounds and more. Anger energized him to keep plucking at the cotton bolls that painfully pricked his fingers until his skin was cut, scabbed and finally calloused. Ezra had lots of time working the fields to remember the cruelties that fueled his anger.

Unanimous Verdict

Ezra remembered how even in Mobile, supposedly a cosmopolitan place for Alabama, he was nearly killed because he stepped across a white painted line on a crowded street car into the section reserved for white people. A dozen or more whites not only let the driver heave him from the car to the concrete curb where he hit his head, but encouraged him to do so – and Ezra was only ten!

Ezra remembered while he was in Mobile that his mother got sick and that neighbors asked the white grower to take her to a doctor. He said he would, but he never did. His mother died. Maybe in some way the grower killed his mother. Ezra cursed the skies at the thought he lost his mother because of simple indifference to her suffering.

His father was a lazy, no-account nigger, Ezra told himself, but he wasn't born that way. Ezra had only to look around the Saturday night barn dance to see young men like him who had no future, worked hard, had little fun and not much reason to stay sober. Dancing, liquor and sex were the only diversions on the farm. When you got older, like Ezra's dad, when even a half a day in the fields was enough to wear you out, only one of those distractions was left. Who was responsible for that, Ezra asked himself for the millionth time? The white man, he answered, also for the millionth time, pulling another boll. The white man, who as a matter of practice, politics and self-preservation kept the black man down with his Jim Crow laws, his violence and his hatred. Even Roosevelt, who some called a great savior, wasn't helping the black farmer. His farm programs, to the extent Ezra knew anything about them, helped the well-off white farmers. Ezra didn't see a nickel

302

Chapter Twelve: Ezra Lowell

of government money in four years of farming and didn't know a black farmer who did.

Ezra heard some say that things were better in the North, but he also knew that the North was no paradise. So how many whites in America *didn't* hate blacks? A dozen? A thousand? A million? There were more than 135 million people in the U.S. in 1934, 80 percent of them white. So what if there were a few good white people? There were some wealthy black people, too. But these exceptions changed nothing. They proved equality was possible. They proved, therefore, that the whites kept most coloreds down.

Ezra also recalled reading both Booker T. Washington's *Up from Slavery* and W.E.B. Dubois' *The Souls of Black Folks* when he was in the sixth grade in Mobile and could borrow them from the Bonhomme book shelf. He read them again when he was older. Sitting in the comfort of the Bonhomme's parlor, Washington's moderate essays about how whites and blacks could work together, yet remain socially apart, seemed like a good idea. Wasn't that how he was working with the Bonhommes – to mutual benefit? DuBois was much more distrustful of whites. His style was more invigorating than Washington's, but he scared young Ezra.

No more. It was difficult to find the DuBois book in the cotton field towns of Alabama. He finally located one he could borrow through the owner of the Negro general store a few miles down the road from the farm. This time, as a mature seventeen year old in 1934, no longer shielded from so much of black reality by the Hudson cars, the fancy bedrooms and the bright parlors of the Garden District, Ezra was astonished at how much he agreed with DuBois. He wondered if DuBois, who worked with whites at the NAACP, went far enough. Perhaps black people needed to be completely separated from whites, not just receive all the rights and respect whites claimed for themselves. Why not their own country? Ezra was attracted to the evangelical oratory of Marcus Garvey and his Universal Negro Improvement and Conservation Association and African Communities League. With the motto "One God! One Aim! One Destiny!" the association sought to unite "all the people of African ancestry of the world into one great body to establish a country and government absolutely their own." Ezra took four dollars more from his four years of savings from the Bonhomme work – originally nearly $200, now down to about $50, which he buried in a can so his father would not find it – and subscribed to The Crisis, which DuBois edited for the NAACP, and to a monthly publication of UNICA. He looked forward to his twice monthly trips to the local post office to collect these publications, which was his only mail.

Ezra hated his life. His destiny was to have been more than a poor sharecropper caring for a dissolute old drunk. He was talented; he was ambitious. He was a good person, like his teacher, Mrs. Washington, told him. Not a bad one like he was treated. But instead of heading for college, or even going to high school, he was hoeing his garden, praying that all the vegetables would come in so he could eat. It was all so arbitrary. Instead of a college student, he was like the rudely carved marionette that entertained the children

Chapter Twelve: Ezra Lowell

at some of the barn dances. Bonhomme and the growers pulled his strings, letting him laugh and play and learn — almost like a white boy — for a couple of years while he was in Mobile, giving him a taste of a civilized life, then they cut the strings and tossed him into the trash based on a mistake.

He hoed faster.

Shit and fuck and God damn.

He threw down the hoe. It was only 3 p.m. — the middle of the day. But Ezra was hot and angry. He went into the shade of the cabin and read, for the third or fourth time, the latest issue of *The Crisis* and wondered, for the thousandth time that day, where his father was.

About three miles away, Ezra's father was being beaten by four white men who intended to kill him.

The old man was drunk, but not so drunk that he didn't want more liquor. His source of supply, the owner of the Negro general store who lent Ezra the DuBois book, refused to extend him more credit. He wanted cash before turning over another quart of his brother's moonshine. One dollar.

The Negro store was about four dirt roads away from the center of the small town. The whites wanted all the colored services in one place, away from the white "downtown," which consisted of a white general store, which was also a feed store, a gasoline station, a post office, and a combination barber shop and beauty parlor operated by a married couple which prominently posted on its window a "whites only" sign. No one knew how the couple survived in business given the scarcity of white women who could afford the price of a hair-do. Most men had their wives cut their hair except for special occasions.

Ezra's father made the mistake of entering the barber/beauty shop when it was occupied by a white customer and the female half of the proprietorship. The word "slattern" was invented for people like the customer, who was having her first beauty parlor treatment ever in preparation for her wedding the next morning. She was a board — a straight one, except for the knots that purported to be her breasts, barely visible under her blue and pink polka dotted cotton dress. Her face was thin, pale and bore no characteristic that would interest anyone except a similarly dull country boy like the one she was going to marry. The union would eventually produce children with the personality of balsa wood.

The proprietor was what men called "sturdy." This meant she, too, was not especially attractive, but did have large hips, a large bottom and substantial breasts. Her hair was well-coiffed, presumably by her husband, with bottle-blond bangs that fell just short of her eyebrows.

The eyes of both women opened wide as Ezra's father stumbled into the shop to beg for money.

"Do you see the sign, Mister," the proprietor said in a loud voice appropriate for her size and ownership position, before Mr. Lowell said a word.

"Ah needs money. Ah needs money fo a drink," the old man said, only barely aware of where he was. In Mr. Lowell's mind, he was begging. He was asking for a handout. But the two women, frightened

Chapter Twelve: Ezra Lowell

that a drunken colored man would barge into the parlor despite the plain language of the sign outside, thought he was intending to rob them. They screamed. Two loud screams in a quiet town. The old man was surprised at the reaction to his simple request. He was frozen in place. The women continued screaming.

Four white men were driving by the shop in an old Model A Ford truck. One of them was the son of the grower who leased Ezra's father his farm. They were not drunk, but they were madder than hell. They just learned from the head of the farm co-op that he could not pay enough for whole chickens to even cover the cost of their feed. The men were outraged at the unknown, unnamed and uncontrollable economic circumstances that caused their chickens to be worth less than the cost to raise them. But mostly they were angry that they were powerless to feed their families. They could not beat up the co-op manager, but they could beat up a black man trying to rob a beauty parlor and threatening two white women. They could confirm they still had power by beating Mr. Lowell – if not power over their own lives, then over the lives of the colored. When they heard the screams, they stopped the car, ran inside, and heard the owner say all they needed to know: "He's tryin' to rob us."

The four men pulled Ezra's dad from the beauty shop and dragged him around the corner to a side street where they punched him and, once he was on the ground, kicked him. Mr. Lowell put up no defense. He was too drunk. He had been beaten by white men several times in his life and survived. He drunkenly focused on those occasions in an attempt to relieve him from intense pain. The key was not to fight back. Just lie there and take it until the white men stopped. Just as he was about to pass out from the combination of moonshine liquor and the pounding of work boots at his head and body, he smelled gasoline. One of the men said, "Let's have us a bonfire. A nigger bonfire."

No one knows if a passed out drunken beating victim is able to feel the pain of death by burning. It is difficult to believe he does not, but Ezra's father made no sounds as his clothing burst into flames. He was reduced to smoldering ash and bones in less than five minutes.

The beating and burning were witnessed. Two white men were in the general store and raced out to see what was going on. One initially suggested that the vigilantes went too far, but he was ridiculed by the other five men with comments on his manhood and an inquiry whether his wife slept with colored men. He retreated. All six men agreed that the colored man tried to rob the beauty parlor and that it was remarkable how God's vengeance visited the thief so quickly with spontaneous combustion.

Another witness was Laurel Field, a 23-year-old Negro woman who was on the other side of the main street walking to the Negro general store when she saw Mr. Lowell dragged out of the beauty shop. Although she knew her best interest lay in moving on, she could not pull herself away from the horror. Thanks to the distraction of the two men from the general store, no one noticed her and she was able to escape without suffering threat or punishment for being a witness. When Laurel reached the Negro general store, she started to cry, shaking and barely able to speak. The store clerk, a colored man about 18, tried to comfort her by putting his arms around Laurel, but she pushed him away, accurately recognizing that he was trying to take advantage of the situation. Her sobbing brought the owner from the back storage room.

She told him what she witnessed, through torrents of tears. The owner walked to the scene of the killing. The body was left where it was burned. The white men were gone. A sign in the window said the barber/beauty parlor was closed for the day. Only the sickly smoking remains of a dead man of indeterminate color remained. A scrap of blue shirt was not burned. It confirmed for the store owner that the victim probably was Mr. Lowell, his most loyal liquor customer, who was wearing a blue work shirt. He returned to his store, advised Laurel Field who had died, and called the sheriff's office.

The sheriff's office asked the race of the victim. When told he was colored, the voice on the other end of the phone snorted and said, "We'll get there when we can." Over an hour later, the body was collected — a shovel was needed to complete the job — and the remains thrown into the back of a truck. A deputy sheriff assured the owner of the Negro general store and Laurel, who waited for the sheriff's deputies to arrive, that an investigation into the death would commence. But, the deputies added, because it was Friday, nothing would be done until Monday, when the sheriff's office resumed normal business hours. Laurel tried to tell the deputy who killed Mr. Lowell — she knew at least two of the men — but he waved her off, promising to interview her next week.

Unanimous Verdict

"Well, at least he's already cremated," the deputy told Laurel as he closed the truck door to leave. Only the other deputy laughed.

Laurel Field knew the Lowell family well. She was the same age as Ezra's older sister. It fell to her to inform Ezra of his father's death.

Ezra had finished reading *The Crisis*. He was on his knees, weeding his garden about 5:30 in the afternoon, still worried about his father, when Laurel approached. He stood, pleased to see her. Laurel was the only woman in the area to whom he genuinely was attracted, but she was six years older and, until recently, lived in Montgomery, which, without a car or wagon to get there, may as well have been San Francisco.

Laurel approached Ezra with dry eyes. She was determined not to resume crying until she had given Ezra her news.

"Hello, Laurel." Her complexion was like his, milk chocolate. Sweet. Soft. Her eyes were pools of light brown, so clear you could see the details of the iris if you were given time to study them. Her features mostly were those of a white girl – straight nose with small nostrils, straight hair, neatly combed. But she had sensuous thick lips which were slightly parted, an unintended invitation to a kiss. Ezra mentally chastised himself for favoring the model of white women. Dubois – certainly Garvey – would disapprove. But neither Dubois nor Garvey knew Laurel Fields. The rest of the day was promising with Laurel Fields as his guest, Ezra thought.

"Hello Ezra. Have you a minute?" She tried to smile. She thought she failed, but Ezra volleyed with a smile of his own.

Chapter Twelve: Ezra Lowell

"Of course. Do you want to come into the cabin?" She nodded her assent and he took her hand. It was soft and smooth. Not like the hands of the local girls who picked cotton and other crops. "I heard you were back home. I guess that's good news for us, bad news for you?" Ezra was terrible at what he heard called "small talk." He wanted to ask her to fuck him. For many local girls that was sufficient foreplay. He had been on the farm too long, Ezra thought. This girl required a more sophisticated approach.

Laurel saw that Ezra was treating her visit like a date. "Ezra, I have some bad news. Your father is dead." She hated the term "passed." It sounded like gas, like a fart. Anyway, being burned to death was not just passing. It was murder. "I saw it, Ezra. He was burned up. Gasoline was thrown on him. He was murdered."

Ezra processed the information. He was deciding how to react. He was surprised at a hint of guilty pleasure, relief that he no longer had to care for a drunken shell that once was his dad. He could finally leave the farm. But such guilty relief was quickly overcome by anger. His father was murdered. That could not go unavenged. The man was nearly worthless, but he was his father. Once, he had been a fine man. A man who was able to marry a fine woman. Who could fault him for recognizing in middle age the futility of his existence and relieving himself with booze?

"Did you see who did it? Why? Where did this happen? What did he do?" Laurel explained all that she saw and heard. She identified two of the four men and described the other two. She told him the

311

reaction of the sheriff's deputies. She held nothing back. She expected Ezra to cry. He did not.

"Do my sisters know?" he asked Laurel. She shook her head. She came to him first. "Don't tell them until tomorrow afternoon, please. I don't want them to know."

"But why, Ezra? They should be told right away."

"Because I need you to be with me." It was not a lie. Ezra wanted comfort, and wanted to lie with Laurel. His father had given him nothing. He helped kill his mother by leaving the entire burden of caring for the family on her. Few would mourn his passing, though many would be shocked by the manner of his death. None of that justified his murder. Ezra would not let the white men get away with the brutal killing of his father. If his sisters, who lived a short distance away with their own families, could honestly claim they knew nothing about their father's death until tomorrow afternoon, they might be safe from the angry white mob that likely would form to seek further revenge after Ezra was finished with his own work.

When Ezra arose the next morning, Laurel was still by his side, sleeping soundly. They had talked deep into the night, about Ezra's father, his family, and the events of Laurel's life. That would have to serve as his sendoff, he told himself. Ezra did not know if Laurel could read, but he left a note on the only table in the cabin, the one that served as desk, dinner table and platform for any other activities. The note said:

Chapter Twelve: Ezra Lowell

"I am gone. I will not be back. You are wonderful. Thank you. Fondly, Ezra."

Before setting out for the grower's house, Ezra dug up the can with the last $40 he saved from his days with the Bonhommes and looked for a weapon. He found one and departed. He estimated it was six o'clock in the morning. It was June, so it was bright out even so early in the day. He knocked several times before the door to the grower's house opened.

"Why, it's Ezra Lowell. What you want bein' aroun' here so early in the 'mornin?" The woman was stout, wrapped in a housecoat, shielding her eyes from the sun, which already was well above the horizon.

"Is Marcus around?" Ezra asked, trying not to sound impatient.

"Well he's still abed. He came in late last night."

Ezra was uncertain what he would do if the owner's son, who Laurel identified as one of his father's killers, came to the door. He intended to kill him, but was put off by the owner's wife, who had never been mean to Ezra and sometimes, when he was a child, had offered him candy and even read to him. She was not really a bad person. Maybe, Ezra thought, it would be sufficient to force the son to drive to the sheriff's office so that Ezra could turn him in. Whatever he was going to do, Ezra considered, it could not wait.

"It's an emergency. I think there's a fire in the northeast section."

Unanimous Verdict

The woman shielded her eyes again, looking to the northeast. "I don't see nothin' Ezra. I hope this ain't some dumb-ass thing from you. I'll get Marcus. You stay here."

Ezra could hear the woman climb the stairs and a few moments later some weary complaining as she rousted her son from sleep.

Several minutes later, Marcus, a blond, blue-eyed, well-muscled and tanned man several years older than Ezra, came to the door.

"Ezra Lowell," he said somberly. "My momma said somethin' 'bout a fire. What's goin' on?"

"Ain't no fire. You killed my daddy yesterday. I'm here to take you to the sheriff." It was harder to maintain a desire to kill a man when he was in front of you, Ezra thought, than when he's just an idea. He could kill him later if, as was likely, the man wasn't punished for his crime through the law. These thoughts calmed him. If Marcus went along to the sheriff and confessed and asked forgiveness, maybe it would be worth waiting for the law to work. Maybe he and Laurel could get together. But Marcus authored the writ of his own execution.

"Yeah, we did have us a little barbeque downtown. But they said your daddy was tryin' to rob the barber shop." Marcus spoke almost offhandedly, as if describing the weather or how to kill a chicken for dinner. He was even grinning at the recollection. "Maybe we done gone too far. But your daddy shoulda' stayed outta' the white part of town."

"This is my daddy you're talkin' 'bout. Be respectful."

Chapter Twelve: Ezra Lowell

"Why, Ezra! I done tol' you we gone too far. But your daddy was a good-fer-nothin' drunken nigger. You know it, too. Reckon there weren't much to respect, now."

Ezra's hand tightened around his weapon. The man had one more chance.

"You come along with me. You can drive us to the sheriff's office and you tell 'em truthfully what happened." Marcus could not miss the threat in Ezra's voice.

"Come on, Ezra. Your daddy was gonna' die soon anyway. That cheap moonshine was gonna' kill him. No need to make a police case outta this." His face lit with an idea.

"I reckon he did some work on that plot of land you're sharecroppin'. He weren't no good picking cotton, that's for damn sure. But I guess any man's worth somethin'. I'll give you a hunnert dollars to leave it alone. That's fair. I'll be right back."

The pitchfork tines punctured his thighs before Marcus could begin to pull the screen door shut. He looked down to his legs, but before the bloody sight could register, Ezra had withdrawn the tines from his flesh and turned the pitchfork 45 degrees so that the tines were at a right angle to the porch floor. He jammed the pitchfork into Marcus's genitals. Marcus then screamed and grabbed his privates.

"I'll be goddamned if you're gonna' buy my daddy's dead body! You fuckin' white bastard! Time you fuckers learned that slavery's over. It'll be the last goddamn thing you learn, boy." He emphasized the word "boy" as he rammed the pitchfork a third time into the white man's bloody body, this time at the chest, ripping through muscle and bone to puncture the aorta. The grower's wife reached the door in time to catch her son's body, spurting arterial blood as he fell. Ezra jammed the pitchfork into his victim's chest another time as the woman dropped to the floor, grabbing her son, pulling him to her. The weapon caught between the victim's ribs. Ezra left it there, an upright sentry posted in the dying son, then turned and ran. He was stoked with energy. He had no fears. He was a superman. He had killed a vicious white man. He had no regrets. No guilt. He felt like he was running a mile a minute as the breeze slipped by his face. His feet barely touched the soft, turned, red earth. It was exhilarating. This was what freedom felt like.

He crossed a quarter mile of open field and entered the rows of corn which were still weeks from harvest. Even as he raced east, he crouched low to hide behind the immature stalks. He avoided roads and open spaces, following the crop rows when possible. He had a destination. His bare feet propelled him through fields of cotton, alfalfa and more corn. After about 40 minutes, breathless and his left side aching, but still feeling triumphal, Ezra reached the Negro general store. He pounded on the door and awoke the store owner.

"You saw my daddy get killed. You the one that been sellin' him that rotgut. I just killed the grower's son. I oughta' kill you," Ezra shouted between gasps for breath. Ezra had no weapon, but none was needed to convey an effective threat to the guilty grocer. "You gimme your car. You can say I stole it. I ain't gonna be aroun' to deny it. But

316

don't call the sheriff until around 11. Then I'll get God in heaven to forgive you."

"Ok. Ok. Here's the keys," the general store owner told Ezra as he reached to a hook that held his key ring. "You know how to drive?" he asked. Few coloreds knew how to drive.

"Sure do. Learned from white folk," Ezra replied, grabbing the key.

His explanation was more than a little exaggerated. He saw Bonhomme, the man for whom he worked in Mobile, drive his Hudson nearly every day for two years, but never himself drove. He had not been in a car of any kind for nearly four years. Ezra was relieved that the store owner's car was a 1927 Chevy with controls similar to the Hudson's, but without the fancy interior and chrome. He stalled the car five times before finally conquering the clutch and lurched away. Ezra did not know where he was going, except that he hoped it was north. He had no map. The little hamlets in rural northeastern Mobile County were difficult to reach. Most roads were dirt or gravel and poorly maintained. Ezra wasted precious time following dead-ends, semi-circles and meandering roads that were endless and went nowhere. He finally came upon U.S. Highway 43, a good paved road, and took it north. He now was in command of the gearshift and clutch. He was growing comfortable with the steering.

Ezra stopped for gasoline at Tuscaloosa and then turned east toward Birmingham. He knew he had to get out of the state and that by now the grocer had reported his car missing. Even the Mobile

Unanimous Verdict

County Sheriff's Department eventually would figure out Ezra escaped in the car. He would abandon it in Birmingham and take a train north. He heard about men jumping onto freight trains. It was a dangerous practice, and the rail yards were policed by employees who would turn Ezra over for prosecution if he was caught. But he had to get out.

Birmingham was much larger than Mobile and it was a challenge for Ezra to maneuver the Chevy through city traffic. He was afraid of causing an accident – another route to capture. He abandoned the vehicle before entering the center of town. A colored man told him how to get to the train station and directed him to a bus stop. He had no time for tourism, but as the bus delivered him to the station he was surprised that the office buildings were not much larger than those in Mobile. The traffic was much worse, however, and the sidewalks were more crowded. When Ezra disembarked he walked quickly to the freight rail yard.

He wasn't sure how to enter the yard inconspicuously. The switching towers were obviously manned and the yard personnel presumably would stop an unknown Negro with blood on his shirt who had no official business walking among the freight cars. He regretted not stopping at a smaller town on the rail line where it might have been easier to hop a freight. Perhaps following the line north along the street would lead him to a place he could board before the train picked up too much speed. He observed the yard until a train departed north. Ezra noted the rails the train used as he watched it disappear behind some distant buildings. He started walking, following the rail line north as

Chapter Twelve: Ezra Lowell

closely as possible along the sidewalks and roadsides. Although the auto journey was a long one, Ezra had been preoccupied with the mechanics of driving and obeying all the traffic laws. He was desperate to avoid calling attention to himself. There was no time for contemplation. His walk along the tracks was his first opportunity to consider his situation realistically.

His pride in killing his father's killer, in defeating a white man, had diminished. Even if a hero to himself, he recognized that he also was a murderer. Worse, he was a Negro who murdered a white man in the Deep South. Ezra didn't know much about the law, but the Bible talked about an eye for an eye. One life for taking another. Ezra was satisfied his killing was just, if not legal. But no matter how just his actions, Ezra knew he would be hanged after a *pro forma* trial – or, at least as likely, no trial at all. If he was caught.

Walking along unfamiliar roads in the warm dusk of June, his destination and his way of getting there both unknown, Ezra also awakened to possibilities in his life. He was through with farming and Alabama and the South. He had no ties. He was only 17, could write and was a voracious reader. If he could get to some northern city, a place packed with colored folk who worked and made things and were paid regularly, he could change his life. He knew from stories told by friends with relatives in the north that there was much hatred of Negroes and segregation by custom. But these same relatives said that if you got a good job – not always an easy thing to find – a colored man could live a good life in the big cities. Days went by, these people said, when you didn't even talk to a white man. Black folks lived apart, not close by whites like in the South. Ezra looked forward to such separation. If white people hated him, then just leave him alone. Ezra would do the same for them.

Finally, a freight train chugged out of the Birmingham rail yard heading north. By the time it reached Ezra, it was starting to accelerate, but still was slow enough to run with. Only a chicken wire fence separated the road from the tracks, which Ezra simply pushed through. Ezra did not try to board the train. Instead, he examined it carefully while there was still a small amount of daylight, figuring out where and how to board. There must have been 100 cars in the train. Not one car had an open door. How could a man board a train without an open freight car door? Ezra wondered. He watched the caboose disappear into the coming darkness.

"So I guess you ain't goin to Atlanta, eh?"

Ezra was startled by the voice coming out of the brush only a few feet from where he stood. Two white boys rose from the brush like Ezra imagined spirits rose in a cemetery. Their clothes were tattered, their faces filthy. Ezra looked to see if they wore shoes. "Yeah, we got shoes nigger." Others obviously had looked at their feet with the same curiosity. They looked at Ezra's naked feet. The one who spoke used the pejorative casually, as if it were interchangeable with "colored." The boys were not threatening. One carried a small valise. The other only a paper sack. Ezra guessed that he was older than either boy.

Chapter Twelve: Ezra Lowell

"Mebbe we kin get ya' some shoes on the rails," the older one said. Ezra didn't respond. He didn't know what to say.

"Don't you talk? Where you goin', boy?"

He could answer the obvious questions. "I'm just waitin on a train. What about you? How did you know that last train was headed for Atlanta?"

"You new to ridin' the rails, ain't ya nigger?" The taller boy, about Ezra's height, did all the talking.

"Don't your friend say nothin'?" Ezra asked.

"When he's spoken to. He's my brother. Lemme ask you agin, you new to the rails, right?"

"Right. This is my first trip."

"I knew it Eddie. I tole you so. Name's Marvin. This is Eddie. Pleased ta meetcha." Marvin and Eddie both extended their hand. Ezra shook them. "You runnin' from or runnin' to?"

"Whatcha mean?"

"I mean are you runnin' away from somethin' or to somethin'? Somebody after ya' or is you jus' hopin' to find some work someplace?"

A locomotive headlight cut through the darkness. "Come on, get down," Marvin instructed firmly. Ezra joined the boys crouched in the brush. "Get ready to roll," Marvin said. "You wanta' head toward Chicago?" Ezra nodded. He had not given his destination any thought, except that it had to be north. Chicago would do.

"Then this is your train."

"But the last one didn't have no open doors."

Unanimous Verdict

"Lots don't. That's when you ride the roof." The locomotive passed by. The train was moving at less than 10 miles an hour. "It's movin' slow. Look, when we jump, you jump. Grab a ladder rail and hoist yourself up. There's one at each end of the car. One person per ladder. We'll see you at the top. Eddie, you first."

The smaller boy leaped from the brush and ran along the train, carefully timing himself so that instead of running after a car, a car caught up to him. He reached for the lowest ladder rung at the front of the car with his left hand and pulled himself to the train, keeping his legs well away from the rolling wheels. Then he pulled himself up the ladder with his arms until his feet could rest on a rung. All the while, the train was picking up speed. As soon as Marvin saw that Eddie had a firm grasp on the ladder, he started running and duplicated his brother's feat several cars behind.

Ezra clenched his jaw and ran. Two or three cars passed as he tried to time himself to grab a rung. With no confidence, but driven by necessity, he reached out and succeeded in attaching himself to the railcar. He struggled to bring his right hand around to the rung to join his left, strongly encouraged by the rolling steel biting into the rails only inches from his legs. After that, it was relatively easy to pull himself up far enough to plant his feet on the bottom rung. He was chilled either by fear or by the breeze kicked up by the accelerating train. He climbed to the top of the car and was surprised to see that the ladder flattened across the car and dropped down the other side. Reaching the summit was easy. Staying there was difficult at first as

Chapter Twelve: Ezra Lowell

the train jostled from side to side, threatening to fling Ezra to the trash and brush along the rails or into a coupling and certain death. Ezra lay flat atop the ladder rails. His hands hurt from hauling his own weight up the ladder, but he gripped the rungs tightly, afraid to move.

"Hey, leggo and move back so's we kin join ya," Marvin said. He and Eddie were standing up on the next boxcar forward, three feet and a dangerous jump across the couplings from Ezra. Ezra was astonished. The car's movement was too abrupt to make standing up possible. He was afraid to even loosen his grip. "It ain't no worse than a boat. You been on a boat, ain't ya?" Ezra shook his head. "Man, you colored got it bad. Ain't done nothin'. Jes' stan' up and you be OK."

Ezra wondered if this was a trick to get him to fall off the train. A white man suckering another nigger. But Marvin's voice was calm and authoritative. Eddie said nothing. Ezra decided to test the jerkiness of the train. He rose to a crouch, holding on to a rung with one hand. He had never been on a boat, but Ezra instinctively captured the rhythmic swaying of the train. What was uneven, unpredictable and harsh now was like a rocking motion. He relaxed his other hand and stood, alternately easing and stiffening his knees to match the rocking right and left.

"Ya ready Eddie?" Marvin asked his brother as Ezra stepped back. Eddie nodded and jumped the gap between cars. Marvin then did the same.

"Now we sits," he told Ezra. "Cain't stand on top o' a freight car too long or you gonna get bounced off. Gotta' lay down or sit down."

"Why didn't you tell me that before I stood up?"

"Cause you wouldna got outta the way if I done that. Eddie n' me, we wanna be yo friends. Hep you out on the rails."

"Why. I got no money to pay ya."

"Ain't nobody got money. We jus' like ta pay back. Other kids taught us. We'll teach you."

"I don't see no other kids."

"Not on this train. Jes' left Birmingham. Start o' the run. It'll be full o' kids and old folks by the time we hit Louisville If you stay'n on to Chicago, it'll be like ants at a picnic. Where you goin' anyways?"

"Chicago, I guess."

"Well this is the train fer' it. Illinois Central. All Illinois Central trains ends up in Chicago, some's faster n' others. No tellin' how fast this one'll git thar."

It was a clear night with a full moon. Ezra examined the faces of his companions, trying to see past their grime. Both had brown hair, blue eyes and were very young.

"How'd you know the other train was goin' to Atlanta?" Ezra enjoyed talking to the boys, but his palms rested flat on the top of the boxcar. He was very conscious of the rocking motion, and still afraid of rolling off the train.

"That was a Southern Railway train. It meanders all aroun' but eventually ends up in Atlanta. Maybe goes on to Washington, D.C. No farther. All Southern. Eddie and me, we don't like Southern.

Chapter Twelve: Ezra Lowell

They's toughest on the hoboes and rail riders. Midwest and west, them's the places to go."

"Where y'all from?" Ezra asked.

"Tulsa. Daddy drilled for oil. Lost his job. No other jobs. We lit off figurin' they couldn't take care of us as well as we could take care o' ourselfs."

"Well, are you right? Are you takin' care of yourselves?"

"We alive, ain't we? You must be runnin'."

Ezra tried not to act surprised. "Why do you say that?"

"Well, you talk English pretty good. Bettern' any nigger I ever heerd. You from these parts since you ain't nevah hopped a train. I only guess you got in some trouble with the white folks."

Ezra kept his silence, which signaled to Marvin his observations were close to home.

"Doan worry. Mos' people on the road is runnin' from somethin'. You don't hurt me or Eddie and we ain't gonna' hurt you." Ezra wanted to believe Marvin. But he was wary. White people had fooled him before.

Ezra completed his story just as Neil slowed the Bel Air, looking for a motel. They were outside of Raleigh. Lou had asked Ezra a few questions about sharecropping and Alabama, but otherwise the narration was uninterrupted. His audience asked him to continue his story, but Ezra was not interested. "The main thing I done was kill that white man," he said. "The rest is not so interesting.

"After a couple months, I got to Chicago. No work. But I was well-spoken and was a pretty good lookin' kid. After a few nights on the streets, I found my way to the Southside, where most of the black folk lived, and fixed myself up with a woman who offered a place to sleep and other, let's say, benefits. First of several kind ladies. I never paid any rent for seven years."

"You musta' done somethin' for money," Lou said.

"I ran some numbers for a gang for awhile. Did a little stealin', but it was all from colored folk. I hardly saw a white man in the Southside 'cept cops. Even had a colored alderman. Only way to get a city job was through the alderman, and then you had to give him part of your pay. That was the way through the whole city. White folk, too. Alderman wasn't interested in me until '38 when I turned 21 and could vote. Then I got a job sweepin' streets in the ward. Didn't do that but a few months before the alderman put me on his staff. Not in the office, but on the streets, talkin' to people, fixin' their problems, you know, makin' people like the alderman so's they'd vote for him again. I was gonna' be his campaign manager in '42. But I got drafted."

Lou interrupted. "See, we need to vote in D.C. Black folk would get jobs then. A vote is worth a job."

Neil was interested in Ezra, not Lou's political views. "Well how'd you get drafted if the alderman was behind you?"

"Well, the alderman tried to get me out, but the board said they had to draft me to meet their quota 'cause there weren't enough coloreds around who could pass the tests. I think another guy on the

Chapter Twelve: Ezra Lowell

alderman's staff was jealous of me and went behind the alderman to get me drafted. Anyway, that's my story of Chicago. You know the rest. In the stockade in Louisiana, then jail in Alabama. I been under the white man's law long enough to know its powerful stuff. That's why I'm tryin' to work with the kids. I don't think knowledge alone is power, but ignorance sure is weakness. That's sort of what the school is about."

"Sounds to me like you got a lot of help from white folks. Bonhommes in Mobile, growers, those kids on the train," Neil said when Ezra had completed his abbreviated version of his biography. "I can see why you'd hate whites 'cause of your Dad and all, but you can't blame all of us for that."

"I told you on the train, I don't hate whites exactly. I don't trust 'em and I sure don't expect 'em to give up their power, no matter how much some talk about equal rights. Push comes to shove – and there's still a helluva lot of pushin' and shovin' to be done – white folk will favor white folk 100 percent. Colored people so far under their thumbs that you can't even count on a black man favoring a black man against a white."

"But you said there was a colored alderman. Colored had power in Chicago."

"Is that a joke? He had an itty-bitty amount of power, limited to his ward and only as long as he went along with the whites on the city counsel who went along with the mayor. Man, we got the crumbs even at that. Street sweeper. Maybe garbage collector. Sometimes a clerical job downtown. The big jobs, the good pay, all went to white guys. Even with the election fraud they got in Chicago, ain't no way a white man gonna' get elected alderman on the Southside. Hell, outside of Hyde Park where the university is, there ain't hardly a white man or woman livin' on the south side. So, they get a go-along, get-along nigger to be alderman and give him a little money and a little what they call patronage to keep him gettin' elected.

"White folk control it all. That numbers racket I was talkin' about? I found out that at the very top it's run by the mob – white guys. Italians. You wouldn't know it on the street. Everybody doin' the work was colored. But if you traced the money, you'd find more'n half of it went to the mob. Left the Southside for some gangster's pocket."

Ezra was relieved to talk politics in the late North Carolina night. He preferred it to autobiography. He warmed to his subject.

"Look, the black man left alone with the same resources as the white man can do just as well. We don't need the white man in our face or throwin' us crumbs. We've got to fight the white man to get our share of economic power, then get him to leave us alone. We got to own real estate, run and own factories and construction companies. Then we can go it alone. White man never gonna share."

"But if the white man won't share, how are you gonna' get the economic power?" Neil asked.

Chapter Twelve: Ezra Lowell

"That's the hard question," Ezra replied quietly. "It's hard to see any way for a black man to get what's his that isn't violent. We may just have to take it."

Neil found a cheap motel. He parked the car far away from the motel office. After he checked in, he brought his companions a roll of toilet paper and two paper cups filled with water and left them for the night. He wished he could hear what they were talking about as they went to sleep.

They would reach Atlanta the next day. If there was to be an answer to the murder of Clayton Van Dyke, it would have to be there.

PART TWO: THE DEFENDANTS
Chapter Thirteen: The Farwell Family, 1904–1922 February, 1922

"Oh God! Oh God! Just end it, please! I can't stand the pain!"

"It's coming now. The head is crowning. I can see it," the doctor said soothingly, grateful for what he expected to be an uneventful birth at the end of the day. "My goodness …." The doctor's voice was suddenly full of astonishment, agitation and anger.

"It's a colored baby!" he screamed. "This is obscene! It's terrible!"

The patient kept pushing the object of the physician's disgust out of her birth canal. No one had told the doctor that his white patient would yield a black child. "God dammit. A pickaninny foaled from a white gal. Now I've seen everything. Who is this patient?" the doctor demanded as he grabbed the newborn by its head and bottom to pull it into its new world. Its mother, exhausted, dropped her head to the pillow, panting.

Reflexively, based on 20 years of deliveries, the doctor cut the umbilical cord and held the child for the mother to see. Of those in the room, only the mother smiled at the brief sight of her baby. She was allowed only a glimpse.

"Put the baby into the layette, doctor." It was a woman's scolding voice. The new mother identified it as that of Mrs. Drucker, the head mistress of the St. Mark's Christian Home. "You know we don't permit the girls to see their babies. Nurse, take him away."

"No! No! I want to see. It's a boy, isn't it?" She smiled and lifted her head, mustering all of her energy to glimpse her child. "Please, let me hold my baby."

"You know the rules, Miss Roach. Take the baby away." Mrs. Drucker was firm, trying hard not to sound mean while performing a mean task. "We bent a lot of our rules for you. Please don't make a fuss."

"But I have a right to see my own child." She spoke in a high pitch, reflecting her own anger and desperation. But also guilt and shame. Guilt because she had agreed to give up her child; shame because she had done so, but not – emphatically not – because her baby was black.

"You are only seventeen, child. You have no rights. And you have known this day was coming for the last six months. You can't change it now. You made your bed, Emily Roach, now you must sleep in it." Mrs. Drucker was calm. She was used to delivery room confrontations. This girl was no different from most in wanting to see her baby. All those babies were white, however. Why this girl wasn't happy to give up her Negro child was a mystery, but Mrs. Drucker was certain the girl's regrets would not last out the day. She soon would be happy knowing the evidence of her shame – shame from the conception itself – was gone from her life for good.

Chapter Thirteen: The Farwell Family

The doctor, his obligations nearly completed, was also angry. "I should have been told I was to deliver a colored child. And to a white woman at that. I don't know that I would have done it. No doctor I know wants to assist in miscegenation, bastardization and adding more niggers to the world. We sure as hell don't need another half breed orphan. Why was this allowed to go to term? Why not hire a nigra midwife?"

Mrs. Drucker retained her businesslike demeanor and a silken Southern delivery that comforted her accuser without granting his argument.

"Why Doctor Hall, I'm surprised at you. You are our principal obstetrician and have delivered dozens of babies here. You know very well how much we value discretion. No one except those of us in this room and the girl's family will ever know about this." Her eyes cast about to the two nurses who assisted in the delivery who were on the Home's staff and who dutifully nodded in agreement. "We could hardly count on a Negro midwife to keep quiet about the birth of a black baby to a white woman now, could we? Birthing a colored baby is not shameful to a nigger woman. She wouldn't understand, or might actually want to spread the news. We trust you, doctor." More shame. This time, a doctor's shame for delivering a Negro child would ensure he kept his mouth shut, along with the healthy retainer he received from the home.

"Please, please let me see my baby. Just a few minutes. No one has to know."

Unanimous Verdict

"Rules are rules, dear. I think you should get some sleep. The nurses will return you to your room after the doctor gives you a final examination."

The doctor's examination was quick and soundless. He quashed his curiosity. He did not want information. He wanted to be gone. In moments, his wish was granted. The patient was young, in good health and the delivery was a clean one. There was no episiotomy to sew up. He packed his tools and started to leave.

"Thank you, doctor." The voice was thin, painfully lonesome. The doctor noted to himself that the patient had no relatives by her side. Even unwed mothers usually had at least one parent present, especially at the Christian Home, which cost a lot of money and was hardly an institution for the dispossessed. Serves her right, messin' with a nigger, he thought. Cute girl, too. Coulda' easily gotten a white guy. He left without responding to her thank you. A few minutes later, the patient was returned to her room for a few days of watchful recovery.

She knew the plan was to have her child adopted in the North somewhere. She had only one night to visit the baby. Its name for a night was Brian, if it was a boy, or Brianna, if a girl, in honor of its father. Had she heard correctly in the haze after giving birth? she asked herself. Was it a boy? Her stomach churned with resignation and resentment. She was giving up Brian's child, a cowardly act borne of necessity. She had no resources of her own. She relied entirely on Papa. But still, she was giving up her baby. Yet, her heart also was filled with joy. She had saved Brian's child from death. This child would carry

334

Chapter Thirteen: The Farwell Family

Brian's genes mixed with her own into the world someplace. It would live. With God's grace, as long as she walked the earth, so would their child.

She climbed out of bed. The pain in her gut from the delivery was already diminishing. She could walk, but needed to put her hand on her belly as if to keep her insides from falling out. She knew where the nursery was for the newborns. She had long suspected it was unguarded. Mrs. Drucker knew that some mothers needed to see their babies before they were gone. Denying such charity was not in Mrs. Drucker's true nature, as long as she wasn't confronted with the offense.

The girl opened the door to the nursery and saw two layettes. Hers was the third delivery the last two days. Where was the third layette? She crept in her bare feet and nightgown to the two layettes. The babies were sound asleep. Both were nearly as white as the sheets in which they slept. The mother panicked. Had they destroyed her baby after all? Had her father and brother lied to her? She looked around the room. There was a closet, presumably for storage. She went to it and opened the door. The buckets and mops and whatever else that were kept in the closet had been removed. Instead, there lay her child, isolated in a dark closed closet, separated from the white children from the day of birth.

The mother picked up her child. Although she had little experience with babies, this one cradled in her arms easily, naturally. She raised the corner of its diaper. A boy! Brian! The precious object now had a name. She walked to the nursery room door, staying just inside the door frame so as not to be seen. The light from the hallway awakened the child. He looked directly at his mother and smiled. His mother pulled him to her warm body. She kissed him. He was light skinned – far lighter than Brian. His skin was a perfect mingling of the mother's fair color and the father's far darker hue – a vital, visually accurate creation of their love. It was difficult to see his eyes in the dim light. Was it her imagination, or did he really have green eyes, with flecks of gold, like his father? It was too early to tell. She held him to her for an hour, even as the lingering pangs of his birth intensified while she stood. She kissed her baby many times through her tears as muffled sobs mixed with joyful smiles and as she imagined his future. Would he be a great man? Would he be adopted by a loving family? What mattered now was simply that he was alive, a gift to her and to Brian. He mostly slept, easy in the care of his mother, as if instinct told him he was safe in her possession. She held him until she was so sleepy she was afraid she might drop her son. She placed him back in the layette, but only after wheeling it from the closet to join the white babies in the nursery. The squeaking of the wheel woke the baby, again smiling at his mother. Only as his mother walked away, did Brian start to cry. She returned to hold him again. On her third attempt to depart, the baby slept peacefully. The young girl returned to her room, her body and soul alike awash in tangled emotions about love, loss, family, race – and resentment that she had to leave her child of Brian to the care of unknown others.

Chapter Thirteen: The Farwell Family

She knew she would not see her son again. She kneeled by her bed and did something she had not done since she was a child. She prayed. She asked God to please protect little Brian.

Two days later, she returned to River's Edge. She had been gone six months. Banished.

MARCH 1919

"Damned telephone; never a minute's peace." John Calhoun Farwell, two-time governor of South Carolina, now retired, muttered to himself as he quickly climbed out of bed, put on his slippers and headed to the magisterial staircase of the grand estate called River's Edge to answer the devilish device at the foot of the stairs.

As was his custom – and reward – the Governor admired his eight-by-three foot oil paintings, stretched between intricately carved four-inch wide gilded frames, which hung along the curved stairway and in the two-story center hall. The Governor marveled that each of the dozen paintings was lighted through the night with its own portrait lamp at the top of the frame, a result of the arrival of electricity at the mansion five years earlier. Four of the paintings were of Governor Farwell's three elder brothers and his father, all of them in the uniform of the Confederate States of America, complete with swords, pistols and, in his eldest brother's case, mounted on a white steed, its front hooves held high above a pile of vanquished Yankees. Other paintings were commissioned portraits of great Rebel victories and revered officers, most of whom Governor Farwell and his father had known personally, including the God-like Robert E. Lee.

The portraits were drawn with attention to the smallest detail, accurate representations of uniform accessories, bridles and bits, horse flanks clearly defined, all in bright bold colors. But the pictures, especially of the battle scenes, were mythical. There was no blood, no sweat, no fear, only the heroism of the principal figure, always a Confederate. Even the Union dead only appeared to be sleeping.

The urgent ring of the telephone did not prevent John Farwell from pausing a moment at the top of the stairs, where all the paintings were visible at once, creating a panorama of valor and victory, a history that, in the governor's view, both was and should have been. As always, Farwell was inspired by the paintings. He self-consciously straightened his back and raised his chin, adopting a military bearing to honor his kin, proud to share their blood and defend their cause. Then he began his own unheroic journey to the telephone table, a tired old man.

Farwell cleared his throat and picked up the receiver. "Hello." The Governor hid his embarrassment at answering his own telephone. He did not like having colored help in the house after the dinner dishes were washed, but a man of his wealth and reputation should not be answering his own telephone. He lowered his voice an octave and added more accent to his southern speech (never call it a drawl) than he used in less self-conscious occasions. Both the deeper timbre and heavier accent were intended as a reminder to

338

Chapter Thirteen: The Farwell Family

callers that he once was the powerful governor of a proud southern state.

"Hello, Governor."

"Hello, Mary. How are you this evening?" He imagined the pleasure his honeyed tones gave the local operator, though she had heard them thousands of times. Courtesies to women, even to the lowly telephone operator in Barnwell, must be maintained. There could not be more than 20 telephones in 10 miles, Farwell thought. He assumed Mary often listened in on the governor's calls.

"The Aiken Academy for Women is on the line. Long distance. Will you accept charges?"

"Why of course."

"Putting you through. Hello? Governor Farwell is on the line now."

"Hello, Governor?"

"Yes."

"This is Miss Austin at the Girls School."

"Yes, Miss Austin. To what do I owe this pleasure?" He doubted very much that the red-haired, large breasted woman whose aggressive artificial warmth for Governor Farwell on his visits to the school was more threatening than welcoming, had called for any reason that he would find pleasurable.

"Is it too late? I'm sorry if it's too late," she said solicitously.

"No, no. I was just reading," Farwell lied. He was ashamed to be pulled from bed at only 8:30 in the evening.

"I'm afraid I have some bad news."

The Governor raised his left hand to his chest. He could feel his heartbeat double with fear.

"It's not Margaret, is it? Is she alright? What's happened to her." The studied mannerisms of his voice were forgotten. He had lost two wives to premature deaths. Please God, not his daughter, too.

"Oh, she is just fine physically, Governor Farwell. Please don't worry about that. But I'm afraid it's her attitude. She has become a great trial to us. She is very disruptive."

"Well, she's only 15 and has been raised on a cotton farm, Miss Austin. I'm sure she has lots of energy that might be hard to contain at your school. Surely you've encountered such in the past and can handle it." Once he was comforted that his daughter was safe, Farwell returned to his more demanding executive voice and hoped the obsequious school mistress would get to her point and then hang up.

"Margaret has many good qualities, Governor. She is smart, perhaps too smart. She is simply not of a type that we can serve here. She is quite disruptive."

"Yes, you said that." Farwell's patience was diminishing. He wanted to go back to bed. "Has she broken something? Has she hurt someone? What do you mean?"

"I mean disruptive in the classroom. She simply refuses to be taught. She challenges everything her teachers say and argues with them. A few of the other girls are taking her side. We've had complaints from parents.

Chapter Thirteen: The Farwell Family

"Governor Farwell, we are in business to train our girls to be Southern ladies. We are not able to deal with views that smack of race-mixing, anarchy and Communism and the like."

Farwell pulled a chair to the telephone table and sat. What was she talking about? When Margaret left River's Edge in September 1918, she was curious about the world, like anyone her age, but the governor was unaware of any radical views. The Aiken Women's Academy was hardly a breeding ground for non-conformist thought. It promoted fine Southern traditions. The Men's Academy had schooled the Governor, his son, his brothers and his father.

"Are you referring to my daughter? I'm not aware she had any political thoughts at all when she began attending your school last fall. I find your claims preposterous. Tell me what she has done, specifically." He felt himself scolding Miss Austin. Perhaps she deserved one, but he reminded himself she was still the head mistress at his daughter's school. "I am sorry if I sound brusque, Miss Austin. But your words do astound me."

"Margaret and this other girl, Nancy, have become their own little radical group. They read Northern publications that put all kinds of subversive ideas in their heads about the colored and the poor. The other day, Margaret even said that the Yankees deserved to win and were on the right side. When the teacher told me this I could not believe it since she is your daughter. But Margaret repeated it in my presence. She seemed quite proud to be defending the Northerners."

Unanimous Verdict

Miss Austin spoke the words faster as she proceeded with her narrative until they tumbled like a waterfall.

"My daughter always has thought for herself, Miss Austin. Surely, this is a passing thing. Margaret must not be the only child who experiments with odd positions in the classroom. The school must cope with such things daily." Even a girls' school should be able to deal with some juvenile dissent, Farwell thought. There must be something else going on.

"She does more than express herself, Governor. She is disrespectful of those who maintain the Southern traditions. She speaks mockingly to the other students and even to the faculty. Even her friend, Nancy, knows to hold her tongue, something your daughter seems unable to learn." The volume and intensity of Miss Austin's voice increased as she described conduct which angered her.

"What do you want from me, Miss Austin?" Governor Farwell sensed that further discussion would prompt tears. He did not want to comfort a tearful Miss Austin. But if Miss Austin expected to stir anger in the Governor, she had failed. Farwell was even slightly pleased to hear that his daughter was thinking for herself.

"I'm afraid we must ask you to come and bring Margaret home."

"You mean she is being expelled?" Farwell's comfort was shattered. Were the school traditions and curricula so delicate they could not tolerate some wayward thinking from a 15-year old?

Chapter Thirteen: The Farwell Family

"We prefer to call it a home leave. Perhaps by returning to River's Edge and your direct care, she will be cured of these ideas. We would happily welcome her back in the fall term with your assurances that our lessons will agree with her.

"Candidly, Governor Farwell, it is a matter of finances and reputation. Nearly a dozen parents have said they will not return their daughters to the Academy next fall if Margaret is a student. They expect their daughters to receive a *social* education, to transmit our Southern traditions, the traditions of Southern bloodlines. They are not paying for us to fill their children with contrary ideas. We must insist."

The spring term would be over in six weeks, Farwell thought. But Miss Austin did not seem inclined to brook delay and Farwell was not interested in negotiating his daughter's future at a place where she was not wanted. Besides, he missed Margaret and would secretly welcome her early return. He also would find out what really troubled her. She could not possibly have become a Yankee sympathizer. She was a Farwell.

The Governor telephoned his son, State Senator Nathan Farwell, who practiced law in Aiken when the state legislature was not in session and was preparing to run for attorney general. The senior Farwell asked his son to remove his daughter from the Academy at once and bring her to River's Edge in the morning.

Unanimous Verdict

<u>1903–1919</u>

John Farwell always had showered his daughter with love and attention. Her mother, Rebecca, John's second and much younger wife, suffered a fatal hemorrhage during Margaret's birth. John loved Rebecca far more than he did his first wife, Nathan's mother, who committed suicide when John was denied the Democratic Party nomination to the U.S. Senate. The first wife, Catherine, hated River's Edge. "Nothin' but niggers and farmers," she often exclaimed. Denied the prospect of life as a Washington socialite or more years as the First Lady in Columbia, Catherine medicated herself with alcohol and ended her life in the Savannah River. The newspapers called her death accidental.

Rebecca, however, was enchanted by River's Edge and took to rural life with enthusiasm. Her energy renewed John, who, at nearly 50, looked forward to a future filled with domestic satisfactions and agrarian success rather than political challenges. Margaret was Rebecca's precious gift to him; a daily reminder that John Farwell's life still had purpose after his wife's death. Margaret did not disappoint him. She had her mother's cornflower blue eyes, corn tassel blonde hair and energy enough for two more girls. By 14, she had lost the chubbiness common to younger children and was showing the beginnings of a fine figure.

Over the years, the Governor grew accustomed to strangers complimenting him on his "granddaughter". It was an understandable mistake. By 1919, when Margaret was sent home from school, Farwell was nearing 70. Still trim and able, but with only a few strands of gray hair atop his head and the beginnings of loose flesh which promised

Chapter Thirteen: The Farwell Family

the wattles of old age, Farwell was the picture of grandfatherly affection with his young daughter.

As a young girl, before boarding school, Margaret traveled everywhere around the state with her father. She loved the attention she received at political gatherings as she sat in the first row of the audience with the wife of the host while her father delivered a speech. The Governor never neglected to point to Margaret and credit her with redeeming his life from two tragic deaths. Although she understood little of the politics, Farwell was confident that somehow just being in the presence of South Carolina Democrats would shape Margaret's view of the world.

Margaret returned the affection. She was proud to be her Daddy's girl. Her half brother was building his law practice in Aiken and preparing for his own political career. She had all the benefits of an only child, including her father's undivided attention. Although she had no mother, Margaret was coddled and cosseted by a series of "mammies" who lived in the former slave village. When she was very young, she was permitted to play with the children of the colored hands, both in the village and in the mansion, because there was only one other white child her age on the plantation, who was the daughter of the plantation manager.

As he had done with Nathan nearly 30 years earlier, Farwell sat Margaret on his lap in the living room at River's Edge and spent hours under the gas and, later, the new electric lights, with photo albums and scrapbooks which detailed the glorious history of the Farwell family.

Unanimous Verdict

The earliest photos were of his father, Edward, who, John told his daughter, made River's Edge even grander than his father before him. There were sketches and daguerreotypes of Edward in his Confederate officer's uniform and, in the most cherished photo in the house, with General Robert E. Lee. One of the large portraits – the one in the position of honor in the middle of the staircase, mastering attention from the main hall – was based on that daguerreotype. Other photos were of John's three older brothers, the most glorified and sanctified members of the clan because they had died heroically for the cause of the South. These, too, had been the basis for the lavish oil paintings which adorned the walls of River's Edge.

The painting of the Governor, which was hung apart from the others in the dining room, was different. It was a portrait of him in the Governor's Mansion. There was nothing wrong with the work, a typical portrait of an executive, except that while the other paintings bore the trappings of war, heroism and passion, John's could claim only the much duller characteristics of commercial and political success. He was only 5 years old when the Civil War began, 10 years younger than his nearest brother.

Too young to spill his own blood in the war, by 1880 John was fully recruited into the political battle against Reconstruction and what Northerners called "civil rights of the Negro." He early vowed that what his elders lost in war, he and allies in the southern legislatures would recover – the right of white people to claim their native heritage, including supremacy over the Negro. In his eight years occupying the

Chapter Thirteen: The Farwell Family

Governor's Mansion across the turn of the nineteenth century — four years as lieutenant governor to Ben Tillman and four years as governor in his own right — Farwell had ensured that while the colored were no longer legal property, in South Carolina they would be unable to enjoy the fruits of liberty. Colored public schools received less than half the funds of white schools and were non-existent in many counties. No money was spent to provide colored neighborhoods with running water, sewers or decent roads. Poll taxes and complex literacy requirements — waived for whites — kept the Negro from voting. Law enforcement at every level rigorously enforced Jim Crow laws that segregated black from white at every occasion that public social interaction could occur. The Democratic Party thrived on fear of the colored. Nearly 60 percent of the state's population was black, a statistic that was regularly used to cudgel even reluctant whites, fearful of Negro rule, into supporting Jim Crow. Whites jealously guarded their power and privilege and were easily persuaded that "niggers and Northerners" wanted to take it from them. John Farwell was a masterful politician who appealed to fearful whites not only to win their votes, but because he shared their fears and beliefs.

Farwell was jealous that his brothers were able to die defending a gallant cause, but he took comfort that his own life honored the same cause and the blood of the fallen. He had instilled the same passion in his son and aimed to do so with his daughter.

As Margaret got older and learned about history and government from her tutors, the Governor dwelled on the clippings in the scrapbook of his own political rise. He never tired of explaining to his daughter how he had helped return the white man to power in South Carolina and restored the colored to their rightful place in society. He left no doubt that his was a moral and heroic platform which protected the integrity of the great white race while providing paternal protection to the savage Negro.

Over the years, the Governor had given his son, Nathan, most of the swords, battle flags and other memorabilia of the Civil War which his own father had acquired and to which John had added. Nathan was a Civil War enthusiast, with a genuine affection for the heroism of the defenders of the South and a pragmatic understanding that display of Confederate swords, flags and uniforms in his law offices in Aiken and Columbia established his *bona fides* as a trusted defender of Southern values. But a handful of items remained at River's Edge along with the massive oil paintings. John Farwell pulled these out with the photo albums and scrap books to show to his daughter. As a small child, the one sword remaining in the mansion pleased Margaret the most. She demanded that it be produced for inspection regularly.

But Farwell could have seen clues to Margaret's still-latent rebellious nature if he were not blinded by the certainties of his convictions.

In 1913, when Margaret was almost 10 years old, Farwell instructed her to stop playing with the colored children of the field hands. This was a rule when Nathan was 10, when John Farwell was 10 and when all the Farwell ancestors were 10. It was the rule

Chapter Thirteen: The Farwell Family

whether the colored were slaves or free. At 10, it was time to erect the permanent social barrier between the races. The urgency of this rule was doubled for Margaret, the first female Farwell offspring, due to the perceived risk from Negro boys incapable of controlling their lust for white women. But Margaret fought the order and enlisted her colored playmates for help. She enjoyed her colored friends. The colored children were more active than most of the white kids. They played in the river. They went hunting with slingshots and homemade bows and arrows. They played hide-and-seek in the extensive woods in and around the plantation. They made her laugh. Margaret was a tomboy. She thought dolls and board games were OK on rainy days, but she preferred the more active outdoor life of the colored boys.

Margaret and her plantation friends made a game out of violating the anti-fraternization rule. They invented secret codes for messages left in hiding places around the outside of the mansion. These messages used crude cartoons to identify times and places for Margaret to meet her playmates, who were illiterate, or nearly so. When her father and Lorelei, her nanny, believed she was napping or studying, Margaret escaped to the old slave village, where the hired hands lived with their families.

Her best friend was a dark-skinned Negro named Isaac Fuller. Isaac was a prankster. So was Margaret. They enjoyed playing tricks on their friends and on adults. Margaret was often in the farmhand village with Isaac, the two of them laughing uproariously at some private joke. They shared the intimacy of co-conspirators and liked each other immensely.

If Farwell suspected his daughter was violating his orders, he never said so. But when Margaret was 14, her home schooling ended and she was sent to board at The Women's Academy. Farwell was sad to send her off because River's Edge was very lonely without her laughter and gaiety ringing in the hallways. Boarding school always was planned for Margaret when she reached an age requiring a more formal education than local tutors could provide. But he had other reasons for sending her away. He worried that his wish for an independent, spirited daughter was too generously granted. Margaret not only was a tomboy, interested in boyish things, but she was headstrong. She questioned everything, including Farwell's rigid racial views. Her questions were reasonable ones for someone her age, such as: Why do we hate the coloreds? (Answer: We don't hate them. We take care of them.) Why don't they go to school with white kids? (Answer: They would fare poorly compared to white children and might drag the white children down with them.) But Margaret was not satisfied with these answers. She doubted that her friends were inferior to herself, and her father encouraged her belief that she was among the best the white race had to offer. Although secretly pleased that his daughter, like her mother, was capable of independent thought, Governor Farwell was confident that The Women's Academy would educate his daughter not only in mathematics and literature, but also in the history of the South and how the Negro had demonstrated during Reconstruction that he was unfit for either self-governance or social commerce. A proper education was the cure to juvenile misconceptions, Farwell told his son, Nathan, who usually reacted angrily to Margaret's questioning of Southern values. Further, the school would teach Margaret how to be a proper lady, a role that a widower could not fulfill.

Margaret went willingly to the Academy. She was anxious to experience life outside of River's Edge. Her father's political gatherings she enjoyed as a child now were dull and attended by people she did not particularly like. But she quickly found the conventions of a Southern girls' school even more stifling.

"The lessons of womanhood are not learned solely in the classroom, dears," Miss Jasmine Austin, headmistress, informed her charges during the first week of the fall term. "You must appreciate the fine things in life. A young lady who does not know the Brevets of Greenville or the Knowles of Charleston (both families well-represented at the boys' school) is simply not fit to call herself a product of South Carolina. You must meet them, and some of you might be fortunate enough to marry them or their like." Margaret had no interest in taking up the challenge. These boys would be lucky to meet her, she concluded.

Sometimes, Margaret volunteered to classmates her unusual views about race. She had found nothing in her studies, she said, that proved the Negro was inferior to the white man. Her research on Reconstruction disclosed hints that the accepted view — that Yankees and Negroes did a poor job running the post-war South — was wrong, or at least debatable. Her views were considered eccentric, but she was not socially suspect until she mentioned having Negro friends she respected, treated as equals, and with whom she socialized back home. Thereafter, on many occasions outside the hearing of faculty and staff, sweetly pubescent blond, blue-eyed gentile daughters of the South dressed in pretty pastel dresses hissed through their soft lips and clean white teeth words such as "nigger lover" and "nigger whore." Margaret was shocked that merely stating she had Negro friends had uncovered such raw animosity. She hoped that most of the girls simply did not appreciate the gravity of their slanders. She resolved to study harder and determined to spend no more than three years at the Academy rather than the standard four.

Two weeks before the Thanksgiving 1917 recess of her second year, Margaret answered a knock on her door. She had roomed alone after her first term. Most girls were resistant to sharing a room with Margaret. She was not unfriendly, but her views were outlandish and isolating. Margaret was happy not to share her room. Answering the knock, she was greeted by a girl who had enrolled only that fall. She introduced herself as Nancy Markham.

"Yes, I know who you are," Margaret said. She forced herself to smile. She did not enjoy interruption of her studies. She was on course to collect all her credits in 18 months.

"I wanted to talk to you," Nancy replied. "I heard you are a tolerant person."

Chapter Thirteen: The Farwell Family

"Is that really what you heard?" "Tolerant" was an odd term to apply to a young person, she thought.

"Well, no. Honestly, some people call you a nigger lover or a Yankee. I'm not sure which they think is worse." Nancy was somber as she spoke, uncertain what reaction her reporting would bring. She welcomed Margaret's laughing reply.

"I don't think they believe there is any difference! Don't worry about it. They call me 'Nigger lover" to my face. It's true I have close colored friends. But I don't have any lovers, black or white. I'm only 15, after all!"

"I don't think they meant it literally, but who knows? You see, I have sort of the same problem here."

"You mean you have Negro lovers?"

"Of course not. You didn't mean that?"

"No. I was kidding. You mean people are suspicious you might even be a Negro yourself, is that it?"

Nancy had dark hair and deep brown eyes, like many other girls at the Academy. But she also had very brown skin, like a permanent deep tan. She was darker than some mixed blood Negroes, but her facial features were more European. To the unprejudiced eye, Nancy was a maturing young girl of great beauty. But to the students, faculty and staff at the Aiken Academy for Women, she was a girl with suspect skin color.

"I'm not, though. I'm half Moroccan. My dad is white. He met my mom while he was with the State Department. He was stationed at the U.S. embassy in Marrakech. It's North Africa. Like Egyptians. We are considered white." Her words were practiced. She had recited the same explanation many times.

"You don't really look Negro, just different," Margaret said.

"Many people see no difference at all. There are not many people in the South from North Africa. Even fewer who are only half North African. You would be surprised how many stores and restaurants refuse service to my mother and me, or how many people expect us to move to the back of the bus or the movie line and to sit in the colored sections. They call us mulattos or half-breeds. My mother learned to drive just to get a license to prove she is legally considered white. It says right on the license: white. Many people still don't believe her and think it's a fake. I'm still too young to get a license to drive. I have no proof I'm white."

"I'm starting to think that the only thing some of these girls here have to be proud of is that they're white," Margaret said, twisting her own blond locks around her left index finger.

"Some of them try to be nice. They're pretty sure the school wouldn't let me enroll if I weren't considered white. But most of the girls are standoffish. I mean, they talk to me when I talk to them, and they don't run away when I walk by, but they are mostly cold. I can tell some don't like me and most of them are uncomfortable with me. I think they are silly and dumb, but it still hurts. I can't change my skin color." By now, Nancy had shoved aside some of the books on the former roommate's bed to sit and showed signs of suppressing tears.

Chapter Thirteen: The Farwell Family

Margaret rose from her desk chair, made more room on the bed beside her and put her arm around Nancy's shoulders.

"Of course you can't. What do you want from me?"

"I want to be your friend."

"Because I am 'tolerant'?" Nancy smiled at the gently mocking tone.

"Yes. And because we are both lonely." Margaret knew that what Nancy said was true. She had avoided confronting her loneliness by throwing herself into her studies and by taking comfort in the justness of her own causes. But she had no one to talk to. No one to share her dreams with. Margaret removed her arm from Nancy's shoulder and the girls began to talk. They exchanged their opinions about the faculty, other students and life in the South. The conversation continued past lights-out and into the early morning. They learned that both of them enjoyed pranks and the outdoors and had been considered tomboys growing up. They went to sleep as fast friends.

Nancy and Margaret were nearly inseparable after that night. Nancy adopted Margaret's goal of learning as much as she could and getting out of the Academy early. She moved in with Margaret and they studied until lights out, their concentration often interrupted by long discussions about Southern myths masquerading as facts in the textbooks they studied. They corresponded daily during Thanksgiving and Christmas breaks, sharing homework assignments and gossiping about the other girls.

Unanimous Verdict

Margaret complained to Nancy at Christmas that she felt isolated at River's Edge and wanted more interesting things to read. Governor Farwell subscribed to several South Carolina newspapers and some farming periodicals, plus numerous journals devoted to Southern history, all of them published by Southern universities and fraternal organizations. But nothing came into the house devoted to thoughtful articles on matters of current national or international interest. Nancy's father, the former diplomat who now ran the family department store in Augusta, was interested in world affairs. His appetite was not satisfied by the local Augusta paper or even *The Atlanta Constitution*. He subscribed to *Harpers Magazine*, *The Atlantic Monthly*, *The National Geographic* and *The Saturday Evening Post*. Nancy promised to bring a collection of issues to school in January.

Margaret was enchanted, especially with *The Atlantic Monthly*, *Harpers* and *The National Geographic*. The first two publications explored issues in a fashion she had never encountered. They raised questions. Facts were marshaled in support of ideas. There often were debates between different authors, the first taking a position that Margaret thought was insurmountable until she read the opposing author. Letters to the editor challenged points presented in earlier issues. Sometimes it seemed that nothing was ever settled and that everything was subject to exploration. Maybe some day I can add my voice, she thought.

John Farwell and the Academy faculty presented every subject as having been finally decided, brooking no room for doubt. Jefferson was the greatest among the Founding Fathers. Senator John

Chapter Thirteen: The Farwell Family

C. Calhoun, for whom Margaret's father was named, was not only a great South Carolinian, but the most important American since Jefferson. Lincoln was an unhappy man – probably insane – with a nasty wife, to boot – who punished the South for asserting its proper rights to self-governance. Jefferson Davis, Robert E. Lee, Stonewall Jackson, Wade Hampton, John Farwell and Pitchfork Ben Tillman – all heroes. And so forth up to the present day.

Rigid thought was infectious, extending to matters far beyond the U.S. Civil War. Europe must fight its own wars. We have no stake there. The Reds will take over the U.S. unless we hang the anarchists and labor unionists. Be watchful of the power of the Jews. Look out for those who think differently. The United States is the City on the Hill, especially now that the Negro is in his place. Don't let anyone challenge the vision.

But these magazines, several months worth that Nancy packed in a large box (her mother was grateful to be rid of them), established that there were differing views that were backed by stronger facts than the ones she heard at school and at home. Margaret's intellectual energy was sparked, invigorated and nurtured by these publications and the freewheeling discussions, mostly with Nancy, that they provoked. She vowed to work doubly hard at school, and to attend a boarding school in the North, where she assumed she would be exposed to a more demanding and more open education.

The National Geographic appealed to her for different reasons. The large black-and-white pictures were fun to examine. The descriptions of far away places with strange customs intrigued her. *The Geographic* usually was respectful of the cultures it reported on. She wanted to visit such places. She wanted to see the world.

All of these influences – Isaac and her other Negro friends at River's Edge, Nancy, the nasty reactions of the other girls at the Academy, the eye-opening intellectual freedom represented in her periodicals and the sympathetic descriptions of other people and cultures in the *Geographic*, plus her own instincts – fostered and encouraged Margaret's childhood inclinations. Margaret Rebecca Farwell – daughter of a two-term race-baiting supremacist governor of South Carolina, granddaughter and niece of heroes of the Confederacy and half-sister of another angry race-baiting politician – became as a teen-ager an ardent opponent of Jim Crow and vocal advocate for integrating the races. Nancy agreed with Margaret and encouraged her with late night, lights-out bedtime discussions, but rarely voiced such views to others. Already suspect because of her dark skin and suspicious parentage, Nancy wished to avoid becoming an outcast. No such bonds restrained Margaret.

One of the first to receive this message was Horace Beckinsmith, Margaret's history teacher. Beckinsmith was a lean, bony man with a sour personality. He seethed with resentment because he was unable to obtain a university position and instead was forced to instruct empty-headed daughters of the landed gentry, nearly all of whom cared little about the history of the state or the nation. Beckinsmith himself lacked a curious mind. He learned what he was taught and preferred to repeat it rather than question it.

Chapter Thirteen: The Farwell Family

He was steeped in the doctrine of the Lost Cause of the Civil War. He was the perfect vessel for squelching even modest thirst for education at the Academy.

"So, class, let's repeat what we've learned this week." Beckinsmith directed oral quizzes at his students each Friday morning. "Why did the North prevail in the War of Northern Aggression?"

"Because the North had most of the industry," said Susannah Moultrie, a petite, doe-eyed girl from Greenville. "That's why it is a rougher, ruder and more base society than the Jeffersonian South."

"Because Sherman and his forces were so inhuman, what with raping and pillaging and whatnot, that the South was too demoralized to fight on. Our boys would not do that, even to Yankees." Michelle Asquith, a striking brunette who also was the tallest girl at the Academy, spoke in the deepest Southern accent, a result of living in Mississippi most of her life. Her remarks brought on applause from the rest of the class.

"Because Lincoln threatened England with war to keep them from supporting the Confederacy," added Lucy Bainbridge, an overweight, heavily freckled young lady from Charleston whose dance card was usually empty at the balls sponsored by the Academy for the boys' and girls' schools. Heads bobbed in agreement around the classroom. Beckinsmith beamed.

"Because the North had a just cause and Northerners didn't rely on the work of slaves to harvest their crops and build their industries like the foolish southerners. They were tougher and more realistic."

Unanimous Verdict

The room was silent. Beckinsmith stared at Margaret Farwell. Margaret might as well have declared Genesis a fiction. Her comments were no less heretical.

"Why, that's what we'd expect from a nigger lover." The doe-eyed Susannah Moultrie spat out her words. "Why don't you just get on the train and head north."

"I'm just stating the truth," Margaret said. "But you won't find it in your book."

Beckinsmith regained his speech. "That's not what you were taught, Miss Farwell. Where did you learn that? I'm certain your father didn't teach you that."

"No, he didn't. But it's obviously so. We were one of the last places on earth to have slavery. Doesn't that tell you something, Mr. Beckinsmith? And isn't it so that no person can own another? Why, it's immoral."

Beckinsmith suppressed his initial desire to silence Margaret and change the subject. Instead, the class engaged in a discussion of the morality of slavery, with nearly all of the girls taking the traditional stance that slavery assisted the black man and woman with a better life than they could live on their own. One or two girls sided with Margaret. Beckinsmith was nervous about permitting the debate, and made sure it concluded with a resounding endorsement of the Southern cause. A few days later he was chastised by Miss Austin for permitting such a discussion. Students had written their parents about the class and Miss Farwell's comments. They said the daughter of the former governor was a Northern radical. The parents lodged their complaints.

"These girls are sent here to refine their manner and to understand matters from the Southern point of view, Mr. Beckinsmith. Anything that counters that view is contrary to our purpose." Miss Austin's manner suggested Mr. Beckinsmith's job would be in jeopardy if he allowed further departures from the accepted ideology.

It was by no means the only time that Margaret was the heretic. She forced her teachers to defend themselves, their textbooks and their scholarship. She engaged her classmates in dialogue, challenging their sloganeering about state's rights, the Lost Cause, the inerrancy of the Bible and the Creation Story. She even expressed vocal support for the proposed Nineteenth Amendment giving women the right to vote – a position on which even her friend Nancy had doubts. Most were unmoved, but some were inspired to take up Margaret's challenges and to debate these subjects. They borrowed her magazines and obtained passes to the Aiken Public Library, as Margaret had done, to supplement their research. Sometimes they were persuaded Margaret was right; more often they clung to their original positions, unable to accept that the previously unquestioned principles of their upbringing could be in error. But even then, Margaret had introduced a germ fatal to dogma: doubt. Parents were not amused when their daughters returned home on holidays armed with curious questions about accepted truths.

But even a vocal, determined young Margaret could have only limited impact on an institution like the Academy. Of over 100 girls in four grades, perhaps ten were willing to pick up Margaret's challenge and debate the issues. The other ninety tried to ignore her and some parents thought she might require institutionalization. Miss Austin did not appreciate academic freedom in what was intended to be principally a finishing school. When parents continued to complain that principles on which the South was built were being challenged in class, she asked Margaret to please allow the teachers to abide by the printed curriculum. When Margaret refused, Miss Austin weighed the consequences of asking a former governor to withdraw his daughter from the Academy against the possible loss of a dozen other students if Margaret remained. Posed as a matter of economics rather than principle, the question answered itself. Margaret was dismissed in the spring of her second year at the Academy. She could be interviewed in the summer for the fall term, if she wished. If, at that time, she agreed to abide by the school curriculum and not raise irrelevant, obstructionist arguments in class, the school would consider readmitting her.

At first, Farwell did not know what to do with his errant daughter. He rejected immediately her request to attend boarding school in the North. He couldn't think of a more preposterous idea. He concluded that Margaret needed a re-education in matters of race, politics and the history of the South. It was obvious to him that the dull, second-class teachers at the Aiken Academy were no match for his daughter's bright, active mind. River's Edge was the best place to revisit these matters. Margaret needed to be challenged by more effective instruction. Farwell was confident his daughter's heresies would fall when confronted by

Chapter Thirteen: The Farwell Family

the indubitable logic reflected in a deeper and sober understanding of history and literature. Farwell could monitor his daughter's education at River's Edge and hire whom he pleased to deliver it. He diligently questioned the county school board, neighboring plantation owners and important men in Aiken, Barnwell and Allendale to identify men or women who could reliably tutor his daughter in high school subjects. He was especially concerned about literature and history. Mathematics and chemistry were not subject to political whim, Farwell reasoned. Biology was not a problem because Farwell himself thought evolution was a reasonable theory and he secretly considered the story of creation in Genesis a myth. The obvious superiority of the white man to other races made evolution self-evident, in his view. He could live with the notion that the white man came from a monkey in exchange for the scientific judgment that the Negro was little more than a monkey.

Margaret wished to subscribe to the publications she enjoyed receiving from Nancy at the Academy. Farwell considered this request for a long time before granting it. He believed wholeheartedly in the principles he espoused as governor and could not fathom that the arguments of Northerners, most of whom had much scorn for the South but little personal contact with the region or its people, could successfully defeat those principles if they were properly taught. He permitted his daughter to subscribe to the Yankee magazines. If his daughter put more trust in unknown Boston publishers than her own father, the thinking of those Brahmins must be shown to be wrong. Still, Farwell somewhat regretted his earlier enthusiasm for his daughter's independent thinking. Margaret at 15 reminded him less of his wife and more of the crazy suffragettes and anarchists he read about in the Augusta newspaper. A restless mind could be tolerated at River's Edge; rebellion against precious traditions of the South could not. He was confident Margaret's tutors were up to the challenge.

Chapter Fourteen: The Roach Family, 1870–1920

In April and May, the Savannah River flows fast with the runoff of the mountains in the west that temporarily disguises the muddy brown that will return to the surface with the lazy rhythms of the hot summer. Breezes that caress the long-leaf pines and live oak gently carry the sweet odors of crape myrtle, cherry laurel and gardenia from cultivated flower gardens on large old plantations and tenant farms alike. Azaleas blossom at every corner around every house in white, red and pink. All of nature's colors are intense in spring along the Savannah. This is when her artistry is nearly perfect. This was River's Edge.

The mansion was built by John Farwell's grandfather, Thomas Edward Farwell. Work began in 1807 and was completed two years later. Grandfather Farwell contracted with a Charleston architect, who designed a three-story mansion in the Greek Revival style built of oak, pine and cedar. T.E. Farwell supervised the construction, using skilled craftsmen drawn from across the southern half of South Carolina and from parts of Georgia all the way to Atlanta. No slaves were permitted to work on the house other than as laborers hauling materials to the site. The completed structure featured a wide porch wrapping around all but the back side and a second-story widow's walk at the front atop four Georgian columns created from southern red oak trees. The Savannah was visible two miles distant, across two gentle ridges. All of the floors were oak planks, heavily sanded, stained and polished.

The interior walls were plaster, with hand shaped plaster ceiling molds, oak chair rails and floor moldings. The library was paneled with polished walnut. Bookcases, also of walnut, lined two walls of the library, reaching to the 12-foot ceiling.

Cotton built River's Edge, and cotton needed slaves. Grandfather Farwell was mildly opposed to slavery when he bought his first 500 acres of what became River's Edge. He had emigrated from England, shortly after the Revolution. Slavery was unfamiliar to him and he was repelled by the notion of one human owning another. He tried to farm the land himself, using hired hands as needed. But due to the farm's isolation, even hired hands required room and board, in addition to wages. Farwell soon learned he could not market cotton at a profit against slave labor. Further, slaves were property to be bought and sold. Maintaining them was a form of investment; feeding white laborers who could quit at any time was only an expense. The need to feed a family competed successfully against principle. Within a few years, T.E. Farwell was buying and selling slaves with the alacrity and skill of a native South Carolina planter. And, like his competitors, he maintained his slave property to the extent necessary to protect his investment, and no more. This meant able slaves (and the valuable young children they produced) were well-fed, had a warm, dry place to sleep and even received medical care in Aiken or Barnwell if doing so would return them to the fields. Old slaves, feeble slaves and chronically ill slaves either were sold for whatever price they could bring or were put on minimal rations and in the poorest housing in hopes they would meet a quick end. Sometimes, rarely at River's End, more commonly on some other plantations, a sick, bed-ridden slave was charged with thievery or other crime impossible for him to have committed in his condition. He was then beaten or whipped so severely that he died, ending the unprofitable drain on his master's purse.

"Slavery hardens men's hearts," T.E. Farwell observed in his quiet, philosophical moments, "but a soft heart cannot prevail against hard trade." He concluded that slavery was a necessity for the white man and a benefit to the Negro. "What can a Negro do with freedom? He will not learn. He is lazy. He will procreate to starvation," he wrote in a letter to *The Barnwell Sentinel*. "But a slave is guided by his master to perform fruitful labors on the land in return for sustenance and shelter for his family. Most of my Negroes say they do not want freedom. In that, they demonstrate surprising and unexpected wisdom."

T.E. Farwell's grandson subscribed to all of these sentiments when he succeeded to ownership of River's Edge as the sole surviving son in 1882. Those same teachings made him twice governor of the state, but took him away from his beloved plantation for long periods – leaving Buster Roach in charge.

By 1919, Roach had been the foreman of River's Edge for over 30 years. John Farwell had hired him in 1888, during his first race for the state senate, when it was clear that politics would keep Farwell and his first wife, Catherine, away from the plantation and unable to make the daily decisions necessary to operate what was now a 3,500 acre farm employing 150 hands, most of whom had families. This meant feeding and housing nearly 400 coloreds in what had once been the slave village. When Margaret was sent home by the Academy, Farwell had been out of politics and residing in the mansion for nearly 20 years, but, except for affairs inside the mansion, River's Edge was run by Roach as if it were his own.

Buster Roach grew up neither a farmer nor a Southerner. He was born in the Five Points slum of New York. His father was murdered by his partner in crime when Buster was a youngster. His mother was not a prostitute, but only because she was too anxious and too ugly to be paid for sex. Why pay for what could be obtained for nothing? Buster inherited her appearance. He possessed a number of unfortunate features, a result of neglect, mistreatment and years of inbreeding among the Irish of New York, mingled with more recent Italian blood and genes of unknowable origin. One eye was green, the other blue. His face was riddled with the unmistakable potholes of chicken pox from his youth. His nose was twisted to the left, the result of multiple breaks that never properly healed. A huge scar crossed his throat, a reminder of a near-fatal knife wound. He limped due to untreated infection from a bullet wound. His skin was a shade somewhere between yellow and orange. It never varied no matter how long Roach was in the sun or in the dark. His coloring was not a symptom of disease. Roach was healthy until the day he died. The Farwells surmised that Roach's skin color and his different eye colors were the product of some genetic mutation. No one really knew. It was assumed he was born ugly. Roach was short, about five feet five inches, but he exercised the strength of four men.

The most remarkable feature of this pockmarked yellow stain of a man was that he spoke English at least as well as President Wilson, if not better. His grammar was proper and there was only the slightest trace of a New York Irish accent. Even this was not noticeable in normal conversation; it appeared only when Roach was excited. When the Farwells asked how he learned to speak properly, Roach lied and told him that he was fortunate to attend a slum school with an inspiring English teacher. The truth was that at the age of eight his mother sold him for one hundred dollars to a gangland captain with a sideline in child prostitution. Some clients cultivated a taste for well-spoken boys dressed in fancy suits or even costumes from the reign of French kings. Kidnapping real upper class boys who spoke good English was an invitation to execution. But the police didn't care about poor waifs. It was less risky to hire a school teacher for extra wages to instruct a few boys in proper English pronunciation for two or three hours a day. The investment was amply returned by the premium price the boys brought once night fell in Five Points.

Buster Roach was educated in this fashion until he was thirteen. He was so skilled at proper sounding English, even sometimes adopting a realistic continental English accent, that he was rumored to be the highest priced boy for rent in New York City. (Buster was required only to *sound* like an English lad. Proper grammar was not critical because his customers were as ignorant as Buster of proper use of the language). But his value plummeted like a racehorse with a broken leg when puberty began and Buster looked less like an innocent, albeit not very handsome, English school boy and more like a Five Points male hooker.

Roach escaped Five Points and New York City in 1884, when he was 14, after a drunken customer nearly succeeded in cutting his throat. He stowed away on a steamship bound for South America but was discovered and put on shore at Savannah. With reasonable spoken English, knowledge of basic arithmetic he had acquired as part of his earlier trade, and a hatred for Negroes learned from the Irish gangs, Roach was a good candidate for field boss on South Carolina plantations. Of course, he had no knowledge of agriculture, but the Negroes and the senior foremen taught him those skills on the job. In less than four years, he acquired a reputation in the Jasper-Beaufort County region.

Among many growers, Roach was deemed a reliable supervisor of colored workers who promptly and effectively addressed disciplinary problems, clearly and concisely explained any matter raised by his bosses, and produced crop yields that surpassed those of anyone else working directly with the colored population on the plantations.

Among the colored plantation workers, Roach was considered the meanest, most vicious, most foul-mouthed and ill-tempered SOB on any plantation or farm. Many Negroes quit when Roach was named their supervisor. Roach just made the remaining Negroes work harder until replacements were hired. Stories about Roach's cruelty were legion. He once hit a pregnant woman in the stomach

Chapter Fourteen: The Roach Family

with a crowbar, causing a stillbirth only minutes later. He tied a man to a large rock and tossed both of them into the Savannah River, intending to retrieve the man after a few minutes. When he was called away by another white supervisor, the man drowned. He tied another man to the saddle of an unbroken horse and laughed while the horse bucked. He laughed until the man broke his back. Then, to hide the injury from the owner, Roach reportedly chopped the man into small pieces and deposited them in a barrel. The Savannah River came to his aid again as a depository for the barrel. Roach denied these stories were true, except when there were white witnesses. Some of them may have been apocryphal, others half-truths. But many likely were true, even if not subject to proof in a courtroom. That such stories grew around Roach and were believed was itself evidence of his behavior.

A large minority of plantation owners and their supervisors dissented from the laudatory views of Roach by other whites. These men thought Roach was nothing more than a transplanted New York hoodlum with the unrestrained judgment of a killer and a strong taste for sadism. One of these owners, accompanied by his foreman, journeyed to River's Edge when he heard the Farwells had hired Roach to tell them they made a mistake. His description of Roach only burnished his reputation in the mind of Catherine Farwell, who hated and feared Negroes. John Farwell, who was more paternal toward his colored hands, decided the matter was not sufficiently significant to challenge his wife's judgment.

Unanimous Verdict

Most of the Negroes at River's Edge resided with their families in the same shacks constructed by former slaves after the Civil War. By World War I, the principal concession to modern living standards was provision of a water pump outside every five or six shacks. Farwell, not Roach, ordered this improvement after repeated requests from the workers, some of whom had to walk nearly a half mile to the nearest pump. The river was even farther. In Roach's view, River's Edge was obliged only to provide four walls and a roof to those living on the plantation. "The principal benefit of the Emancipation Proclamation is freedom," Roach told employees when they complained about living or working conditions. "You are free to leave if you don't like it and I'm free to fire you if you keep complainin'."

Roach was not so parsimonious with his own quarters. He expanded his house as his family grew and upgraded amenities as they became available. By 1919, his house had full electrical service, indoor plumbing, two bathrooms, a furnace and a hot water heater. Roach made sure that the mansion received any improvements he desired for his own home so that all upgrades were approved (and paid for) by Farwell.

Neither Catherine nor John Farwell expected that Roach would find a bride. He was ugly and his physical appearance was not offset by any charm which they could perceive. But after several years of isolation at River's Edge in which his only human contacts were the Farwells and their employees, Roach started attending services at the nearby Baptist church. The congregation was rural, white and poor. The preacher was

372

Chapter Fourteen: The Roach Family

a sharecropper who had founded the church a few years earlier. He was a powerful preacher. He combined the poetic English of the King James Bible with the rough, profane speech of the dirt poor. Each service was a roller coaster ride of hellfire fear and heavenly promise. After a two-hour service, the congregation felt cleansed of their sins and fearful of what God had in store for them in the coming week. The church was a great success, with a congregation of nearly 100 worshipers. Buster Roach often skipped the service because he didn't care to be cleansed of sins and was not afraid of any God, but he religiously attended the fellowship hour each Sunday and the monthly pot luck socials. He was looking for a mate.

Roach was not without some features a poor woman could appreciate. He was foreman of the largest plantation in the region and was handsomely paid. He made sure to give generously to the Baptist Church. He knew the preacher would spread the word that Roach was able to make such contributions, a sign of both wealth and piety. Roach also knew the basic rules of etiquette and was able to ingratiate himself easily with both the men and women in the congregation. He had made a living for himself and his pimp for years by acting the role of a British school boy for the sexual satisfaction of wealthy New York perverts. It was nothing to turn such skills to more pedestrian uses such as squiring poor farm girls. Roach offered these girls a chance to move up the economic and social ladder. Roach was so skilled at playing the role of a God-fearing suitor that no one suspected the pain and regret that life with him would bring his wife.

Unanimous Verdict

It required only a few weeks of attending services for Roach to identify Celestine Grove as his target of opportunity. She was one of seven children of Patience and Jacob Grove, who farmed a parcel of land about four miles from the northern reaches of River's Edge. The family never had more than five dollars at any one time. They put a dime in the offering plate every week for the whole family. Their regular contribution to the pot luck socials was boiled beans. The preacher often offered prayers from the pulpit for God to look over the Groves because they were the poorest family in the church. Other members of the congregation responded by giving the Groves their cast off clothing and offering them foodstuffs. The Groves responded with appropriate humility and grace. They were not a bad family, just a very poor one. Roach knew the congregation would rejoice in his marriage to Celestine. He only needed to persuade her.

Roach knew his limits. Celestine was not the prettiest girl in the congregation. She was plain. But with thin reddish hair, freckles and a mild burn from the sun she could be appealingly cheerful. At 19, her parents had nearly given up on her finding a husband. They were grateful for the attentions bestowed upon her by a prosperous, responsible man like Roach. Roach moved cautiously, knowing that several pot lucks and Sunday social hours were required to overcome first impressions. But he was a patient fisherman. He achieved his goal with a kind, sympathetic and entertaining personality which was entirely artificial. Six months after his first visit to the Baptist Church, he and Celestine announced their engagement. They were married two

Chapter Fourteen: The Roach Family

months later. Two months after that, Celestine was pregnant. Long before the birth of her first son, she knew her marriage was a great mistake.

Roach desired marriage for only one reason: he required a wife to bear him children. Roach told himself that all sex was disgusting, but he was more inclined to sex with men than women, a desire he denied to himself and repressed all of his adult life. His drives may have been the product of an early life servicing pedophiles, but smothering them engendered a mean and angry spirit that profited River's Edge but destroyed any prospect of a happy marriage. Roach refused to make love to his wife after she was pregnant. He resumed relations with her after their son was born, but stopped when she was again pregnant. Roach believed three children were enough, so after the birth of the third child, a daughter, he never had sex with his wife again. She was only 24. He was not yet 35.

Roach was continually aware that his livelihood depended on maintaining the respect and trust of the Farwell family. This acted as some restraint on his natural inclinations. Although he frequently threatened Celestine with violence, he rarely acted upon the threat. He knew that the Farwells would be appalled if he beat his wife, so he did so only on those occasions when the mansion was to be empty for a long period. Celestine made it a point to learn the travel plans of Catherine and John Farwell and dreaded their absences. Her life was made especially miserable during the eight years Farwell was governor and lieutenant governor and lived most of the year in Columbia. Even then, Roach took care to hit his wife only in ways that her face would not disclose an injury.

Celestine informed her father and mother of the beatings. There was nothing they could do. Celestine begged them not to confront Buster because he would be angry and the beatings would be worse. Wife beating was commonplace among the rural poor. Women fretted about it, but men accepted it as a husband's right and duty. Jacob Grove never beat Patience, but they knew many other families in which the husband was not so considerate. They advised their daughter that if Roach's beatings became life threatening, she and the children should come to live with them. Roach's beatings never were that severe and the prospects of bringing four more mouths to feed to the Grove house were daunting. Celestine stayed with her husband. The family's physical wants were well satisfied by an ever-expanding and improving home, a full pantry and even central heat in the winter. A poor woman could expect nothing better.

Roach raised his sons, Robert and Matthew, to be like him – mean, tough and disrespectful of human life. As small children they accompanied him on his rounds of the plantation village where the hired hands lived. They saw him discipline the workers, sometimes with corporal punishment, including beatings with a stick. They heard him call the hands "nigger" and "burr head" and "darkie" and other racial slurs. As if his example was insufficient, Roach instructed his children that emancipated colored people were less valuable than a mule because a mule had a market value and a colored man could just up and run.

Chapter Fourteen: The Roach Family

Women, white and black, fared even worse in Roach's vocabulary. He regularly used terms like "cunt" and "bitch" and talked about "pussy" and "poon tang", both when women were present and when they were not. Although he always was highly respectful of the Farwell men, on occasion he referred to Catherine Farwell and later even young Rebecca as a "cunt," – outside their presence, of course. He applied such words to his wife, even in front of his children.

Celestine witnessed the steady and intentional twisting of her handsome young tow-headed sons and protested that they should be raised in a Christian home, with love and kindness, as Jesus preached. Her protests were to no avail, prompting more cursing and, if the Farwells were absent, a thorough beating around her ribcage. The Roaches stopped attending church. Celestine became more sullen and isolated. She thanked God for her daughter, Emily, because Roach took no interest in her, leaving mother and daughter to live in a separate world of cooking, sewing and housekeeping. Celestine knew it was against God's teachings, but she hated her husband. As her sons grew into his image, she began to hate them, too, which caused her great guilt and pain.

The Farwells were not ignorant of Roach's personality and methods. John and Catherine appreciated his discipline of the colored help, even if they sometimes reprimanded him for extreme behavior. But the women, Catherine and, later, Rebecca, could discern from conversations with Celestine and the boys' behavior that Roach's soul was as ugly as his appearance. Catherine was too busy tending to her husband's political career to give Roach much thought, but she avoided him when she was at River's Edge. She insisted to her husband that she never be alone with Roach.

Rebecca, who was of Celestine's generation, was more judgmental. She made no effort to hide her distaste for Roach. Rebecca wanted her gestating child to live in a kind and gentle world at River's Edge, a world that would not include Buster Roach and his boys. She believed that the hands could be made to work with gentler treatment; that rewards are more effective than punishment. Celestine, who was pregnant with Emily, knew better than to share with Rebecca the stories of her mistreatment, but even in her few months at River's Edge, Rebecca could see that Celestine was withered by unhappiness and aging far beyond her years. She repeatedly demanded that her husband fire Roach before her own child was born. John Farwell promised to do so, but secretly hoped he could avoid making good on the commitment because he valued Roach for his skill at running River's Edge profitably. Roach knew Rebecca wanted him fired. He hated her for that. He was relieved when she died in childbirth. But her death was not free of consequences for him. Every time John Farwell spoke to Roach or thought of him, he was reminded that his wish to keep Roach in his employ was granted at a high and bitter price.

Buster Roach's respect for his boss declined after Farwell's failed attempt at a Senate nomination and his return to River's Edge. Among other things, Farwell could not control his females. His first

Chapter Fourteen: The Roach Family

wife shamed him with what everyone knew was a suicide and now his teen-age daughter was questioning core principles of race relations that had made Roach and River's Edge a commercial success for many years. "A man who can't control his bitches ain't worth two niggers," Roach told his sons. Farwell also was a lousy plantation manager. Roach had been skimming hundreds of dollars a month from the crop proceeds for years and Farwell never noticed. Roach persuaded him he didn't need an accountant to keep the books. Roach could do it. Farwell was a fool, he concluded, as well as an easy mark.

Roach was more clinical about Margaret, who was nearly 16 when she returned to the plantation. She was going to be a fine looking woman soon, "a handsome pussy between her legs and two firm handfuls of tit," he told his sons. She had a pretty smile, bright blue eyes and neatly bobbed blond hair. What else could a man ask for? She would be a perfect gift for his son, Robby, when he got back from the war in Europe. A couple good fucks is all. Unless Robby came back a changed man, she'd never marry him and Farwell would rather shoot Roach than let his son near her. But times changed. A couple good fucks, anyway, would be a good gift to Robby. Put him in a right frame of mind after the fighting. Might make the girl have a little more respect for the Roach family, too. She couldn't hold her head so high if she carried some of Robby's cum. Maybe a blow job, too. Roach hated her, even more than he did all women. He wanted to punish her for being who she was: pretty, rich, unattainable and a "nigger lover" to boot.

Unanimous Verdict

Buster was so obsessed about the Farwells that he failed to notice that his own daughter was attractive, blessed with her mother's genes plus improvements from suppressed generations in the past. Hers was a gentler, earthier appearance than Margaret's brassier blond coloration. If Margaret was a strong, fizzy cocktail, Emily was comfort food, no less appealing, but different. Her skin tanned easily in summer, complementing chestnut hair she maintained in long tresses which she believed disguised the soft roundness of her face. Her breasts and hips were larger, rounder, and more ample than Margaret's. Emily invited the notion of family and hearth, of safety and well-being, even as she lived under the harsh domain of her father. While Margaret dreamed of far-away places and studied the issues of the day, Emily wished only to find a man better than her father to take her away from his nightmarish ways. Confined as she was to River's Edge, forbidden to attend church and pulled from school after the eighth grade, even this slight goal was challenging. Though Emily's face, in which were fixed light brown eyes under long brown lashes, seemed made for laughter and cheer, there was little chance for such pleasures in the Roach household. When Emily left her house to churn butter, beat rugs or take walks, her expression was uniformly grim, finding no joy in her life and expecting none. Though they had been playmates as children, Margaret and Emily had grown apart, and John Farwell no more wanted his daughter to associate with a Roach than he did with a colored man.

In November 1918, armistice was declared in Europe. The Continent was again safe for travel and the dollar ruled commerce.

Chapter Fourteen: The Roach Family

Margaret suggested to her father after she was banished from boarding school that they take a Grand Tour of Europe. Farwell, who had never traveled north of Washington, D.C., told her he had many years in which to travel and that River's Edge required his full attention. But Farwell was almost 65 years old and Roach managed River's Edge. For the first time in her life, Margaret sensed that her father was afraid of new adventures and challenges.

The tedium of River's Edge was relieved for Margaret only by anxiously awaited periodicals and her old playmates from the farm worker village, especially Isaac. Margaret visited the village frequently, no longer bothering to hide this friendship from her father. She was curious about the lives of the farm hands and lobbied on their behalf with her father and Buster Roach for better wages and living conditions. She had small successes, and the colored families came to trust her. As in any community, some were more thoughtful than others. A few parents and nearly all of Margaret's contemporaries could read at least a little bit. Some, including Isaac, were more diligent. With a little schooling and much self-teaching, they were literate, able to read books. Margaret loaned them books from the Farwell library and passed along her magazines, pointing out articles she thought might be of particular interest. *The National Geographics* were especially popular, with their pictures of foreign lands and frequent articles and pictures about African cultures.

Farwell initially worried about his daughter's safety among the farm hands, clinging to the notion that Negro men become uncontrollable beasts in the presence of white women. His concerns diminished over the span of a few weeks when Margaret returned to the mansion every afternoon, her virtue unharmed. He did not like her fraternization with the colored, but the only other diversion was the Roach family. Farwell accurately perceived those Roach boys to be a greater risk than the colored.

Buster Roach seethed at the undermining of his previously unquestioned authority caused by Margaret's visits to the farm workers. The workers registered complaints with her that they would not dare raise directly with Roach or his sons, who were now his foremen. Occasionally, Margaret challenged Roach directly over a disciplinary action or work assignment. Roach ignored her, but knew that she brought these same issues to her father. Farwell usually supported his manager, but on one or two occasions suggested Roach use less corporal punishment to discipline the workers. In Roach's view, this was one or two times too often. He and his boys took to referring to Margaret as the "queen cunt". The Roach men lusted after and hated her; the Roach women feared for her safety, but were silent.

Robby Roach was discharged from the Army in time to celebrate Christmas of 1919 at River's Edge. He was physically fit, but nearly two years with a combat unit in Belgian trenches only reinforced the character he acquired from his father. Five farmhands packed up their families and quit River's Edge within only a few weeks after Robby's return to the fields. Robby believed that the men and women under his supervision worked hard only when threatened, and that threats

Chapter Fourteen: The Roach Family

only worked when they were validated by action. He thought a kind word of praise was a weakness the workers would exploit. As the days of spring grew longer, he extended the working day to match without raising wages. Even Matthew Roach, three years younger than Robby, was deemed by the hands a more tolerant and sympathetic foreman than Robby. Margaret heard bitter complaints about the older Roach boy which she took to Buster and to her father. Farwell told Buster to caution his son and that the Roaches would be judged on their ability to retain help as well as to increase farm production when their salaries were reviewed. The Roaches nodded their heads dutifully in front of Farwell, but were privately furious with Margaret, whom they accurately blamed for causing them to be chastised.

As Roach predicted, Margaret, fully 16 in 1920, was a classic Southern beauty. She had her mother's figure and the sharp chin and high cheekbones of a Farwell. Her breasts had grown to more than a "handful", but they gently called attention to themselves under the bodice of the long dresses Margaret preferred; they complimented her body rather than dominated it. Her hips and bottom curved gently and firmly, their outline visible when the fragrant spring breezes swept her loose cotton clothing tightly around her. Robby Roach regularly stiffened in his crotch when Margaret was in view, but the feeling was the opposite of love. He imagined dominating her, violating her most intimate parts. He wanted to get inside her, to force her to open herself to him. Like his father, he envisioned that Margaret would not be so haughty around the Roaches once she carried his seed. She would be at their level, even if only Margaret and the Roaches ever knew it. It would be a shared secret, warranting repeat visits. He would threaten her with death if she told her father, but Robby expected that the shame of being raped by a Roach would be enough to guarantee her silence. The whores of Europe told him he was a good lover. Perhaps Margaret would think so, too. He began to watch her carefully. He began to stalk her.

A gravel road separated the compound containing the mansion and the Roach house from the farm hands' village nearly two miles away. The road mostly separated fields of cotton and a few acres of cornfield, but sometime early in its 100 plus years, chestnuts and magnolias had been planted along the roadside, providing a canopy of welcome shade. About half-way down the road, the tree line expanded into a large grove, dividing what was called the Southeast 100 from the Southeast 80, identifying the fields by direction from the mansion and the acreage on either side of the grove. Margaret and her friends played in the grove when they were small. It was possible to hide in the grove, but a scream could easily be heard from the road. In Robby Roach's violent fantasy, the only sounds to come from the grove would be low moans of pleasure. Robby imagined that once Margaret relaxed and enjoyed his prowess, she would beg for more.

Margaret usually completed her tutoring by lunch time. She studied her lessons until about 4 o'clock, when the field hands were dismissed. This included those working under Robby after Margaret complained to her father that they were working longer hours than they

Chapter Fourteen: The Roach Family

had bargained for. Margaret then walked to the village, sometimes pulling a wagon with books and magazines. Her schedule was erratic. If she was immersed in an interesting article, or if the weather was inclement, she skipped the trip. But most weeks she visited her colored friends two or three times.

Matthew Roach usually was foreman for the southern fields at River's Edge while Robby commanded the north fields. Buster rode circuit between them and addressed extensive paperwork at the plantation office next to his house. In late April, as the sweet spring weather approached and the azaleas were in bloom, Robby asked his father to change assignments, which he did immediately. Robby did not hide his reasoning. There was no reason to do so. His father often asked him if he had "fucked the queen cunt" since he had returned from the war. They had even discussed how to keep the rape a secret in case Margaret took no pleasure from the encounter.

Robby looked for an opportunity and in the first week of May he found it. He was walking home from the southeast fields at the end of the workday when Margaret approached him, heading for the village. He slowed his gait so that he would meet her at the grove of trees. She was wearing a blue polka-dotted sun dress that had straps across her shoulders and a square bodice that revealed the foothills of her breasts. Her exposed skin was slightly reddened, a necessary prelude to an early summer tan. Margaret was deep in thought. *Harper's* had published a long profile of W.E.B. Dubois titled "Angry Scribe of the NAACP". She was anxious to show it to Isaac. She noticed Robby approaching her when he was only about 50 feet away. She wanted to move to the other side of the road, but decided doing so was impolite, even if he was a Roach.

Robby was focused on controlling himself. He needed to initiate the approach carefully. He had to try to be a gentleman – at first.

"Good afternoon, Miss Farwell. How are you today?"

"I'm fine, Mr. Roach."

"Do you have a minute? I need to ask you something?"

Margaret was suspicious. All of the male Roaches scared her. Robby sensed her fear and knew it would come in handy.

"I suppose so. But only a minute. I need to get to the village." Robby grabbed her elbow and maneuvered her to the side of the road. "Please don't touch me," she said forcefully.

"I'm sorry ma'am." He did not release her elbow. "I wanted to talk to you about one of your nigger friends. Isaac. I think we'll have to let him go."

"They are Negroes, Mr. Roach, not 'niggers', and I'm sure there is no reason to let Isaac go. He is a very smart man and I suspect he's a hard worker. Now, please let go of my arm."

The combination of Margaret's favorable remarks about a colored man and her evident disdain for even being touched by a Roach fueled the deep hatred he felt for Margaret and ignited these passions so that they overwhelmed Robby's caution.

"Whaddya do with those niggers down there anyway, Margaret? You can get what you need from me. I'm all white meat." As he spoke, he put one beefy arm around Margaret's waist and with his other hand he reached for a breast. At the same time, he pushed her toward the tree grove. Margaret resisted and grabbed a handful of Robby's hair, forcing him to release her breast to wrest her free arm from his hair and hold it in a hammerlock behind her back. Her upper torso and arms locked in his grip, Margaret's legs went slack. She hoped that her dead weight would cause Roach to drop her, giving her a chance to run. But her 110 pounds was barely more than a full picker's bag of cotton that Roach threw onto trucks all day at harvest time. He picked her up and carried her deep into the grove. Only when Margaret began to scream did Roach throw her to the ground, himself on top of her, and put his hand over her mouth. He was panting hard, less from carrying Margaret than from passionate anticipation.

"Now I'm gonna' fuck you, you bitch. You know what fuckin' is don't you? I'm gonna' stick my big cock inside your cunt and you're gonna like it. And then if you're good, I'm gonna let you put it in your mouth. You walk around like you are the greatest thing on earth but you're just a pussy waiting for a piece of Roach cock."

Margaret barely heard the river of hate flowing from her assailant's mouth. She was focused on fighting back. Roach's hand was pushed hard against her mouth and close to her nose. She felt herself suffocating. She kept her legs tight together. He would have to kill her to invade her, she vowed to herself. His breath on her face was hot and she thought it smelled of bacon and cigarettes. A working day's worth of sweat soaked through his shirt and onto her skin. His dampness made her shiver. Roach released his hand from Margaret's face and used it to pull the bottom of her dress up to her waist. He rose slightly to do so and then rose to his knees while he ripped off her panties and unbuttoned his fly. Margaret tried to raise a leg to knee him in his privates but Roach kept his legs tight on either side of hers, making the defensive motion impossible. He reached into his pants and pulled out his penis. It was the first one Margaret had ever seen. She thought only that it was ugly and unclean. Roach fell onto Margaret and as he did so he placed one knee between her legs, forcing them open. She continued to resist. Her fighting only increased Roach's intensity. He was certain she would be worth the battle.

"Now you're going to feel it, you bitch. You're going to like it. Open up. There, you feel it on your leg. Now we'll get it inside. Roach and Farwell fucking. Like it oughta' be."

Margaret felt herself tiring. She could not maintain the tense resistance in her legs. She could feel Roach pushing to enter her body. He was having difficulty because there was no lubrication, but knowing his entry would hurt her increased his excitement and further hardened his penis to push past Margaret's resistance. Margaret suddenly realized she could scream. She did so until Roach again covered her mouth. His other hand maneuvered his penis to find the entry.

Suddenly a black arm reached around Roach's neck and pulled him away from Margaret. A 250 pound load had suddenly been lifted. She heard Roach cursing, and then screaming in pain. She tried to raise herself to a sitting position, but could not do so. She turned her

Chapter Fourteen: The Roach Family

head and saw Isaac and his friend Petey pummeling Roach with their fists. Roach's pale white penis hung limply outside his pants as he used his hands to fend off repeated blows to his face from the two Negroes.

Knowing she had been rescued, Margaret was able to cry, even as the beating of Roach by her friends continued. She occasionally interrupted her sobs with cries of "God, oh God" and "Kill him. Please kill him." After a minute that felt like ten, Roach was left on the ground, bleeding from his nose and mouth, holding his head with one hand while reinserting his penis into his pants with the other. Isaac and Petey ignored his impotent threats of death and torture to tend to Margaret. Isaac held her head to his chest, speaking words of comfort, while Petey pulled her dress down to where it belonged. Margaret gave no thought to the fact she was exposed to the Negro boys. She had nearly been raped. She was abused. And by a Roach.

Roach finally arose and left the area, mumbling that Margaret's rescuers would regret their actions. Margaret shrieked to his back that he would be sent to prison. Petey ran to the mansion and asked her father to bring the horse-drawn wagon to take Margaret home. When Farwell suggested that one of the Roach boys join them, Petey told Farwell what happened. Farwell quickly hitched the wagon himself and he and Petey hurried to the grove.

After Margaret was safely in her bed, Farwell made two phone calls. He first made sure to warn the operator in a stern voice that these calls were confidential. One call was to the doctor and the other to the Aiken County Sheriff. Both men arrived at River's Edge about the same time. The sheriff himself responded to the call from the most prominent planter and politician in the county. Margaret described what happened after the doctor examined her. She already had told her father, so she was able to complete her narrative, with difficulty only at the end. Her voice was soft and slow as she told her story methodically, like a witness in court, until the point at which Roach pulled off her underwear. Then Margaret lost her composure, describing the rest of the assault rapidly, raising her voice in both volume and octave, until her body shook at the recollection and her face was wet with tears.

Isaac and Petey sat on the glider on the front porch, waiting to be interviewed by the sheriff. No one had approached the Roach residence.

The doctor pronounced Margaret fit, but for some bumps and scrapes. He assured Farwell and his daughter that she had not been penetrated. Margaret was still a virgin. But he cautioned Farwell privately that there were psychological consequences to such an attack. Farwell must not blame his daughter for the attempted rape or in any way make her ashamed. Failing to heed that advice, the doctor said, could have long-term consequences. Farwell agreed to do as he was told.

The meeting with the sheriff was more disappointing. After interviewing Margaret and her rescuers and learning the results of the physical examination, he ventured to the Roach residence and questioned Robby in the presence of his father. The sheriff then returned to the mansion. He advised John Farwell that although

Chapter Fourteen: The Roach Family

there was sufficient proof of attempted rape to take the case to a jury, the chances for a conviction were very slim. A South Carolina jury would heavily discount the testimony of Negroes against a white man. Robby Roach would take the stand. He claimed in his interview with the sheriff that Margaret and the Negroes had conspired against him to lodge false charges because he was a hard taskmaster, Margaret had complained about him, and that the entire incident was manufactured in revenge. The sheriff did not rule out that Robby also might tell the jury a different story – that Margaret had flirted with him and wanted to have sex. Buster Roach claimed to have seen his son fend off advances from Margaret, testimony which even the sheriff thought unlikely, but could not disprove. It would be the Roaches' word against hers, as far as the jury was concerned. Reasonable doubt.

Farwell could not disguise his contempt for the sheriff's counsel. Any jury would believe his daughter, who was a picture of integrity and virtue. The Roaches, all of them, were poor white trash who would lie for a dime. The sheriff held his ground. He would arrest Roach if Farwell insisted, but then the case would have to go forward. It could not be dropped unless Margaret and the boys changed their stories and admitted they lied. It also would be a matter of public record that the daughter of a former governor and sister of a current candidate for attorney general claimed to be the victim of an attempted rape and was rescued by colored friends. If Farwell or his daughter did not press charges on a weak case, the family's privacy could be preserved.

Unanimous Verdict

Reputation was of critical importance to Farwell. Attempted rape would tinge his daughter's reputation. Her chances of marrying into a prominent political family would be diminished due to the publicity. His own reputation would be amended to become the former governor "whose daughter was raped" or, worse, "whose daughter falsely charged a man with rape." It would also hurt his son's political future. An acquittal for his sister's rapist would not help his campaign to be the state's chief lawyer. Governor Farwell calmed down and thanked the sheriff for his advice. He would handle the matter internally at River's Edge. The sheriff warned Farwell that he could not resort to violent revenge. Even a former governor can be arrested and sent to jail, the sheriff warned as he drove away.

Farwell decided not to act hastily. He wanted to focus on his daughter. Robby Roach could wait one more day.

The assailant informed his family of the day's events. His father was disgusted with him, but only because two young colored men had prevented him from completing his mission. Robby tried to regain his father's confidence by describing the attempt in detail up to the point at which he was attacked by Isaac and Petey. Celestine and Emily left the room soon after he began. Even Matthew, 18, lowered his head. Only Buster and Robby enjoyed the retelling. By the time Robby finished, both men were laughing over the botched rape, convinced that Robby's threats would silence Margaret and the hired hands. They were more somber after a visit from the sheriff, but congratulated themselves on telling the sheriff a reasonable story.

392

Chapter Fourteen: The Roach Family

Before the Roach men set out for work the next day, the telephone rang. It was Farwell. He wanted to see Buster and Robby immediately. All of the Roaches knew the rare summons to the mansion could be only about one thing. Buster chided his son. "You're in a big pile of shit now."

But Farwell's options were few, having surrendered the right to bring criminal charges. He could expel the entire Roach family, but Buster Roach knew more about the workings of the plantation than Farwell did. Even if someone equal to Buster's talents could be found quickly, he would have to learn the farm's operations. There already was talk of a post-war agricultural recession. Working in a new man would aggravate difficult conditions. And only Robby was guilty of attempted rape. Farwell had no reason to know that Buster encouraged the crime. Robby would be fired, of course. Buster might threaten to quit, but no one would pay him as handsomely as Farwell and he would require a reference. No one would hire him if Farwell said Buster was fired because of misconduct by members of his family. Buster Roach was stuck at River's Edge as much as Farwell was stuck with him.

Robby denied the allegations and Buster defended his son, but both knew Robby was lucky to escape with only the loss of his job. Farwell added that Robby could never return to River's Edge and that if he ever put himself in the presence of his daughter again, at the plantation or elsewhere, there would be grave but undefined consequences. Robby didn't care. There were other jobs and other women. He told himself he was tired of River's Edge and wanted to be independent of his parents. He had seen New York, Paris and Brussels. There were much better places on earth than South Carolina. Buster was less sanguine. He would miss Robby. Matthew was too close to his mother. He didn't blame Farwell for wanting punishment. He blamed Isaac and Petey. They had no right to interfere with a white man getting his due. Who were they to say it was rape? Didn't the colored rape their women all the time? He would get even somehow.

Farwell had left one loose end. He did not consult with his daughter before deciding not to bring charges against her assailant.

"When is the trial going to happen, Daddy?" Father and daughter were eating breakfast. Lorelei, Margaret's nanny, was now a cook. She heard the question and quickly retreated to the kitchen after setting a plate full of eggs and bacon on the table. Farwell served his daughter and himself before answering.

"There won't be a trial, sweetie. It would not be in your best interest. But I'm confident you never will see Robby Roach again." The Governor felt the matter was now closed. He had made an executive decision.

"What do you mean? Did you kill him, Daddy? Is he dead?" Margaret was excited by the idea that her father had honored her by slaying her attacker.

"No, child. He's not dead. He's just gone. I fired him."

Father and daughter were silent while Margaret contemplated this news. Surely there was more to learn.

Chapter Fourteen: The Roach Family

"Well, of course you did. Is he in jail? Did he – how do they say it? – enter a plea or something?"

"I don't know where he is. He's just fired and he's never allowed to return to River's Edge." For the first time, Farwell sensed that his daughter would not be satisfied with his action. She needed a fuller explanation. "There will not be a trial because he was not arrested.

"Look, honey, I felt it was for the best that your reputation not be damaged. Arrest and trial would be public. You are the daughter of a two-term governor. It all would be in the newspapers. Why, we would probably have reporters from Columbia, Aiken, Augusta, Charleston and God knows where else coming to River's Edge to interview you and me and maybe even Buster's family. We can't have that now, can we?"

Margaret could not believe her ears. For the first time in her life, she saw her father as weak, as a coward. "But Daddy, he tried to rape me! And you're letting him go? Because you are afraid the lawn will be damaged?" She pushed her plate away to emphasize her anger.

"No, of course not. The sheriff said it would be your word against Roach's. That's reasonable doubt. It would be horrible if a jury voted to acquit. It would mean they thought you were a liar and a temptress at that. A Jezebel, we used to call it. Think of your reputation."

"So you have so little confidence in me that you think there's a risk I'd be called a whore? That's outrageous. Do YOU think I wanted to be raped by Robby Roach? What about Isaac and Petey? They saw the whole thing."

"The sheriff told me the jury would discount Isaac and Petey because they are colored and Robby is a white man. He's even a veteran."

Margaret would not let him evade her other question. "Like I said, do you think I wanted to be raped? Do you think I gave him some cause to believe I wanted to have sex with him? Do you?"

Farwell was flustered and red-faced. It was not proper for a father to talk about such matters with his daughter. He had instructed Lorelei to explain the facts of life to Margaret years ago. This conversation was not chivalrous.

"No. Of course not. I know you have no interest in Robby Roach." He paused and saw that his daughter was tight-lipped, a sure sign of her anger. He wanted to regain the offensive. "But it's your reputation that has to be preserved. You weren't really injured. There's no real harm. Why make it public?"

"No harm? I was attacked, beat up and nearly had a penis stuck in my vagina by one of your hired hands. No harm?"

"Please, Margaret. You don't have to use such language. I'm ..."

"You're a coward." The whole picture suddenly became obvious to Margaret. She would enjoy stripping away the hypocrisy to reveal the truth and embarrassing her father. "It's not my reputation that you are worried about. It's not getting my name in the papers that would bother you. It's your name. Our name. Nathan's name."

Chapter Fourteen: The Roach Family

She rose suddenly and walked toward the center hall which was essentially a gallery of Civil War heroes. She lifted her voice so her father, and everyone else in the mansion, could hear her clearly.

"This is the reputation you're worried about Daddy. All these dead heroes on the wrong side of a war to keep men enslaved. The great Farwells. It isn't about me. It's about them. And about you and about Nathan.

"All of this stands for nothing, Daddy. It stands for nothing if it makes you too cowardly to even prosecute the man who tried to rape your own daughter." She raced up the grand staircase in tears and locked her bedroom door. She remained there the rest of the day. She met her father's entreaties with silence for days.

Margaret was too smart and too familiar with John C. Farwell to believe that he consciously would hurt her. He was blinded by his own upbringing and unyielding myths about the South. John Farwell's older brothers and his father had fought gallantly in the Civil War. John himself had kept their flame lit, as would his son. Nothing could be permitted to tarnish that heritage. As with many Southern traditions, the living had to suffer for the memory of the dead.

Chapter Fifteen: Brian Carter, 1921

Although she loved her father and knew that, in his way, he loved her, Margaret's heart hardened against him as she continued another two years of tutoring at River's Edge to complete her basic education. Margaret distanced herself from Governor Farwell and observed him objectively, rather than as a proud and loving daughter. She saw an aging rich man whose life had been spent insuring that the Negro was dispossessed for the purpose of reinstating a dusty old society that was both evil and irrelevant to the modern day.

Margaret boldly ridiculed both her father and her half-brother, who was now the attorney general based on a campaign much like her father's had been, playing on white fears of race-mixing which would dilute the greatness of the white race and threaten Southern womanhood. She was especially vocal when she visited the village of the hired hands, which she frequented more often because it was difficult for her to be alone with her father. He was weak. He had even retained the Roach family on the property, except for Robby. Margaret shivered whenever one of the Roaches was near, including Celestine and Emily, who always bowed their heads in her presence, ashamed of what Robby had done. Margaret wished they all would move on, but her father relied on Buster more than ever as the farm economy suffered even as the rest of the nation prospered in the 1920s.

One small good thing did come out of the attempted rape. In gratitude for saving his daughter, Farwell promoted both Isaac and

Unanimous Verdict

Petey to the mansion staff and out from under the Roaches. Margaret came to feel even more at-home in the village with the Negro hands than in the mansion or even with her few white friends. She was pleased that Isaac was now a member of the house staff. They sat in the parlor or the library for hours discussing the issues of the day until Farwell or Lorelei summoned Isaac for chores. Both Negroes were happy to join Lorelei and two other hands greeting guests, cleaning the mansion, caring for the surrounding yards, grooming the horses and keeping the wagons and carriages repaired and the automobile clean. Farwell had finally purchased a car in 1920. He was among the last of the plantation owners to do so. Even the Roaches had a car before the Farwells. But it was rarely used except for occasional travel to Aiken. Farwell preferred old-fashioned horse-drawn transportation for local trips. He was happy for Matthew Roach to teach Isaac how to drive a car so that Farwell did not have to learn. Isaac taught Petey and Margaret.

Margaret was finally nearing the end of her high school tutoring in the spring of 1921. A small "graduation" ceremony was planned for early May. She had been admitted to the University of Pennsylvania, Northwestern and Cornell, but her father insisted she attend the University of South Carolina. Her friend Nancy, with whom she kept in touch and visited regularly during school holidays, was a freshman at Smith College. She reveled in the intellectual ferment of the Northeast and lamented only that Smith was an all-women's college. Margaret read her letters with envy. Most of Margaret's tutors were graduates of South Carolina. This fact alone caused her

400

to cringe at matriculating there. It also convinced her father that it was the ideal institution for Margaret.

Margaret stood at the back of the small audience while her father welcomed their guests. The upright piano had been moved to the widow's walk above the front porch of the mansion, only about 40 feet from the lawn where the ceremonies were conducted. Margaret paraded down the aisle, a graduating class of one, to the sound of "Pomp and Circumstance" played by the Aiken Episcopal Church organist. She thought it a silly touch, but the tutors insisted that the graduation be as close to one at a real school as possible. When she reached the podium, she turned and sat in a chair, facing the audience. She immediately looked for Nancy and Isaac, but her eye fell instead on a handsome black stranger. She scanned the rest of the crowd, pretending to listen to the mildly humorous and wildly adulatory remarks of her tutors. She cast her eyes to the black stranger again, this time catching his own eye, which prompted his mouth to widen into a grin, teeth white as Ivory Soap jumping from a face dark as the cloth in Margaret's graduation gown. He nodded to her and she nodded back before she could think about doing so. She resumed pretending to direct her attention elsewhere but his presence stayed in her head. Not surprisingly, Margaret was the valedictorian. Her speech was a dull recitation of the expected platitudes, extending routine thanks to family and tutors and offering bland promises to help make a better world. She had magnanimously allowed her father to edit the speech. Predictably, he cut out the paragraphs in which

Margaret called for an end to Jim Crow, unions for farm labor and U.S membership in the League of Nations. He added some adulatory comments about the attorney-general brother, who was planning on a run for lieutenant governor. Margaret did not protest very much. She thought the entire ceremony was more for her father's satisfaction than for herself.

During her delivery, she repeatedly lifted her eyes from the text, looking in only one direction, as though this new black boy was her only audience. When the ceremony was completed, Margaret anxiously and quickly completed mandatory courtesies with her father's friends and made a beeline to Isaac, Nancy and the newcomer. Isaac introduced her to his cousin, Brian Carter.

"Miss Farwell." He bowed slightly as he spoke, his grin still in place. "That was a very nice speech." His voice was firm; his diction clear, with no trace of the South; his manner was direct, neither deferential nor superior, but the voice of an equal – unheard of from a Negro on being introduced to a white woman, especially the mistress of a large plantation.

Margaret suppressed her surprise and delivered a practiced curtsey. "Not at all Mr. Carter. I thought it was rather plain." She tilted her head slightly, looking into eyes several inches higher than her own. They were hazel, with little flickers of another color it would require closer observation to identify."

"Perhaps it was the delivery more than the content, Miss," Brian responded. "A rose makes even a plain water glass beautiful."

Chapter Fifteen: Brian Carter

"Are you flirting with me, Mr. Carter?" She determined the other color was a golden yellow and also knew that this young man was not from the South. No Negro she knew would have rendered her such a forward compliment.

"No, ma'am. I'm told that would be dangerous down here." He grinned at Isaac, who was somber and began tugging at his cousin's sleeve, urging him to leave before the conversation resulted in trouble.

"And where are you from?"

"Harlem, ma'am. In New York."

"No wonder you are so frank. A northerner. I've read about Harlem. I should like to talk more with you about it," Margaret said, turning slowly while keeping eye contact with her new friend. "Perhaps later. How long are you staying with us?"

"At least a month. Isaac's mom is my aunt." Margaret completed her turnabout and walked toward the other guests, but she made a mental note to visit the slave quarter the next day to find out more about Isaac's cousin.

"They lynch colored down there," his mother warned him when Brian announced he was visiting South Carolina. "You ever heard the term 'uppity nigger'? When I say it to you, nothin' bad happens. If some cracker even *thinks* that where you're goin', you could be dead. No tricks, hear? You shuffle and scrape no matter how much it hurts."

Brian told his mother he understood, but his mother replied she saw no reason why he should. "You hear it, but you don't believe it, son. They's people down there that hates you just 'cause what you are."

Unanimous Verdict

Brian was a junior at City College of New York, the free university. He read about the South and Jim Crow. But he resented the need for such warnings from his mother. He was over 21 years old, able to vote, buy liquor and own property. He should not have to stifle his playful spirit. The South claimed to be part of the United States, after all.

He was dark as a coffee bean, darker than Isaac. His lips were thick, full, vaguely pink and slightly protruding. He had high cheekbones and a jutting, wide jaw. There was no sign of fat in his face or in the rest of him, as Margaret noted when she quickly glanced at his body while moving away. He was over six feet, but not too tall for Margaret, who was nearly five foot ten. She noted that his face was lively and expressive. In fact, his whole face and body were expressive. His was in motion as he spoke, moving right to left and even bobbing up and down on the balls of his feet. When she glanced his way and saw him talking with Isaac and other farm workers, his hands were in constant gesticulation when he had the floor, pointing, balling into fists and opening again to emphasize what he was saying. He seemed to move even while standing still. When he grinned, that perfect set of teeth was framed by his luxuriously soft lips. As she thought about him in her bed that night, Margaret wondered if the rhythms of Brian's body and face were jazz.

She disclosed her excitement about the new guest to Nancy, who was staying overnight before returning to Augusta.

"He's fascinating and handsome."

Chapter Fifteen: Brian Carter

"Yes, but be careful. You don't want to be lovin' a black man in South Carolina, you know."

"Well, he lives in New York. We could live there."

"So you're already setting up house! Let me tell you, Margaret, mixing blacks and whites of the opposite sex isn't much liked in New York or anywhere else in the U.S. It's called miscegenation and it's illegal in most states."

"Oh, quit raining on my parade, Nancy. I just met him. I'm sure nothing will come of it. It's just fun to think about for a night. Imagine.... New York ..... Harlem!"

The frequency of Margaret's visits to the village increased with Brian's arrival. It wasn't long before all the hired hands knew she was infatuated. There were mixed feelings. The younger women were jealous. Brian certainly was as attractive to them as he was to Margaret, and he offered them an opportunity to get out of rural South Carolina and be a part of the renaissance that was Harlem. Why should a white girl who already has more than anyone in the village ever could have, win the heart of such a fine colored man? It was not fair. They were right, but their mothers reminded them that if life were fair, lots of things would be different. These same mothers and their husbands had a different concern, one which they expressed to both Brian and Margaret. A white woman befriending a Negro, especially an attractive male Negro, was difficult for people to accept. An interracial *romance* always led to a bad end. Brian and Margaret swore they were only friends in the same way Isaac and Petey were Margaret's friends.

Unanimous Verdict

They told themselves that for most of May. They avoided holding hands, or kissing or even hugging each other. Brian understood. New York was not the South. But he affirmed Nancy's report that even there, interracial couples were neither common nor accepted except in the most liberal quarters of Harlem and Greenwich Village. Initially, Brian decided simply to enjoy Margaret's friendship until he left River's Edge at the end of June. He did not want trouble. He had no interest in breaking down racial barriers on a short summer vacation. He was not indifferent to the racism inflicted on his cousins, just biding his time.

Brian sometimes called himself "the white man's nigger" because he fit none of the negative stereotypes and did all the things white men thought a "good" Negro should do. He went to school. His liquor consumption was modest and occasional and he avoided drugs, and prostitutes. He didn't play the numbers. His goals were a good job, a pretty wife, a nice home and beautiful children. When his parents heard Brian denigrate his goals and achievements by calling himself "the white man's nigger," they scolded him. Success was colorless. Family was colorless. Education was colorless. In the United States – hell, his father said, in Western civilization – the white man made the rules for such things, but that didn't make these goals and institutions white. "Don't let the white man shame you into shuffling subservience," his father instructed. "Opportunity is color blind. The white man's stolen it. We have to steal it back. You are a frontline warrior, son, not an Uncle Tom. Some folks say a big nasty nigger is a white man's nightmare. But an educated, talented black man who can take the white man's job is his real nightmare."

Brian discussed his goals and his feelings with Margaret, who listened intently, encouraged him, and made little effort to hide her growing affection. By early June, she trusted Brian enough to describe the attempted rape. Two days later, she found herself opening to him about her fear of sex and her shame. Brian listened. He did not lecture. It was the first time they violated their rules about touching as Brian held her close to him and she sobbed while recounting the fears engendered by Robby's attack. He kissed her. She kissed him back. It felt right. But they told each other it was only to comfort Margaret, not a sign of things to come.

Margaret wasn't the only white iron filing drawn to Brian's magnetic Negritude. Brian saw that Emily Roach, pretty, lonely and living in fear of the harsh prejudices of her father and brothers, looked at him with what he sensed was more than curiosity about an exotic northerner. She was introduced to Brian at Margaret's graduation, but, unlike Margaret and Nancy, she said nothing in his presence. She clung silently to the crowd, which included Isaac and Petey, and to Brian, for the rest of the afternoon, unable to participate in most of the conversations about matters of the day with the white guests because she was ill-schooled and poorly bred — a real white "nigger", socially estranged.

Brian was unnerved because Emily never took her eyes off of him. She was not staring; she was admiring. This was confirmed when

Brian occasionally returned her look and Emily's normally stern face broke into a wide, gap-toothed smile that, in turn, made Brian smile. He looked over her body, with no attempt at subtlety as when he first eyed Margaret's figure, and enjoyed what he saw. Margaret noticed the diversion of the new visitor's attentions, but never considered that her interests might intersect with those of a member of the Roach family.

Emily, however, was flattered by Brian's brief but favorable attention and did not hide her affections from him, dangerous as they were. Aside from rare shopping trips to Barnwell, she had been a virtual prisoner at River's Edge since she graduated from the eighth grade. Her only company was her family and the farmhands. Her brothers and father paid her no attention except when they demanded meals or found fault with the housekeeping. Her father made it clear to the farmhands that he would kill any man that befriended his daughter. But not only was Brian not subject to her father's command, he was handsome, well-spoken, educated and clean. A man who worked with his head, not his body. But for his skin color, Brian was a better man than any white man likely to court Emily Roach.

Emily found occasions to meet the exotic young green-eyed black man from Harlem.

"Why hello, Mr. Carter." Emily's light brown eyes brightened, reflecting the late spring sunshine, as she used her right thumb to move a shank of long chestnut hair over her shoulder and let it fall suggestively over her bosom. They were on the grassy lawn between the mansion and the Roach house. Brian had just left the mansion, visiting Margaret

Chapter Fifteen: Brian Carter

and Isaac. Emily had been watching for his departure, planning the "accidental" meeting.

"Miss Roach." Brian tipped his cap cordially.

"Can you walk with me?" Emily spoke quietly. Even so, her timbre was shaky, revealing her uncertainty about how to approach a man of any color. She was also frightened. Her 17-year-old heart, taken with the sweet but daring notions of forbidden love, drove her in ways that surprised her in more reflective moments. In this way, Brian's effect on Emily was the same as on Margaret.

"You're father would not approve, Miss Roach. He would not approve at all."

"He doesn't have to know. It's just a walk, Mr. Carter. Let's go to the front gate to check for mail." Walking the half mile to the front gate not only was pleasant, under the magnolia and elm canopy, but it was much safer than walking a road to the Negro village or the fields, where the couple was likely to encounter one of the Roach men.

Brian was touched by the appreciation of a second white woman at River's Edge, and was attracted to Emily's generous proportions and gentle manner. He was tentative and somewhat overwhelmed in the presence of Margaret Farwell's wealth and aggressiveness. Emily's company was warmer, more comforting, despite the presence of her father not far away. Margaret was in charge. With Emily, he was in control, less tense, less worried, despite her father's reputation. Being with Margaret seemed a high reach. Emily was closer to the ground.

"I feel more relaxed with you than I do in the mansion."

Unanimous Verdict

"But that mansion's so very nice. And I'm sure Margaret is nice to you, too." Emily was embarrassed by her limited vocabulary in Brian's presence. It was their third walk to the mailbox in five days.

"But I feel I'm kind of on display. Margaret's always eyeing me and pushing at me. She wants to go to New York with me."

"So do I."

"You know I can't take either of you. Your daddy and Margaret's daddy would come after us. It'd be really bad."

"Do you love Margaret?"

"I'm not sure. Maybe. I like her, though."

"Do you love me?"

"Look, I just met both of you. And you're both white, as if you didn't know."

"You didn't answer my question."

"I like you, too."

Emily lay awake nights planning her next step. Whatever else, she wanted him. She wanted to feel him on top of her and inside of her. She would finally get at least one thing she wanted in life, even if she had to share him. A sweet dream was made deliciously sweeter because the mingling of black and white skin she imagined while lying in bed was anathema to her father's prejudices. A touch of resentment and payback informed her feelings and made them stronger.

"There is a place down by the river I'd like to take you. We won't be seen. Let's show how much we like each other down there." She turned to Brian, pulled his head to hers, and they kissed. Emily felt

Chapter Fifteen: Brian Carter

her heart racing – or was it Brian's? They skipped to the river as best they could through the high grass.

Buster Roach was generally aware that Margaret Farwell was seeing a great deal of Brian Carter, though he knew no details. It never occurred to him that his own daughter might be attractive to any man or that she would defy him by socializing with a Negro boy.

Roach met Carter at Margaret's graduation and saw instantly that Carter was repulsed by his appearance. Roach was used to that, even from coloreds. Brian heard stories from Isaac's family about Roach before they met. He knew Roach was a brutal foreman who had no respect for the farm hands. But he was polite when he spoke to Roach, giving the man no cause to dislike him. Nevertheless, Roach concluded Carter looked down on him. All of his life Roach believed that people somehow knew he was sold by his mother and once made a living serving the needs of pedophiles. He knew it couldn't be true. He never even told his wife about the life he led in New York. But Roach never could shake his belief that his past was revealed in his face. Shame and anger were his constant companions and the driver of his many hatreds.

Brian and Margaret were not worried about men like Roach. Margaret believed they were falling in love, a love in which their color differences merely added to the intrigue, attraction and romance. Brian enjoyed Emily's company, but even he could see that a future with Margaret, difficult as it would be, would be impossible with Emily. Margaret would fit in with New York, even in Negro Harlem – with a lot of help. Emily never could live outside the rural South. Emily would be a summer fling; with Margaret, there could be more.

The wall Brian and Margaret built to block their natural attraction to each other was like a dam against rising water. When the dam broke in the middle of June, pent up emotions electrified their love and drowned their common sense. While Brian kept his relations with Emily a total secret, he followed Margaret's reckless lead as the mistress of River's Edge. They held hands in the village. Isaac arranged for them to meet at the mansion. Initially, Margaret, Brian and Isaac met in the library to exchange ideas and learn from Brian about life in Harlem and New York. Margaret usually brought the discussions around to the continuing consequences of slavery, industrialization of the South, state's rights and the rights of women and the colored. At first, Isaac and Brian sat in chairs while Margaret sat on the davenport. After a few days, Brian moved to the davenport. A few days after that, Isaac stopped attending the sessions, which were now less about any ideas other than the idea of Brian and Margaret. He warned his cousin to be careful. He invited him to the mansion thereafter only when Margaret demanded it, which was nearly every day. "This is dangerous," he told Margaret. "Nonsense," she replied curtly, "I'll protect him." Brian held off Margaret's advances for a time. He released his sexual tension with Emily, who resigned herself to secret couplings but reveled in defying her father and even in sharing a man with Margaret Farwell.

Brian was simply irresistible to Margaret. He was a mimic. Brian could imitate the high-pitched snarl of Buster Roach and the heavy southern accents of both Farwell and his daughter. He went right to Margaret's heart by ridiculing Jim Crow, the southern belle traditions and Civil War pride in a way that made her laugh.

"Heah are awwwwll mah relations," he said, standing in the stately center hall, his right arm extended toward the portraits of honored Farwells and other heroes. "Some say we lost the Great Wah Against Nawthern Aggression," he continued, as if delivering a speech to a convention of the Sons of the Confederacy. Margaret and Isaac already were convulsed with laughter at both his exaggerated accent and the wildly unrealistic picture of a Negro owning the mansion and claiming the Farwells as his relatives.

"We done fooled the evil Yankees. We won that great wah. These brave men fought to keep the nigga' beholdin' to the great and glorious white man. You don't see no niggahs here do you? No niggahs in the statehouse, or the schoolhouse or – may the Lord strike me down if it ain't so – walkin' with ouah lovely Southern daughters." Brian took Margaret's hand and they danced around the polished oak floor of the center hall in the manner of a lord and lady at the ball, laughing at the absurdity of Brian's performance. They were sobered only when Lorelei arrived to investigate the source of so much comedy.

"Y'all better stop that right now. You don't know when Master Farwell gonna' arrive. He ain't gonna' like you makin' fun a' his relations." She gave the trio a stern look that dampened their enthusiasm.

Unanimous Verdict

Brian was bright, educated, funny and handsome. Margaret was accustomed to being close to Negro men at River's Edge. She had come to equate Negro features with hard work, common sense, strength and kindness, not brutality, shiftlessness and stupidity that most whites assumed was reflected in dark skin and African features. But Brian brought something new: sophistication, worldliness, education and a chance for romance. Brian's black city skin had not suffered from hours in the hot sun that could turn skin leathery and wrinkled, or the punishments levied by the Roach men, which could leave ugly scars and bruises. His skin was supple and smooth, as were his lips when they enfolded Margaret's.

Margaret loved Brian. Like Emily, she wanted to make love to him. And like Emily, she wanted to run away with him.

Brian was more cautious. "This is crazy," he told Margaret as they kissed on the library davenport. "We have to stop."

Margaret pulled away. She was tired of these discussions. "But it's right, Bri. Don't you feel it's right. I love you."

"And I love you. But this is dangerous. God knows what your father or your brother would do if they found out we were even kissing. Black men get hanged for less." Rutting with Emily in an obscure untilled field near the river did not bring the same fear as snuggling in the mansion at mid-day.

"Oh, Daddy wouldn't do that. He loves me. And Nathan is the attorney general of the state. They'd just send you home. I'd follow you to New York." She returned her mouth to his lips, trying to again

414

end the discussion in the usual fashion. But Brian did not respond in kind, instead pushing her away.

"Maggie, that would be crazy, too. You have wealth, a profitable cotton plantation and, of course, beauty and brains. You'd lose the wealth and your right to this gorgeous place if you ran away with me. And your daddy wouldn't sit still for it. He'd hunt you down and force you to come back."

Margaret became petulant. She hated the nickname "Maggie," except when Brian used it. And she could not envision being made a slave in her own house.

"I'll be 18 very soon. He can't do anything to me after that. And New York is an exciting place, I know. I won't miss the South. I hate the South for what it's done to the Negro."

"Ain't no paradise in the North, neither. My parents raised my sister and me in a four-room apartment and were happy to have it. They work for the city. Steady jobs, but we had to watch every nickel. Whites in New York are nearly as bigoted as in the South. Black man goes into a downtown jewelry store to buy an anniversary present and in no time flat he's got the manager in his face demanding to know what he wants, afraid he's gonna rob the place.

"You're still a child, Maggie. You got the body of a woman but you ain't got the experience of one. There's no magic in this world. We'd have a damned hard time wherever we lived. It's impossible."

The couple was still and silent, staring at the books in their shelves. The beautiful blond and the strikingly handsome Negro were only inches apart, each with the same thought: Yes, it is a dangerous world, but I love this person. Soon, they looked in each other's eyes, received the same message, and resumed their embrace.

Three days later, Brian and Margaret were sitting on the glider bench on the side porch, holding hands and sharing an occasional kiss on a sparkling blue afternoon. They used the side porch so that they could not be seen from the Roach house. Margaret knew that her father was in Columbia to deliver a speech that night for some Democratic club. After dinner, they would have the house to themselves as Lorelei, Isaac and the staff departed for the village.

"Stay for dinner, Bri."

"In the kitchen?"

"Of course not, silly. As my guest. In the dining room."

"With your father watching? I thought it was against house rules for a Negro to eat with the family in the dining room."

"I already told you, Daddy is gone for the night. Oh, you mean the portrait. I'll take it down if it makes you nervous."

"No, it's OK. That was a joke. But I'd feel uncomfortable. And Lorelei would spread the news, that's for sure."

"What if I also invited Isaac. Would you come then?"

He thought for a moment. "Of course."

Margaret did not, however, inform Isaac of this plan.

They dined in the large dining room at a table that sat twelve and could be expanded to seat 22. Margaret and Brian sat next to each other at one end. They ignored the portrait of Governor Farwell staring

Chapter Fifteen: Brian Carter

down at them from the dining room wall. When Brian inquired why Isaac was absent, just as Lorelei was serving the soup, Margaret looked sharply at Lorelei and said Isaac was sick. Lorelei, who knew Isaac was healthy as a horse when he left the mansion, got the message and remained silent. After Lorelei departed to retrieve the main course, Margaret ran her hand along Brian's thigh. Now Brian got a different message. He looked at Margaret, her blue eyes pleading to proceed. He wanted her.

When Lorelei came into the dining room to deliver the main course, no one was there to eat it.

Margaret was a virgin with a recollection of a terrible act. Despite her aggressive flirtation at the dining table, she was nervous and uncertain how to proceed when the couple arrived at her bedroom. Brian proceeded slowly and gently. Margaret expected him to throw her on the bed in a fit of passion, as Robby had thrown her to the ground. But Robby acted out of hate. Brian held Margaret close to him as they stood by her bed. He whispered to her that he loved her. They kissed, sharing their tongues, alternately pushing themselves together, breast to chest and belly to belly, and then separating themselves slightly to begin all over again. At first their movements were tentative, random and experimental, but shortly they united in a rhythm, rocking their bodies back and forth together. There was no force; there was no pressure except of one body accepting the gentle touch of the other.

Margaret felt Brian's penis stiffen against her gut. She stood on her toes, allowing Brian to lower himself so that his penis rubbed against her where it belonged. She felt herself dampen. Brian's tongue was sweet. His light perspiration was clean and manly. A recollection of Robby Roach entered her head but was quickly dismissed. This was nothing like that. This was love. This was soft and warm. This was special. She desired Brian. Her lower body ached with excitement. She wanted him inside her. She wanted Brian to be a part of her. She wanted Brian to be her first and only.

"Let's lie on the bed." Together, they moved to the bed and Brian lowered her to the mattress. "I love you," she told Brian. She allowed him to remove her dress and her underwear. He made no effort to enter her until both of them were naked. He was very black. An inkblot in the darkness. Margaret felt his firm, smooth, skin and muscle along his back as she held him tight. Brian admired Margaret's breasts, her stomach and her legs on the bed before mounting her. She was a gift. He wanted to pleasure her and to protect her. She accepted him willingly and felt him inside her. The piercing of her hymen was a welcome announcement of the excitement and joy of his presence deep into her body. She felt his black stiffness inside her. His penetration was warm. It filled her womb. Made it whole. She explored the intensity of his green eyes reflecting modest light from a half moon and responded in kind to the gentleness of his kisses. "I love you," he said repeatedly between kisses as his lips moved to her breasts where he suckled each one alternately, still moving deliberately, rhythmically inside her. She responded with equal passion, her hips rocking to match his movements. Finally she felt his tremor and his body shudder with the release of his seed. Margaret moaned. It was a sound of pleasure, mixed with regret that the act was completed. Then Brian, who had been supporting himself with his hands and elbows on the mattress so that he could explore her body with his kisses, collapsed into her arms, his penis still inside her.

They kissed and agreed that they were excellent lovers. Margaret wanted him to stay with her all night. Her father was not due home until noon the next day. But Brian was insistent. This was too dangerous, he said. People would talk. Word could get back. Both of them could be in trouble.

Margaret knew it was easier to agree. She was not unmindful of the dangers. But she expected that their love was blessed and would survive. It was sinful to think otherwise. They made love again. The second time was better than the first. Then Brian returned to the village. Falling off to sleep, Margaret made love to Brian a third time, but the fantasy could not match his presence.

That was the only time they made love in Margaret's bedroom. Her father, by now long out of office, had few speaking engagements, and even fewer that took him far from home. But it was not the last time Brian and Margaret made love. They made love by the riverbank, but not at the same spot Brian used with Emily. He was not ashamed — Emily knew the situation and confessed that if she could not have Brian alone, she would share him. But he did not wish to seem disrespectful by using her "bed" by the river. Margaret and Brian also borrowed Isaac's cabin while the family was in the fields, until Isaac's mother found them and scolded them for risking the lives of the entire family. Although Margaret was worried she would be reminded of Robby, they ventured into the grove of trees where she was assaulted. After a tentative beginning, they made love with special abandon because they were exorcising the devil Roach. At night they even made love amid the rows of growing corn. They had an insatiable desire to mingle their bodies. Brian retained his reservations, but they were a useless defense against Margaret's tenderness and the pleasure she gave him, which he returned to her. They were vigorous young lovers who were certain their affections were a part of God's plan and would not be torn asunder.

After Farwell expelled his son from River's Edge, Roach decided it would be prudent to recruit an informer among the hired hands. Roach could learn who was complaining about him to Margaret before he heard it from Farwell. He would be prepared, and he could punish the complainer. Roach was careful in his recruiting. If he offered the job to someone who rejected it, word would get out among the colored and his plans would be defeated before they began. He knew the best way to find a candidate was to look for someone with a vice that Roach could satisfy. He found such a man. He was a new employee who called himself Slim because he was so fat. Roach quickly learned that Slim had a serious drinking problem: he couldn't get enough liquor. Roach offered to provide Slim a bottle of moonshine every Saturday. Slim agreed to provide information he thought might be of interest to Roach. Many weeks he had no valuable information. Often his information was wrong. But even Slim could understand the gossip about Margaret and Brian that raced through the village in June.

The colored girls were angry and the colored mothers worried. The colored men, having delivered their warnings to Brian earlier, accepted that a man's nature would take its course and admired him for bedding the squire's daughter. They even kidded him about it in Margaret's absence. Isaac and his mother told Brian every night to stop his nonsense. Isaac's mother even ventured to Barnwell to place an expensive long distance call to ask Brian's mother to order him home. She telegrammed him to return, but Brian responded he would stay until the end of June as originally planned. He did not tell her that he intended to bring Margaret home with him.

Slim informed Roach that the romance had advanced to intercourse when he picked up his bottle on a Saturday afternoon.

Near the end of June, as Margaret and Brian planned their departure north, the frequency and intensity of their lovemaking increased. Convinced their love was unchained from limits imposed by culture and custom – and that it was blessed by God or gods – they grew reckless. They held hands openly, even around the mansion. They exchanged kisses in front of anyone but members of the Roach or Farwell families. They drew the conclusion of amorous young couples of every generation: Something so right cannot be wrong.

Unanimous Verdict

Nathan and his family took a break from his duties as attorney general and arrived at River's Edge for a vacation through Independence Day. Margaret introduced Brian to Nathan on the veranda. Nathan noted to himself that she bubbled with enthusiasm about the boy. He still thought of her as his "little sister," however. He sensed Margaret had a schoolgirl crush on Brian, but he never imagined that any Farwell woman would fall in love with a Negro. Certainly not the little sister, who was rebellious, but plainly not stupid.

On June 27, 1921, Buster Roach had his chance. Slim told him days before that a favored spot for Margaret and Brian to make love was about 200 yards behind the mansion, amidst a few magnolia trees behind a hedgerow. Buster set up a viewing post on the other side of the trees, even farther from the mansion. He armed himself with a Brownie camera to capture the image of the lovers embracing. For two days, his efforts were to no avail. The couple had chosen other locations. But they showed up on the 27th, only three days before they were planning to escape to New York.

Margaret and Brian were well into their love making on the soft, grassy ground.

"What the hell!" Roach's panting, caused by both running toward the couple, awkward with his boyhood limp, and his own excitement, shattered Brian's intense focus on pleasing Margaret. He pushed himself off of the ground and his lover to confront the mad man snapping their picture.

Chapter Fifteen: Brian Carter

"Get the hell out. What're you doing. Get away." Roach pushed the button on the Brownie, turned the handle to advance to the next frame, and snapped again. The very brazenness caused Brian to pause. It was difficult to absorb why Roach was suddenly present. His confusion gave Roach the chance to photograph Brian standing, fully naked from his waist down. But Brian's pause lasted only for a few seconds.

"You ugly yellow bastard!" Brian had been careful for nearly two months not to lose his temper, despite the many peculiar and demeaning practices he encountered on his visit to River's Edge that would not be tolerated in New York. He was a guest. But now he was livid – and frightened. He charged Roach and grabbed at the camera Roach pulled away. Brian was nearly a foot taller and 30 years younger than Roach, but the older man had the advantages of surprise and decades of hard labor on a cotton farm. He also was fueled by the one emotion equal to self-preservation: hate. As Brian lunged again for the camera, Roach turned and ran. Brian tackled him at the legs. Roach pulled the camera to his body, and curled into a ball, his concern for his camera greater than that for his own safety.

"Get off, nigger! I got you now. I got you and that bitch! I got the evidence!" Roach laughed triumphantly even as he was pummeled by fists. He curled into a tighter ball, like a caterpillar under attack. "You better run back to New York, nigger, 'cause otherwise you ain't never leavin'!" Roach's taunts and laughter infuriated Brian. Margaret, meanwhile, had instinctively pulled down her dress to regain her modesty. She was now standing, but otherwise paralyzed by confusion and shock. She had been so focused on loving Brian that she neither saw nor heard Roach approach the couple and was terrified when Brian suddenly withdrew and forced her to let him stand. She watched the fight helplessly.

Just as Roach was about to succumb to Brian's attack and release the camera, Matt Roach entered the clearing and jumped on Brian's back. He pulled the Negro off of his father, pinning him to the ground. This allowed the voyeur to run with his evidence past the mansion to his own home. When the older man was safely distant, his son released Brian, who was still half naked. Margaret had now regained sufficient composure to speak.

"Matt Roach! What are you doing? What's your father doing? God, I hate you."

"My daddy's doin' what your daddy oughta' be doin'. Keepin' that nigger away! You oughta' be shamed a yousef. Who'd ever consider a Farwell woman fuckin' a nigger? Everbody knows it so 'cept your daddy. He wouldn't believe it without pictures."

"You go to Hell, Matt Roach," Margaret screamed. "Your brother tried to rape me and now your ugly daddy is tryin' to kill me. My business is my business. My daddy's not gonna' look kindly on spyin' and snappin' ugly pictures of Brian and me. He's decent man. He loves me. Your daddy will be makin' a big mistake if he shows those pictures to my daddy. Y'all gonna' be tossed outta that house five minutes after he sees 'em."

Matt Roach said nothing. He merely offered a smirk and turned to return to his father's house, leaving Margaret and Brian to assess the damage.

Chapter Fifteen: Brian Carter

"You gotta' get outta' here right now," Margaret instructed Brian, trying to take command and convey urgency to Brian, who had taken advantage of Margaret's verbal attack on Matt to put on his pants. "At least get out of Aiken and Barnwell Counties, Bri. I'll get the car and take you to the train station right now."

Brian pulled Margaret to him and they embraced. Summer was in full flower. The air was sweet with lilac and the clearing surrounded by a profusion of colorful plants. The sun was bright, its heat tempered by a gentle breeze. A yellow butterfly fluttered briefly around the young couple. Not ten minutes earlier, the small clearing was a place of enchantment. Even the Roach men could not destroy the beauty. Peace returned with their retreat. But now the clearing was only a refuge, a place to hide, no longer enchanting, but foreboding.

"I'll leave tomorrow, Margaret. Roach won't go to your father without his proof. He'll have to take it to Barnwell or Aiken to develop that film. It'll take a couple days, at least. I need to say good-bye to my aunt, to Isaac, Lorelei and Petey. I ain't gonna let those Roaches make me rush away like a runaway slave. And we still have hours before you have to return you to the mansion. Let's enjoy them."

Despite her anxiety, Margaret consented. It was an easy decision when made in Brian's arms.

Brian had underestimated Roach. Roach knew nothing about photography, but arranged with a neighboring farmer who made photography his hobby to develop his film. Usually these were pictures of Roach's children or vacation scenes on the South Carolina shore, but this time he told the farmer they were pornographic pictures of intercourse between a black man and Margaret. The farmer developed the film promptly. By morning, Buster Roach was in the mansion presenting his evidence to Farwell.

At first, Farwell could not believe what he was seeing. He accused Roach of doctoring the photography, something he read was done by the New York tabloids. Roach brought forth his son, who testified to the fight with Brian. The three of them walked to the magnolia grove behind the hedge. The grass was matted: inconclusive but suggestive evidence. Farwell went to his daughter's room and awakened her. He told her to dress modestly and come down stairs.

When she reached the top of the stairs and saw that Roach was in the house, she knew Brian had to be warned. She raced down the stairs and out the front door past her father and Roach. She ran 50 yards to the stables, where the car, wagons and horses were housed. She jumped in the Packard and turned the ignition switch. The car roared to life. Before she could put it into gear, Roach was in the passenger seat and grabbed her arm. Margaret screamed. She immediately pictured another Roach who had grabbed her arm two years earlier. She could not free herself from Roach's grasp. Seconds later, her father stood beside her, outside the car.

"I guess your actions have answered my question," her father said sternly. "But I'll ask it anyway. Is this you in this picture?" He shoved it under her chin. It was fuzzy and unfocused. Brownie cameras were not tolerant of motion, but Margaret filled in the details in her mind.

"Yes! Yes! Yes!" she screamed. She would not be shamed by her father this time. "I love him. I'm going to run away with him and there's nothing you can do about it."

Her father was silent. He was straight as a post, his fists clenched at his side. His blue eyes burned into Margaret's. He frightened her. For the first time in her life, she thought her father hated her.

"Take the car and bring the Negro here," he told Roach. "No, I changed my mind. Don't bring him here. Get your pistol, your camera and some rope." Farwell's voice was cold, emotionless, instructing Roach as if he was providing information about crop rotation.

"No, Daddy! No! Don't hurt him. You can't hurt him! If you hurt him, you'll have to kill me. These Roaches did a terrible thing, Daddy! Isn't it terrible to take such awful pictures. It's not Brian, Daddy! He's not at fault! You should be mad at the Roaches! This is like a second rape, Daddy! Please! Brian will go home today. I'll stay here. Just don't hurt him!"

Farwell ignored his daughter. He turned to Matt Roach. "Bring Nathan out here, please, Matt. I want him to come with us."

Nathan! Nathan would help her. Nathan would stop her father. He would protect Brian. He was from a younger generation. A responsible man, the attorney general. He would not permit their father to perform an irrational act such as harming Brian. It would be illegal. Nathan had no truck with the Roaches. He would see.

Unanimous Verdict

Margaret opened the car door and ran ahead of Matt Roach to find her half-brother. He was in the kitchen, eating a bowl of cereal.

"Nathan! Daddy's going to hurt Brian! I think he might kill him! You've got to stop him!" Nathan put his spoon down. His sister was hysterical.

"What are you talking about? Daddy's not going to kill anyone. Why would he want to kill Brian?"

"Roach. That horrible Roach. He took a picture of Brian and me together. Daddy's going to kill him. Help!" Matt Roach entered the kitchen.

"Mr. Farwell wants to see you in the stable," he told Nathan.

"Do you know what Margaret's talking about, Matt?"

"I think you'd better talk to your father. He's out there with my Dad now."

"Be calm, Margaret," Nathan advised her as he rose from the kitchen table. "Why would father be upset about a picture of you and Brian? He knows you two are friends. He doesn't like it much, but he's not going to kill anybody over it."

"It's not that kind of a picture. Nathan, I love him. I am going to marry him." Margaret burst into tears and ran to her brother for comfort. Nathan grabbed both of her shoulders and held her away from him, rejecting an embrace. He spoke to her harshly, demanding she deny an act for which there was no atonement.

"Do you mean you've had relations with a nigger boy? You've had sex together?" Nathan could not believe he was asking his sister

428

such a question. When Margaret nodded her head as she sobbed, he was stunned. Suddenly he drew the mental picture of his sister in the arms of a big black man. It quickly turned pornographic. Nathan was sickened by it. It was like his sister had sex with a monkey or a dog. He pushed Margaret away. He was unable to speak.

"Oh Nathan. You have to help. I'm sorry. I'll do anything. But please stop Daddy from hurting Brian. I'll be good. I'll go to a convent. I'll say bad things about the Negroes for your campaign. I'll do whatever you want." Her thin, high voice followed Nathan and Matt out the door. Margaret ran outside to join them, continuing to plead for Brian's life.

Roach returned to the garage with his pistol and rope. He put the rope in the trunk of the Packard along with the Brownie and a hatchet.

Margaret renewed her pleas. Her father finally spoke. His manner was still stern, cold and controlled. He looked at Margaret with the same hatred as before. "I'm not going to kill him. I'm going to send him home, as you suggested. We'll take him to the train station in Aiken. We don't intend to hurt him, if he goes peacefully." Farwell had a sudden idea. "It would help if you wrote him a short note telling him to go with us. I know he would want to say good-bye, but that obviously is impossible. A note will do."

Margaret almost collapsed to the ground with relief. She then rose and hugged her father, who did not return the gesture but continued as before, fists at his side. "Oh Daddy, thank you. Thank you. I'll do whatever you want. I'll write the note right away." Whatever made her think her father, who was not a violent man, would kill Brian? Margaret asked herself as she went to her bedroom to write a note. Daddy even protested when Roach beat the hands. He was sending Brian home. That was a fair result. She would join him in a few months, after things had calmed down.

She scribbled a quick note, scented it with her perfume, and put it in a sealed envelope addressed to "Brian." It said:

> Dearest Bri,
> Roach told Father about our affair, and has a picture to prove it.
> Roach is a nasty man, but Father is being reasonable for a man of his views. He insists that you return home now. He is going to take you to the train. Please do as he says.
> I wish with all of my heart that I could see you off. I so want you to hold me in your arms. That will happen. We will be together for the rest of our lives. I will come to New York.
> Please write me every day. I will do the same. I love you so much. Have a safe trip.
> Love forever,
> Maggie

When she returned to the front door she found the Packard in front of the house. Roach was in the driver's seat. Her father was also in the front. Nathan and Matt were in the back seat. She handed her father the envelope and asked him to say good-bye to Brian for her. She

430

Chapter Fifteen: Brian Carter

wanted to ask him to give Brian her love, but knew he never would do so. The men drove off. Margaret went to her room and cried. Then she began writing a letter to Brian in New York.

Later in the day, she asked Isaac what had happened in the village. He told her that everyone was surprised to see the Packard and more surprised to see the two Farwell men in the car. They stopped in front of Isaac's cabin and demanded that Brian come outside. The men were polite, with the senior Farwell doing all of the talking. He did not appear to be angry or upset. Isaac described him as "businesslike." He explained to Brian in front of a crowd of farmhands that Brian had to return home a few days early. He said he hoped Brian would not require an explanation why this was so in front of so many people. Brian said he understood. Farwell gave Brian a sealed envelope, saying it was from Margaret. Brian went inside the cabin to pack his belongings and returned to the Packard. Roach put his suitcase in the trunk of the Packard. Brian was sandwiched between Nathan and Matt after giving his aunt a good-bye kiss. They drove off.

The men were gone for several hours. Margaret assumed that they took advantage of the trip to do some business in Aiken. When they finally returned, she was pleased to see that her father's mood had much improved, presumably the result of Brian being off the plantation and on his way to New York. She asked if Brian got on the train without any problems. Her father said that yes, Brian got on the train. He said Roach even took a picture of Brian on the train station platform.

Unanimous Verdict

"I reasoned with the boy on the way to the train. He was a sensible fella'," Farwell told his daughter. Both were sitting on the front porch of River's Edge. "I told him I didn't want any further contact between the two of you and no nonsense about you leaving River's Edge. I told him that after you completed college, there wasn't much I could do, but that you are still under age and I'd have him sent to prison if there was any further communication with you."

Tears welled in Margaret's eyes. She felt her body stiffen, then her shoulders sagged. "What did Brian say?" John Farwell crossed the room and brought his daughter close to him. She put her arms around him, smelled his shaving soap which always reminded her of when she was a little girl and her father told her stories of the Confederacy. Her world was small and safe in those days; she was protected by her Daddy.

"He agreed. He apologized. He said he wasn't used to southern ways, but he knew he was wrong by any standards. He also said he was too ashamed to go home and probably would head to the West Coast, San Francisco maybe, once he got to Atlanta."

"No, Daddy. You're wrong. He's going to write me every day. Just like I asked him to. You'll see." Margaret then ran to her room and cried. A few hours later, her father brought her a print developed by Roach's friend which portrayed a sober looking Brian, his suitcase in his hand, standing on the train platform under the "Aiken, S.C." sign. The side of a Southern Railroad passenger car was visible on the right side of the picture.

Chapter Fifteen: Brian Carter

She did not leave her room again for nearly a day, and then only to check the mailbox.

There was no letter. There never was a letter. Her own letters were returned from New York unopened. Margaret was inconsolable the rest of the summer.

Emily Roach did not write any letters to Brian Carter. She did not receive any, either. She bore no one ill-will. She locked away her memories of May and June of 1921. She took them out to cherish on occasion as the best months of her life.

Chapter Sixteen: Atlanta, May 7-8, 1954

Thursday night, May 7, Neil, Lou and Ezra arrived in Atlanta. They acquired a city map at a gasoline station. King told Neil to drive to the local NAACP office near Hill and Decatur Streets. "Why go there at this time of night?" Neil asked. It was nearly 8 p.m.

"I make it a rule when I visit a city in the South to first stop at the local NAACP office, if they got one. Many reasons. Two of them is to find out the town temperature and the second is to find a good place to sleep that will take Negroes."

"What do you mean by finding out the town temperature?"

"How bad do the white folks treat the colored. Some towns are worse than others. Key thing is the cops. You can't tell about any individual cop, but in some places the police as a rule don't hassle people of color. Other towns, they make a point of making life more difficult."

"Don't go to Mobile," Ezra chimed in. "They are tough down there."

"*The Crisis* famously called Georgia the Empire State of Lynching," King added.

"I saw some statistics once somewhere. Georgia's lynched nearly 500 Negroes, and that's only the ones folks know about. Only Mississippi is worse," Ezra said.

Neil, not wishing to be left out, added the political angle. "I know the governor of Georgia, Herman Talmadge, is a huge race baiter. So is the senator, Richard Russell."

"So we know the temperature," King said. "Hot. But all the more reason to consult about finding a place to stay. Ezra and I ain't slept in a bed in three days."

After several false starts, Neil located the NAACP offices in a semi-commercial section of town that mixed shops and houses. The NAACP occupied a street level storefront with office space or a residence on the second and third floors. As expected, no one was in the office, but a handwritten sign, legible only because of a nearby street light, told visitors to contact Miss Masters in an emergency. A phone number was provided.

Neil prowled the streets in the Bel Air until he found a public telephone. King got out, found a nickel in his pocket and called Miss Masters' number. He returned to the car in less than two minutes. "She said she'd meet us back at the office. Told me it would take five minutes for her to get there. Very nice lady."

Miss Masters was waiting for the trio when they returned to the office.

"That was fast," Neil exclaimed after introductions were completed.

"I live upstairs temporarily. I need to find a place to live. I just started working here." Laura Masters was a young woman with skin the color of a vanilla milkshake with bits of cinnamon, otherwise called freckles. She did not appear to have taken in any of the spring sun. She had brown eyes and curly brown hair that barely reached the nape of her neck and was pointed in all directions. Neil assessed her as plain, but her smile was warm and welcoming.

"What can the NAACP do for you gentlemen?"

"I'm sorry. Yes, we are in Atlanta for a day or two. Mr. Endicott and I are private investigators. Mr. Lowell is assisting us." Lou, whose idea it was to visit the NAACP office, seized the lead in representing the group. While he spoke, Neil and Ezra looked at the spare office. A couple of desks, filing cabinets and telephones with some old protest posters on the walls. Nothing more. Four fluorescent fixtures hanging from the ceiling cast a harsh light on the gray-on-gray furnishings. Only a bouquet of yellow mums in a vase on one desk broke the monochromatic scene.

"What are you investigating? Do you want our help?"

"Only in our accommodations. Mr. Lowell and I have been sleeping in our car the last three days during our journey. We would dearly love to sleep in beds while we are here and wondered if you could help us with a recommendation for lodging."

"Sure. I can help with that. You are on the edge of the colored district now. There's a decent colored hotel just down the street. It's about three dollars a night." Neil winced. He had been paying about seven dollars at the motels along the road from Washington. They were barely livable. He could not imagine a "decent" room for only three dollars. But King and Lowell didn't show any sign of skepticism.

Turning to Neil, she recommended the Peachtree Hotel downtown. After obtaining directions, the men agreed to meet the next morning at the same location.

Lou obtained his reading of the Atlanta police the next morning from Lydell Wilkie, who headed the NAACP Atlanta office. As expected, it was not good. The men decided it would be wise to let the NAACP know the nature of their mission. The organization might be an important ally if there was trouble with the police.

Neil and Lou spent much of morning explaining the details of the Clayton Van Dyke investigation to Masters and Wilkie. They left out the break-in at the Childress Agency, saying only that the records were obtained. King added a detail occasionally, but mostly allowed Neil to take the lead. Ezra, who made it clear he was only an unofficial member of the team, stood by silently.

"So, we need to find out what is in Clay's file at the Christian Home," Neil concluded. "That's why we're here."

"I don't see how that's possible," Wilkie said. He was a short, stocky Negro man, about 30. "Those records are sealed."

"We know. We're hoping you can recommend a solution," Neil replied.

"You don't even know what you're looking for. At least in Chicago you knew the baby was adopted by the Van Dykes. You don't even have a name to go on down here."

Chapter Sixteen: Atlanta

"We know he was born on February 20, 1922 and was sent off to Chicago four days later. There can't be many children with files at the Christian Home that fit that description."

"There's something about all this that doesn't make much sense," Laura said. "The Christian Home only takes pregnant white girls. I'm pretty sure they have a firm policy against Negro women. Didn't you say that Clay thought his mother was raped by a white man?"

"That's what happened," King interjected. "But we want to find and question the mother, if she's still alive."

"How is that going to prove who killed this Van Dyke kid?" Wilkie asked. He was met with silence. "If that's the case, why not just drop it?"

Finally, King spoke up. "It's all we have. But we've got this note that was left on Clay's body and the words of the guy who beat up Neil. We know there is a connection. There has to be. We're going to pull this string to see where it leads or until it's so balled up we can't go any farther. Can you help us?"

"I don't have any contacts at that agency," Wilkie said. "We work with some orphanages occasionally, but the NAACP ain't high on the list of helpful contacts at homes for embarrassed pregnant white girls. What is it you want, actually?"

"Just to look at Clay's file, or the file of any kid born on February 20, 1922," Neil replied.

"That's a long time ago. Maybe they don't have it anymore."

"We have to find out." The five people in the room, two of them standing, were again silent for a few minutes. Finally, Laura spoke up.

"I have a goofy idea, but it might work. We need to find out how the place operates, where the files are, the old files." Laura explained her plan. All agreed it was preposterous, but no one had any better ideas. Fortunately, Neil had packed his sports jacket. Miraculously, it was fairly clean.

Later that day a couple walked up to the front door of the Christian Home. A sign on the door said "Deliveries and Colored Please Use Rear Entrance." "I guess asking nicely shows they're Christian," Neil joked.

"No jokes. This is serious," Laura scolded. She was dressed in her most conservative clothing, a black dress buttoned primly up to the top of her neck, trimmed with a narrow strip of lace, black flats on her feet and a black veiled hat. She called it her "funeral outfit." She already had worn it to the funeral of an outspoken NAACP member who was murdered – no suspects in custody. Her hair was now neatly combed. With lipstick and a little makeup Laura's appearance had changed from mousy to professional. She reminded Neil of many women in Washington, but doubted her's was a fashion statement common in Atlanta. Neil wore his jacket and charcoal slacks with a white shirt. Wilkie had dropped them off in the Bel Air two blocks from the Home. The car's D.C. dealer tags were too conspicuous to park the car near the Home. King staked out the back of the building to look for colored employees

Chapter Sixteen: Atlanta

he could question while Neil and Laura were inside. They rang the doorbell. A young colored girl in a maid's black uniform opened the door.

They identified themselves by their real names, in case identification was required, but Neil said he was Laura's brother. They had telephoned earlier for an appointment with the chief administrator of the home, Mrs. Dorothy Crabtree. The young colored girl led the pair to a set of raised panel double doors, opened them and announced Neil and Laura to a grey-haired woman of indeterminate middle age whose head was bent over her desk. The room was immaculate. It reminded Neil of pictures of the Oval Office at the White House, except he doubted that the White House walls were lined with baby pictures. The Childress Agency offices were a dump compared to the Christian Home. A few more trips like this one, Neil thought, and he could write a Baedeker about homes for single women and their babies.

Mrs. Crabtree lifted her head to scan her visitors and rose to greet them with a handshake and introductions. She invited the couple to sit at a long conference table near the double doors. When all were seated, she asked the purpose of the visit.

As agreed beforehand, Neil would do most of the talking. He and the rest of the team assumed that a loving brother would take over arrangements for his pregnant sister. They were wrong.

"This is my sister, Mrs. Masters, who is divorced," Neil began. Mrs. Crabtree cut him off.

Unanimous Verdict

"I always prefer to hear from the expectant mother, Mr. Endicott. I realize you have your sister's interests at heart, but I'd like her to speak." Laura was game for the job.

"I'm afraid I made an absolutely dreadful mistake, Mrs. Crabtree. I hope you can help me."

"Now, now. We are here for girls – I mean, ladies – who make mistakes. I must admit that you are a little older than our usual client, Mrs. Masters. We also rarely encounter divorcees. They should know a little more than our typical teen-ager."

"Yes. Yes, I should have known better. I'm too old to let my emotions get me into such trouble." Laura pulled a hankie from her purse and brought it to her eyes. Neil was tempted to roll his own eyes at Laura's overacting, but resisted the impulse.

"Tell me what the problem is. No details are necessary." Some girls wanted to describe their fling, such as how they maneuvered The Act with a steering wheel in the way, how they felt the snow melting under them, threatening to chill the moment of passion, or how they had to keep slapping mosquitoes up to the point of withdrawal. Mrs. Crabtree, who had not had sexual relations since 10 years before her husband died, preferred not to hear such information.

"Well, I am divorced from a man of some means and reputation. I had not had relations for a year – since my divorce, of course. There was a man I hired to care for my gardens and lawns – I have a fairly large estate, vengeance on my ex-husband for his philandering. You can imagine what happened." Laura regretted she had not practiced more. Her eyes were watering as she struggled to keep from laughing. She made gentle sobbing sounds instead and covered her face with the hankie.

"I understand. But having a baby is not the worst thing that can happen. Since the war, our country's morals have suffered a serious decline. I'm not trying to put you off, but people are more accepting of children born out of wedlock, especially to older women who are single and want children before menopause but who lost their husbands in the service of our country."

"Yes ma'am. I mean, I can imagine what you are talking about. Menopause and all."

Neil was blushing. He had never been in the presence of women speaking about menopause.

"So, perhaps you don't need to be confined to a place like this. Your friends might be more amenable to your pregnancy than you think."

"Oh, Mrs. Crabtree. It's much, much worse than you think. Melvin, the father, is a Negro. A very black Negro." Neil put his arm around Laura to comfort "Sis."

"You can see why she is so upset," he said. "I am humiliated. We must keep this secret and then get rid of the child." Now who was overdoing it, he thought to himself.

Mrs. Crabtree was visibly taken aback. She did not know whether to be disgusted or sympathetic, so picked both. "Oh, Mrs. Masters. How awful. Rape. I certainly understand why you want to get rid of this child. How horrible. You have all my sympathies. That nigger should be hanged! A Negro. How disgusting!"

Her moral rectitude satisfied, Mrs. Crabtree returned to her role as businesswoman. " Of course, you can't press charges. Not and also keep the secrecy you want. I certainly now agree that you need our services."

"Of course, it isn't enough for me to have the baby privately," Laura said, easing the emotional content of her acting and focusing instead on the information she needed from Mrs. Crabtree. "Once the baby is born, it will have to be placed with the utmost discretion."

"We have handled these situations in the past. These — what should we call it — mixed race situations. Not often. Perhaps a half dozen times. We also wish to be discreet. We do not want to get a reputation for birthing colored babies here."

"A half dozen times. My word."

"Well, we don't keep a count. Some of them happened before I got here. I've been here 20 years. You see these filing cabinets?" She waved her hand toward a half dozen filing cabinets lining the Oval Office walls beneath the baby pictures. "These are the births and adoptions we have cared for over only the last eight or 10 years. There are many more files in basement storage. You can see that even if the number of Negro babies is as high as six, it is a very small percentage of our clientele."

Basement storage. Bingo! Neil thought.

Chapter Sixteen: Atlanta

"Well, what do you do to maintain discretion when the baby is born?"

"Whatever you would like. I have heard that one woman wanted her baby placed anonymously outside the South. I assume she was so embarrassed to have had relations with a Negro that she didn't even want the baby in the same region. Perhaps she thought the existence of a bastard half-breed, a spawn of rape, was an insult to Southern traditions. That would be my reaction, certainly."

Neil wanted to slap her. So did Laura.

"Do you have people who deliver babies to other states? I mean, how does that work?"

"No. It is up to the mother or her family to find an agency out of state and arrange transportation. It happens so rarely, I really can't provide much information."

"So someone else would have to know?"

"Someone else always has to know. We need someone to contact in an emergency. We can keep your name anonymous from the staff of the Home and, certainly, the adoption agency. But we do need a contact. What if something happened to you, or, God forbid, the home burned down or something.

"You needn't be concerned. Your brother already knows your situation. He can be your emergency contact."

"I see." Now that they had what they came for – the location of the files – Laura and Neil were tired of pretending and wanted to make a graceful exit. But Mrs. Crawford was not about to let them get away without closing the deal.

"Of course, it is very expensive to house a pregnant woman through birth. There are nutritional needs. A doctor must be available for regular checkups and emergencies. Six or seven months is a long time to be confined to a home, especially one as nice as this – and you won't find better – so we have to entertain you. All this costs money. Let me give you a price list. From what you have told me, I assume cost is not a problem? If it is, I can recommend some cheaper facilities, though they are by no means as professional. But if our facilities are satisfactory, we can sign the papers today." Mrs. Crawford was dripping sincerity now that economics were being discussed.

" I just want this to be over." Laura's ambiguity was intended.

"If that is all you want, and you aren't concerned about the baby – and why should you be concerned about a pickaninny – we could do something about that much more cheaply and quickly." Mrs. Crabtree's tone turned conspiratorial. Now it was Neil's turn to be self-righteous. He also saw a way to a quick exit.

"Mrs. Crabtree! You are not suggesting my sister terminate her pregnancy, are you? That is illegal and against our religious values. I am shocked that a place calling itself the Christian Home would suggest such a thing."

Mrs. Crabtree retreated. "Of course the Home does not recommend it or perform the procedures and we counsel against it.

Chapter Sixteen: Atlanta

But wouldn't you prefer your sister to have it done in a sanitary, safe place, if she was to have it done?"

"No. I would rather she be infected and die. Imagine, killing a baby. Even a colored baby is one of God's creatures. We will be going now. I really don't think we want to patronize a place like this that counsels killing babies." Neil harrumphed and pulled at Laura all the way to the front door. They kept their backs to the building and stood straight as they walked away until they were out of sight. Then they burst into gales of laughter.

"That was wonderful!" Laura exclaimed. "Imagine, that old biddy is pushing abortions! You were great. What a show of disgust! 'I would rather she be infected and die!' *That* was over the top. She's probably scared we'll turn her in."

"I bet she gets a big cut out of every abortion referral. I wonder if whoever owns that place knows about it?" Neil asked. "Jesus, what a fraud!

"You did great, too, Laura. 'He's a Negro. A very black Negro.' Great work, Laura." Neil was doubled over with laughter.

They found the Bel Air and Wilkie where they had been dropped off. King did not return for over half an hour. They spent the time debating how to obtain Clay's adoption papers. Wilkie and Laura wanted nothing to do with a break-in. When King finally arrived, he had a big grin on his face and could not wait to reach them before he started shouting. "Success! Success!" He was waving a sheet of paper. All four boarded the car with Wilkie in the driver's seat.

447

"I got it. I got it." King said loudly.

"Got what?" Laura asked.

"I saw the file. I saw the file on the birth of the baby that's got to be Clay."

"What?" Neil was stunned. "The files are in the basement. How the hell did you get to them?"

"Doesn't the Bible say something like the right folk gonna' win? That's what happened."

"I don't think the Bible says any such thing or the world would be a lot different," Laura said testily. Lou had trumped the comedy in the Home with real results. "Get to the point."

"The record of a baby Negro boy born on February 20, 1922 says his mother was Emily Roach, white. The father is listed as "unknown, colored." The record also says the baby was the result of a rape. It says "rape" in big black handwritten letters. There's another copy of that agreement we already got with the Chicago agency. There's another document that says to give the baby to a 'Mr. Roach.' It also says that this guy Roach is to be called if anyone inquires about the birth or adoption. That's about it."

King paused to look expectantly at Laura and Neil, his chin jutting forward at an impossibly abnormal angle. "The forces of the righteous shall triumph, led by the wise," he said, another phony Bible passage. The other three in the car laughed. King joined in. "I think that's from the Psalms," he added.

Chapter Sixteen: Atlanta

"I think it's from bullshit," said Laura. The whole car was joyful. The riddle of Clay"s adoption was almost solved.

"How did you get it?" Neil asked. "We just went through a whole routine worthy of Sid Caesar and Imogene Coca but only found out the file was in the basement. What did you do?"

"Just like we thought. I found a colored guy entering the building. He's the janitor at that place. He was taking a lunch break. I started talking to him. Nice young man, maybe 22 years old. He just graduated from Morehouse College. He's pissed off. He's got a degree in sciences, biology, I think, and can't get a better job. He's had this one while in college.

"He hates that Christian Home. He says it ain't Christian for them to be white only. He says that the head lady is mean to all the colored help. Treats 'em poorly."

"We can believe that. You should have seen how she acted when I told her I was knocked up by a Negro. I didn't know if she'd faint or shoot me," Laura said as she resumed laughing.

"I'll bet. Anyway, he remembered Clay. He don't often get approached by black folk to look at papers for white bastards. Clay gave him twenty bucks and the fellow let him look in the basement all day. When Clay found what he wanted, he gave the guy another ten-spot to store the folder so Clay could get it when he came back. The guy's been waitin' for him to come back for two months."

"Amazing," Neil exclaimed.

"I told him I'd give him fifty for the folder, but he wouldn't give it up. He said if two colored guys were interested in it, then it must contain something the white folk would be interested in and he didn't want the folder missing. Made sense. I said I'd give him the fifty if he just let me look at the folder and take notes. He was copasetic with that. So he goes inside and comes back out with the folder. I sat on a boulder and took notes, then gave it back to him. Easy as pie."

"What was the mother's name again?" Neil asked.

"Emily. Age 18. River's Edge, Aiken County, South Carolina."

"Oh my God. That's the Farwell plantation!" Laura put her hand to her mouth after shouting her information. "You know, the Supreme Court justice."

"I've heard of him. But the name is Roach, not Farwell." Neil said. "Wasn't Roach the name that woman gave when we called the phone number in your office the other day?"

"Sure was. It's all fittin' together now," Lou replied. "So this River's Edge is some kinda' plantation? Owned by the Supreme Court guy? What's the Roach name mean?"

"I have no idea. Never heard the name. Maybe it's a hand on the farm or maybe a distant relative. I don't know. I think I know where the plantation is," Laura said. "It's probably ninety miles away. Maybe a little more. It's east of Aiken and west of Barnwell. In its day it was one of the most legendary plantations in that part of South Carolina." Laura glanced at the Christian Home price list for the first time. "This Roach must have had money to afford this place to have her baby."

"No point in wasting time," Neil said.

"Let's go there tomorrow." King agreed.

"I'm coming with you," Laura said.

"Why not? We may need a great actress," Neil laughed.

All four in the Bel Air had talked themselves into a victorious mood when they arrived at the NAACP office. They quickly told Ezra what they had learned. He declined to join the celebration.

"No wonder Clay was so down after coming here," Ezra said, his sadness deflating the mood of the others.

"You all are so happy for no reason. Don't you get it? Think it through. Clay thought he had a white father, maybe a rich guy. Maybe a powerful guy. Maybe this Justice Farwell or some governor. He didn't know, but after Chicago he had a reason to think it was possible. White man rapin' a colored gal, that's bad for a man's reputation 'cept among the white trash, who ain't got no reputation to worry about. *Or* among the rich whites, who got the means to keep it all secret. Clay wouldn't be ashamed of bein' the son of a prominent white man, not in his own view, anyway. He'd be lookin' for payback from a white man who raped his ma. But that ain't what happened. Clay found out a black man raped a well-to-do white woman, a 17-year-old, maybe 16 when it happened. His ma was a victim, but a white victim of a black crime. It just confirms all the negative images whites got of the colored. The rapin' black bull. Nothin' to be proud of.

Only thing come from making that public is to embarrass the white woman. Maybe even Mrs. Van Dyke.

"This ain't nothin' to celebrate. This is Clay's tragedy." The group paused for a moment to consider Ezra's conclusions, their joyful helium balloon suddenly punctured.

"He's right," King said. "We oughta' wrap this up now and go home. This puts that note they found on Clay's body in a whole new light. It was just somebody's sick idea of a joke. Makin' fun of a colored boy unhappy in his skin. The note ain't a clue about nothin'. This whole adoption stuff was a wild goose chase for us as well as Clayton Van Dyke. He mighta' been killed by some drunk at a bottle club who couldn't stand Clay bein' high yella or maybe 'cause he didn't like Clay's unusual philosophy about blacker is better. Based on what we know now, coulda' been a black killer or a white one. We're back to square one."

"Wait a minute." Neil's voice was unusually authoritative. "We aren't just some posse. We've been hired to do a job and we've spent a lot of Mrs. Van Dyke's money coming down here. We need to pull this string until we reach the end."

"Look, white boy, you don't know shit about the South and the black man. This ain't gonna lead to nothin' good for Mrs. Van Dyke." King's voice was dismissive. But he underestimated Neil's commitment and command.

"No, you look, King. I may just be a white boy from Chevy Chase, but that doesn't mean I'm stupid or a coward. There's something wrong here. A woman has a baby in a home for unwed mothers. Let's say it was a rape by Clay's father. Why the hell would the mother, or her parents or whoever be leaving notes to be called if there was some inquiry? And why the ruckus after 30 years? Why would I get beat up? Why would they care? It's not like the mother's name is gonna' be broadcast on the radio. These places keep the information a secret. And hell, the mother might be dead by now anyway."

King was weary with this boy. King was the voice of experience. "You don't get it, do you? Ain't nothin' worse for a white woman than to be raped by a colored man. Even that little white slut in Jonesboro nearly got a few colored boys lynched. Nobody'd care if those boys were white – just a little sowin' of oats with a little whore. But the very idea of a black penis in a white vagina drives most white folk nuts – north and south.

"Learn the lesson, boy," he concluded.

"I'm gettin' more than a little sick of you belittling me, condescending to me, when it comes to race." Neil's face was red, but this time not with embarrassment. He was angry. "I'm getting more than a little sick of you and Ezra ganging up on me and hiding things from me and making decisions without me. Maybe prejudice is not a one-way street. Maybe you guys are so full of stereotypes and legends that you can't judge things as they are or accept things as they might be. When I was on the force we learned not to reach a conclusion until we had the proof. When I was in Korea we learned not to claim a victory until we counted the casualties. Now you want to quit when we're nearly there. It doesn't make sense."

"Of course it makes sense." Ezra's deep bass demanded the floor. "It makes sense, but it isn't right. Mr. King is afraid of more embarrassment. More disappointment. We black folk have seen it plenty. Just when we get optimistic, just when we get hopeful and even joyful about some black man or woman makin' his or her mark, we get wounded again. I wish I could put all the blame on the white man, since he's the one caused it. But the fact is that black folk disappoint all the time." Ezra paused. He clearly was not finished. He was emotional. For a moment, it seemed possible the black bear might cry. He shook it off.

"Whites make blacks figure they ain't supposed to succeed. So when some of us are able to fly close to the sun, we tear off our own wings and drop to the ground. Mr. King knows it. He's an exception. He done raised a good family that's circling the sun. He knows how hard it is. How hard it is for his kids. The expectation is that all of them will fail. They're aimin' too high. Too white. Even black folk, in their heart of hearts, want 'em to fail. If a black person succeeds, then there ain't no excuse for the rest of us. It's like crabs in a bucket. One tries to reach the top, to get out, it gets clawed back down by the others.

"So we're ready to assume that any colored man born of a white woman is rape. Reason high yellas get their heads so far up their asses about color is 'cause they assume some colored grandma of their's was

Chapter Sixteen: Atlanta

so damned sexy and smart that even a white man wanted to love her. But it also means a white man – a slave owner – could control the best women available. If a white woman has a colored child, it must be the result of violence. What white woman wants a black man? We been taught not to even imagine such a thing. Lou don't want to confirm Clay Van Dyke's own sad conclusion that his mama was raped by a vicious black man. It's almost certainly a true fact. But provin' it's so will hurt too much."

Silence ruled the room as everyone contemplated Ezra's soliloquy.

"I think you are wrong, Mr. Lowell." The tiny, tentative voice was Laura's. "I know a white woman can love a colored man. I know it's a fact. I've been in love with a colored man myself."

Another silent preface before King replied. "That's a mighty gladdening thing, Miss Masters. You are a fine Christian lady, I'm sure. But you ain't no daughter of a plantation owner in 1922 far as I can tell. I'm sure you genuinely loved this colored man, but even in modern day 1954 ain't one percent of white women who'd be in that situation."

Laura's eyes were wet, but she was unblinking. "It is not impossible, Mr. King. If it was love, not violence, that resulted in that baby, then that young woman believed anything was possible, even loving a colored man and having his child. She was wrong. It wasn't possible for her. But that doesn't make it rape." Laura's determination failed her at the end of her short statement and she wept soundlessly. "I'm sorry," she said quietly and left the room.

Unanimous Verdict

Those remaining turned to King, but he was silent. No message could be read from his face. But after a couple of minutes, he delivered the last word.

"Alright. We follow this string, as Mr. Endicott calls it. I think it will end in misery for Mrs. Van Dyke, but she's paid out a lot of dough. We got no other leads to follow. We're less than a day's ride from this place where Emily Roach lived. We got to finish it."

Chapter Seventeen: The Chief III, May 8 - 11, 1954

The time had come for the Chief to write the majority opinion in its final form for presentation to his colleagues. All of the opinions would be proofed, printed and announced on Monday, May 17, only nine days hence. There were to be three of them: The majority opinion written by the Chief, a dissent written by Jackson, joined by Clark, and another dissent by Farwell. The Chief sighed as he examined the evidence of his failure to bring home a unanimous verdict in *Brown v. Board of Education of Topeka Kansas* and the other four school cases. He had been able to persuade several million Californians to vote for him for governor, but he couldn't win the votes of three colleagues on the Court. A one-third vote to sustain school segregation, roughly proportionate to the number of states in the Union that had such laws, would be read by the South as comforting support for continued resistance to making the Negro a full citizen. After all, the warriors of the "lost cause" had turned defeat into victory many times before and surely could do so again against six old men. Hoping for a miracle, or at least a change of heart, the Chief postponed the formal vote on Brown until the last possible moment, Saturday, May 15. He had given up early on getting Farwell's vote, but thought he still had a shot at persuading Jackson to join the majority. Clark would follow. If his prayers were answered by an 8-1 decision, the print shop could work overtime on Sunday.

The Chief visited Justice Jackson on Saturday afternoon, May 8, at his home in McLean, Virginia, where the justice was recuperating from his heart attack of a month earlier. If politics is the art of the possible, he said to himself as he rang the doorbell, being Chief Justice is the art of alchemy – creating wisdom and leadership from the base material of nine old men. He was greeted at the door by a young Negro housekeeper.

The Chief found Justice Jackson standing in his living room, dressed as if he was going to work in a dark three-piece suit and tightly knotted tie. The Chief, who was in slacks and a striped sports shirt, felt underdressed. Jackson was holding a thick volume open in his hands when he greeted his visitor.

"Hello, Chief. Nice to see you again. What's it been? Two weeks, I think, since you were last out here."

"You look a helluva lot better. Don't even look like you've been sick. I think maybe you're just loafin'." In truth, the Chief thought his colleague did look better, but he still looked sick. His face, a pleasant one that for some reason reminded the Chief of the young man who sold him his first life insurance policy, was drawn, its color drained away.

"Thanks, Chief. Since I left the hospital a couple weeks ago, I feel like I've been doin' anything but loafing. You've been here a couple of times and everybody else. Even Farwell came by once. He gave me one of those damned Civil War rounds he likes so much. Felix has been here so often I thought I'd get him to cut the grass! I like to think they were social calls, but somehow everybody wanted to talk about *Brown*."

Chapter Seventeen: The Chief III

"Well, at least the boys are interested." The Chief wanted his own pressure to seem light, though his goal was the same as the others — get Jackson to vote his way.

"I was just looking again at Myrdal," Jackson said, indicating the book held in his hand. "It's sad that we need to look to a Swede to tell us what's wrong with this country." Gunnar Myrdal had written a mammoth study called *An American Dilemma: The Negro Problem and Modern Democracy*. Although the book was published a decade ago, it was still considered the most thorough study of the subject.

"Yes, a Norwegian would have done a better job," the Chief joked. "Why are you looking at Myrdal? Are you considering a change of heart on *Brown?*"

"I go back and forth. It's a troubling matter. Set aside the legal issues. There's no doubt the Negro is punished by segregation, whether it's the legal kind in the South or the practices in the North. The data in this book proves it, if there were any question. I doubt matters have improved much in 10 years. In some ways, I give the southern whites credit for putting it all in black and white, so to speak. We northerners prefer to practice our discrimination without acknowledging it. The statistics in this book are appalling. Even the poorest whites fare better than the colored. I hate the idea that I might vote to uphold this bigotry and the pain that comes with it."

"You don't have to, Bob. You can join us. With Frankfurter on board, the best-known advocate for judicial restraint is saying the decision is OK. You won't be giving up your legal philosophy."

Unanimous Verdict

"I don't know. Frankfurter's an immigrant. He's a Jew. Given what Hitler did, he's got almost a religious obligation to vote as he will. Farwell is the same way on the other side, if you are willing to give religion a bad name. He really thinks he's the modern-day Lee or maybe Jeff Davis. I feel I'm the one in the middle. Clark feels the same.

"But what really worries me is that we are going to start a race war in this country. I don't know how bad it will be, but it's going to be bad. People will die. Some of them might be children, black and white. Do we really have the right to do something to spark such a war?

"I won't be around for it, Chief. Don't tell our colleagues, but the press has been misled. My heart attack wasn't a mild one. It nearly did me in. It was a bad one and a signal. My heart is weak. I could go soon."

"Bob, don't say that. You look awfully healthy now. Just relax over the summer. You'll be fine."

"Didn't know you were an M.D. as well as an L.L.D., Chief. I doubt I'll relax when I read all the reaction over the summer to the *Brown* case. Why now?"

"If not now, Bob, when? Wait another 300 years? The U.S. stands on top of the world right now economically and, at least in most of the world, politically. The South will never volunteer to integrate the schools, at least not until many more generations of Negroes are ruined. The change must begin now. It will happen one step at a time, but fast.

Chapter Seventeen: The Chief III

First the southern schools, then northern, then housing, then jobs. I don't know if it will all be the Supreme Court or if the Congress and the President will step in. But it's got to start somewhere."

The Chief decided to take advantage of Jackson's knowledge that his remaining life might be brief. It was a cheap trick, but the stakes were high.

"If what your doctors tell you is true, do you really want one of your last acts to be a vote to sustain segregated schools? I think the answer is 'no,' Bob."

Jackson sat down on his sofa. The two men had their brief debate while standing, and Jackson already was exhausted. He offered the Chief a seat, but he declined. He felt lousy having used Jackson's health as a chip in the debate.

"It's not a legal point, but it's a damned good practical point," Jackson replied dolefully.

"I've scheduled a court conference for Saturday, May 15, to take the formal vote. Your dissent will be in galleys and ready to go, but I hope you will change your mind by then."

"It's hell being a mortal asked to make these God-like decisions over the lives of millions," Jackson ruminated. "And I feel especially mortal right now."

"I can see that, Bob. I know that however way you vote, it will be the way you think best." Jackson's vote wasn't set yet. There was still a chance to bring him around. He shook Jackson's hand. The return handshake was weak, childlike, yet his heart attack was over a month ago. "Are you coming to our lunch with Truman on Tuesday? Douglas invited him. It's a command performance, the ill excepted, of course."

"No, I think I'll have to pass. Maybe he wants to bury the hatchet on the *Sawyer* case. There's a good example of overreaching, but not by us." *Sawyer v. Youngstown Sheet and Tube* had been decided two years earlier. Truman had ordered government seizure of the U.S. steel mills during a strike, citing the need for steel during the Korean War. The Court held 6-3 that the action was beyond the powers of the executive branch. "I heard he was hopping mad that all the liberals and Frankfurter and I voted against the administration. You remember that John Davis argued for the steel companies in that case."

"I wasn't on the Court," the Chief gently reminded.

"Oh, of course you weren't. Well, Davis did a better job in that case than he has representing the states in the school cases. Can't say as I'm surprised. A lawyer skilled in business law sometimes lacks the passion needed in a civil rights case. Davis gets the law down alright, but sometimes has a problem with the justice part."

"Keep that justice part in mind as you think about *Brown*. And don't worry about what the doctors say. They're wrong more often than right." The Chief departed before Jackson could reminisce over more cases from the past.

Conflicting thoughts battled in his head as he made his way to his limousine. For the first time in years, the Chief had been treated like a young man as Jackson started to recount old cases for the newcomer.

Chapter Seventeen: The Chief III

But the Chief didn't feel young. He was melancholy. Jackson, one of the great justices, was in decline, physically and perhaps mentally. *Brown* and other cases before the Court were more important than any one justice, the Chief thought as his chauffeur drove him home. But the law was written by men, and could ill-afford the loss of a fine man like Jackson.

Former President Truman joined the justices for lunch in the Court's conference room the following Tuesday. Douglas acted as host. Truman was jaunty and in good spirits. As expected, Jackson did not attend. Truman said that as President he resented the Court's decision in *Sawyer*, but now that he was a private citizen, he didn't think it was so bad, "especially now that we have a Republican in the White House."

Everyone obeyed the unwritten rule not to discuss pending cases before the Court – except Farwell. He asked the former President if he didn't agree with his former Secretary of State, and a former Justice of the Supreme Court, South Carolina Governor Jimmy Byrnes, that the schools should be closed rather than integrated by order of the Supreme Court. All those seated at the long conference table enjoying their lunch froze, again except for Farwell. Truman's dark brown eyes widened behind his horned rims and his jaw muscles worked back and forth. He clearly resented Farwell's obvious attempt to enlist him in the cause of segregation. Didn't Farwell know that Truman desegregated the military by executive order? What a damned fool, the former President thought. FDR's worst appointment.

"Sometimes politicians say things that they know as a good human being they would never do, push come to shove, Justice Farwell. Jimmy Byrnes is a good politician. But he's also a good human being. He won't shut down the schools." A few minutes later, Farwell excused himself, claiming he had important business to tend to. He was the only justice to leave before the former President did.

PART THREE: THE VERDICT
Chapter Eighteen: River's Edge, May 9-11, 1954

Aiken was abuzz with excitement when Ezra, Lou, Laura and Neil arrived. They soon found out the reason: The United States had just opened the first phase of a huge new facility for manufacturing plutonium and tritium along the banks of the Savannah River. It already was starting to add what was expected to be thousands of jobs to the region. There was talk of new subdivisions and schools, both white and colored, that already were under construction. One entire town was destroyed to make room for the acreage required by the Savannah unit along nearly 30 miles of riverbank and stretching several miles inland. Many federal and state dignitaries, bureaucrats and engineers had crowded into available lodging for the grand opening of the plant. Although the colored motel had rooms for Ezra and Lou, Laura and Neil had to stop at several lodging establishments before they found one with two available rooms.

For all the talk of Aiken becoming a modern center for nuclear science that Laura and Neil heard while dining at their all-white hotel, there also was griping that the plant was attracting Negroes to Aiken at the same time many blacks were leaving other parts of South Carolina. Although the twentieth century finally had come to Aiken, it seemed Aiken wasn't ready for it.

River's Edge was between Aiken and Barnwell. Part of it had been claimed by the government at a high price for the Savannah River nuclear site, but the mansion and a couple of thousand acres of cropland were still owned by the Farwell family. As Neil and Laura gleaned this information from a helpful desk clerk, a matronly gray-haired woman in line behind them interjected that Margaret Farwell was a menace to Aiken and South Carolina and wasn't it a shame she bore the Farwell name. Her reaction to mention of River's Edge was spontaneous. She declined entreaties to elaborate. The desk clerk, who bore no trace of a southern accent, smirked and said Miss Farwell was known to promote Negro causes.

Neil, Ezra, Lou and Laura picked up the road to Barnwell, which swung around the west and north of the Savannah nuclear site, until they reached a county road and then a gravel turnoff at a postal box reading "River's Edge." A second, smaller box was labeled "Roach." The road to the plantation was canopied by magnolia trees and elms planted in the last century. They framed the mansion ahead. It gleamed in the beautiful spring morning, evidence that it was well-tended, which was confirmed as the Bel Air drew closer. As the car emerged from the magnolias, a second, newer brick home was visible across a wide lawn from the original mansion. It had two wings which had been added to a central two-story colonial. The building was painted white to match the mansion, but it was utilitarian, of no architectural interest and bare of landscaping, other than the lawn. The mansion was surrounded by plants of many kinds, most of them in colorful full bloom.

As the party emptied the Bel Air, they heard the steady clop of horse's hooves. A moment later, a handsome black stallion rounded the

Chapter Eighteen: River's Edge

corner bearing a woman in full riding dress, including a black riding helmet. Her tailored suit complemented a handsome figure. She sat upon the stallion with great dignity and command. She reined the horse to a stop a few feet from the visitors, but did not dismount.

"May I help you?" she asked. Her voice was wary, not welcoming. Her face, partly hidden in her helmet, was tanned, a collection of sharp angles surrounding cornflower blue eyes. Her age was difficult to discern. Laura jumped in as spokeswoman for the group.

"Yes, my name is Laura Masters. These are my colleagues." She introduced each one by name. "We are looking for an Emily Roach. We have business with her."

"I am Margaret Farwell. The Roaches work for me. What is the nature of your business?"

Hearing the same name that was the target of the old matron at the hotel, Laura decided it was safe to disclose her affiliation. "I am with the National Association for the Advancement of Colored People. Our business is personal to Miss Roach."

The rider laughed. "Well I welcome the NAACP. I'm a great supporter. But I can't imagine what you want with Emily Roach. She hasn't even been a Roach for years. Her name is Lunker. Emily Lunker. Can't you tell me what you want with her?" Margaret Farwell eyed the brick house across the lawn. She saw Buster Roach peering past a curtain in the window, as she expected he would. Visitors were rare at River's Edge, and Roach still kept a watch on everything, even in his late seventies.

"I'm afraid it is very private," Laura replied. "But I'm sure we appreciate your support."

"I don't recall a Laura Masters working for the South Carolina NAACP."

"Oh, I don't. I work out of Atlanta. I just started."

"Of course. Y'all do good work down there. You can find Emily Roach Lunker living with her parents right across the lawn there. She's a widow now. She's been back with her parents a couple of years." Margaret lowered her voice. "Her father's been watching us from the house. He's very mean and won't take well to the NAACP. Be very careful. Good luck." With that, she gave her horse a gentle kick and headed off for the stable, which was visible down a short trail. The quartet from Atlanta moved as one across the lawn and Laura, who had taken charge without opposition, knocked on the Roach's door. It opened immediately.

Age had taken its toll on Roach's appearance, though it would be difficult to mount an argument that he was uglier than in his youth. But age had not diminished his capacities. The outdoor labor was sufficient to keep him fit, but he accommodated his advancing years with shorter hours and enjoyed a home with comfortable amenities. He was proud that he weighed only five pounds more than when he had arrived at the plantation nearly 60 years ago. He was unchanged in other ways as well.

Roach continued to run River's Edge at the direction of the Farwell siblings. Margaret Farwell had demanded to have him fired

Chapter Eighteen: River's Edge

many times, but her father's will specified that final authority rested with Nathan until her half-brother died.

"Well, if it ain't Uncle Remus and King Kong," Roach sneered by way of greeting, referencing Lou and Ezra. Any restraints in publicly displaying the biases adopted in his youth, and there were very few, were discarded in the irritability and impatience of old age. Laura prepared to scold the old man, but Lou put a hand on her shoulders to signal calm. They had a mission to accomplish. Laura controlled herself.

"My name is Laura Masters. We are looking for Emily Roach Lunker." Roach was quite possibly the ugliest man she had ever seen. She had never met someone with yellow skin. He wasn't Chinese or other Oriental. They didn't really have yellow skin, anyway. This man actually was yellow, or close to orange. The blue and green eyes were even more disorienting. It was hard for Laura to focus on the discussion looking at such a man.

"She's my daughter. Whadda' you want with her? She got no nigger friends."

Laura again ignored the insult. "May we please speak to her?"

Roach knew why the group was visiting River's Edge. He was prepared for them. Mrs. Childress telephoned him when Clay Van Dyke visited and again when Neil Endicott made inquiries. He knew all of Emily's few friends. The white guy at his door fit Mrs. Childress' description of Endicott. He guessed the others were friends of Clay Van Dyke. He glanced over to the stables. There was no sign of Margaret Farwell.

469

"I'll get her," he said, retreating to the parlor. He returned in seconds with a shotgun and stepped outside, pointing the weapon at his visitors and forcing the group onto the lawn.

"Now get outta here afore I blow you all to kingdom come. You got no business here."

"You're Roach, aren't you? You're the guy everybody was supposed to call about your daughter's baby, aren't you?" Neil wasn't sure where he got the courage to challenge a man holding a shotgun to his face, but he was going to complete this assignment. "You know, the Negro baby born in Atlanta 32 years ago?"

"I don't know what you're talkin' 'bout, but even if I did it sounds like a private matter." Roach pointed the shotgun to the Bel Air and back, signaling the group to leave.

Neil pressed on. He would know the truth before he left River's Edge. "And then that baby grew up and wanted to find out who his parents were and you killed him, or got someone to kill him, isn't that true, Roach? His name was Clay Van Dyke and he was a good son and a good man and you killed him. You hanged him. All just to keep from bein' known your daughter was raped by a colored man."

Roach did not wish to admit to anything, but he could not contain his anger at the young white man who obviously had all the benefits of education and economics that Roach lacked, but who was defending a Negro.

"These niggers get the idea they can be like white folk. Sleep with white women or claim the blood of proper white southern heroes.

Chapter Eighteen: River's Edge

They deserve to die. There ain't a jury in this state that would convict me of anything. This nigger was ruttin' aroun' tryin' to find out who his real mammy and daddy were. He had no right. Hell, he was lucky he weren't pulled right outta his momma with a pair of pliers and thrown in the trash.

"I weren't gonna' let him tarnish the names of good white folk. My son, Robby, he done took care of things. He lives in Washington. He done it fine.

"Now you're doin' the same ruttin' 'round and you'll get the same treatment. Only this time we'll just shoot you and make you food for the Savannah River fishes. Nobody'll ever know.

"Matt, come on out here."

Roach's younger son, now middle aged, with a large belly and folds under his chin, did not boast the athletic look of his much older father. He kept his eyes focused on the ground. He did not seem happy to be at his father's side.

"So the Supreme Court guy had Clayton killed. Is that it?" Ezra spoke for the first time. He felt oddly powerful, once again confronting a vicious bigot at his front door. He hoped it would not end in the same way. He had too many responsibilities now. But he wouldn't back down if it came to that.

"Naw. Robby did in the kid, jes like I tole' him to do. I couldn't resist tellin' him to leave some kinda' note. Send a message to all those niggers up there. Whether the Justice knew about will be our little secret."

"So now you're a killer, Buster? Not for the first time I imagine."

The voice came from behind Roach, who turned at the sound and kept the shotgun level, now pointed to Margaret Farwell. She had returned from the stable indirectly, hoping to eavesdrop on the conversation. She knew that a confrontation between Roach and the NAACP could not have a good ending.

"Mr. Roach has an especially loud voice when he's going after the Negro. Like I told you before, he's a pretty mean guy." Roach shifted his shotgun, gesturing Margaret to join the others.

"Too bad for you, you nigger-lovin' cunt. I've wanted to call you that to your face the last 40 years. You heard my little confession, now you'll have to go with them." Matt finally raised his head up to look at his father. His eyes seemed to bulge with either horror or surprise. He ran back to the house. His father, focused on pointing the shotgun at the group, now numbering five, and shouted. "Little fuckin' coward. You never did have the balls of your brother." The obscenities hung in the air, answered only by a screen door slammed shut.

The sun was bright on the green manicured lawn. The temperature was rising into the 80s. A yellow butterfly fluttered across the lawn between Buster and his hostages. It was a beautiful day by the Savannah.

" I'll have to kill all of you. It complicates things, but I can't trust you to keep this secret. You, too, Miss Farwell." Even in threats to kill, and even after using horrible expletives to describe her a moment

Chapter Eighteen: River's Edge

earlier, Roach returned to custom, using the nominal courtesies with his boss.

"Tell me," Margaret addressed the visitors, "do they have the death penalty in the nation's capital?"

Neil admired her strength. She showed not the least fear of Roach. But her disdain for Roach and his shotgun was like a hot poker striking a rabid animal.

"No need to go to Washington for justice, Miss Farwell," Roach replied, clearly struggling to stay in emotional control to keep his shotgun steady. "I think we can do the death penalty right here in front of the mansion, right where you last saw your lover boy. Your brother won't like it, but he'll understand. He's said many times he'd like to throw you off River's Edge. He don't like you no better 'n I do.

"'Nuff talkin' anyway. I got chores to do. Can't spend more time on cunts and niggers." All five hostages were collected in front of his shotgun. "I might 'kin get alla' yus with a single shot from this ole' double barrel," he laughed. He was confident – perhaps even happy – about his plan. He lifted the gun and peered over the barrel, preparing to shoot. Of the five targets, only Ezra had a plan. He would drop to the ground and hope the old man fired both barrels, then Ezra could grab him. He could see Roach's finger on the trigger only 10 feet away.

A shot was fired, but not from the shotgun, which Roach dropped to the ground. He and everyone else turned to the source of the sound. Emily Roach, no longer the picture of young maternal comfort, but a shapeless mass of flesh, her chestnut hair unkempt and now gray, stood in the doorway with a pistol. An even older version of Emily, Celestine, stood behind her, along with middle-aged Matt. "You fat bitch," Roach roared, staggering toward the house. Emily fired again at her father. Neither her mother nor brother moved to interfere. Again, and again and again she fired until the chamber was empty and Roach lay dead on the lawn, blood oozing from his head and chest.

"You killed our baby, you bastard," Emily cried. Her tone was level. Revenge served cold.

"I apologize for my husband," Mrs. Roach croaked. "You can call the sheriff." She turned and with her daughter and son entered her home and closed the door. The living on the lawn were speechless for a moment.

"He's mistreated her and her mother for 50 years," Margaret Farwell said. "I think she was just looking for the right time."

The group then caucused to decide what to do. Later, they talked to the Roach family. Matt expressed mild regret for the death of his dad, but both Celestine and Emily were relieved that Buster finally was out of their lives. Margaret and Emily disappeared into a back bedroom for a long time. Both were drying tears when they returned. There was further discussion, along with some more tears from all three women of River's Edge. Only then did Margaret telephone the sheriff.

According to the account in the Aiken newspaper the next day, Buster Roach, a long-time resident of Aiken County and native of

Chapter Eighteen: River's Edge

New York, was killed by his wife in self-defense as he threatened her with a shotgun in a confrontation on the front lawn at River's Edge. Mrs. Roach's adult children, Matthew Roach and Emily Lunker, confirmed that their father threatened bodily harm, causing Mrs. Roach to retrieve the family pistol and shoot Mr. Roach. Nathan Farwell, former state senator, attorney general, chief justice of the South Carolina Supreme Court and now a justice on the United States Supreme Court, was in Washington, D.C. attending to his duties, the newspaper reported. He told the paper by telephone that he would have no comment on the domestic incident. His half-sister, Margaret Farwell, told the sheriff she was out riding at the time of the shooting and called the sheriff when she found Roach's body on the front lawn. The sheriff said the facts would be presented to a grand jury but that the evidence in favor of justifiable homicide was strong.

There was no mention of visitors at River's Edge. There were none when the sheriff arrived.

Neil drove the Bel Air all the way back to Atlanta, but he did not stop shaking until two hours into the journey. A direct personal confrontation with a shotgun was even worse than the anonymous danger of combat, and Buster Roach made Chicago's Lester Bark seem no more threatening than Howdy Doody. His companions complimented Neil on his courage in confronting Roach, but Neil was convinced he was foolhardy. Lou couldn't resist a bit of advice.

"That was a brave thing to do," he told Neil from the back seat. "You're the first private investigator I ever heard of outside the movies and cheap novels to get a gun pulled on him, and a double-barrel at that. Ain't no fee worth that. I'd of been out of there like a shot myself as soon as he came to the door with that gun." Was Lou saying Neil was brave, or was he saying he did a dumb thing? Neil didn't ask, but he doubted the ambiguity was accidental.

On arriving in Atlanta, Neil dropped Laura, Ezra and Lou off at the NAACP offices. Between all the driving and having his life threatened, he was beat. He apologized for rudeness and went to his hotel. When he reached his room, Neil pumped his fist and cheered. The mystery of Clay Van Dyke's death was solved.

Justice Farwell lived in an apartment at the Kennedy-Warren, a luxury building next to the National Zoo. The Aztec Art Deco architecture, featuring Aztec Indian eagles carved into the limestone façade, was an impressive structure on Connecticut Avenue. Other well-known public officials had lived at the Kennedy-Warren, including Roosevelt's principal aide, Harry Hopkins.

Although most justices and many other Washington officials and politicians listed their home address and telephone number in the phone book, Farwell did not. The Supreme Court police, the clerk's office and his own small staff were instructed not to give out the address or phone number. Even Farwell's sister was required to contact him through the Court and did not know his address. Too many angry civil rights advocates and admiring racists wanted to call or visit him, for very different reasons. Farwell preferred quiet evenings at home, usually keeping up with the many new books on the Civil War, which never lost its attraction for novelists and historians. Now widowed, Farwell did not miss his wife's companionship. She was a bore. As were his children. The genius of his father and his fathers before him was missing from the youngest Farwells. They were successful businessmen, but not one of the three boys had any interest in the Civil War and two of them even voiced support for repealing Jim Crow laws. Even their World War II service records were dull, lacking both battles and heroics.

Nathan often thought to himself how he was like his father, who had died 15 years earlier. Nathan, too, was now a faithful and powerful guardian of the Lost Cause. It was a comforting thought. In one important respect he was better than his father: For all their lack of interest in the South's heritage and its protection, none of his boys made love to any Negroes.

On returning to Washington in the early evening of May 13, Neil telephoned Lisa McCartin, who was still in at work in the Senate office building. He played on her liberal conscience by telling her he was working for the NAACP and needed to send a last-ditch plea to Farwell about the schools case. It was outside the work of the lawyers, he told Lisa. He wanted to send it to Farwell's home address to be sure he saw it. Lisa asked a few questions and told Neil she was impressed that he was working for the NAACP now and involved in a genuine cause. It was only half a lie, Neil told himself. Although clearly against policy, Lisa checked the Judiciary Committee files and gave Neil the address.

Neil met with Ezra and Lou King at King's office late the next afternoon. They joined Margaret Farwell, who had flown to Washington from Atlanta, outside the Kennedy-Warren after dinner. The men all wore sports shirts and slacks. Margaret Farwell wore a black dress and white gloves. This was to be a kind of funeral for her lover and her son and a punctuation point on the end of an important and emotional part of her own life. As well as revenge.

She was especially beautiful, even in funeral garb. Her clean, angular face was topped by a blond pixie cut. At 50, she looked no more than 40. Like her half-brother, she was the product of an active outdoor life in an otherwise comfortable environment where all physical needs were met.

The group entered the aluminum and glass doors of the apartment building and went directly to the reception desk. A middle aged man vaguely resembling the actor Peter Lorre raised his head at the sharp noise of Margaret's high heels on the marble floor.

"May I help you, Ma'm?"

"Yes. We wish to see Justice Farwell. I am his sister. He is not expecting me. It is a surprise visit."

"Are the colored gentlemen with you?"

"Yes." She spoke firmly, in a voice accustomed to giving direction. It demanded obedience.

Chapter Eighteen: River's Edge

"I shall have to ring Justice Farwell before letting you pass," the Lorre look-alike said sheepishly. He did not relish any sort of confrontation.

"Nonsense. I told you this is a surprise. These men worked with my brother before he came to Washington. We will go up without an announcement." Margaret turned on her heel without awaiting a response and headed to the elevator bank. The men followed her, not having spoken a word.

Margaret lifted the heavy knocker on the door to Farwell's apartment. It was quickly answered. Farwell opened the door only a couple of inches, the distance permitted by the chain lock.

"Yes?" he said.

"Nathan? It's Margaret. I was in town with some friends and thought I'd drop by. Is it an inconvenient time?" She maintained a cheerful tone and smiled at the man behind the crack in the door.

"No, I guess not," Farwell responded as he unhooked the chain holding the door. "There is such a thing as the telephone, you know, and I..." The thought was left unspoken. Farwell's graying eyebrows leaped in surprise at the sight of Ezra Lowell walking in after his sister, followed by a second, older black man and a young white man. Farwell started to speak again, to continue scolding Margaret, but caught himself. He visibly changed tactics.

"Anyway, welcome Margaret." The siblings did not kiss or exchange hugs. "Who are your friends? I'm afraid I have court tomorrow, so you can't stay long." Lou later said they were "as welcome as polio at a picnic". It wasn't that no Negroes had been in Farwell's apartment. But no Negro had been in the apartment who was not a servant. No one could mistake Ezra Lowell for a servant. "Take a seat, please. Can I get you something? A soda? I believe I have some Coca-Cola."

The living room was surprisingly small, barely room enough for a sofa and a couple of Queen Anne chairs. But there was no doubt the inhabitant was an enthusiastic fan of the Confederacy. As in his chambers, Farwell had covered the walls and shelves with paintings, armaments and memorabilia of the rebel armies. Neil inspected one bookshelf as he declined the invitation to sit. It contained picture books about the South and the Civil War along with a few law books.

"No, thank you, Nathan. These are my friends, Mr. King, Mr. Endicott and Mr. Lowell. They seem to have stumbled into a little of our family history, Nathan. They found out some things I never knew. Of course, as the head of the Farwell family, you ought to be brought up-to-date, too."

Farwell, who was dressed in a red woolen shirt and dark slacks, looked uneasily about the room at his four visitors. He only tolerated his sister and her liberal politics because she owned half of River's Edge. He knew she felt the same about him and his politics. Whatever the purpose of her unusual visit, it was not to offer him a favor.

"I don't know what you're talking about."

"We have the picture, judge," Neil said, reaching into his shirt pocket.

480

Chapter Eighteen: River's Edge

"What picture? I still don't know what you're talking about."

"You know, Nathan. The picture Buster Roach took of Brian Carter? You remember Brian, don't you? That wonderful young black man I met on my graduation day at River's Edge?" Margaret maintained a forced cheerfulness. She had cried for three days after the confrontation with Buster Roach, and would cry much more. But she would not give her brother the satisfaction she knew he would take from seeing her in pain now.

"Of course I remember him. He left behind a lot more than memories." Farwell smiled at his joke. No one responded. "Buster took his picture at the train station. I think I gave it to you. Did you lose it? Did these men find it? What does it have to do with me?" Farwell didn't like riddles or other people wasting his time. His sister was angering him on both counts.

"Not that picture, dear brother. I still have that picture. This is another picture Roach took that day. Please show it to him, Mr. Endicott." Margaret had dropped her artificial friendliness. Her rosebud lips were parted, the picture of a snarl, without the sounds. Her cornflower blue eyes widened and her voice was even more commanding than at River's Edge. She knew what was coming. To her brother, it would be punishment more dreadful than he could imagine — worse than death. Still not enough, she thought, but sufficient.

Neil handed him the photograph.

Chapter Nineteen: Birth, 1921 – 1922

"What did you and Nathan do with Brian?" Margaret demanded.

"We put him on the train. I don't give a damn what happened to him after that." John Farwell tried to return to reading the Aiken newspaper as his daughter circled his armchair waving the letter from Brian's mother.

Margaret wrote letters to Brian daily. No matter what her father said, she could not believe that Brian would not communicate with her. They were in love. She would go to New York to be with him. It was all arranged between them. She walked to the end of the long driveway to the main road to check the mailbox early every morning. Her diligence was rewarded about 10 days after Brian's departure with a letter addressed to her and postmarked New York City, Harlem Station. She ripped it open as she stood by the mailbox, her hands shaking in anticipation.

The letter was not from Brian, but from his mother. She said that Margaret's letters had been delivered and were being saved for him, but that Brian had not come home. His aunt, Isaac's mother, had telephoned the day of his abrupt departure to say he was being sent home and describing the reasons, which were no secret in the farm worker village. Brian had been expected home two days after he left Aiken, which would have been a week ago, his mother wrote.

She asked Margaret to please call her if she had any information about her son's whereabouts.

Margaret had to read the letter twice before its full weight registered with her. She continued shaking with the letter in her hand, but this time with worry and anger. What had her father done with Brian? She raced to the stable and opened the trunk of the Packard. The gun was still there, but the rope and hatchet were missing. Perhaps Roach had needed them for something else. Their absence was proof of nothing, but it frightened Margaret. No outlandish imagination was required to know that angry southern white men and rope were a dangerous combination for a Negro. She pressed her father for more information about the day Brian departed.

Farwell again put his newspaper on his lap to address his daughter, anxious to put the entire bitter experience of Brian Carter behind both of them. "I told you three or four times. He told us he probably would not go back to New York. Look, he's a young guy. Probably pretty talented for a colored, and he obviously has a wandering eye for pretty white women and adventure. Why go back to his mammy and pappy? It's like the song says, you can't keep 'em on the farm after they've seen Paree." Realizing the metaphor comparing New York to a farm and a cotton farm to Paris might not be persuasive; Farwell coldly expressed his true feelings.

"You really have to share in the blame, kitten. You gave him a taste of white women. That's gotta be like opium for a nigger boy. What do you expect?"

Chapter Nineteen: Birth

Margaret slapped her father across the face for the first time in her life and fled to her bedroom.

Margaret missed her periods in July and August. She remained in her room except for taking meals. She did not visit the village or spend time with Isaac or Petey or her other friends. She wept often and continued to write to Brian, hoping some day to receive a letter from him in return. In early August, his mother wrote to say that there was no trace of Brian. She asked pointed questions about his last day at River's Edge, which Margaret answered as best she could. A final angry letter from Harlem blamed Margaret for Brian's disappearance. Margaret was a Southerner, Brian's mother wrote, and knew the danger to her son. She suggested that Margaret had used Brian for her own pleasure and then discarded him. Margaret's letters, she wrote, were the product of a guilty conscience. She asked Margaret to stop sending them.

The sheriff stopped at River's Edge in mid-August. He apologized for bothering the family, but the New York Police Department had asked him to investigate the disappearance of a New York resident named Brian Carter. The sheriff's questions were perfunctory. He was easily satisfied that Brian had been put on the train in Aiken and was safely out of the sheriff's jurisdiction before anything could have happened to him.

Other than her father and the servant staff, Margaret's only visitor over the summer was Emily Roach. Margaret was reluctant to see her. Their childhood friendship, a product of necessity between the only white children at isolated River's Edge, was quickly over when Margaret started boarding school and Emily ended her education altogether. Although Emily could not be blamed for the actions of her father and brothers, the Roach association inevitably destroyed whatever chances were left for even casual friendship despite class distinctions.

Emily wore a bright colored sun dress she had made herself that revealed her full figure. It was daringly cut two inches above the knees. Margaret thought to herself that Emily was common and coarse, advertising herself in the way she dressed.

Emily was blunt.

"Miss Farwell, is it true that you were attracted to Brian Carter? That you were intimate with him."

Margaret's face reddened with both blush and anger. How dare this daughter of a farmhand confront her with this? Emily saw she needed to continue her advance if she was to obtain candid answers.

"Don't be embarrassed or ashamed if it's so. I made love to Brian myself. He told me you and him was lovers. I loved him, too, Miss Farwell." Margaret was stunned to see Emily begin to cry.

"I don't believe you. Brian and I were going to run away together."

"I know. He told me." Emily spoke through her tears. "He said we could never be together; that I had too many bad breaks in life, with my family and all. He knew I'd hate a place like New York. Miss Farwell, I know the difference. You're the princess and I'm just a

Chapter Nineteen: Birth

peasant and that's the way God made it to be. Brian thought you could make it in New York among all the fancy people. But I'm jes grateful for the chance to have been with Brian for a time. I'll never forget him. Like I said, I love him. Jes like you do, I'm sure. I know I'll never be with as good a man as Brian."

Shocked, Margaret dismissed Emily from the mansion. How could Brian have done it? At first Margaret denied it happened, and called Emily a liar as she talked to herself in her bedroom. On further reflection, she concluded that her father was right. Once Brian tasted love from a white woman, he wanted more. She concluded it was possible Brian made love to both women. He was fun-loving, had no real duties at River's Edge, and while wary he was also careless. She could forgive Emily. Margaret found Brian irresistible; how could Emily not also? She summoned Emily back to her bedroom.

"You may as well know I'm pregnant."

"I thought so. There are lots of stories goin' round about why you stayin' in bed. Lottsa folks think you must be pregnant."

For the second time in as many visits, Emily caused Margaret to blush. "Do these folks think Brian's the father?"

"'Course they do Miss Farwell. The coloreds is kinda proud of it, actually. I'm happy for both of us."

"Does your daddy know?"

"Is there anything aroun' River's Edge he don't know," Emily replied.

"Does he know about you and Brian?"

"No. We know'd from the start it was a temporary thing. We kep' it secret. But I'll remember it forever. Miss Farwell?"

"Yes, Emily."

"Don't hate Brian for what he done with me. He loved and respected you. He done tole' me so. He liked me, but he also I think felt sorry for me, livin' practic'ly like bein' alone with my family as it is. He was gentle and kind and funny. He made me laugh. Don't be hard on him. He was 'gonna spend his life with you. You oughta' remember that, not the other stuff."

Emily's word picture of Brian flooded Margaret with the recollections of two wonderful months. Even if Brian violated every moral code Margaret grew up with, he had brought laughter and joy to two very lonely young women at River's Edge and now he was gone. Margaret held out hope he would return, but for now she wanted to share her memories with someone, someone who would help to keep them real, before they became inseparable from fantasy and the memory of the real Brian was lost forever.

Margaret rose from her bed and approached Emily. They hugged each other.

"We shared Brian. We can share our memories of him, Emily. I'm going to have his baby. It could have been you instead of me. I'm going to call him Brian. He will be *our* baby. Raised at River's Edge."

Margaret redirected her emotional energies to her baby and away from the loss of Brian. At first she tried to hide her growing belly. Her face

Chapter Nineteen: Birth

brightened and her skin glowed from the additional hormones pregnancy created. Her father commented that she was gaining weight. Her breasts grew. By early September, Margaret was concerned that she had not seen a doctor. She wanted a healthy baby. She gave thought to running away to have the baby rather than confide in her father. Emily might join her. Surely she wanted to abandon her family, too. But she had no money of her own, only a small weekly allowance. She had no skills. She didn't need either at River's Edge. Emily could sew, but she had even less money than Margaret and was practically illiterate.

She waited until a Sunday evening when her father was relaxing with a book about the Civil War. Farwell was pleased his daughter had come down from her room to spend some time with him. He had tried to put out of his mind the fact she had slept with a colored man, but every time he saw his daughter, the picture of them flashed in his head. He couldn't trust her. But he still loved her. He had decided privately that she would not attend the University for at least another year. He wanted to keep her close to him. He wanted to watch her. He was surprised his daughter had not inquired about her schooling.

Margaret opened the conversation politely by asking about the book. Farwell provided a précis, describing how the author, a Northerner, completely misinterpreted the causes of the war. Margaret pretended to listen intently.

"Daddy, I have something to tell you. Promise you won't get mad?" Farwell knew instantly that this was no longer a casual conversation. He did not respond to her question directly.

"Is there something wrong?"

"Not exactly." There was no easy way to say it. The only thing to do was say it quickly. "Daddy, I'm pregnant."

Farwell's eyes narrowed to slits. He turned his head away from his daughter. She was a slut.

"Do you know who the father is?" he asked matter-of-factly.

"Daddy!" Margaret threw her hands to her mouth. "Of course I know. I've only made love to one man, Daddy. How could you say that!"

"So it's a nigger's baby, is that right?" Farwell had gotten what he wanted by remaining calm when the problem of Brian had arisen before. He forced himself to quell his anger yet again, his fists clenched as before, even while continuing to sit. Would there be no end to this filthy mess? He thought. "You have to get rid of it," he added without waiting for confirmation. "I know a doctor in Columbia who can do the job. I never thought anyone in my family would need his services."

"What do you mean 'get rid of it'? I'm going to keep it and my baby will be part of the Farwell family."

That dissolved Farwell's resolve to remain calm. He jumped out of his chair, walked quickly to his daughter and slapped her hard across the face, as she had done to him a few weeks earlier. She screamed. "There will be no nigger blood in the Farwell family. You disrespectful little bitch. If your mother were here she would be ashamed. I'm ashamed. You're filthy and vile. A disgrace to the Farwells." Her father's voice shook the old walls of the mansion. Margaret was grateful

Chapter Nineteen: Birth

that the help had Sunday afternoons off. "We'll kill that baby before it's born."

"Then you will have to kill me first. I'll kill myself if you try to take me to some abortionist. Are you going to keep that secret, too? Are you going to say I got on the train and never was heard from again? Is that right, Daddy? You won't get away with that again. I won't kill myself privately. I'll go down to the Aiken County Courthouse and use Roach's gun to shoot myself in the head. And I'll leave a note explaining everything – especially that I was going to have a Negro baby. It'll be just in time for the elections. Nathan won't have a chance and the Farwell name will be a joke in this state."

Margaret hardly knew what she was saying, but she saw it was having the desired effect. Farwell let her finish. His most immediate problem was hiding Margaret so that no one would know she was pregnant. He had spoken hastily. He didn't care if the baby lived as long as no one knew about it. He had room to bargain with his daughter. There was a moment of silence while he considered a response.

"Perhaps we can reach an agreement that will allow your baby to live. You must agree to keep your pregnancy a secret; to never disclose you had this baby. You must also agree to give it up for adoption. I will not pay a nickel to support you or it if you don't give it away. This way, you can have the baby and someone else will provide it a home."

"You want me to give up Brian's child?" Margaret shrieked. "That's dreadful. I can't do it."

Unanimous Verdict

"You better think about it. The only other choice is that the baby dies. I hope you won't kill yourself, but that's your decision. If you tell anyone else about this, anyone but your brother, I'll have to disown you completely. I'll throw you off River's Edge and your baby, too."

Margaret hardly heard her father's words after he discounted her threatened suicide. She raced outside, through the center hall lined with Civil War heroes. She wanted to kill them over again, kin or no. The ancient breath of these dead men was oppressive in the mansion; in her own life. Her father was willing to see her die rather than bring a black child into the family. Another sacrifice for the long-dead of the Lost Cause. She stopped her crying only long enough to throw up in the hallway.

Margaret considered her choices on the veranda glider. There was no way she would allow her baby to be murdered. But she also had no means to provide for him. Nathan would not take her in and she had no other close relatives. Nor could she guarantee the baby a good life even if he was adopted; it wasn't likely she would know who adopted her baby. But maybe there was a way to better the child's odds in life, or at least to keep him from the rotted blood-thirsty corpse she viewed as the South and South Carolina. She cursed her father and her ancestors. The Civil War. Jim Crow. The mean spirits and narrow minds. She wanted her baby to be away from all these things. She returned to the study, clattering across the bare floor of the hall, noise enough to alert her father to pretend he was continuing to read his book.

Chapter Nineteen: Birth

"I will agree to your plan," she told him. "But you have to agree that the baby will not be put up for adoption in the South. It has to be adopted by a couple who lives in the North."

Farwell was happy to oblige his daughter's request. One less pickaninny for the Confederacy to worry about, he thought to himself.

The next morning, Farwell set about to find a place to put his daughter until her baby was born. He shuddered to think that the beast growing in her womb could be considered his grandchild. He would never see it. He called Nathan for help. Nathan had handled adoptions early in his legal career, and even on one occasion found a home for a friend's daughter secretly to give birth out-of-wedlock. The complicating factor in Margaret's case was that the baby would be a Negro.

Nathan Farwell was devastated by the news that his sister was carrying a Negro child. Even more than his father, Nathan was ashamed for the family name. He recommended his father simply expel Margaret from River's Edge, making her a public example of the moral turpitude that results from social friendship with Negroes. He could not respond directly to his father's question about whether such banishment would harm Nathan's political career.

"I don't care," Nathan answered. "Sin of this magnitude, a sin against the white race, South Carolina, the Confederacy and the Farwells, should be punished."

John Farwell eventually convinced his son that it was preferable to minimize the disruption to the family than to aggravate it.

Nathan's political career could go unharmed, unburdened by a black baby born anonymously and sent north.

Nathan called the Christian Home in Atlanta. He explained the situation without giving his name. The Home's director, a Mrs. Drucker, agreed that the unidentified woman could have her baby at the home, but that the child would have to be removed immediately to a place that accepted Negro babies for adoption. Nathan was assured the Christian Home would be discreet. It had handled the births of bastard offspring of many famous South Carolina families without incident, though none of those babies was a Negro. The risk to the Home's reputation would have to be recognized by additional compensation, Mrs. Drucker explained. Nathan agreed.

Nathan gave his name, which Mrs. Drucker, though in Georgia, recognized. Nathan cautioned her that he was merely the family's lawyer. There was too much risk that Mrs. Drucker would recognize his father's name, even more than 20 years after his political career. The family could not be associated with the birth in any way. Buster agreed to allow his daughter's name to be used instead of Margaret's. He never told Emily of the arrangement, but did collect an extra one hundred dollars from John Farwell as compensation, contending that his family was "takin' the risk of havin' a nigger baby. Comes out, it'll damage the Roach family name," he said. Roach heard Nathan Farwell snicker over the telephone at the notion the Roach family had a name worthy of protection.

Chapter Nineteen: Birth

Five days later, Margaret was resident in the Christian Home under the name Emily Roach. By the end of the year, Nathan had arranged for the Childress Agency in Chicago to take the baby. As the due date approached, Roach was told to be prepared to take the baby to Chicago. Roach was at the Home when the baby was born, but under strict instructions not to be seen by the birth mother.

It was Roach who suggested to Nathan that a note be placed in the baby's file at both agencies to call him if anyone inquired about the birth or the baby's placement. Nathan might become governor or even the President. A man in the public spotlight attracted attention and press, including reporters who specialized in looking for dirt. You couldn't be too careful nowadays, he told Farwell.

Chapter Twenty: The Reckoning, May 14, 1954

Justice Nathan Farwell looked at the picture presented to him in his Washington living room for a few seconds, at first uncomprehending, then surprised. Then he tore it into small pieces.

"So much for the evidence," Farwell chortled. "Now it's time for the police."

"Oh, we made prints. We have lots of prints," Neil replied, pulling another from his pocket.

"We're colored, but not stupid," Ezra added. Farwell stopped laughing and turned serious, staring up at his sister. She was tall, strong and beautiful. For a brief instance, Farwell was reminded his sister was a physical credit to his own bloodline. But she also was a traitor to the Lost Cause. She was a whore. It was good she knew his deepest secret. Now he could hate her without compromise.

"What do you want? Are you trying to blackmail me? Do you want all of River's Edge? Is that it? Well, you won't get it. This is the end of the road for all of you. Nobody will believe you. I'm a Justice of the Supreme Court of the United States and son of a two-time governor of South Carolina. It's blackmail. But you haven't a chance. I believe the penalty for extorting a federal official is 20 years."

The threat had weight. It was delivered in the stentorian voice of a practiced attorney used to having his way. If Farwell was afraid, he did not betray that fear in his voice or manner. Now that they were in Farwell's apartment, the serious risks of the confrontation to Neil, Lou and Ezra were much more real than when they were discussed at Roach's house or, later, at Lou's office among friends. The justice was no longer an abstract figure, but a flesh and blood human, vigorous and fit. Farwell was a formidable man of considerable public achievement. Neil felt small in his presence. What he and his friends were about to do could earn him a long spell in prison, shame his family and friends and even damage the civil rights cause. The extensive Civil War memorabilia in Farwell's apartment further weakened his courage. It graphically reminded him that men fought and died horrible deaths over these issues, then and today.

"We think of it more as bargaining." The deep voice was Ezra's. It, too, was steady and fearless. "And you haven't got much to bargain with." Ezra harbored no doubt that what he was doing was right. Everything was a question of power. Here was one time he had power. Finally, a Negro owned power over a prominent white man who intended to do the Negro wrong. He saw Neil tremble with uncertainty and fear. Ezra would use the power. It was his job, not a white man's. Not even Margaret Farwell's.

"In this room that celebrates the obscenity of a war required to end slavery, we are going to honor as best we can the memory of an innocent black man you murdered. You, Mr. Farwell, are going to be the first casualty in a new war. Only this time, your side is really going to lose." Ezra was surprised by his own speech. He hoped all of it was true.

Chapter Twenty: The Reckoning

Farwell visibly shrunk back into his chair as the large black man joined his sister looming over him. "Bullshit," he said. "You don't even have evidence. That picture could be tampered with. Faked."

Ezra did not see a man who was either formidable or admirable. He had studied Farwell's history in the short time since he returned to Washington from Atlanta.

"You and your daddy rode the backs of black people all the way to the governor's mansion and the Supreme Court. You Farwell men were nothing more than demagogues. Your power and your father's power were only as strong as the fear, anger and ignorance you spread among your own people. You should carry yourself in shame."

Shame associated with Farwell men? His sister, yes — she is nothing but a bag full of shame. Farwell abandoned his even but threatening tone. He would not stand disrespect from an ignorant Negro. "Get this nigger out of my house. Get out now. I'll call the police and you'll all be in jail before the day is out. Margaret, how can you let him insult your own father like that? Leave!" No one moved.

"I'd be careful how you talk to people right now, brother," Margaret said. "You're outnumbered here."

Sensing a physical threat from Ezra which his sister would permit, if not actually encourage, the justice began negotiations. For the first time that evening, there was a tremor of fear. "Let's be reasonable, Margaret. That Brian Carter boy died 30 years ago. It's done. What is it you want now? Money? Maybe I could buy you out of River's Edge

499

and we wouldn't have to even see each other again. It's worth a lot, especially with that weapons plant and the growth and all."

Despite his office and his wealth, Ezra thought, Farwell was no different from any shantytown bigot. In groups, bigots are dangerous. Alone, they are cowards. Farwell was soft. He was pampered. He was lavished with praise by wealthy contemporaries and surrounded himself with sycophants. Ezra was sickened by the apartment. It was a celebration of an evil that even today damaged the lives of millions. But alone with a big Negro, Farwell was just a scared old man.

A thousand visions raced quickly through Ezra's brain. His mother working the cotton fields, her hands cut, bruised and calloused picking 200 pounds of cotton a day. His mother starving. Other mothers barely able to keep their children alive. His sisters, kept unschooled and pregnant so the cycle could be repeated. His father reduced to impotent alcoholism and then burned to death to humor some white boys. The Mobile streetcar. He could still call up the pain in his head in memory of that occasion. The incredible poverty and indelible fortitude among the railroad hoboes. Chicago, with its successful containment of black men and women to the poorest areas of the city. The Army's raw racism against men who volunteered to fight for their country. Farwell was never even was in the military. A coward pretending he was better than all the millions of black men and women for whom every day living required courage. Ezra hated him. He would not hesitate to kill him. He would enjoy doing so. But that would waste the power now held in his hands. Greater things are to be achieved. Maybe.

Ezra didn't know if a Supreme Court decision was important. Others had little impact. But it was enough for him for now that Farwell was against it. He suspected the decision would be yet another example of the white man holding out promise to the Negro and delivering disillusionment. A civil war, an Emancipation Proclamation, Reconstruction, two world wars for "democracy." All promises and no results. Bonhomme, his master in Mobile, was like that. Four years of good service and even affection, only to be abandoned due to the lying of a white boy. Whites were like that. No commitment, no trust and no forgiveness. Ezra didn't have any power over Bonhomme or the lying white boy or the men who killed his mother and father. He held it now over another white man. Regardless of the result, Ezra relished the occasion.

"I don't want your money. And you're never going to set foot on River's Edge again," Margaret said evenly, hiding a struggle to stop from shaking in anger. Old wounds had been savagely reopened by the photograph. Once again, her life was fundamentally altered by hateful prejudices shaped long before her birth that were incubated and nourished in her native South. She, too, enjoyed exercising power over her brother – her father's favored child who symbolized all of the grievances Margaret had suffered as an intelligent, curious female in a world dominated by men who preferred to live in a world that never was and never could be.

Unanimous Verdict

"We want your vote in the schools cases," Ezra said. His eyes were aimed like a cannon shot into Farwell's. Farwell blinked and looked away. Ezra knew he was in charge.

"Y'all workin' for the NAACP? I tell you what. You leave now and don't cause me any problems in the future and I won't report the nigra lawyers to the bar association or my colleagues on the Supreme Court. That's my bargainin'."

"No lawyers for the NAACP know a thing about this," King interjected. He had enjoyed watching the tableau unfold in the Kennedy-Warren. He suspected that big-time Washington politics often operated through threats and blackmail. He was glad that for once, at least, black folk could join in for their own cause.

Farwell addressed his one possible ally. "What happened to you, white boy? You gonna let the nigras do all the talkin'?"

"They're doing fine without me. You should listen to them." Neil was genuinely admiring of the way Ezra took charge. Maybe they would get out of this without going to prison.

"His name was Brian Carter. His son's name was Clayton Van Dyke. We know you killed Brian. Did you have Clayton killed, too?" Ezra spoke in a flat, cold tone. All traces of Alabama were missing from his voice.

"I never heard of this Clayton fellow. Who is he?"

"He's your sister's son. Your nephew. He's dead. Roach told his son to kill him. He was on the trail of finding out who his parents

502

were. It would have led to your family, of course. That's why Roach killed him."

"And you killed Roach, you bastards. Blackmail and murder. You SOBs will rot in jail."

"We'll enjoy reading behind bars all the stories in the tabloids and in the magazines about the Farwell family. Not just racists, but also killers, father and son alike. The great gentry of South Carolina in the same boat with the goofy grand dragons of the Ku Klux Klan and every poor cracker who hangs niggers and runs a still on the side. Except the Farwells will be worse because they pretended they were something different." Lou King was warming to his topic. "Americans don't like frauds, whatever their color. Especially frauds who try to show and tell everyone they are the elite."

"I didn't know about this Clayton fellow. I never knew what happened to that baby. Roach took care of it."

"But you sure as hell knew what happened to his daddy. You were there. Picture shows it." Ezra forced himself to keep emotion out of his voice as he shoved another print in front of Farwell.

"Did my father and yours kill Brian Carter?" It was the first question Margaret asked the Roach family when they gathered in the Roach house with Mrs. Van Dyke's investigation team after Buster was killed. Matt Roach did not answer directly. Instead, he pushed a davenport aside and pulled up a floorboard. He reached into the space and pulled out a handful of papers. He handed the top paper, a photograph, to Margaret.

"I saw Daddy open this hiding space a couple years ago," Matt mumbled into his double chin, embarrassed at addressing such a large group. "He never know'd I knew. I looked at the stuff. He kept this stuff."

On later examination, most of the documents were old daguerreotypes, with descriptions carefully hand written on the back. One picture was of a large, formidable looking woman. The back was labeled "Mother." Several others were of a child. The child could have been a boy or a girl, but was dressed in frilly pantaloons and what appeared to be a heavily patterned sleeveless jacket that exposed the child's midriff and navel. The writing on the back said "Me."

The picture Matt handed Margaret was not a daguerreotype, but an old Kodak Brownie print. It was in black-and-white and the definition wasn't very good. But it clearly showed a colored man hanging by the neck from a tree beside a river, with two white men smiling on either side, as if the dead man were nothing more than a catch from the river of which they were extraordinarily proud. There was a dark blotch at the crotch of the victim. It took no imagination to know why the crotch was bloody.

For a few seconds Margaret examined the photograph as merely a curious object. But then her outdoors complexion faded to that of a winter-time shut-in. Her mouth dropped as her jaw sagged. Her shoulders slumped and her body collapsed farther back

Chapter Twenty: The Reckoning

into the old brown overstuffed chair. Finally, the full import of the picture fully registered, she let out a shriek as she jumped to the floor. "Oh God no! God no!" Then she began to sob. She passed the picture to Emily, who duplicated Margaret's reaction except that she had sufficient outrage-driven resources to rise from her chair and begin clawing at her brother's face. He did not block her hands, but he backed away, and began explaining in a jumbled, rapid-fire fashion, the events which resulted in the yellowed black-and-white Brownie print. He was, finally able to disclose his horrible secret to his own family.

"We stuck his dick in his mouth but he spit it out right 'afore we hanged him," Matt said. "Them's the Farwells on either side. Old man is John and the younger guy is Nathan. Damn fools. They was so pissed off at Margaret and so proud o' themselves for stringing this kid up they let Daddy take a picture. Day later, they had second thoughts. They tole Daddy to destroy the negative. He done give it to Mr. John Farwell, but he kep' a couple copies. Robby done got a job with ol' Nathan right after Daddy showed him this picture a few years back. Workin' at the Supreme Court now as some kinda cop."

Margaret first tried to speak, but nothing came out of her mouth. She rubbed her eyes and tried again. Unlike her dowdier, fatter contemporary, she found no energy to take physical revenge on Matt. "Was he dead before you hanged him? Did you shoot him first?"

"No ma'am. He was hanged alive. He was alive when we cut him at his privates."

Ezra grabbed the photograph from Emily as she flopped back into a chair. Margaret also sat down. Both women were drained, their faces drawn, too saddened and surprised by events of the day to continue the examination. The 33-year-old picture had not lost its capacity to shock and anger. But Brian Carter's lovers did not have the emotional energy necessary for further tears. Both had assumed the worst over the years. Confirmation ended a long journey of false hopes, but was insufficient to avoid the shock from learning of the violent end to the only young man either of them had genuinely loved.

After a few moments of silence — none of the visitors felt it was their place to comment — Emily spoke to her brother. "Why didn't you tell me, Matt. I loved Brian."

Now it was Matt's turn to be shocked. He found shelter in the prejudices handed to him in his life. "I can't believe that. You made love to a nigger? Why, it's even better we killed him." Matt was again on his knees at the space where he had retrieved the documents. Ezra pushed him in the face with his boot, knocking Matt backwards and bringing blood from his mouth. Too fat and afraid to fight back, the younger son of Buster Roach crawled away into the kitchen. Ezra's show of violence was met with no disapproval, even from Matt's mother, but it broke the gloomy silence. Those left in the room discussed what to do next.

❖ ❖ ❖

Chapter Twenty: The Reckoning

"Nowadays they can make a picture show anything," Nathan Farwell told his accusers surrounding him in his apartment as he examined the second copy of the photograph. "Look at our new vice president. Nixon faked a picture of his opponent and got to Congress with it. Who are people going to believe? A Supreme Court justice or a bunch of nigger blackmailers with access to scissors and paste? The question answers itself."

"Justice Farwell," Neil said sharply. "You're in no position to call anyone a nigger. You're the killer, remember?"

"You're right, Nathan. A picture can be toyed with," Margaret said. "But I will be a witness against you. And so will Celestine Roach and her daughter and Matt. Matt was there when it happened. He told the entire story in front of his family and us."

"You wouldn't do that. Think of the shame it would bring down on the family. On your father."

Margaret moved her head slowly and dramatically so that her eyes could encompass the memorabilia around the room before responding to her brother.

"I see it's the same old Civil War crap you and Daddy loved so much. I never understood it. A war to defend slavery. Why celebrate that? Shame? It's a little late to worry about shaming our family, isn't it Nathan? Daddy got his votes baiting white folk with fears of big black Negroes taking women and jobs. You only got the droppings from his table. Do you really think you'd be doin' anything except slip and fall cases in Aiken if your name was Nathan Jones?

Unanimous Verdict

"This Lost Cause stuff is just like kid's dress-up games. It isn't real manhood, waving the Stars and Bars and yellin' about state's rights or Confederate Culture whenever somebody suggests the colored got some rights, too. Three wars in your lifetime and you didn't have the balls to be in any of them. But you still have wet dreams over the Confederacy, right? General Nathan Bedford Farwell, defender of the lost cause of the South. Does that cause include killing defenseless black boys? Did it take a man like Buster Roach to sew some balls on you, Nathan."

She glowed with the same outdoorsy coloring as her brother, the same blue eyes and sharp chin. There was not an ounce of fat in her face. She was still gorgeous in an appealing, athletic way. She could even use the language of the outdoors and the barnyard if called upon, as now. Margaret was determined to have fun at her brother's expense and let him know it.

"I guess you heard about Roach. His daughter killed him, not his wife like the papers reported. Not an ounce of remorse, either. After all these years, the women are taking over River's Edge. Roach is dead and after next week, I think you'll be in retirement. Not a quiet one, though. You'll be explaining to every racist in the country why you voted to kill Jim Crow. They may not even let you back into South Carolina."

"You can't do this, Margaret. Dad and I were very kind to you. You tested us in every way."

"That's a laugh. You and Daddy killed the man I loved. Then you smothered every ambition I ever had, including to get the hell out of River's Edge and the South. Then you killed my son, or at least gave

508

Chapter Twenty: The Reckoning

Roach the reason and means to do it. And I learned from Roach just before he died that you even found a good job for the man who tried to rape me. Is that true?"

"I had to. Roach was blackmailing me with that picture. I put his son on the police force. You never had to know."

"Just like I never had to know that my poor Brian was murdered. Tell me about it. Get it off your chest. You're the big Civil War hero — in your dreams. Why, killing my poor young lover must rank as your greatest victory. You and Dad. What a pair! Did you buy some fake campaign medals to celebrate?" She chuckled bitterly. "Roach was a better man than either of you. At least he didn't hide behind the trappings of a big mansion or filter his feelings through politics. With Roach, you got what you saw. You and Dad were just like him. You just hid it better. I hate both of you." There were still some loose ends she needed filled.

"How did you get that picture of Brian at the train?"

The evident joy his sister felt in his betrayal and the news of Matt Roach's confession drained Farwell of all his bravado. He slumped farther into his chair.

"It was easy. We had your note, remember? That persuaded him to come with us. We took him to the station like we promised and took his picture. Said we'd give it to you, which Roach did. Roach then stuck a pistol in the boy's ribs and told him to come with us. Dumb nig — he coulda' run and we wouldn't shoot him at a train station, of course. He coulda' saved his own life. But he went along quietly."

Unanimous Verdict

"Matt Roach said you cut him up after you hanged him and fed him to the fish." Margaret was standing directly in front of her half-brother.

"Roach did. You don't think we'd leave any chance his body would be found, do you? My God, Margaret, the boy was an invader. He disrupted our life." Farwell started to rise from his chair, recovering his anger at the thought of Brian Carter at River's Edge. "Think of our family. Think of our father. Think of me. In fact, think of yourself. You couldn't have kept that baby. You couldn't have run off with that nigger boy. Hell, if these colored guys over there hadn't gotten involved, you wouldn't know any of this now and you'd be happier for it. Don't ruin everything. Don't ruin the work of four generations of Farwells."

Margaret bent slightly, made a fist and punched her brother squarely in the face. His lip started to bleed before he could raise his hands to protect himself from another blow. None came.

"Shut up," she said sharply. "I'm sick of your whining.

"Now you're going to do what these boys tell you to do. Do you understand? Except you have to agree to one other thing. You can never return to River's Edge. You can stay here or wherever you want, except not at River's Edge. In return, though I hate the thought, we will keep our family secrets a secret. Father's name and reputation will not be altered, at least not by this. History will catch up to him later. You will be known as a traitor to your own cause, but not a murderer. I doubt you will ever regret killing Brian and my baby, but maybe you can one day talk yourself into believing that voting for school

Chapter Twenty: The Reckoning

desegregation is the right thing. You'll be able to say you did the right thing for once in your life before you lie in your grave. I doubt it, but you'll have the chance."

"Don't do this Margaret. I can't vote for coloreds going to school with white folk. I can't be away from River's Edge. These are the hallmarks of my life. These are the things your whole family has stood for practically since the Revolution. They are your heritage, too. River's Edge would be nothing without slavery and Negroes. It would be nothing if our Daddy had not been governor and the voice of reason all those years. I would be nothing. These are our principles and our birthright."

Ezra could not take it any longer. "You ARE nothing, Farwell. You never have been anything. If it weren't for the Negro, you and your family would be nothing. Everything you have you owe to the Negro. Your family stole its wealth from the work of the Negro. Your father and you won office only because of the Negro. Hell, even your apartment decorations are due to the Negro. There wouldn't have been a Civil War without him. Look at it this way. You vote for desegregation, you're only payin' a long-overdue debt to the Negro. The bill must be paid. It's personal. You're going to pay it." Ezra took a step toward Farwell. Neil and Lou restrained him. "I ain't gonna hit him. His sister done that. He's a powerless little bug. Not worth steppin' on."

"You won't win, you know." Farwell spoke softly. He had lost the battle, but he would not surrender his sword. "White and Negro ain't interested in being together. I'll vote like you say, to save Daddy's honor. I'll sacrifice myself. But it'll just start a war, not end one. The North will adopt the ways of the South. The black man will lose. The Lost Cause has prevailed before. It will prevail again."

Chapter Twenty-One: The Chief IV, May 15, 1954

The conference of the justices of the Supreme Court of the United States opened as usual with the ritual of the handshakes, each justice shaking the hand of each of the other eight justices before they were seated at the conference table in order of seniority, except that the Chief sat at the head of the table. To his right sat the most senior associate justice in tenure, Hugo Black. To his left sat the second most senior, William O. Douglas. To his right again was Felix Frankfurter. Farwell, fourth in seniority, sat next to Douglas.

Only one matter was on the docket for resolution – the five cases to be known forever as *Brown v. Board of Education*. Final versions of all opinions were circulated earlier to all of the justices. There was the majority opinion by the Chief, a dissent by Justice Jackson in which Justice Clark concurred, and a dissent by Justice Farwell. The Chief's trips to McLean were in vain. Justice Jackson was not changing his vote.

The Chief formally introduced the cases by their docket numbers and said the occasion was for a vote on how the appeals should be resolved. He announced that he would vote to reverse the decisions of each of the five courts below, which ruled in favor of the defendant school boards, and hold that segregation of public schools on the basis of color was unconstitutional. He agreed to schedule argument on the appropriate relief in the cases for the next term of the Court rather than immediately remand the cases to the district courts, as was customary.

Unanimous Verdict

No school desegregation would be required in the fall of 1954. Jackson's fear of a race war was effectively postponed, at least.

The Chief turned to Black, who announced that he would join the Chief's opinion. Douglas and Frankfurter quickly voted in favor. Sixteen eyeballs turned to Justice Farwell. Frankfurter later recorded in a note that Farwell was much paler than usual and looked worn and sick. His lip was swollen. He did not join in the usual jocularity of the justices during the handshakes, remaining seated and silent, forcing each of the other justices to approach him to shake hands.

Farwell kept his head lowered, staring at the dark mahogany tabletop. A fig leaf had been presented by the Chief. He took it. "In view of the fact that the Court agrees it will not enter a formal order desegregating the schools until after a hearing on relief next year, I have decided to support the majority, joining the Chief's opinion."

The room was silent for several seconds. "Congratulations, Nat. That took guts. It's the right thing to do." It was Douglas, Farwell's worst enemy on the Court, save perhaps Frankfurter. Douglas knew Farwell hated to be called Nat. Farwell lifted his head and turned to glare at Douglas before turning to again examine the conference table.

"In addition, I want to take this opportunity to inform you, my colleagues on the Court, that I will tender my notice of retirement to the President at the conclusion of this term." This news was met with a longer silence. Farwell was only 70 years old. It was assumed he would remain on the bench another ten years. Even 80 was no worse than an average age for a justice to retire.

Chapter Twenty-One: The Chief IV

The Chief broke the tension by standing to congratulate Farwell on his retirement. The other justices came around the table to do the same before the voting resumed. None suggested that Farwell reconsider his decision to retire. None expressed regret that he would be gone.

Jackson used the time to confer with Clark. Jackson was next to vote.

"I am not going to stand against the desegregation of the schools of this country," Jackson said, his voice firm. He was relieved of the need to counter Farwell's dissent. He could vote his conscience. "In view of Justice Farwell's change of heart, I see no need to dissent. I join the majority." Clark did the same when his turn came. So did all the justices. It was a unanimous verdict. The Court was overturning nearly sixty years of precedent and 300 years of history. Everyone at the table – and two days later, all thoughtful people in the country – knew that legal segregation was a dead letter, not just in schools, but in every aspect of public life. It would take time, a long time for the burial, perhaps, but segregation under law was dead.

Only two justices at the conference were not surprised by Farwell's sudden change of vote. One was Farwell. The other was the Chief.

After his meeting with Black nearly three weeks earlier, when Black scolded him for asking for dirt about Farwell, the Chief had called his Negro messenger, Louie, into his office. The Chief suspected from soon after he arrived at the Court that Louie channeled confidential court information on race cases to the NAACP. By March 1954, it was practically an open secret between them.

"Hello, Louie," the Chief said when his messenger arrived on that Saturday morning in April. "You know I enjoy talking to you sometimes about our civil rights cases. I like to get the Negro view." The Chief resisted an urge to wink.

"Yes sir, I appreciate that. I'm always ready to help."

"I know you are Louie. Now you know about these school cases. I think Justice Farwell is going to dissent. It would be better if the decision were unanimous, don't you think so?"

"Well, yes sir. I guess so sir. Depends on which way it goes."

"I can't tell you that, but I think Justice Farwell might be the only one to dissent. Of course, there's nothing we can do about that. Each justice is entitled to his own views. But you know what we used to do when I was governor, don't you?"

"No sir. What was that?"

"If somebody wasn't toeing the line like we thought they should, we'd sometimes use a little pressure. Nothing terrible. Maybe a little logrolling. Like I won't sign your bill on this if you don't go along with that. Sometimes we had to be a little more devious. I never did it myself, of course, but I understand that sometimes a legislator had something in his past he didn't want brought up. Some people would use that to get what they wanted. Not blackmail, really. Just bargaining."

Chapter Twenty-One: The Chief IV

"Yes sir. I understand. Like if Justice Frankfurter had a bastard child."

The Chief roared with laughter. Frankfurter had no children. Of that, the Chief was certain. "Yes, kind of like that. But don't go around saying that about Felix."

"No sir. It was just an example."

"Well, we can't do such things on this Court. It's too bad, maybe. Anyhow, Louie, thanks for taking the time to discuss these things with me." He could barely resist adding "Now don't tell the NAACP about this conversation."

The day before the court conference, the Chief received a call from an intermediary who had friends at the NAACP. He said that Farwell was going to change his vote. The Chief didn't know why, didn't ask why, and didn't want to know why.

The Chief chuckled to himself as he opened the door to his chambers after the conference vote. Critics in both parties attacked him when he was nominated because he had no experience as a judge. He's "just as a politician" they said. "Exactly right," the Chief said softly as he closed the door, anxious to pour himself a private toast to a rare success for both justice and politics.

Chapter Twenty-Two: Judgment Day, May 17, 1954

Ezra stayed in Washington over the weekend waiting for the *Brown* decision. He joined Neil and Lou King early Monday morning at the Supreme Court, hoping to get a seat for the 10 a.m. session at which the day's opinions would be read. The Court rarely announced in advance what decisions were to be handed down and *Brown* was no exception. But the term was nearing its end and only a handful of cases remained on the docket for an opinion to be announced. Hopes were high in the crowd at the Court that this would be the day for *Brown*. By the time Ezra, Neil and Lou got to the Court, the line to enter the building stretched to First Street and around Maryland Avenue. They waited outside with the television camera men and their bulky equipment.

Shortly after 10 a.m., word raced quickly through the crowd that the Chief Justice had begun reading the decision in the schools cases. There was a buzz of anticipation in the crowd for about ten minutes awaiting word of the Court vote. Then people at the front of the crowd began to cheer and word was quickly passed. It was unanimous. Segregation of schools violated the Equal Protection Clause of the Fourteenth Amendment. Newsmen raced outside to file their radio and television reports. Soon, Thurgood Marshall and the rest of the NAACP legal team joined the crowd and were interviewed on the courthouse steps midst loud applause.

Unanimous Verdict

Hugs were exchanged all around on the plaza in front of the court. Blacks hugged whites, whites hugged blacks. For a brief moment, no one was a stranger and people of all colors were treated alike. All were fighters for the same cause. Everyone wanted to celebrate. Neil invited his friends to his parents' house in Chevy Chase for a party later in the afternoon.

While still on the Supreme Court steps, Neil and Lou agreed it was time to report to Mrs. Van Dyke. They took a taxi to her house. During the short ride, they discussed how much information they should disclose. They decided she was entitled to know everything, even at the risk that if Mrs. Van Dyke angrily disclosed Farwell's role in her son's death it would mean prison for the two detectives and Ezra.

They found a private limousine and chauffeur waiting at the curb in front of Mrs. Van Dyke's house. The puzzle was solved when Mrs. Van Dyke ushered Neil and Lou into her living room, where they were greeted by Margaret Farwell. Both women were using tissues to dry their reddened eyes. Margaret greeted the men warmly.

"A unanimous verdict!" she exclaimed. "Hallelujah!" Her joy was genuine; her cheery demeanor was obviously forced.

Mrs. Van Dyke remained somber. "At a high cost for both of us," she said quietly, knowing the observation was not news to anyone in the room. "We both lost our son." Neil and Lou felt they were intruding on the mothers' grief and interrupting the sharing of recollections.

"I am so grateful to the Van Dyke family," Margaret said, rising into the arms of Mrs. Van Dyke. They squeezed each other tight. "The

520

Chapter Twenty-Two: Judgment Day

guilt I've carried most of my life is lessened a bit knowing that Brian — I mean, Clayton — was raised by a wonderful family."

"I've been telling Miss Farwell that she shouldn't feel guilty at all. We are the ones to be grateful. Her decision gave us our son. His death wasn't her fault."

Mention of Clayton's murder raised a difficult issue. The men had decided on the way to the house that Lou would take the lead on the subject.

"There is still the matter of your son's killer, Mrs. Van Dyke." He ignored the fact that Clayton was Margaret Farwell's son, too. Mrs. Van Dyke was paying the bills. "We will have to turn him into the police. This fellow Robby Roach could unravel the whole thing – make it public. It could get us and Miss Farwell in plenty of trouble for . . ." Lou looked for a gentle term, "persuading Justice Farwell how to vote."

Mrs. Van Dyke looked squarely into King's eyes and spoke sharply. "That has been taken care of. It is not your concern. You will drop the matter immediately, Mr. King. You, too, Mr. Endicott." She seemed upset that King had interrupted the sentimental recollections of Clay's two mothers with the subject of their son's killer.

Lou could not disguise his surprise. "What do you mean, Mrs. Van Dyke? This is a serious crime. It needs to be handled properly."

"It has been, Mr. King. I won't discuss it further."

"Is that your view, too, Miss Farwell?"

"Robby Farwell got what he deserved. He should have gotten it a long time ago. Yes, I'm happy with the resolution." Margaret smirked after she spoke. Her blue eyes were hard as diamonds. Lou thought it was a strange reaction by women prominent in two versions of high society to what sounded like a violent end for Roach.

"I hope you didn't do anything illegal," Lou said to the two women.

"We didn't have anything to do with it. I'll leave it at that," said Mrs. Van Dyke.

There was an awkward silence. Neil and Lou felt like strangers in a house of secrets shared by the two mothers. Neil tugged at Lou's sleeve. It was time to leave. Lou had other ideas.

"There is still the matter of the fees and expenses," Lou said.

Mrs. Van Dyke rose to fetch her checkbook. Neil quickly calculated that his time and expenses for a month long investigation clearly exceeded the thousand dollars he had received from Mrs. Van Dyke. Forty dollars was in his wallet and less than one hundred dollars in his bank account. He still owed the grocer and some of his friends money. And he would owe a lot on the Bel Air. But he had no heart to extract more from Mrs. Van Dyke. He would consider the difference his contribution to the Negro cause.

"You don't owe me anything else, Mrs. Van Dyke. You've been very generous," Neil said.

"You owe me two thousand dollars," Lou said. "Expenses were high and a lot of time was spent." Neil glared at his colleague. Lou's people achieved a great victory, in part thanks to Mrs. Van Dyke, and at the cost of her son. Neil had covered the expenses. How could he charge her more money?

"Are you sure I don't owe you anything, Mr. Endicott?"

Neil had committed himself. "No ma'am. Thank you."

"Well thanks to both of you," she said as she wrote the check to King. They said goodbyes to Margaret Farwell, who extended the courtesy of River's Edge to the men if they ever were in the neighborhood, an offer everyone knew was not expected to be taken literally. Mrs. Van Dyke escorted the men to the door. Formal and dignified as always, she shook their hands firmly and said goodbye.

Neil and Lou quickly walked the short distance to a newsstand on Florida Avenue and purchased both *The Daily News* and *The Evening Star*. The ink was still wet as the papers rushed to distribute the news about the *Brown* decision. The men ignored the front page, searching for something that related to Clayton Van Dyke's murder. Neil found it in *The Daily News*. It was a short, routine item.

Court Cop Suicide Victim

Robert P. Roach, 60, a 10-year veteran of the Supreme Court Police, died Sunday. He was found hanging from the rail of his walkup apartment's back porch at The Paradise Apartments on Second Street, S.E. Detective Robert Jeffords said the death appeared to be a suicide.

"Well I'll be damned," Lou said when Neil read the paragraph to him. "Justice is done sometimes after all."

"How could this happen? Who knew about our investigation? Who knew about what happened at River's Edge besides the Roaches and Margaret Farwell?" Neither man believed Roach killed himself. The Roach men had no guilt. Neil was troubled by the vigilante nature of his death. Even Roach deserved a trial. Neil also felt betrayed. Someone was an informant. Lou was suddenly silent and contemplative. This non-reaction stirred other suspicions Neil was harboring.

"You guys are hiding something from me, aren't you? What did you have to do with Robert Roach's death? Don't tell me it was a coincidence he died like Clayton on the eve of the decision." His Negro colleagues were ganging up on him again, keeping him out of the loop. "I risked going to jail on this thing. I deserve to know everything. What is it."

"I don't know who killed Robert Roach."

"God damn. I've been a reliable part of the team all along. But I guess I wasn't fit to be included in everything. I think I'm owed an apology." Neil felt the joy of completing the investigation and obtaining a good result ebbing as he contemplated the lack of trust on the team.

"Maybe you are," Lou said diplomatically. "But not from me."

"And by the way, how could you take another two thousand dollars from Mrs. Van Dyke? Hell, I picked up most of the expenses anyway. The car, the gas, the motel rooms, the meals – I paid for most of that."

Chapter Twenty-Two: Judgment Day

Lou was glad to change the subject. "If you are going to make a living in this business, you have to set aside sentiment when it comes to billing. After you turned down more money, I knew it was because of some white guilt or misplaced pity for Mrs. Van Dyke, 'the poor Negro lady.' I put in for both of us. After I cash the check, I'll give you half."

"I'll take it."

Lou returned to his office. Neil went to his father's office to pick up the family car. He needed to shop for the party. He called the Henshaws and Lisa McCartin from *The Star* newsroom and invited them to the party. They accepted. He left the Bel Air in front of his apartment on Capitol Hill and called Mike Q to pick it up. Mike was angry, but relieved when Neil told him the car suffered no damage other than the wear and tear of a thousand miles of travel. He also was disappointed when Neil did not offer to purchase the vehicle after such a long test drive. Nevertheless, a big chunk of the money Neil was to get from King would go to the Chevy dealership. "You half paid for it, I tell 'ya," Mike chided.

Neil completed his shopping by late afternoon and picked up Ezra and Lou for the trip to his parents' house. He immediately demanded that Ezra tell him everything he knew about how Robby Roach was murdered.

Lou, who was in the front seat, turned to look at Ezra. "I think we should tell him."

"We have so many secrets between us already. What is it? What about Robert Roach?"

" I didn't know he was dead until we looked at the newspaper this afternoon," Lou said.

"Laura Masters. She knew about everything," Neil said, an idea dawning. "So she told somebody at the NAACP. Then they got down and dirty and probably killed a man. Probably to reward Mrs. Van Dyke for all her NAACP work. No honor there. I'd hate to think any court decision justifies murder."

Ezra erupted. "Don't be such a namby-pamby. This is a war, a war for Negro rights. Like the Civil War all over again. You set the justified killing of Robby Roach on a scale against 300 years of violence against the black man, including Clayton Van Dyke, and Roach don't even register. You killed people in a war. That was for people far away we don't really even give a shit about. This war is for people in your own country. Don't be so prissy now."

"I do know that a helluva lot of young guys died or lost their limbs who were friends of mine. War is a waste and it means somebody failed. Maybe you'd know that if you hadn't spent your military career in prison." Neil was glad he was driving. He could focus ahead and not turn around to grab Ezra by the throat, initiating a fight he would surely lose. No one responded to Neil's insult. Neil was agitated. He needed to keep expressing his feelings.

"Sure, the coloreds have suffered 300 years. And it ain't over. You heard Farwell. He thinks the bigots will just get stronger. Like you said, Lowell, Supreme Court decisions are just more paper. But damn it, that paper has to have some weight, some kind of honor, some moral impact. What's the alternative? Race war? You and Farwell think that's inevitable. But it's not. There's whites who want to give the black man all his rights. Its doable some day. But not with a war. Not with violence. You got the honor. You got the weight of history. You've got the high ground — the moral power. If the blacks start taking up arms, all that's lost. And the result will be like Korea or most any other war — just more folks dead for nothin'."

"So now you're an expert on the subject, huh? Listen, I'll admit it. I like you, Neil. I thought you were ballsy when you attacked Lester in Chicago and again at River's Edge with Roach. But I damn sure ain't gonna' be lectured to about race relations by a white boy from Chevy Chase who hardly talked to a black person until a few weeks ago.

"Sure there're whites that'll help. But there's a helluva lot more that won't. How many white folks say 'tut-tut' when they read about lynchings and segregated movies and restaurants, but won't send their kids to schools with black kids? I don't know if we need a race war, but we need power, and the only way to get that may be through violence. How many coloreds on the Supreme Court? How many in Congress? I wish we could each get three-fifths of a vote 'cause that's more than no vote, which is what we got most places."

Lou was silent. Other voices were not needed as Neil and Ezra staked out their positions. Neil drove in silence for several blocks before concluding it was ridiculous to believe the NAACP had killed Robby Roach. He realized he already knew who did.

Unanimous Verdict

"You killed Robby Roach, Ezra." He stated it as a fact and without emotion.

"Guilty. And proud of it. Clay's murder needed to be avenged. Mrs. Van Dyke's grief needed to be answered. Even the grief of them white women in South Carolina needed to be avenged. The NAACP had nothing to do with it. Clayton was my friend. He was my fellow soldier."

Neil was silent. He both wanted to know the details, and didn't. Lou King wasn't torn. "How'd you go about it, brother?" He could have been asking him about a bowling score.

"Roach's name and address were in the phone book. I waited outside his apartment building Saturday night until the bastard came home. He was still in uniform. I followed him through his apartment door. He was big, but he'd gotten soft sittin' around the Supreme Court all the time, I guess. I strangled him with a belt, waited until the middle of the night and wrapped the belt around the balcony railing with him hangin' from it. Damn good thing he had a strong belt. Guy was heavy."

"Did you get Jeffords involved?"

"Oh yeah. I left a note in Roach's pants pocket. A variation on the one left on Clayton's body. Something like 'We Know Our Place – Now You Do Too.' I called Jeffords at home from Roach's place – his number's in the book, too – and told him Clayton Van Dyke's death was avenged and where he could find Roach. I figure the note confirmed for him that the killings were related and that Roach's killer was someone who knew about the note on Clay. I figured he'd want to close the investigation quick so none of the higher ups would get wind of the note. They'd figure Jeffords leaked the information about the note on Clay. You told me Jeffords said that would kill his career. Self-preservation is always the best way to be sure someone keeps their mouth shut.

"And by the way, if you knew anything about the big war – as opposed to your little war – you'd know that colored guys weren't allowed to fight until after D-Day. If I wasn't in jail, I'd have been sweepin' out the generals' quarters or something equally gallant. I fought my war as best I could against the racist bastards who ran the Army."

They arrived at the Endicott home and piled out, each passenger carrying a bag of groceries or liquor into the house. They were greeted by Neil's mother. She did not try to hide her surprise when Neil's two companions were introduced as friends of her son and not delivery men from the DGS store.

"I didn't know you had colored friends, son," she said. As soon as the words came from her mouth, Mrs. Endicott's indoor white face acquired a pink tint. "I mean, I think that's wonderful. It's nice to meet you gentlemen." Lou and Ezra merely smiled and extended their hands, which Mrs. Endicott shook with an exaggerated enthusiasm, as if to prove to them she could touch Negro flesh without cringing.

"Your father has to work late on an extra edition because of the Supreme Court decision, dear. He says there will be hell to pay.

I mean, it's a grand decision certainly." Uncertain what else to say, Mrs. Endicott decided to retreat from the room. "Everyone should make themselves at home," she urged as she departed. Neil wished he had warned his mother that some of his guests would be Negroes.

The Henshaws and Lisa McCartin arrived a short time later. Alice and Lisa went to the kitchen to prepare snacks. Neil entertained everyone else in the den, where the new TV was located, to watch the local news at 6:30.

Neil prepared drinks for everyone. He offered his hand to Ezra Lowell in peace, recalling the first time he did so Ezra rejected it. Ezra took it warmly and grabbed Neil's arm with the other hand. Max Henshaw was in animated conversation with Lou King. Neil was glad. He wondered if his relations with the Henshaws could be the same as before. The women brought the snacks into the room in time to watch the news.

The local CBS television station, WTOP, broadcast a long story about the impact of the school decisions on Washington. The school superintendent vowed that the District would not wait another year for the Supreme Court to rule on appropriate relief. The schools would be integrated in the fall. A camera crew filmed man-in-the-street reaction, which was mixed but muted.

The telephone rang twice and then stopped.

Douglas Edwards and the News came on at 7 p.m. *Brown* was the lead story. Edwards narrated the essentials of the decision and then CBS showed film of Thurgood Marshall on the steps

Chapter Twenty-Two: Judgment Day

of the Supreme Court earlier in the day. Marshall, who seemed exhausted even through the black and white of the camera lens, pronounced how pleased he was with the Court. "A unanimous decision means that the Court is united and that the message is clear. This land can finally be the land of the free." Everyone in the room cheered. Neil went off to find his mother so she could join the celebration. He found her in Neil's old room, which was now a spare bedroom.

"Yes, they're invited guests. They're friends of Neil. They seem alright and haven't caused any trouble." Mrs. Endicott said into the telephone, her back to Neil. "But I guess I should count the silverware after they leave," she laughed. "No, they won't be staying in the neighborhood overnight." She paused to listen. "I understand. I'm sure they will be quiet and won't cause any trouble. I don't want them here long, either." How could she say such things? Neil thought. These were his friends. But he was not surprised. He resisted the urge to reach around his mother to hang up the phone and give her a stern lecture. It was still a glorious day and not to be ruined by another family battle.

Instead, Neil returned to his "invited guests" before his mother ended the conversation. The television account of the decision was still being broadcast. Marshall's coffee-and-cream face was being shown in close-up, now conveying authority and resolution.

In a way the world had moved, Neil thought. But in another way, maybe in the most important ways, nothing had changed. Elijah

Unanimous Verdict

Lincoln's face flashed through Neil's mind. He was still pleading not to be left behind.

"I think Thurgood Marshall could be on the Supreme Court one day," Neil said, trying to recover his earlier good humor by focusing on the TV picture. Peals of laughter answered such an incredible proposition.

"Sometimes you are an idiot," Lisa said, rubbing her hands playfully through his hair.

Epilogue

Included in the report by *The New York Times* on May 18, 1954, about the *Brown* decision was the following:

> Two principal surprises attended the announcement of the decision. One was its unanimity. There had been reports that the court was sharply divided and might not be able to get an agreement this term. Very few major rulings of the court have been unanimous.
>
> The second was the appearance with his colleagues of Justice Robert H. Jackson. He suffered a mild heart attack on March 30. He left the hospital last week-end and had not been expected to return to the bench this term, which will end on June 7.
>
> Perhaps to emphasize the unanimity of the court, perhaps from a desire to be present when the history-making verdict was announced, Justice Jackson was in his accustomed seat when the court convened.

Justice Jackson suffered a heart attack on October 9, 1954 while driving to work. He returned to his home, where he died. His death came less than a week after the Court opened its 1954-55 term.

Unanimous Verdict

President Lyndon B. Johnson nominated Thurgood Marshall to be an associate justice to the United States Supreme Court in 1967. Marshall served until 1991. He died in 1993.

A Note On Sources

Unanimous Verdict is a historical novel. As such, some characters and events written about actually happened, but many did not. Unless the reader knows something mentioned is true based of other sources, he or she should assume anything described in *Unanimous Verdict* is *not* true. Justice Farwell in particular is a completely fabricated character. In the novel, he replaces Justice Stanley F. Reed, who was a willing supporter of the *Brown* decision and in no way resembled the fictional Farwell.

The best non-fiction account of *Brown v. Board of Education* and the civil rights legal struggles leading to it is Richard Kluger's *Simple Justice*. The author consulted that book, as well as other sources, for general and specific information incorporated in *Unanimous Verdict*. The reader is asked to rely on *Simple Justice* (Vintage Books, 1977), not *Unanimous Verdict*, for a truthful account of *Brown*, real civil rights heroes and villains, and related matters. Of course, any factual errors are the author's.

2809914